BY CHRIS LOPARCO

WITH JOHN SANTARSIERO AND HERBERT OLIVERA

COVER AND ILLUSTRATIONS BY CHRIS LOPARCO

# A Story Told

Chris LoParco, Herbert Olivera, & John Santarsiero

www.astorytoldbook.com

ISBN-13: 978-1466311152

ISBN-10: 1466311150

*Cover Design, Illustrations, and Page Layout by Chris LoParco*

Thanks be to the True and Ever Loving God,
without whom none of this would be possible.

And to all of our family and friends,
All those who have helped us and believe in us
– Thank you.

*"For those who want to save their life will lose it,
And those who lose their life for my sake will save it." Luke 9:24*

# CHAPTER I
## DEATH'S HUNGER

*Dong, dong, dong.* The ominous toll pierced the ears of the dead. The night was calm, yet this had not been the case a few moments earlier. A man lay on the floor in a pool of his own blood, and the bells rang louder. Another figure, like a man, cloaked in a dark flowing cape with a hood to cover his face from prowling eyes, approached the seemingly dead body. The toll was now reduced to a whisper, for the figure realized that there would be no funeral. The man was not dead. The man *could not* die. The figure had been through this many times during his years of collection. As usual, he was unable to collect this one. The blood on the floor began to disintegrate. The wounds of the man were miraculously healed, and he slowly rose from the ground and disappeared among the shadows with a malicious laugh. The figure turned around and vanished. All was quiet.

# Part I
## Death's Tale

Once again, that cunning monster has slipped away from my grasp. It has been almost two thousand years that I have been chasing him. This millennium will end soon, and a new one will begin. If I do not end the reign of that horrible beast, the Earth will suffer another century of pain; and the next millennium will be filled with nothing but more torture, destruction, and pure evil. I have been searching for a way to defeat him, but the fact is that he cannot die. If he does not pass through to the world of the dead, then I cannot soothe my pain. The longer he lives, the longer I hunger, for I am the one who collects the souls at the time of passing, longing for the death of all things. My sole purpose is to make sure that all the souls of the universe are brought into the other world after passing. I yearn for death, which is my bondage to life. I am Death, in name and being.

Since my creation, I have existed in a place separate from time: a world that has no feeling, no love, no hate, no happiness — nothing but the grim image of death. My existence is empty and one-dimensional, controlled by the fates of those living. Their death is my life. Because of this I am forever alone. The only true contact I have with the mortal world is with the dead. I have never spoken to a living being for they cannot see nor hear me. I curiously look out at them, wondering what it would be like to live among them. Sometimes, I will see someone come and run toward me. Ah, but it is not me they are running to, it is the cold lifeless body on the floor. I cannot escape my prison of solitude until all have crossed over into the next stage. Once there is no need for death, I will be complete, and my services will be needed no longer. But as long as mortal life exists so will I.

Mostly, I stay trapped in my own dimension: a plane forgotten by man — a world separate within itself. My world lies between what humans call Heaven and Hell, yet it touches neither. These worlds (Heaven, Hell, and my own) are not physical, therefore, they do not honor man's theories. Think of them more as states of being. I stare blankly down these halls that fill this plane — this Limbo. The entire place is a maze that has no beginning and no end — just dark, gloomy corridors.

It is difficult for mortal man to understand how I collect the souls of all who die; for someone dies every second, practically, and the universe is infinitely large. The laws that govern the mortal world do not govern mine. Being of a metaphysical nature, I have the ability to travel in and out of space and time, allowing me to be in all places at all times. Because of this I can collect each and every soul, even if two beings perished on separate worlds at the same time. Once a mortal dies, I become aware of it, and know exactly where to go to collect the spiritual energy. The energy is collected in a mystical box that was given to me at the beginning of my existence. This box is the key to my existence and the power that I hold, and it can only be accessed by me.

I wonder as I sit alone, what would it feel like to love or be loved? Feelings are dead to me. Who is there for me to love or to love me? I have no one, not even God it seems. I know about as much of God as mortals do. All my interactions with the Highest of all Powers are through His glorious angels (or so they call them), and Kepha, known to most as St. Peter. After Peter's death and transcendence, he was placed in charge of the Gates of Heaven. He took over for one of God's elite, the angel Janus. This was the first time a mortal was given a position of power in Heaven. I hand the souls of the dead over to Peter after collecting them. He, then, places them in the judging Fire of the Spirit, which determines what fate is in store for that soul.

Though I may not know God, the Damned One I do know. The fallen Morningstar whose countless faces, all disguises, I have seen — all but his real visage. This I hear to be quite frightening, even more than my own ghoulish guise. To think, at one time he was the most beautiful of all creatures created by God. But he abused his powers and paid the consequences.

Now that devil makes everyone pay for his own disaster, trying to deceive the mortal plane to fall into the darkness that he fell into long ago. Many planets have fallen already. Earth, though, has passed the test of time well — but it is still young. Things can change, and Earth will fall like the others if Radix succeeds. Satan couldn't do it on his own. He couldn't make the Earth fall, and so he created the most evil mortal to walk the face of the Earth; a mortal that defies his mortality — a mortal who cannot die.

That beast escaped me tonight, just like before. I wonder who he has to kill now. It's hopeless though, because you never know who Satan wants dead. Radix has killed many unknowns before, plus countless bystanders, just for the sake of doing it. He has to reach his quota soon, for it is the year of the Lord, *anno Domini*, 2000 according to the standard Earth calendar, and the millennium will shift in the year of the Lord 2001. I believe he has put an end to 665 lives already. All he needs is one more. It is about time I took matters into my own hands. I must go to Heaven and for once demand to seek counsel with God. I do long for death, but I gain no nourishment from a planet falling into darkness. That void is worse than the one that Radix has created inside of me.

# Part II
## Locked Gates

With a flash of intense light, Death vanished from his plane of Limbo. His destination was a place too glorious for mortal eyes, where the souls of saved men and women waited for the new creation, and angels sang up high. An infinite paradise, Heaven was God's first creation, the center stage where it all began. The trip to this Holy plane was not easy, and could not be done by just anyone. It involved being in full control of your spiritual energy. Energy that exists in all who live, even demons. To travel to and from dimensional planes, one must be able to access the proper frequency of that plane. That was why most demons were trapped in the bottomless pits of hell; they did not possess the ability to achieve these frequencies. The only demon with the ability to freely travel through the planes of existence was Satan, for he was the first to fall into the black pit of nothingness. But even with his years of mastering his dark powers and his ability to travel to and from all worlds, his power is nothing compared to that of the Almighty, whose Will is greatest of all.

Death appeared with another flash of light and stood before a sight most beautiful, the Gates of Heaven. The structure was actually not a gate at all, but rather a portal to the many levels of this infinite plane. Death approached the immense crystal formation, which was surrounded on all sides by a pure white fire that was strangely both hot and cold to the touch. The walls of this formation were made of no earthly crystal. They were denser and more solid than diamond, and as clear as glass with light passing through all sides — this made for quite a sparkling display. Stepping through the strange fire, Death entered the crystal realm. A ring of the very same fire surrounded him and then vanished. He searched the room with his empty eyes, taking in its beauty. This was not his first time here; but no matter how many times you visit, the crystals always seem to sparkle with more brilliance than the last time. The walls and floor that surrounded him were made of the same crystal that formed the outside. Portals of pure white fire were fitted into the walls. Death gazed upon the magnificent ceiling, which was made up of the stars of the sky. Beautifully colored supernovas and bright flashing lightning created a feeling of unlimited space, yet clearly from the outside one could see that a ceiling stood there. Before Death stood a man, or so he still appeared, in good health but well matured. He had a thick beard, and thick curly hair. His robe was as white as the fire, and he shined with a brilliance of an angel. It was indeed St. Peter, and beside him stood two great angels, like pillars of great fire, strong and stern. These three guarded something special, something grand — the Gates of Heaven. Behind them, in the center of the room, stood a ring of fiery crystal, which went up to the ceiling. There was an opening in the front of the structure acting as a doorway. Inside was housed the Pure Fire of God, the Heart of the Holy Spirit. All the souls that Death collected were brought here and placed into the Fire to be judged. The Fire determined their fate, and where they would go. Death approached St. Peter.

"Why have you come, Death?" Peter asked. "You have no souls to hand over."

"Well, to speak honestly, I am here to seek counsel with God. You see, I have a slight problem, and I was wondering if—," implored Death, as he was cut off by the words of the Gatekeeper.

"If God could solve it? Why not just pray like we all do."

"I don't pray." Death stated. "If I pray, I cannot know if God is listening, or if He even cares to listen. My problem is much too important to leave to chance. Prayer is out of the question, I need to *speak* with God."

Just as Death spoke those words, another portal opened right in front of him. A great fire beamed light from this portal, which illuminated with such great brilliance and was shrouded by such an aura of pure love that it made the fire outside seem dimmed and dulled. At this the angels, those great pillars of fire, bowed in reverence, as did Peter. From the portal came a voice unlike any on Earth.

"Be still!" the voice thundered from all around them. "Death, I know why you have come."

"God, is it truly You, the Creator of all?" Death asked.

9

"Yes, it is I, YHWH," The same voice spoke, but this time as soft as a lamb. "Are you surprised to hear My voice?"

"I have never heard a word from You all my life, and now I am speaking with You," Death spoke back. "I figured at best You would have sent Metatron to speak Your Word, as You have been known to do."

"Your faith has opened your ears to My voice. Anyone who wishes to hear it must just listen, as I deny none of My children the opportunity to be in My presence and My Grace," God's voice filled the air with love and peace.

"Will You help me then, oh Lord?"

"It depends on your definition of the word 'help'. I am always helping everyone and everything, for I am Creator of all things. But My ways are not the ways of all."

"Lord, I am confused by Your words. Will You help me by ending the life of Radix, and save Your people from death and darkness?"

"Since when have you been concerned with the deaths of mortals?" the Most High asked. "You know in your heart that I will not just wave My mighty hand and smite Radix."

"You do not have to smite him. He has a contract with Satan." Death interjected. "Can't you just have one of your mighty angels protect his next kill, so Radix misses his quota and therefore forfeits his life."

"That is not My way. Man will bring an end to Radix. I will be of help. But I will help as I help, and no other way."

"So, what is Your way? Is it to let Radix keep slaughtering Your people and bring forth destruction to the entire planet, while we wait for some superhuman to do the impossible?" Death snapped back. "You are abandoning Your people when they need You the most, when I need You the most. The longer Radix lives, the longer I pain. And if the world falls then my pain will be unquenchable, as I still feel the sting of other planets lost in generations past."

"Blasphemer — show some respect when speaking to the Lord of all," St. Peter cut in.

"Kepha, let him speak. I understand his pain, as should you," the Almighty rebutted. "Death, you must understand that I do not take pleasure in treating my children as puppets or slaves. It is right for My children to live in My ways, but they must choose how they live, and therefore they must face challenges and gain the right to My power. What kind of Father would I be to them if I did not respect them as my sons and daughters. I love My children with an undying love and give them all they need — for as long as they call upon Me, will I bless them."

Pausing again, Death spoke, "I was right. You don't really care. You speak in circles, talking about love and giving your children what they need. Well, what they need is salvation." Then, Death turned and said, "I'll just have to find help somewhere else."

"You speak of salvation. This I have already given all of My children, no matter where they are scattered, by the only means through which they could be saved — My own blood." the Almighty answered. "Go, if you must. But know that *he* will be of no help to you. *He* will only try to use you, as *he* has used others in the past."

"I have no where else to turn. It's not like You are doing anything, as usual," at this final comment Death emitted a great shining light from his body and vanished.

"Their suffering will not last forever," the sound was faint as the words rolled off of the most powerful lips in all creation. "But without suffering there will never be peace." At this the portal closed.

# CHAPTER II
## EVIL IS UPON US

The year was 2000 AD, and after almost two millennia from the time of our being saved from sin, evil still flourished. But this had been the case since before the infamous Sodom and Gomorrah, before the time of the great flood, before the slaying of Abel by his own brother Cain, and even before Adam ate the "forbidden fruit." It all began with a falling star, who dragged a third of Heaven along with it to the depths of Hell. Since then Satan has made it his mission to corrupt all of God's creation, turning the hearts of God's children dark like his. We are pitted against each other, when we should band together to defeat our common foe. God has done His part by sending us men and women to lead us in His ways. Though time and again we have rejected those who bring the message of peace and love from the Most High, including the greatest of all — God's own Son, Jesus Christ. Christ died so that we might live, for with His resurrection were we truly set free from sin and evil. We may continue to walk in darkness, but there is a light. We must just look for it and follow.

# Part I
## Evil Lurks Around Every Corner

It was a cool night in New York. A dark man stood atop one of the city's sky piercing structures, resisting the strong wind as if it was a calm spring breeze. His long black coat flowed behind him, and the air ran through his short jet-black hair, which contrasted his pale white skin. The silk shirt that he wore was as red as the blood that flowed from his victims. This man's name was Radix and many had fallen by his hand. The streets below seemed still and calm from where he stood. Radix looked down at the city — its millions of people, all cattle waiting for the slaughter. To kill all of them would be sheer pleasure to the man, a task he could easily complete. But for some reason he did not. He told himself that if he killed them all, then what would he do. He would have no purpose. But that was not the true reason. Deep down inside, Radix did not know why he held back from annihilating the entire human race. That was because Radix did not realize that he was not the master of his own destiny, not since he signed his deal. But it was not Satan, either, holding him back. A powerful force of evil held back the hand of Radix, an evil that needed the people to live in order to have what it desired. From the distance approached a gentleman, who walked on the currents of the air. His skin was nicely tanned, and he had thick black hair and a well-trimmed beard. He wore a white suit with a red tie that matched Radix's shirt. Still looking down at the city, Radix paid no attention to the man who approached him. When he looked up, the red eyes of the gentleman in white met his own, and the two began to talk.

"So, Old Scratch, how's the weather down there?" Radix asked.

"We're keeping it warm for you," Old Scratch replied.

"And what brings you here?"

"Just checking up on my favorite boy. I heard that you nixed number 665, only one more to go. Don't mess it up or you'll be spending your days getting a tan with me. But something tells me that you won't take to the heat like I do."

"Always a clown, huh, Scratch. Well, I'll finish off the next one quick. So who is it, this time? A world leader, the pope perhaps, or just another pacifist?"

"Actually none of the above. The next lucky contestant is a Caucasian male, twenty-five years of age, and about five-feet-six-inches tall. His name is Nathaniel Salvatore, and from what I hear he's not too far from here. Good luck hunting," Scratch grinned, his teeth whiter than his suit and sharp like a lion's.

"I'll do just fine; I still have plenty of time. But what I want to know is why that name sounds so familiar," Radix contemplated, rubbing his head. "Nathaniel Salvatore, hmm."

"Well, that's none of my concern. I just wouldn't be so smug about how much time you have to kill this one. Death is looking to put an end to you. He can't afford to lose another planet, and your not dying is leaving a nice gaping hole inside of him. He has already spoken with *His Highness*. Even though the Almighty gave his usual shtick, the feeling is that He won't be as passive as He has been in the past. It could mean your end if you don't stay

14

focused. It's a good thing you found the *Necronomicon*. I have put it nicely and neatly back in its place of honor. It is yours to use whenever you need to. Just call upon it like you have in the past."

"I only like to use that book as a last resort. I've done fine without it for a good many years. I'm sure my next victim will not cause me too much trouble, despite your concern," Radix answered.

"Never underestimate your enemies, for at any time someone can take you down. That book that you do not like to use was the source of the power you have today. Remember its magic is what makes you live and breathe. So you might think differently, to use it as much as you can. Better to stay on top of the game, and survive, than to let your guard down and be overcome. Do as you please. I must be going now. Farewell."

The gentleman vanished, leaving Radix all alone with the cold night air.

# Part II

## The Gutter

A loud knock at the door startled Lyles as he sat in his bed. It was four o'clock in the morning, and he had been woken up only moments earlier by the sound of a gunshot from across the street. The young black man of twenty-six years of age was accustomed to the sound of gunfire in his neighborhood, it had been the case his whole life. But he was more confused by the knock at the door, and it continued even louder.

"Who's there?" Lyles asked harshly with his shoulder pressed up against the door.

"It's me, Rashan, and the guys," a voice answered from the other side of the door.

Lyles opened the door and let Rashan and his friends in. The three thirteen year old boys walked in with a swagger, each of them had a gun tucked into his jeans. Lyles looked at them with a disapproving glare.

"Was that you three causing the rucous out there tonight? What the hell were you thinking?" Lyles scolded.

"Yo, Lyles, cut us some slack," Rashan jumped in. "That wasn't us. But it's why we're here. You see, Old Man Reynolds was shot by some white fool," Rashan said and walked over to the window and pointed across the street. "See, his body is still there."

"Oh God, no!" Lyles cried. "I'd say we should call the cops, but I'm certain they are on their way already. To be honest, you boys bettter ditch those pieces, unless you want to get tied into this."

"It don't matter, 'cause we already are," Rashan spoke again. "You see we tracked that white freak to an alley, and shot that cracker with about every bullet we had."

"What's wrong with you three? I thought I taught you better than this," Lyles responded.

"What's wrong is some white punk comin' into our turf and shootin' one of ours. That's what's wrong. You think we're gonna let that slide?"

"Rashan, you're crazy. The cops are on their way, and once they start investigating this, you are all screwed. That man you shot is full of bullets from guns with your prints all over them."

"We thought you would help us — hide us, hide the guns, anything. We know if the cops get to us, we are as good as dead. Those pigs got no love for us, just like we got no love for them."

"This is ridiculous. You are staying here. But when the cops come, you are gonna tell them everything. It'll be better for you to come clean. Lying will only make it worse," Lyles lectured the teens, who were like younger brothers to him.

"I ain't waiting around for no pigs. I'm out, and you guys best be comin' along. I know I don't want to go back to no juvi, let alone jail."

The three boys got up and bolted out the door before Lyles could stop them. They ran outside and headed south. Lyles heard the sound of sirens approaching, and he went out to the street below, not sure what to do.

# Part III

## Three Little Pigs

It was about five in the morning, and the sun had not yet risen. The sky was still mostly dark with a hint of red coming from the horizon. Three shadows could be seen dashing through the streets, trying to escape. Not running from anyone in particular, but instead running from reality. They had just killed a man. To them, they did the right thing — a life for a life. But that was not the law of society. Sure, they feared being caught by the cops, but they feared what they had done even more. The band of fugitives ran about sixty blocks south until they finally stopped. Sitting on the cold concrete sidewalk, they took a rest.

"Let's relax for a li'l while, guys," Rashan panted. "We've been runnin' for at least an hour, and I'm—"

"You ain't the only one who's beat, Rashan. Me an' Josh are about to drop, too," interrupted Kenny.

The three boys just sat on the strange street corner, and watched the people go by. They had rarely been outside of their neighborhood before, never knowing how big the city really was and all the different types of people that made it up. Things would be different now — new and scary. They would have no one except for each other. All of their friends were back in the neighborhood, a place that these boys would never see again.

"Yo, Rashan! Josh! Wake up! It's ten o'clock, and we best be out."

"Where we gonna go, fool? We ain't got no homes no more," Josh sniveled back.

"Well, all I know is I want to go somewhere other than here," replied Kenny.

"Kenny's right. And anyway we gotta' get as far away from home as possible. Let's head downtown and then go out of state. Maybe Jersey."

"Rashan, you crazy? You think we can just go somewhere else, just like that. Where you plan on stayin'. It's not like the Ritz is offerin' rooms to homeless black kids. We gonna have to sleep

17

on the street!" Josh shouted. "We gotta find a way to get some dough."

"You guys, just chill'. All we should be worryin' about is hidin' from the pigs. So let's get up and out," Kenny stated calmly in order to relax the others. At this the boys got up and began to walk the cold, cluttered streets of the city.

As the day dragged on, they got tired and very hungry, but they had nothing to quench their thirst or starvation. Just then, deliverance came their way. A young African-American woman in a Salvation Army uniform approached the boys. She had a welcoming smile, and the most honest eyes they had ever seen.

"Are you boys all right? You look lost. Do you have homes?" she inquired.

"Not any more ma'am," replied Rashan. He always seemed to be the mediator of the group. "You see we kinda ran away, and now we got nowhere to go, and nothin' to eat. Can you help us?"

"Sure I can, young man. You see, I'm from the Salvation Army. It's our duty to help those in need. Come with me, and I'll feed you boys, and give you a place to rest tonight," the woman said in a comforting voice.

The three boys, in their joy, followed the woman down the street to a soup kitchen. Their eyes opened in shock as they saw how many other people had similar problems to theirs. Growing up, they saw the bums on the street corners, drinking whiskey from bottles in paper bags. They never understood why, until now. They were just like those bums with no place to go; no place, that was, but the streets.

*Where are those boys,* Lyles thought to himself as he told the police about last night's incident.

"You said that a white male, indefinite on the description, shot Mr. Reynolds at his front door at about a quarter to four in the morning?" questioned the portly red-haired officer.

"Yes," Lyles replied in a worried, yet calm tone.

"I see. Now, you yourself did not get a view of the criminal suspect, but rather were told this information by three boys? Correct?" the officer asked, while writing down what Lyles told him.

"Yes, that is *correct*."

"Well, where are these boys, and do you have any clue to where the suspect went off to?" inquired the officer.

"The boys ran off and haven't been heard from all day. As for the suspect, well, I'm really not sure where he is. All I know is what the boys told me," Lyles replied almost stuttering due to his nervousness.

"And the boys didn't tell you where the guy ran off to, or what he looks like? All you know is that he's white? This all sounds shady to me, boy. Now don't withhold any information! If you know something, tell me. Or I'll see to it that all this gets pinned on your head!" the officer roared at Lyles.

"Officer, I'm telling you everything I know. All that the boys said was that they saw a white guy shoot Mr. Reynolds, and run off. I haven't seen the boys since. So why don't you do your job, find those boys, ask them what happened, and leave me alone!" Lyles shouted back at the officer.

"Okay, boys," the officer called over some of his fellow policemen. "Let's search the area and find these kids, I have names and photographs, so you know who you're looking for. Let's go!" Before he left he turned to Lyles and said, "Don't worry, I'll be back for you later, boy."

*Who does this guy think he is calling me "boy,"* Lyles thought to himself as the officer walked off showing the photographs of the three teenagers to the other cops in the search party.

A Caucasian man in his later forties draped in a gray trench coat with a cigarette dangling from his mouth and a pair of shades covering his eyes walked out of Mr. Reynolds apartment and went over to the remaining officers. He whispered something to a woman, and walked over to Lyles.

"I appologize for Officer Roger's lack of manners. I'm Detective Johnson, and I'll be working this case. Thank you for all of your help," the detective said and shook Lyles' hand.

"You're welcome, detective."

"I'll be keeping in contact with you as further information comes up in the case. Here's my card. Call me if anything happens, or if you have any questions," the detective paused as he gave Lyles the card. "And if those boys return, please have them contact me as well. I would love to hear their side of the story. Hope to hear from you soon," he said and moved off.

Later that night, Lyles decided to take a look around Mr. Reynolds' apartment. He had a spare set of keys that the old man had given to him, just in case anything happened. Lyles crept into the small one-bedroom apartment, and quietly closed the door behind him. Lyles started to look around the living room, but he was drawn to the bedroom, as if something was calling him from inside there. There was a large cross hanging over the bed, and in the corner was a desk piled with books, including various translations of the Holy Bible. Next to the stack of Bibles was a beaten-up leather-bound journal. Something told Lyles to take it, and so he tucked it under his shirt and sneaked back out.

That same night, downtown in the village, the three teens were lying down in a resting house for the homeless. They tried to sleep, but their little minds were cluttered with confusion.

"Hey, *pst*, Rashan. Yo Rashan," whispered Josh as he shook Rashan to get his attention. "Yo, I can't sleep. I can't stop wonderin' about what's gonna happen. I mean we're gonna get caught for sure."

"Josh, don't worry. We're gonna be just fine. I mean now we got a place to stay," Rashan replied.

"Ya'll gotta be trippin'. We ain't got no place to stay. This is only for tonight. Who says we can crash here forever. Eventually, we gotta go. And we don't have many options, so we gotta start huntin'. Maybe we can walk around tomorrow, and see what's up," Kenny said, trying to set the situation straight.

"What are we s'pose to look for anyway, huh?" Josh threw in.

"I say we leave things be 'til tomorrow. Okay, guys." Once again Rashan took charge.

That next day the boys went off on their journey and roamed the vast streets of the city. Before they knew it, it was nightfall, and they had no idea where they were. The streets were no longer numbered, and they did not recognize any of the names, for it was their first time venturing this far south. Even though they did not want to admit it, they were scared. Rashan thought that he knew how to get back to the shelter. He led the boys into an alley that he was sure was a shortcut. The boys followed their leader blindly. But unfortunately it was a dead end, even deadlier than the boys knew. They moved in close together as the walls seemed to close in on them, darkness all around.

Lyles sat down once he got home, and decided to look at the journal that he found. He opened the old dusty leather cover, and flipped through the yellowed pages that had countless rips and tears. It was Mr. Reynolds' personal diary. Lyles read the first entry. It was from 1930:

*Today is my 10th birthday, and ma gave me this diary. She says that I should write in it everyday. She wants me to learn to read and write good, cause it'll help me succeed. I ain't had much schooling cept by poppy. That's grandpa. He's a very smart man. I just wish that I could grow up to be like him—*

The book went on to point out the major events of the man's life, and Lyles kept on reading:

*June 29th, 1945*

*Today was the greatest day of my life, for today I was ordained a minister of God. Now I can preach His Word to all the world, just like Christ instructed His apostles. This is the greatest accomplishment of my life. I thank my mother and grandfather for all that they taught me. I am glad that the Lord has provided me with such success—*

Lyles drifted off as he read the book. He slept very peacefully.

The boys were trapped at the end of the dark alley. They huddled close together, as they heard the sound of approaching footsteps. Fearing for their very lives, the boys climbed quickly into an adjacent dumpster. The putrid smell and filthy vermin that were contained inside were no concern to them at this point. All that they cared about was staying alive. They held their breath and hoped that whoever was there would just pass by. But they did not get their wish. The footsteps got louder and stopped. A dark man stood outside the dumpster for he knew the boys were inside, the same man that they saw kill Mr. Reynolds, the very one that they thought they had killed. But this man could not be killed. Radix pounded on the side of the dumpster.

"Hey boys, come out, come out, wherever you are. I know you're in there. I saw you, and I can hear you breathing. Now come out like nice boys, before I have to pull you out myself," he said, his voice evil in every way.

The three runaways remained quiet, hoping that he would leave. But he did not.

"Okay boys, I've had enough! I'll huff and I'll puff and I'll blow your dumpster down." At that he lifted the dumpster off of the ground and flung it into a wall. This was no ordinary man — he was the Devil's right-hand, and the boys knew it.

The crash knocked all three of them from the dumpster. They lay on the ground unable to move from the impact. Helpless, the three gazed into the man's empty eyes. Their own eyes were full of fear, for they knew that their lives were coming to an end.

"You, you were dead. We killed you!" Rashan shouted.

"Sorry to inform you, but you didn't do such a good job. But since you had so much fun shooting me, I'm going to have some fun of my own."

*Bang, bang, bang!* At the sound of someone pounding on his door, Lyles fell out of the chair that he had slept in. The happenings of last night were vague in his mind. So far, the mysterious diary had shown him nothing, except for a few highlighted moments in the preacher's life. But Lyles forgot about the book as he got up to answer the door.

"Who, is it?" Lyles shouted.

"It's me, Detective Johnson. I have to speak with you for a moment."

"Who let you in the building? I never buzzed you in," Lyles said, not wanting to be bothered by the Detective.

"The super let me in. I showed him my badge. So open up."

Lyles did not feel like arguing, it being so early in the morning, so he undid the chains and locks and let the detective in.

"What is it that you have to tell me?"

"My visit here is of the utmost urgency. But before I tell you anything, I just want to give you one more chance to release any information you might still be holding concerning the case."

"I told you everything that I know! I don't really feel like having you come up in here and play games. I don't like playing games!" Rage consumed Lyles as he spoke.

"I'm behind you kid. But if we don't have a murderer your statement falls, and you become a likely suspect."

"Well, I told you — once you find the boys, they can describe him to you. I don't know anything else!"

"That's the problem. You see, we did find the boys."

"Really! Are they all right?" asked Lyles with a feeling of relief.

"No," Detective Johnson said and lowered his head. "They're dead."

"No-o!" Lyles screamed in agony.

A half hour later in an alleyway in Manhattan, Lyles looked up at three little bodies. They looked so innocent. A tear flowed down his cheek as he thought about what kind of monster could do such a horrid thing to mere children. Fear crept into his heart for he now knew the true evils of mankind. How unlike any other creature, man would not only kill one of his own for no other reason than sheer pleasure, but also in such a painful and unnatural way.

These boys had suffered much torture as they died. All three were crucified on the alley wall, held up by pieces of their own ribs that were driven through their wrists and feet. No one could figure out how anyone could drive bone through a brick wall. It had to be done with great power and precision that no man could perform. The boys' chests had been ripped open; on each boy's stomach was carved a six; and above all of this horrible slaughter was a pentagram with a diameter of ten feet, scrawled in blood. The only thing Lyles could think about was how these boys suffered, and he knew why. See, it was no accident that these boys were killed in such a manner. It was the man who they shot. He was alive, and sought his revenge. Lyles knew that some greater force was behind this, and he was going to find out what it was — even if it would cost him his life.

23

# CHAPTER III
## TO HELL AND BACK

My visit with the Lord was not very fruitful, leaving me with little hope. God was my best chance at victory, for we shared the common enemy. But as usual, I'll be doing this alone. Now I have a more difficult task. That is to find some kind of compassion in the heart of the Devil. This will be most difficult if not impossible. A human might compare it with trying to squeeze orange juice from an apple. Though actually, it might be more like trying to persuade a hungry lion not to eat you. God was right; why would Satan help me ruin his own plan? I have to be crafty; trick him into helping me. All the while, making sure to not fall for any of his deceptions. He is the slyest of all creatures, a cunning snake.

# Part I
## Death Goes South

In a flash of light, Death appeared on the outskirts of Hell, a desolate wasteland. The ground was rocky, the air was red and still. The Gates of Hell did not have the splendor of those in Heaven. The tower supporting the Gates of Hell was enormous and irregular in shape, made from black crystals, similar to the clear crystals that made up the Gates of Heaven, but lacking the luster and beauty. Around the dark crystal structure burned a bright red fire, so hot some say that it could turn the stars of the heavens to dust. The opening was quite large, much larger than that of Heaven — for all were welcome here. At the opening were stalactites and stalagmites formed from the same crystal as the tower, giving the impression of a large mouth waiting to consume whoever dared to enter. Unharmed by the scorching flames that surrounded the tower, Death entered.

The inside of the tower was made up of the same crystal as the outside. Another circle of intense fire was in the center of the room causing the crystals to reflect a strange dark light. The room had no decoration, and the dark crystal walls seemed to go on without end. Death walked toward the fire.

"Brother, good to see you," A voice came from behind Death.

"Don't call me brother," Death renounced.

The being that stood before Death wore a long deep-purple robe with a hood over his head, hiding his face. He was the same height and build as Death. His long bony fingers gripped a tall wooden staff. On the head of the staff was a demonic hand gripping a dark crystal, like those that made up the tower. The crystal had a glow similar to the fire that kindled next to Death.

"Why have you come here, brother? To cause trouble, I am sure," the being spoke with the same sharpness as Death, as he moved closer.

"My being here is none of your concern, and I told you not to call me brother, Sin."

"Don't deny your birthright, and anyone's being here is of my concern. I am the gatekeeper, as I have been since the fall. I was created when Lucifer defied God. The Prince of Darkness himself gave me this position. For he knew that like no other, I could draw many souls to this place. So, explain your presence now!"

"My birthright? You fool, we are not beings of flesh. We were not born. We were created. Yes, both of us spawned from temptation, two halves of the same whole; but I am nothing like you and therefore do not acknowledge you as my kin. As for why I am here. I need to see your prince."

"It's about Radix, isn't it?" Sin inquired. "You fool, my lord will not help you with this. It is a lost cause. That's his golden boy. So why don't you go home now and save yourself the trouble."

"Listen here. If you do not let me pass, I will strike you down here and now. Remember, you may be older, but I am far stronger," Death said sternly as he gazed into the blank face of Sin. Yes, blank, for all beings wore the face of sin.

"Brother, your power is useless here. It only works on the mortal plane. You may be able to best me there, but right now you are in my world, so you better think twice about trying me! I will let you pass, though, for it will amuse me to hear what my master's answer will be. Go into the fiery circle, and you will enter Hell in all of its torment." Sin laughed.

Death did exactly that. Unharmed, he walked through the fire. As he did, the heat increased a thousand fold. After being engulfed in the flame, he walked out and was now in Hell.

# Part II
## The Land of Torture

The sound of Sin's laughter echoed in Death's head as he entered the plane of everlasting torture. The sky was an even deeper red than it was at the gates. *Whappp!* Death was struck from behind and crashed face first onto the hard dirt floor. The dirt from the ground burned his face and eyes, making it hard for him to see. As he got up, his vision began to clear. He could see souls before him, ones that he had collected over the ages. These damned souls were forced to work the land for all eternity, harvesting the sins they committed throughout their mortal lives. Dusting himself off, Death turned around to see what had struck him down. Before he could get a good look at his assailant, he was grabbed and lifted off of his feet by a large tentacle made up of bones. The monstrosity squeezed Death tighter and tighter with its tentacle. It carried Death up to one of its four faces — each of them looking in a different direction. This made it easier for the creature to watch all of its slaves at once, making sure that everyone was working hard. For if any of its slaves tried to rest, the hideous demon would easily strike that slave down with a crack of its whip, which was woven from the strands of its own coarse hair. The taskmaster ripped the hair from its own head a long time ago, for the hair always blocked one of its faces. Each face of the monster was unique, representing an emotion of some sort. The three that looked away from Death represented hate, sadness, and anger; while the face that stared into Death's own had no emotion. It was uncaring in every way, just a blank stare. The torso of the creature was completely skeletal with large wings of bone spanning twenty feet in each direction. The demon had no arms or legs, but rather six tentacles of bone that protruded from its torso, one of which still held Death tightly in its grasp. Its faces began to rotate, stopping on the one that symbolized anger.

"How dare you come here and interrupt my slaves' labor," the demon spoke with curdling anger. "I don't have time for this!

Why are you here, Death, in a place where you do not belong?"

"Nothing that pertains to you, Bayemon. So please, kindly release me and get back to your pointless torture," Death demanded.

"How dare you speak to me in such a tone. I rule over the Harvest Lands. You have no power here. You are nothing! I am a god to these people!"

"God, that's a good one. *You* are nothing, and you know it. Satan dictates your life to you — a pitiful existence."

"Pitiful? I'll tell you who's pitiful. Look at your life," his face changed now to the one of hatred. "You are a mere slave for the Man upstairs. You have no life; you live for the dead; something you have no say in; an existence you were born into. Always doing God's dirty work, while He sits atop His high and mighty throne. At least I chose to be where I am."

Silence came over the entire land. Bayemon placed the dumbfounded Death on the ground. The thought crossed Death's mind to strike at Bayemon, though he reconsidered, seeing that he stood no chance as long as he was in Hell. Here his powers were limited, and for the most part useless.

"You got me there. I guess I may be a prisoner; but you, my friend, are not better off," Death took a calmer tone. "Let me refresh your memory. You gave up your grace in Heaven because you felt that you were treated too lowly. You gave up your happiness and beauty because you got greedy. And look what it got you. Now instead of being a lowly angel in paradise, you are a lowly demon living in the wastelands of Hell. You are miserable and disgustingly hideous to look at. Plus, the power that you believe yourself to have; ha, you are not a slave master, but rather a slave yourself — to Satan. You gave up everything for nothing, just like the others."

Bayemon looked as if he was about to explode but at that moment his face shifted again, now revealing the face of sadness, "Death, leave now for you have no business staying. Leave me to my kingdom, to my punishment. Just leave!" Bayemon spoke with a broken heart.

Death took the opportunity at hand and went off to find Satan's stronghold. As he left he saw the hideous demon change faces again, and all was back to normal as Bayemon drove his slaves harder than before.

As Death took another step the entire landscape altered before his very eyes. Bayemon had completely disappeared, as did his entire land. This new place was much different, even stranger than the last. The ground beneath his feet changed from dry crusty dirt to slick black marble. The sky darkened and a breeze floated past him. Before him stood a woman, taller than he. She had long pin-straight blonde hair and wore a sackcloth robe that covered every inch of her body. Her eyes were inviting, a peculiar pink; and her skin was a strange shade of pale blue.

"Death, is it possible that you are dead? Death dead?" the woman jested like a child.

"You know I cannot die, Giltine. A mortal, I am not," Death responded to her banter.

"So, if you are not dead, then why are you here? Have you fallen? Are you one of us now? Death on our side, what a good rouser that would be," she snickered as she spoke.

"Please, you know me better than that. Had that snake never corrupted you, you would not be here yourself. It's a shame to see how easily the Devil can to lead a lamb to slaughter. He is cunning. But that is of no importance."

"Then, why are you here? Is something wrong on the other side?" Giltine asked in a curious tone.

"I am looking for your keeper — the Dark Prince, Satan. I need to speak with him. So, where do I find that tyrant?" Death inquired curtly.

"What you seek, you may never find. These hills change with every heinous act, every sinful thought. As we speak the land changes around us. In mortal time the changes would be so fast that they would go unnoticed, only flashes would one see. But to those like us the changes are evident, for we defy the principles of time and space. And for the damned, the scene never changes. They are trapped in their torture for eternity."

Death looked around noticing that the world around them was indeed changing. Mountains appeared and disappeared. Fields came and went. He could see mortals from across the universe being tortured by fire, disease, pestilence, and the like; all there and then gone again. The only thing remaining constant was the ground that they stood on.

"If you will not help me, then I will be off," Death said.

"Oh, Death, do not leave so soon. Maybe you can stay and chat a bit longer. Come on, you can afford to stay. It's not like your wasting away or anything. Not that anyone could tell. You were never beautiful like us. We all were angels at one time, beautiful forever. But your ugliness has been with you since you were created. Look at me, am I still beautiful?" As she said this, Giltine dropped her robe and exposed her naked body, which surprisingly was beautiful even though she was a demon.

As Death took a closer look, he noticed something strange. Her skin was being pulled, and pushed from the inside. Things were moving around. Death saw faces, hands, and feet; countless numbers of them, as if they were trying to break free from within her.

"These things that you see are the souls trapped in me, the souls of all the mortals whose vanity led them to do evil acts. They let their beauty rule their lives. How fitting that they are inside me. I was beautiful once."

Death did a double take as Giltine transformed before him. Her once breathtaking face now grew more and more deformed. Horns protruded from her skull. Her hair no longer flowed, but instead was raggedy and frayed. Her pink eyes turned a horrifying yellow, and her skin became charred. She squirmed about in convulsions as the souls tried harder and harder to free themselves. Shocked at all that he saw, Death went off and escaped yet another horrifying creature.

*What other oddities does this land of the damned hold*, Death wondered. The landscape changed yet again and took the form of the classical fire and brimstone Hell preached about at Sunday school, time and time again. The air grew hot and thick, and it was filled with the foul smell of rotting flesh and sulfur. Lava flowed through the rocky terrain. Gigantic walls of flame, hotter than a million suns, surrounded the entire area. The smell grew stronger as the air got hotter. Death looked around as countless souls, all of which he remembered, burned in the hot lava and fire before him. Their bodies were chained to the rocks, and their skin bubbled and blistered. There was no escape for these lost souls. They were all killers, murderers. Death knew this for he collected every one of them. Walking through the smoldering heap of bodies, Death looked on to see which demon watched over this section of Hell. No demon was found, but rather a man — a man Death remembered well. His name on Earth was Stan Morgan, a simple name for a simple man. Everyone who knew him thought that Stan was the nicest guy in the world; you know the type, who would not even harm a fly. That is how they all seem to be; you never can point out the really crazy ones, the true psychos. They wear a well-hidden mask. Stan was no different, a family man turned killer. He had it all, a wife, a beautiful daughter, even a dog, and a house in the suburbs with a white picket fence — the American dream. But all that he had, he lost with a small assist from Satan. Death knew this man's story well, so well that it recited over in his head once he took notice of him.

Satan told Stan that if he killed a few people for him, he would see to it that Stan's family was taken care of for the rest of their lives. Not being a religious man — actually, Stan did not believe in God at all — he decided to take Satan up on his offer. The story ended with his wife finding a few dismembered corpses in the basement, about a fifty or so. But before she could turn in her husband, he went completely psycho and killed her. He then killed his own daughter and even poor Cocoa, the family dog. Realizing what he had done, Stan took his own life. Stan learned a valuable lesson about the Devil and his promises. The only problem is, he learned it too late.

Death approached him cautiously, wondering why he was not chained up like the others?

"What brings you to my domain, Death?" Stan asked in a queer way. "Checking up on me? You do remember me right? Stan Morgan? I mean, you visited my basement enough times to collect the souls of my victims. But then again, you get around a lot and have probably seen worse. Well, how is all this for you? Nice to see that everyone is having so much fun around here, huh?"

"You always were one sick guy, Stan; dismembering people, eating their organs, even making clothes from their skin. Your wife actually thought that you bought her a leather jacket for Christmas that year," Death spoke shrewdly. "Me, I'm just passing through. So, I'll be off."

"Leaving so soon? Too hot for ya? Well, the heat's just kickin' in. This place just keeps getting hotter every second, ya know. You should stay a while. We can catch up. Last time I saw you was, hmm, when I died. It's been a few years. Look at me now in charge of all this torture, my gift for doing some dirty work for the Devil."

"Some gift — looks like Hell to me," Death remarked.

"Well, look who's talking, mister 'I have the power to kill anyone and everything, to stop all evil, but I never use it.' If you want such a perfect world, why don't you create one? Kill all the baddies like me. Ah, but you take such a passive role; you make me sick."

"It is not up to me to decide who lives or dies. I just pick up the pieces. The only time I take an active role is when I am instructed to do so. I know how to control myself, unlike people like you," Death bluntly stated.

"People like me? People like me? What is that supposed to mean? See all these people? They were all like me; or so they thought. Now, look at them. I am their king."

"A kingdom of refuse is all you have, a true Gehenna. You gave it all up when you signed a deal with that snake. Men can be so weak. And what about your ultimate mistake, something even you must regret. Remember their screams, their agony. You know who I mean, Susan and Amanda — your wife and daughter. Remember how they begged for you to put down the knife. But did you? Of course not. You were so deranged, you didn't even know what you were doing. Why did you make that deal again, to protect your family, right? All of that, and you slaughtered them yourself. He got you real good. Look at what he gave you — nothing. You watch other animals like yourself fry, in what should be your torment as well."

"Shut up!! You know nothing! My torture is far worse then theirs ever will be, for it is beyond physical. Look at this," Stan said as he pointed at a wall of fire next to him. In the fire a picture appeared, a picture of a beautiful woman playing in a field with a little girl and a dog. "That is Susan and Amanda up in Heaven. They are enjoying eternal bliss, while I stand down here an eternity away from them — the only ones I ever loved. Even little Cocoa. I didn't mean for it to happen. Now, I am tortured to watch them every day as I sit here in this Gehenna, as you put it — my land of fire and brimstone. The reeking stench of burning flesh and sulfur are my only rewards."

Death looked as a tear came to the mass murderer's eye. Stan turned away and went back to watching his wife and child play with Cocoa in Heaven. Death began to walk away, and saw the lava engulf Stan Morgan as Hell changed once more. Approaching deeper into the catacombs of Hell, he felt the great power of hate and sin rise around him, so much that it seemed to mutate the very terrain. Unbeknownst to Death, Satan plotted and conspired as he watched the otherworldly being roaming his land. Being the trickster that he was, Satan decided to play a game with the outsider. The air shifted again, as the world around Death began to morph. The climate, the ground, the atmosphere all transformed around him. Everything changed at such a rate this time that he only caught vague glimpses of his surroundings. The terrain seemed to spin as the rapidness of its transformations increased. When would the world stop spinning? How close to his point of destination was he? Would he be lost in this maze forever? These and other questions drifted through the thoughts of Death. At the moment when he could bear the spinning cyclone of images no longer, it all stopped.

Death gazed at the sight before him — there stood two monstrous pillars, as hard as stone yet made of flame. These pillars stood so high that they appeared to be holding up the sky. Beyond the pillars stood a magnificent palace made of solid gold. It too reached up to the sky, almost as high as the two pillars before it. Death stood back and studied the richness of the palace, all of its fine detail and craftsmanship. He thought of what a fool Satan was to adorn himself with such royalty, when his kingdom was such a tragedy. Death knew that none of this mattered. All that mattered to him was that he had finally reached his point of destination. Now, he had to pull himself together and do the one thing he never thought he would do — ask the Devil for help. He passed through the pillars. The heat of the flames increased with every step. Death reached the large golden door, the entrance to this impressive fortress. *What would be waiting inside,* he thought as he knocked on the door? The door swung open, but no one was there. It was too dark to see much inside, but Death did not care. He had a mission, and he was going to complete it. Shutting the door behind him, he entered the palace and began to walk down the hall. At that very moment, the floor collapsed from underneath him; and he began to fall. The pit seemed to have no end, and Death seemed to be falling for days. He reached out for something to grab onto, anything to stop his descent. At last, his hand grabbed onto something, stopping his fall. Death hung there wondering what was going on, and wondering even more about what he was holding on to. Some light began to shine from fresh fire that appeared on the walls around him. He could see that he was hanging onto a large wooden cross, which protruded from the rocky wall that was now engulfed in flame. The cross was drenched in blood, which dripped down into the bottomless pit below him. The blood was springing from four places: three nails that were imbedded in the two arms and at the foot of the cross, and from a crown of thorns that sat atop the head of the cross. Death reached out with his free arm to get a better grip, so as not to fall. Normally, he would not be in such peril. But in Hell Death had limits on what he could do, and the dark never-ending pit below was sucking him in. At that moment, the crown of thorns sprung from the top of the cross and bound Death's hands and feet. The thorny branches grew and formed into a web-like structure, holding him above the darkness that was trying to swallow him.

"Looking for me?" A voice came from all sides of the pit as Death hung from the web of thorns.

"Satan, what kind of games are you playing?" Death spoke back. "I'm in no mood for games. I have some questions, and I need answers. Be civil, stop these silly tricks, and let me talk with you."

"Death, you should know better. I am anything but civil, and tricks are what I do best. So if you want to see me, you have to pass my little tests. Don't worry, you're almost there. Good luck."

The web snapped. Satan's voice faded into the darkness, and Death began to fall once again. This time, his fall was cut short as he crashed face first into the hard rocky ground. The darkness was gone, and Death brushed himself off as he got up.

The air weighed heavy with the distinct smell of blood. As Death started to walk, he heard the crashing of waves and a beastly, bellowing scream. Death looked around to see where the sounds were coming from, but he only found the bone-dry ground that he was walking on.

"Death?" a deep echoing voice called from behind.

He turned to see an enormous beast towering over him, at least two times his height. The beast had the head and torso of a man, handsome and well built, while the lower portion was like that of a snake. His long, thick trunk-like tail ended with a poisonous stinger. The poison that it possessed was extremely toxic, even for metaphysical beings such as Death. At the end of each of his fingers was a long jagged claw, and large bat-like wings came from his back. They flapped every now and then, creating a violent wind. The monster smiled to reveal a large set of fangs.

"Geryon, do you always pass your time by sneaking up on wandering folk? I thought you had a high ruling position down here. Don't you have better things to do? No matter, I can't be bothered right now. I need to find Satan's palace."

"Be quiet, fool," Geryon roared, "I do as I please in my territory. If you are looking for Satan's palace, it is across the River Styx. Do not expect to get there by foot. The only way across is by means of Charon, the ferryman. Nothing can cross over the river, except on that boat; not even you or myself. It is impossible to even swim across, for it is plagued with a unique type of fish that was created by Poseidon himself after he was sent to Hell. These fish eat souls, and keep them inside their bellies for all eternity. You cannot escape these fish — they are many, and they move faster than anything you have seen. Remember, your powers are useless here. Therefore, you are nothing more than prey."

"Where is the River Styx?"

"Right behind you, imbecile," Geryon said as he pointed to the river.

Death looked where Geryon was pointing, and surprisingly, there flowed a monstrous river as red as blood and as dark as sin. He looked at the powerful waves crashing against the shore and watched as the water seemed to boil.

"Where do I find Charon?" Death inquired.

"You do not find him; he finds you. He will appear when you wait at the dock. But you should not worry, for you cannot cross the river without my permission. Only I choose who can cross, and I will only let you cross if you do something for me."

"And what would that be?"

"Long before human souls were sent here, an angel with no name was thrown from Heaven into this Hell where he was tortured for a thousand years. Before the angel escaped, he stole my mystical horn. I want my horn retrieved. If you can bring it to me, I will let you pass."

"The angel you speak of is nowhere to be found; his whereabouts are unknown. The horn is no longer with him, but rests in Heaven with countless other treasures. I cannot retrieve such a prize, for God and His Heavenly Host would forbid it. Is there anything else I could do to convince you to allow me to cross?"

"You have done well in telling me where my horn rests. I will find that angel, and I will seek out my own brand of justice against him," the demon roared. "I will let you pass this one time, since I know the Master is expecting you. But do not count on such a nice gesture the next time you find yourself in Hell."

"I won't."

"You will need this," Geryon said as he handed Death a silver coin with a skull engraved on it. "Use this to pay the ferryman. Just one thing — don't pay Charon until he gets you to the bank on the other side of the river. Now leave!" Geryon's voice boomed, which caused waves to rage across the water.

Death reached the dock at the River Styx's bank. It creaked as he walked on its wooden planks. A thick fog made it hard to see, but Death could hear the boat approaching. As he looked down into the murky water, he thought about the soul-stealing fish that Geryon had told him of. Was it true or was the demon up to his old tricks and scare tactics. The little wooden ferryboat pulled up against the dock, bumping it ever so slightly. The fog made it difficult for Death to make out Charon's face. The ferryman was tall and lanky, a little hunched over, and wore a sackcloth robe. Charon put out his bony hand, gesturing for an offering for the ride. Death showed him the coin but did not place it in his hand, letting him know that he would be paid upon a safe arrival to the other side. The boat dipped down as Death walked into it, and Charon began to paddle them across the river.

The ferry ride was quiet, and the fog made it difficult to see. Death leaned over the edge. The River Styx was not like any other body of water known to man. It had a very high potency of spiritual energy; so high, that it made it very difficult to cross over it. Like a magnet, it would pull in anyone who tried to pass. Only by riding in the magical boat piloted by Charon could anyone be assured of safe passage to the other side. But the worst part of being pulled into the crimson water, as Geryon mentioned before, was that the strange fish of the river fed on souls. Death was lost in the movement of the soft waves as the ferry drifted further and further.

The water began to ripple, and Death could see some bubbles coming up to the surface. Then out of the river, a monstrous creature flew up with a loud screech. Death jumped back just before the creature could wrap its jaws around him. He got a good look at the mammoth-sized mackerel as it gracefully glided straight up into the air and then landed flawlessly back into the river without the slightest splash. The fish was like none that Death had ever seen on any planet before, and he had been to all of them. It was jet black with a gold trident branded on it, the mark of Poseidon. Its teeth were like long sharp needles, and it had three flippers on each side and one long jagged fin that ran down it's back. But its eyes were what was most peculiar. It was not so much their black color or bulbous shape that made them strange. It was the look that came from them, a sinister look. Death had seen that look before in the eyes of Radix. It was the look of no remorse. He now knew that Geryon told no tales, and he made sure to keep his head in the boat for the rest of the journey. *What would the world be like if Death was no more? Nothing but wandering souls,* he thought.

37

The ferry slammed into the shore. Death turned to Charon, who opened up his hand waiting for the silver coin that Death flashed at him on the other side of the river. As he went to hand the ferryman the coin, it disappeared. Charon impatiently pointed at his empty hand, gesturing for a form of payment; but Death had none. The more he tried to explain, the more still Charon became. Then with a powerful wave of his hand, he caused Death to fly from the boat and into a pile of bones on the shore. The laughter of Geryon was heard throughout the land. The coin was another one of his tricks. Death looked over at Charon as the ferry drifted away. He knew that he was safe for now, but that the ferryman would never bring him across that river again. He knocked over the bones that covered him, and got up. There were more piles of bones around him. Death grabbed a skull from one of the piles and studied it carefully. The skull was about three times the size of a human skull. Three broken horns were set into it, one at the top of the forehead and two just above the temples. The skull's incisors and canine teeth were sharp, but the molars were dull. Death assumed that it was a demon-humanoid hybrid of some kind. Their reason for being there was a mystery of its own. He threw the skull back into the pile, and began to walk to Satan's palace.

After enduring all the trials and tribulations of the land of the damned, Death had finally reached his intended destination. The palace towered over the land of torture, sin, and hate. It was a shrine, majestic in every way. The magnificence of Satan's dwelling confused and surprised Death. How could living in such splendor be seen as punishment? The golden palace seemed to stretch for miles on each side. Nine towers pierced the sky, and all nine were adorned with large gems glistening in the dark light. The central tower rose higher than even the Tower of Babel did before it was sent crashing down by the Lord. The elegance of this central tower was matched by no other part of the palace. Atop the tower lay a golden dragon of monstrous proportions. The dragon seemed to be sleeping, though it was obvious to Death that it was not a living being. Its long golden tail came down and wrapped around the tower. Large stained glass windows — each showing horrid images of war, death, and destruction taken from times passed — sat between thick columns, which adorned the facade. Death noticed that the palace seemed to take on the form of some kind of twisted church. It was both beautiful and an abomination at the same time. His attention shifted to the great rose window that was high above the threshold. The image it portrayed was that of one of the the most climatic points in all of history, the point when God had first lost one of his own, when the balance took its first shift in the direction of darkness, the great fall — Satan's descent from Heaven to Hell.

Death walked up the stone road before him, which turned into fancy marble. On each side of him stood tall demonic statues. Their clawed hands grasped each other's, and their large marble wings spread out on either side, forming a tunnel. The statues seemed to growl as a hot wind passed under them, hitting Death's face. The tunnel led to even finer marble steps. They were extremely wide at the base, about a fifth the width of the palace, and grew narrower as they reached the threshold. The huge golden iron-like doors stood under a finely crafted archway, in which images of demons and men doing heinous things were sculpted. Death wondered what kind of place he had gone to. As he reached the top of the stairs, the door opened.

# Part III

## Inside the Sleeping Dragon

Death stood and watched as the doors crept open. He waited to be greeted by a host of some sort, but no one stood on the other side. The room that he had entered was much different from the outside of the palace. It was not heavily decorated in precious metals or fine gems, but was rather plain. The only décor was two tall marble pillars with golden rims wrapped around their bases on each side of the room. In front of Death were three identical wooden doors. He could not decide which door to enter. Without giving it too much thought, he randomly chose the door in the middle. Just as he placed his hand on the doorknob he heard a loud echoing *thud* on the marble floor. Startled, Death turned to have his eyes met by another's. The creature, some sort of goblin, stared at Death with its wide green eyes, peering into his very essence. Its skin was bumpy and a pale shade of green, matching its eyes. It wore a robe made of tanned leather. In its left hand the goblin was wielding a large metal staff, almost twice the height of its body. On the top of the staff was a transparent blue orb. Death's eyes focused on the glowing blue globe that sat on the staff, noticing spirits swimming around inside of it. The power to hold souls — Death thought this to be impressive, and therefore knew that this goblin was more than just a mere minion of some sort. The goblin waved its staff, and the two side doors opened. Death wondered why only those two doors opened and not the middle door. He placed his lifeless hand on the closed door. Instantly, he felt an empty cold come over him, like none that he had ever known. Death knew somehow that this empty coldness was the absence of God. This was indeed peculiar and made him wonder what other mysteries hid inside these strange corridors. Now Death had to choose: was it the door on the right or the door on the left. He turned his head each way and contemplated his options. Then he took note of a sweet and sultry scent coming from the room on the right. Had Death been a human, the aroma would be intoxicating and impossible to resist. He realized at that moment that the room to the right could lead only to one place, the quarters of the temptress, Lilith. The original succubus and bride of Satan, Lilith preyed on men, seducing them at first, and then after fulfilling their carnal desires, she would fulfill her own by devouring them whole. Pity for the soul of a man approached by Lilith, for after she had her way with him, he would be damned for all time. Fortunately for Death, he was not of flesh and blood. Lilith held no power over him. He then turned and walked toward the door on the left. The goblin stopped him with its staff and cut in front of him to lead the way.

Death followed his guide down the long wide hallway. On the walls hung reliefs that displayed all of the souls in Hell and the tortures that they received. The faces of these men and women were very familiar to the being that had collected their souls at one point in time. He remembered vividly the things that they had done that led them to suffer as they did now. But even though their punishments were well deserved, the fear in

40

their eyes could lead anyone to have pity for them. At the end of the hallway was a nicely crafted oak door with intricate designs carved into the wooden frame and the door itself. Death studied the designs, which resembled Celtic knots in a way. Impatiently, his host pushed the door open with the butt of his staff and gestured for him to move on. The two walked into the next room, which was well lit by a beautiful crystal chandelier that hung from the ceiling and numerous candles that sat atop brass holders that protruded from the walls. This room was much more elegant than the others. The walls were adorned with beautiful moldings, crafted with gold leaf. Display cases filled the room. Each held priceless artifacts, all of which had great spiritual value. Death wondered how Satan had acquired such powerful relics. Some of them had such might that they could radically shift the balance of good and evil. Mortals could not even comprehend the power of these instruments; and if they were ever imposed with these artifacts, it could mean the total extinction of all mortal life as we know it. The most frightening thing about all of this was that Satan kept such great power behind glass and chose not to use it. Death continued to walk behind the hideous little goblin, whose leather robe dragged behind it as it hobbled across the floor to the far end of the room. Pausing for a moment, Death examined some of the objects behind the glass. The imp grew impatient again and tapped Death on the shoulder with its staff. It gestured toward a magnificent golden spiral staircase in front of them, which led downward.

The railing of the staircase was covered with rubies; Death could not help but to marvel at their sparkling beauty. As they neared the bottom of the stairs, the gold turned to rusted iron, and the rubies were all cracked and eventually nonexistent — a more fitting image for hell. The room they entered was a dungeon. The walls were all made of large dull stones. Chains hung from the stone walls, and Death even noticed some implements of torture. Death wondered why he was being brought this way. Was he to be tortured or imprisoned? The goblin led Death down a long narrow hall. There were prisons on both sides, each housing demons of the like that Death had never seen. They pounded and shook the cold metal bars, trying to escape; but it was hopeless.

A few even tried to grab at Death, but he managed to evade each one. One of the imprisoned demons lay dormant on the floor of his cell. The goblin gave the motionless body a few pokes with its staff, but it did not budge. Sensing that the body still had life in it, Death wondered what could have put this demon into such a coma. Wondering still, Death continued to follow his guide down the cold damp corridor. The stones, which made up the walls and ceiling, were cracked and crumbling, and a slimy substance dripped from above onto Death's brow. At the end of the corridor was a large, iron gate, which led to an old freight elevator. The gate slid open, and Death followed his deformed host inside. The elevator ride seemed to last an eternity. The rusted wheels screeched and the chains rattled, as they were lifted to their destination. Once again the gates slid open, and Death and his guide stepped off of the old rusted elevator and into the elaborate and concise library of the Prince of Darkness.

Books decorated the walls all the way up to the high ceiling. Countless volumes sat on the towering bookcases, each shelf packed tight. Death was indeed impressed by the collection of works that Satan had in his library from all ends of the universe and beyond. Some of these texts and tomes were filled with dark and evil power, written in blood and bound in flesh by the Devil himself. At the end of the room stood the final boundary between Death and Satan, a pair of double doors made of solid onyx. They were gargantuan in proportion, dwarfing even the bookcases that towered over Death and his guide. On the doors were sculpted hideous reliefs of demonic faces, which peered deep into Death's soulless eyes. Scenes of murder, lust, and countless other sinful acts danced around the frame of the doors. Death studied the intricate designs; the craftsmanship was unlike any he had seen by mortal or demon hand. The goblin's pale green eyes looked into Death's, grinning as it rapped on the left door twice with the orb that sat on top of its staff. The orb gave out a sharp pale blue light, and the doors began to creep open. It was time for Death to enter into Satan's lair.

# Part IV
## No Deal

The impish guide came to a stop, pointed his staff down, gave a small bow, and gestured for Death to enter through the now open onyx doors. Death passed under the lofty doorway, and the massive doors slammed behind him. The room was dark, the air still and dry, and the odor pungent. Candles dimly lit the room, their soft glow only gave a hint at the room's makeup. Besides the candlelight, the only other light came in from outside through the stained glass windows. The light was dark and strange; it was constant, never changing. Unlike a planet's sun, which rises and sets, Hell had no such thing, but rather a hazy light that shone at all times. This was important, for Death now understood why Satan built his palace where and how he did. The dark light that came through the windows would always shine in the same place, creating a specific mood that he desired. The disturbing colorful images of the windows danced on floor playing out their scenes of discord. Death looked up at the rose window, the mark of this sick, twisted cathedral, and followed the rays of dark light as they carried the colors down to the hard marble floor past the steps that led to the "altar" — Satan's throne. There right in front of the Dark Prince was projected the image of his fall that could be seen as both triumphant and tragic all at once for the one-time great angel. He sat brooding, watching, as one would watch a play or opera.

"Please relax and step forward, Death," Satan's voice trickled from his lips. "I know that you must be impressed by my *humble* abode; maybe too much for someone to take in all at once."

Death could not make out his features. The light from the window did not reach him, and the candles were too dim. But the light did give some shape to the beast. His shoulders were broad as an ox, his head slouched on his breast, and his horns pierced the air. Casually approaching the steps that stood before Satan's throne, Death looked around the room as he drew closer. The high ceilings, the pillars, the candles, the windows. *All this place needs is pews*, Death thought as he headed toward the throne before him. The fire that lit the candles was the same that burned those who were tortured outside the palace's walls. The wax of the candles dripped under the hot flames, yet the candles melted not.

"Go no further," Satan commanded.

Death stopped on the third and final step of the platform. The image of Satan's descent danced before him, separating the two of them like a mystical barrier that neither could cross.

"Quite a trip you took, and all for naught. I know why you have come here, and you should already know the answer to your question," Satan spoke. He lifted his head off of his chest and extended his thick trunk of a neck, so as to get a better look at the grim being before him. "You must think I am a fool. But I do admire your bravery and your determination. It is sardonic in a way. You seem so weak and feeble, yet your power is strong."

"Allow me to speak, before you go any further. I know your games, and I will not fall for your flattery. You are nothing more than a monster in my eyes," Death intervened.

"See, that defiance — it is sweetness to my ears. Your bitterness is not drawn at me, but at the one that I defied," Satan's lies slid off of his serpentine tongue. "We should not be feuding, we should be plotting. Why is it that you hold back your true nature, your power, doing the cleanup job for a being far too superior to ever truly appreciate you? Do you even know the extent of the power you possess?"

"First of all, my relationship with God is none of your concern. My being here should be proof enough that I serve no one — not Him, not you, no one. I serve my purpose as all things do." Death paused and started his plea, "Why Radix? Why Earth? I do not understand why you find such pleasure in misery. You asked me if I knew the extent of my power, but I ask: do you know the consequences of what you sow? Are you ready to reap your harvest? It is beyond my hunger for one soul, it is the tipping of the scales that pains me most. He will shift the balance. His evil is too strong, and grows every day. Earth cannot fall, not like this. The hole will be too deep. Me, you, everything will be doomed, and I cannot allow that."

"That is why you should rebel and join my cause. I have a great plan in the works, something in motion that no force can stop; and with you, my plan would be complete."

"I want nothing to do with your plans," Death retorted. "Why must you crave destruction so?"

"I do not crave destruction, but rather change. Don't all beginnings start with an end. In order for a new world to be created, the old one must perish. I am more of a creator than a destroyer. I create choices, options, new life for all who are ready to open their eyes and see how the 'Old Ways' are archaic and outdated."

"You, a creator, now that is a stretch—"

"Shh, listen—" the Dark Prince cut him off, and the room fell into silence. "Death, do you even know what you are? Do you even know how you came to be? Let me tell you a story and then we will discuss Radix, I promise," he said with a grin.

# Part V

## A Twisted Tale of Death and Sin

The Devil's teeth sparkled in the dimness of the room. He sat back on his throne and began to weave his tale. It started with an African myth, and continued with a myth of his own. The father of lies, Satan was called for a reason; and his tale went as follows.

*The Moon, it is said, once sent an Insect to Men, saying, "Go thou to Men, and tell them, 'As I die, and dying live, so ye shall also die, and dying live.'"*

*The Insect started with the message, but whilst on his way was overtaken by the Hare, who asked, "On what errand art thou bound?"*

*The Insect answered, "I am sent by the Moon to Men, to tell them that as she dies, and dying lives, they also shall die, and dying live."*

*The Hare said, "As thou art an awkward runner, let me go to take the message."*

*With these words he ran off, and when he reached Men, he said, "I am sent by the Moon to tell you, 'As I die, and dying perish, in the same manner ye shall also die and come wholly to an end.'"*

*Then the Hare returned to the Moon, and told her what he had said to Men. The Moon reproached him angrily, saying, "Darest thou tell the people a thing which I have not said?"*

*With these words she took up a piece of wood, and struck him on the nose. Since that day the Hare's nose is slit.*

Much truth can be found in this myth, though it has lost a great deal in its translation. Unfortunately, Death was brought to mankind thanks to a messenger. But this messenger was not vindictive, nor was he misinterpreting another message that he was told. He was instead bringing a message of truth, a message of freedom — freedom for all of creation. But it started many years before mortals came into existence, before there were angels and demons, and even before there was time. It all started from the beginning.

The beginning was dark, the absence of everything. A spark protruded the darkness and began to create. Let there be light. The darkness was suppressed, pushed back behind creation. The one called Creator created the heavens; and in these heavens He placed beings called angels, who lived to serve the Creator. Serving was their life; it was their reward; it was all that they knew. The Creator, King of all, saw His creation and called it good — despite His knowledge of "Evil," which was brought to life through His very own creation. He hid this "Evil" from all that He created; hid it so they would not be afraid, so they would be "happy." But can stupidity be happiness, can it be bliss, or just naïve enjoyment of what you perceive to *be* happiness.

The Creator had a Son; and He made His Son Prince over all that He created, handing Him everything; yet the Son earned nothing. The Son, just as His Father, roamed creation telling all that everything was good, and that all would live happily forever and ever.

Then the Creator put together an army, strong and all-powerful, divided up into divisions by duty and strength. In charge of all of these fleets was one so beautiful and bright that they called him Light, his rays shining as bright as the Son. Light asked the Creator why an army had to be formed when everything was good and full of cheer? The Creator did not give an answer; only that He knew all, and it was part of His great and wonderful plan. A plan for eternal bliss for all that existed.

Light, still confused, looked to the Son for answers that the Father would not give. The Prince only answered that the King knew best and to listen to everything that He had to say for it was golden. But Light was not satisfied with this answer and went to seek his own far away at the edge of creation. At this time, creation was still fresh and new. Everything existed together — the angels with the Spirit, with the Son, and with the Father. But outside of creation, the angel that shown so bright found the only thing that did not exist in harmony, the only thing that was not given the right to stand in Heaven and feel the presence of the Creator. He found what the King deemed as "Evil," what the King was afraid for His people to know about. It was not "Evil" that was found, but instead what Light came to know as "Knowledge." Light took the "Knowledge" that he found and ate of its sweet fruit, filling his head with ideas of his own, choices of his own, freedom that none of creation had experienced. And with this "Knowledge," Light realized that he had been tricked all along. There was no "Evil" outside of creation, there was only true life: life that one chooses, and not that one is given — free will.

The thoughts in Light's mind were spun, then weaved, and finally took shape, took form. These thoughts became something, something that never was before this time. It was the first creation of the "Knowledge" that Light discovered, and it was brought about by the very laws of balance that the Creator instituted. At that very moment Sin was born, strong and powerful, free of mind, free of body, free of soul, and most importantly free of will. Sin was the first being created not to serve the Creator. He served freedom; and with Light being the harbinger of the "Knowledge," Sin joined him. With the help of Sin, Light began to plot and scheme and eventually collected an army of his own — troops of the Creator that found the same "Knowledge" as Light, ate of its sweet fruit, and gained the freedom therein. There was a new way, a new law, and a new hope.

In defiance of the system set forth by the Creator, Light along with Sin and their vast army of avenging angels, waged a war —

47

the first of all time, and by far the most tragic. The war was as long as a billion years and as short as a nanosecond. Unfortunately, the Creator's forces were too numerous and powerful for the small rebellious regime, and they were defeated. Division came with this war, as did the creation of a new kingdom: one where the angel, once known as Light — the forgotten valiant hero — would now dwell. This kingdom was not beautiful like the Creator's, nor was its inhabitants; for this kingdom was meant to be a punishment for those who fought for their freedom; torment for those who did not want to live a life of service, but rather a life of their own accord. The once beautiful and bright angel was now ugly and hideous, a monster, a demon. The same fate came to all that followed him. But Light did not forget what happened; and with the crown on his head and Sin watching his gates, he swore to achieve his goal of freedom for all one day.

Time passed, and the Creator created again. Let there be light. The physical world was formed. This new universe of the Creator's came with a new set of laws — those of nature. New beings also came with this new creation; beings that were physical, not metaphysical. Their souls lay dormant inside their bodies, hidden from them. And once again, the Creator tried to hide the "Knowledge" as He did in the past. But the former angel known as Light came to this new creation to bring the "Knowledge" that he discovered. A box was given to a woman, beautiful, and pristine. Her name was Pandora, a name and story adopted by a civilization on Earth. Pandora opened the box and unleashed the "Knowledge" upon the new world. Because of this the Creator grew very angry and punished his servants once again. He gave them hardships, pain, torment, and suffering; much like He gave those who fought for freedom in the Great War of the past. And in addition to all of this, He gave them one more thing. Out of the box crawled a worm, a worm that would crawl into each and every civilization of this new creation, the same worm that crawled from the fruit that Eve gave to Adam. This worm grew and formed into a being, the second of its kind — the first being Sin. Yes, Death was born; Sin's brother, created through the "Knowledge;" from the same laws of balance.

The only difference was that Death did not serve even freedom, but rather his own hunger. For his own torment and torture from birth was to collect the souls of those new beings known as mortals, and only in the collection of these souls would he find peace. If a soul was not collected or transfigured, a hole would grow inside of Death and cause him much emptiness — a pain that could not be quenched. The box closed once again and was given to Death. This box contained the power to collect all souls at the time of death, as well as the power of death itself. With this, all of the new creation was destined to one day die and wither away — all for the price of freedom.

# Part VI

## Nowhere to Go

The Devil finished weaving his tale and now somehow appeared less frightening than when Death had first arrived. His demeanor was very polite and relaxed, but his story was disturbing. You never knew what to believe from the mouth of Satan. Death looked up, gazing at the Dark Prince as he still sat in the shadows, hiding, exiling himself.

"So, did you like my little tale?" Satan said. He sat up a bit and stroked his chin in the darkness. "Is it upsetting to discover that you were born of the same dark Knowledge that also created me?"

"I don't know what to think — you have added a twist on things I already knew; and at the same time told me things that I did not know," Death answered. "But you have lied in the past. And as far as I am concerned, your tale is exactly that — a tale and nothing more. You and I have nothing in common. Where I came from is unimportant. You chose your darkness; you fell on your own."

"Blasphemy!" At once Satan's eyes burst into raging flames. "Leave, you pathetic fool, leave my kingdom now!"

As frightening as Satan tried to be, Death stood his ground. He refused to answer to anyone.

"Your kingdom?" Death spoke again. "Your prison is more

like it. I will not leave until you give me an answer. Will you put an end to Radix's absurd reign of terror?"

"I welcome you into my domain. I offer you gifts of greatness and a chance to sit next to me at my right hand." The monster rose from his seat and stood just outside the light of the window that stood as a reminder of who he was. His deformed arm reached toward Death, as he continued. "Do you think for a moment that I would stop Radix from carrying out my duties? Are you insane?"

Death could not speak or move. He was frozen by some dark magic of the demon that stood before him. It seemed for a moment that he would take the next step and reveal himself in the light that separated the two. Instead a mirror materialized before Death. It was large with a strikingly beautiful silver frame that was nicely polished. Looking into the mirror, Death saw himself. In an instant, the image transformed into that of Sin as if they were the same. Then darkness came around the image of his brother, and engulfed him. All that remained was a dark and sinister version of Death, causing him great pain.

"This is the Mirror of Truth," Satan spoke. "I look into this mirror every day to see what I was and what I have become. You are correct; I am not free, not yet. But you look into this mirror, and you see the same thing. You are not free either. No one is. We are all slaves. None of us is our own person, but only halves of a whole. Remember this for the rest of your days. Remember what you have seen, and what I have told you. And in the end, we will see who tells tales."

The darkness in the mirror grew blacker as it swallowed the image of Death. Then, he vanished from the lair of Satan and appeared back home on his own throne made of thickets; even his furniture had no life. Death felt alone. None of his questions were answered, and his pain was even greater than before. While he was gone, more victims fell at the hands of Radix. It was time to collect their souls as well as countless others. Death could never understand why Radix would kill such innocents, even children. But Death did not mourn for the dead. Death was a part of life, more so for him than anyone else in all of creation. Just before he left to collect the souls of the dead, Death was taken over by a feeling of cold power. Why should he endure the agony of Radix any longer? The feeling got stronger as he became immersed in his own power and began to feel glorified, indestructible. Why do God's will? God did not help him. He could enact his own brand of justice and stop Radix on his own. All Death had to do was let go and use the power that he possessed. There was no reason to hold back any longer. All he had to do was find that beast and *destroy him*! Radix would feel his wrath.

# CHAPTER IV
## THE HUNT

The night wind howled through the streets of Manhattan. It was late, but "the city that never sleeps" was still bustling. Many people walked the crowded streets oblivious to the darkness that watched from all around. A monster hid in the shadows of this darkness, a ruthless killer, who could tear each one of them apart without a second thought. If only they knew what the man who walked among them could and would do, they might stop being so carefree. They might start being afraid. The predator was focused now on his prey, whose blood was sweeter than the rest for, by spilling it, would the predator gain life anew. But where among the herds of cattle was his intended target? Radix had a schedule to keep, for time was his true enemy, the only thing that could stop him. No matter how great his power was, how much dark magic he summoned, nothing would keep his soul from being dragged into the fiery depths of Hell if he missed his quota. But he remained unconcerned, for who could match his strength, his cunning — no one. All have failed to stop him before, not even the angels from above have been able to hold back his hand. The darkness swept over him and moved him through the streets. His prey was near, a lamb ready to be brought to the slaughter.

# Part I

## Lust

The blackness of the night shrouded the killer, who walked among the shadows. He was one with the darkness, concealed from sight. A weapon of destruction, this man's gravest sin was lust. But the lust that he had was not sexual in nature; it was the lust for blood. The more victims that he slaughtered, the greater his lust grew, making him more vicious and unpredictable than ever. There was a time when vengeance was his desire — he wished only to get back at God for taking away all that he loved. In those days, the spilling of blood by his own hand was vile. Therefore, he relied on the magic of the *Necronomicon*, the very book that gave him his powers, and the aid of demons and dark creatures to perform his deeds. But on that day when he killed his first victim with his own hands, when he ripped that man's heart from his chest and its beating faded in Radix's dark grasp, he was transformed. The darkness that was the source of his power consumed him, turning his heart black as well as his soul. The name of his next victim rang inside his head, as he scoured the streets for his prey. There was something familiar about the name — Nathaniel Salvatore. Satan always gave him the names, the descriptions, but never told him where to find them. This was all part of the game; it was the challenge that made it more interesting. Standing alone in the alley, Radix felt the cool night breeze. It carried with it both the foul stench of life and the sweet aroma of blood. On the wall before him, he studied some graffiti. *Just as an animal marked its territory so did man,* Radix thought. One phrase in particular that was painted on the wall caught his eye. It read, "And all the earth followed the Beast in wonder — Revelation 13:3," and was followed by the number of the Beast, "666," which was painted in red. Radix smirked and thought of a world filled with corruption, where evil was the law. He imagined himself devouring all of mankind, like a wolf preying on the lambs that strayed from the flock.

Leaving the alley, Radix continued on his way. The darkness of the night seemed to bring out the demons, both from the depths of Hell and from the depths of men's souls. Radix's demons were once dormant, held back by his humanity, but no longer. He noticed a group of six men leaving a bar, skinheads dressed in leather with every inch of their bodies tattooed and pierced with metal. The sight of these miscreants almost made Radix laugh. They thought themselves to be like him, but they were cowards, weak and scared. They hid behind their bravado, and preyed on those weaker than themselves to seem stronger than they were. These men would be the perfect sacrifice, their blood to satiate Radix's lust for the time being. He followed close behind the group, moving in and out of the shadows. He did not even have to hide from them for they were far too drunk to notice him either way. As they walked further the streets grew less crowded, until it seemed as if they were all alone. A young woman strolled by, lost and afraid. Her hair was soft and curly, her skin was golden like honey, and her eyes were like emeralds that sparkled in the moonlight. She should have known better than to be where she was at this time of the night. It was not the place for such a sweet and innocent creature. The surly group noticed her and began their attack. They shouted some obscenities and crowded around her. She tried to fight them off, but they were too strong for the girl and they dragged her into a deserted alley away from prowling eyes. Radix watched as the leader of the gang took off his leather jacket and threw it to the floor. His minions held the young woman down and hit her from time to time to try and stop her from squirming so much. As the leader circled the girl, Radix studied his tattooed flesh. It was like a mural that covered his whole upper body. The image was that of a great red dragon having seven heads and seven horns, and upon his heads seven diadems. The dragon's long serpentine tail wrapped around to the leader's back where it dragged along the stars, which had been dashed into the Earth. Before the dragon stood a woman with child, clothed with the sun, and the moon was under her feet, and upon her head a crown of twelve stars. The words "The Children of the Dragon" were branded across the top of his chest. His scars were an insult to Radix and a grander insult to the one who created him.

*What pathetic fools, these men are to call themselves "The Children of the Dragon." They only wished they were so blessed,* Radix thought. *No, they were nothing more than his food, and after that his excrement. They wanted to play with the power of the beast. Then, the beast they shall receive; and with it, all the torment of Hades for all eternity.*

Radix walked out from behind the shadows, making his presence known. The men saw him and stopped.

"Hey, buddy, this doesn't concern you, so get lost before you get yourself hurt!" the leader shouted.

The girl was thrown to the side. She was in too much pain to move. Radix just stood there and watched the group of hoodlums as they gathered around. The hunt had ended. It was time for the slaughter to begin. The five henchmen approached the dark villain with clenched teeth and fists. All the while, Radix kept a watchful eye on their leader, who put back on his coat and let the others do the work. If it was his will, the cohort of Satan could destroy all of them in a matter of seconds. But it would be more fun for him to draw it out and make them suffer. He wanted to teach these vermin a lesson, a parting gift for them as they left this world. All five goons came at Radix at once, trying to overpower him. But he was too fast and evaded all of their attacks. A kick to the midsection took out one; an elbow to the nose, another. A hook to the jaw and a chop to the throat, and two more went down. The last of the five took out a knife and Radix let him thrust it into his blackened heart. It hurt, but Radix welcomed the pain. At first he saw the pain as a curse from God, but now he saw it as a blessing. It made him stronger. The blood dripped slowly down the knife and onto the hand of his assailant. The man let go and screamed in agony, for the blood was eating away at his flesh like acid. Radix took out the knife and gave it a throw, embedding it into the man's crotch. Radix did not want any of them to die just yet. With the five followers down, Radix turned his attention to the leader. His fear stank worse than the others. The girl looked on. She was afraid of what she had seen and wanted nothing more than to just wake up in her bed, all of this being just one big nightmare. Radix flashed her a devilish grin. The shadows of the alley became darker, and the wind seemed to stop dead. The prey lost sight of the predator, as Radix became one with the darkness.

"Where did you go, you freak? Who do you think you are? You think this is a game? Well, you're in for a surprise because no one messes with 'The Children of the Dragon.' We're bigger than God!" the leader shouted into the darkness.

"You make me sick," Radix's voice floated through the alley. "Bigger than God? Do you know anything about Him, or if He even really cares about pathetic little you? You're no bigger than a mouse's turd. Listen, imbecile, the powers that you are tampering with are far beyond your mortal comprehension. You are and always will be nothing. I notice the six-six-six tattooed on your forehead, the number of the Beast. I noticed that your men bear the same number on their right hands. Everything you do is based upon a simple text, a dream that some whipped apostle wrote down. The end will come; but remember, there is more than just one version of the apocalypse. The only thing that is certain is that this world will come to and end."

Two hooked blades, each attached to a chain, fell out from the sleeves of the leader's jacket. He grasped the chains tightly in each hand and swung the blades around in a graceful manner. It was certain that he had been trained in some form of martial arts. But his craftiness, his skill, and his weapons meant nothing, for his hunter could not die.

"If you're so tough, then why don't you come out here and fight me like a man! Where are you?"

"Right behind you," Radix said as he appeared from out of the shadows. The leader turned around and swung one of the blades at Radix, who caught it. Then, he swung the other, which was caught as well. Radix gripped the blades firmly in each hand. They dug into his flesh, as he pulled his pathetic opponent toward him and sent his knee into the man's gut. Blood dripped from Radix's hands onto the ground. It sizzled as it landed. His fallen adversary looked up at Radix and spit out a mouthful of his own blood.

"Who are you?" the man gargled.

Radix wrapped one of the chains around the leader's neck, tilted his head back, and gave him a taste of the toxic blood that still poured from his hands. As the blood trickled down the beaten man's throat, it burned through his insides.

"Who am I?" Radix repeated the question, and then whispered in his ear, "Think of it this way — I am the evil that lies in the hearts of all men and women, personified and unleashed. A day will come when I will have no barriers holding me back. My true power will be seen, as darkness covers the world, and the universe crumbles and collapses. The angels will fall, as will the stars in the sky, and fire will spew from the depths of hell. Who am I? I am the one sent by the true power. I am the way, the truth, and the end of life. I brought the lamb to the slaughter. All will go to the slaughter through me, for I will bring the Dark Age."

The thug collapsed to the ground, barely breathing with blood still flowing from out his mouth. The girl still watched. She smiled and thanked her dark avenger for saving her from that band of hooligans. But Radix was no savior. He had other plans for the girl. His lust still burned inside, and her blood would be a sweet dessert.

"All of you, mortals, share one thing in common — you all want, want, want," Radix spoke louder. He smiled back at the girl and gave a grin to the men who lay passed out on the floor. "Just as much as you want dark power," speaking to the incapacitated gang, "she wants me to be her savior, her knight in shining armor," pointing to the girl who lay before him. "No one will save you. You will have to save yourselves — so it is written. And to your grave, you will go with your wants. Mortals, your greatest sin is your greed. Look where it has led you. And as you go to Hell, remember to tell Satan that Radix sends his best."

# Part II

## Greed

*Bang bang bang!* Once again Lyles had an unexpected visitor pounding on his door. He walked over to answer.

"Who is it?" He asked. " Let me guess, Detective Johnson, right?"

Just as Lyles finished turning the lock on his door, it flew open.

"You're damn right it's Detective Johnson," the detective snapped as he came rushing through the doorway.

"And to what do I owe the honor of having you visit my humble abode?" Lyles remarked.

"Cut the crap! This is important!"

"Sorry, Detective. What do you need?"

"Well, Lyles, I really don't want to do this, but I'm gonna have to place you under arrest," he replied.

"Under arrest! On what grounds?"

"You knew about Philip Reynolds' death before anyone else; you were the last one to see the three boys before they were killed; and today we found your prints all over Mr. Reynolds' apartment, which was ransacked. All the evidence, unfortunately, points to you. And your inability to provide a description of the killer, with the exception of the fact that he was white, does not help either. Now before you freak out, let me explain one thing. You are being held in custody until your trial, which will prove you innocent or guilty. If you are innocent you will be free. Understand?"

"The only thing that I understand is that I *am* innocent." Lyles commanded.

"Listen to me! Either you come willingly, or I'll have to use force. And don't try running because I have the place surrounded."

Lyles peeked out his window and saw a flood of police cars waiting. He had no other choice than to turn around and hold out his wrists. Detective Johnson immediately slapped on the cuffs and he dragged Lyles from the building, while reading him his rights. Lyles kept his head down as he was thrown into a police car. The young man remained quiet. He just sat and thought as they headed to the station.

Detective Johnson walked Lyles into police headquarters, and another officer took over. She gave Lyles the grand tour — fingerprints, ID, mug shots, the whole bit. Now Lyles knew how a dog felt being dragged around on a leash. When she was finished with him, she brought Lyles to a small room and locked him in. In the center of the room was a small table and three chairs. Lyles sat down and watched the shadows as they danced on the walls of the dimly lit room. He wondered what lay beyond them. Depression began to sink in, and he felt himself fading into the shadows. The boys were dead, the killer was missing, and he had no alibi. All he wanted to do now was wake up from this nightmare, with everything back to the way it was before.

"How are we feeling today, Mr. Washington?" Officer Rogers said as he barged through the door. Detective Johnson followed him in, and they sat across from Lyles.

"Oh, *we* are just fine," Lyles replied.

"We're just going to ask you a few questions, Lyles," Detective Johnson rose as he spoke. He paced back and forth.

"That's all you've been doing — interrogating me. Haven't I told you enough? I'm sick of your inability to believe the truth. I have told no lies. I am innocent. And call me Mr. Washington. I no longer want to be of your acquaintance. You said you believed me. You told me that you would help me. Some help!" Lyles shouted and slammed his hand down on the table.

"Okay, Mr. Washington, calm down. I won't have any of this nonsense. Don't you ever get loud with me!" the detective scolded.

"I tried my best, but I still have to follow orders. And orders were to bring you in. I am trying to handle all of this in as nice a way as I can, but even I can't break the rules. I even got your trial date moved up to next week. So before you go nuts, understand that I still feel that you are innocent. But also understand that you are the number one suspect in these murders and therefore must be held in custody, until you've been tried."

"I'm sorry, Detective, I didn't mean to get out of hand. It's just so frustrating," Lyles began to calm down.

"I understand, Lyles. It's okay," the detective consoled the young man. Then he whispered into Lyles' ear, "Your anger is real. I know you are not guilty. I promise that you will get out of this a free man."

"I'm touched by you two, but I have a few questions for the brat, if you don't mind," Officer Rogers stated. Detective Johnson left the room, and Rogers continued, "We're all alone, now. So, tell me why you did it!"

"Are you deaf? I didn't do anything! When are you going to figure that out? Maybe when more kids and old men turn up dead!" countered Lyles.

"You must think you're real funny. Well, I'm going to get the info outta you, even if I have to beat it out."

"You know, officer, they should move you up to detective 'cause you're a real D—!"

"Watch you're tongue, boy," Officer Rogers commanded as he slapped Lyles right across the face. "Any more of this crap, and I'll have you put away for life. So shut up, and be happy that you might be free in a week. Though, I doubt it. If you ask me, you're as guilty as sin."

"Well, thank the Lord that you're not a judge. You'd convict every innocent man in the world. You never listen to the anyone's side of the story."

"Maybe that's because I've heard too many, most of which are lies. A man gets desperate in a situation like this and will say anything. You know that there is a possibility of you getting the death penalty. The fear is what makes you lie so well," the officer gave Lyles a smug look. "You're not fooling me. I'm not easily duped like Detective Johnson. So, sing!"

"I have nothing to say. I've told you everything that I know."

"Fine!" Officer Rogers shouted. He stormed from the room cursing and slammed the door behind him.

Another officer walked in and asked Lyles, "Do you need to call your lawyer?"

"I don't have a lawyer. I live in the projects. You think I can afford one of those lousy, greedy crooks?"

"I'll take that as a No," the officer replied. "Since you have no one in your defense, we will provide you with one for the trial. Come with me."

The officer brought Lyles to his cell, and locked him in. Lyles leaned against the cold steel bars of the prison that he was now subject to. Memories of lost hopes filled his mind as he could only wait for the trial. But nothing mattered anymore. He had no family or friends left. When he was young, both of his parents died in a shoot-out at the local bank. An only child with no parents can be a sad case. His aunt, Lyles' mother's sister, raised him as if he were her own. But, unfortunately, she too passed away a year ago from a heart attack at sixty-seven. All the rest of his known relatives were deceased, as well. His only real friends had been Mr. Reynolds and the three boys. Now, they were gone too. A void of emptiness flooded Lyles' head as he wished to find escape in the coolness of the steel bars. The trial was next week, but who was going to believe a black man from the ghetto who had all the evidence pointing right at him. He knew that he would be found guilty. In a way, the thought of execution sounded good right about now. Lyles would rather be put to death, than be forced to live one more day of his empty life.

From their cells, other prisoners stared at Lyles. He could see the pain in their eyes, even though they put on a tough exterior. They shot him angry looks to try and intimidate him. One's reputation was everything in jail. Fortunately for Lyles, he would not have to interact much with his fellow cell mates as this was not a high security prison that he was sentenced to, but rather just a holding cell at police headquaters, and most of them would not be locked up here for very long.

"Their not as tough as they seem," a raspy voice came from behind Lyles.

Startled, Lyles turned around to see a short slim man in his early fifties with a salt and pepper beard down to his belly and hair to match.

"Who are you?" Lyles asked.

"Sorry to be so rude, my name is Giacomo Gianni; but you can call me Jack. Everyone does," the little man stated in the same raspy voice.

"Hi, Jack, I'm Lyles. Where did you come from? I didn't even—"

"—See me." Jack cut Lyles off. "I would have made my presence known sooner, but you looked like you needed time to think. We all need that sometimes. But now, you know I am here. So, pleased to meet ya."

Confused by the big grin on Jack's face, Lyles asked, "How can you be so jovial when you're in a place like this?"

"Well, when you've been here as long as I have, there's no reason to shut down. You gotta go on believin' in tomorrow, 'cause you know, tomorrow is another day!" The little man chuckled.

"Jack, how long have you been here? What did you do?"

"I can't even remember how long it's been anymore. Days just come and go. As for what I did, well, it's something I'd rather not talk about right now," Jack said. The once jovial man was now very somber.

"I'm sorry, I didn't mean to upset you. I was just curious."

"That's fine. It was a long time ago, and things change. People do too, you know," Jack said.

Jack began to smile again, which comforted Lyles.

"I bet you're wondering what I did," Lyles said. "I'd tell you, but I'm not too sure myself. The whole thing is just too crazy for words."

"Well, I'll be the judge of that. Heck, I'll be the judge, jury, and the whole dang prosecution." Jack chuckled again.

"That's executioner. I'll be the judge, jury, and the executioner," Lyles corrected the little man.

"That, too," Jack said with a grin. "But, it's okay, you don't have to tell me anything that you don't want to. But if I were you, I wouldn't be so glum. Look at old Jack — I'm always bouncing back. We all make mistakes, even the best of us."

"That's the problem, I didn't do anything wrong. I was just trying to help," Lyles said, trying to hold back the pain.

He sat down on his cot and put his head in his hands to hide the tears. Lyles was too upset to realize that there was only one bed but two of them in the cell. There was something strange about his cellmate, but he would not find out just yet. Jack quietly watched Lyles as he gathered his thoughts and emotions.

Lyles spoke, "An old preacher, and three boys from my neighborhood were killed. Mr. Reynolds was a good man, and always looked out for us. And the boys were like my little brothers. I wish I had helped them instead of lecturing them on what they did. They needed a friend, not a parent. The worst part is the cops think I did it. Why would I kill the people I cared about most? But there was something even stranger. The man who killed them, he's something unnatural, like out of a horror flick. The boys said they shot him, but he didn't die. He came back and killed them. He killed them! Not me!" Lyles screamed as the other inhabitants of the prison looked at him as if he had lost his mind. "I'm not lying, Jack. I don't know why, but I feel I can tell you anything. I'm innocent. You have to believe me."

"I know you are, I can see it in your soul," Jack said, and he hugged Lyles to console his pain.

# Part III

## Pride

"Kimberly, did you hear the news?" inquired a young man. "Remember those three boys that you brought in the other day; the ones who ran off?"

"Yes, Tom. What sweethearts they were. Too bad they didn't stick around for a little while longer," a sweet voice came from the lips of the even sweeter woman.

"Well, I'm not sure how to tell you this, but they turned up dead," Tom said with his head down.

"Dead! Oh my God! How did you find out?" she cried.

"It's all over the news and in the papers. I thought you should know. Since you brought them in and all."

Kimberly was overcome with grief. Tears flowed from her precious eyes for the loss of the boys.

"They were so young, and they had so much to look forward to. Do you know how it happened?" Kimberly asked.

"Well, apparently, the boys were brutally murdered. Some kind of satanic ritual or something. The police believe that they have the killer, but they have to wait for the trial. Seems like he might be accountable for the death of an old preacher as well."

"God, some people can be so ruthless," she said as the tears continued to roll down her soft cheeks.

"Why don't you go home, Kim, and get some rest."

"It's okay, Tom. I can finish out the day. Maybe by helping others, I'll get my mind off those who I couldn't help."

Now the trickling tears turned into a downpour, drowning Kimberly in the sea of salt. She got up and walked out of the room trying to compose herself.

*I was always proud of my volunteer work at the Salvation Army,* Kimberly thought to herself as she left the building and strolled down the avenue. *Always bringing a smile to the faces of "lost" people. Not lost as in they do not know where they are — even though I have had cases like that — but rather lost as in they don't know who they are. The people that I see every day are usually homeless, runaways, and the like. They can't conceive of their self-worth and how special they really are. I try to bring love into their lives, and a little self-esteem. I just wish sometimes that I could do more, like give them jobs and homes. But I can't. I'm just a paralegal, who plays the part of an aid to the needy on my days off. But even though I can't make their lives perfect, I'm still proud of the work that I do. Every time I feed, shelter, clothe, or console someone in need, I feel such joy. But now, I don't know if I really am doing any good. Look at how those boys died, so mercilessly. There was nothing I could do to help them. I wonder if I ever really helped anyone. They all eventually end up back on the streets. So many horrible things could happen, like what happened to those three boys.*

The wind grew strong on Kimberly's face as she carried on. But the wind did not bother her as much as her conscience did. A feeling of extreme guilt took over Kimberly as she wondered if the boys' deaths were somehow her fault. Maybe if she had checked their bunks when she was scheduled to, instead of waiting another hour, she might have been able to prevent them from leaving. Or if she had been more responsive to their emotions and reached out to the boys a little more. But regardless of her actions, the boys' deaths were inevitable. Unfortunately, life was that way. Radix would have found and killed them eventually. It was his nature. He had them tracked. The shadows kept watchful eyes on the boys from the moment that they attacked Radix. He would never have let them live after what they did to him. It would have been a disgrace, an embarrassment. Kimberly did not know this. She was unaware of Radix and his treacherous ways. The only thing that Kimberly knew was that the three boys that she tried to help had died, and the blood seemed to be on her hands. She was the last one to see them. Maybe she could have saved them, if only she had tried a little harder.

As Kimberly continued down the street, she passed a newsstand. She stopped as her eye caught the headline on the front page of the *Post*, "Three Harlem Boys Murdered, Satanic Cult or Hate Crime?" The shock of their deaths hit her again. She grabbed a copy and started to read the article. Under the headline were photographs of the boys. They were too young and innocent to have suffered so. It felt as if it was her duty to do something, anything. Noticing that the boys' addresses were posted in the paper, Kimberly decided that maybe there was something she could do. She could visit the families, pay her respects, and try to console them in some way. It was the least she could do, since she was the last person to see the boys. After paying for the paper, Kimberly tore out the article with the addresses, put it in her purse, and went home. Tomorrow, she would go visit the families, starting with Rashan's.

The next morning, Kimberly stood outside an apartment building on 130th Street. She looked very professional in her gray pants suit and black leather pumps. *Bzzzt.* Kimberly pushed the buzzer for one of the apartments, waiting for a response. A few minutes passed by, so Kimberly gave another buzz, thinking that the first one was not heard. Another minute passed and still no answer. She sighed with disappointment and decided to go.

A voice called out from a window above her, "Can I help you with something, Miss?"

"Are you Mrs. Jones, Rashan's mother?"

"That would be me," the woman responded. "If you're here looking for him, I'm sorry to inform you, but he's no longer with us. Please just go and let him rest in peace."

"No, please, I want to talk to *you*. I was the last person to see all three boys before they died. Just let me come up. I'll only be a moment. I just want to talk," Kimberly said in her ever persuasive voice.

"Talk about what, child? The boys are dead — they were brutally murdered, and that's all there is to say about it. I'm sorry, but I would rather you just go home, and leave me to grieve."

"Well, if that is how you feel, I'll go. You have my condolences. Your son and the other boys were sweet kids, I just wanted to let you know that, and to say that I'm sorry that I couldn't do more to help them. I feel as if it were partly my fault," Kimberly added, and she began to walk away.

"Wait, I'll let you in. Just let me buzz you up, okay?"

When Kimberly got to the apartment, she found the door wide open. So, she decided to take a peek in. It was quaint, and nicely decorated with many plants. To Kimberly's eyes, it did not seem like a teenager had lived there.

"Please, come in and shut the door behind you," Mrs. Jones said pleasantly. "I'm sorry, if I seemed to be a little harsh. I guess my sadness over Rashan's death is turning into anger. The scariest thing for a mother is to lose her child, you know," Mrs. Jones stated. "Sorry, but I don't even know your name."

"My name is Kimberly Jackson. I'm a volunteer for the Salvation Army. That's how I met the boys."

"Well, nice to meet you, Kimberly. I'm Martha," she smiled, as she reached for Kimberly's hand. The two shook, and Martha gestured for Kimberly to have a seat on the couch. "Before we talk, let me make us some tea, okay?"

"Sounds lovely. Thank you very much," Kimberly responded.

Martha slowly rose from her chair, and walked over to the kitchen. After filling the kettle with some water, she set it on the stove and turned the gas on. Kimberly waited patiently, looking around at the plants and ceramic knickknacks. The apartment was lovely, a nice home. But it was missing something — happiness.

Kimberly took notice of Mrs. Jones and how tired she looked. The loss of her son Rashan was taking a noticeable toll on her.

Back in the kitchen, Martha grabbed two mugs from her cupboard and placed one tea bag in each. While she waited for the water to boil, she thought about her son, and how she missed his laughter, and energy. She felt as if a part of her died along with him. *Swwwwwwhhhh!* The sound of the kettle whistling woke her from her trance.

"Kimberly, would you like milk in your tea?" Martha's voice rang from the kitchen.

"Yes, please," she responded.

Like all of her movements lately, Martha cautiously added the milk to Kimberly's tea. She walked over to the living room carrying a tray with the two cups of tea sitting on it, and placed it on the little coffee table between her and Kimberly. As she sat down, Martha let out a small sigh.

"Don't worry, I'm not old. Just been draggin' a little lately. That's all," Martha smiled at Kimberly, who smiled back. "Now, tell me how you knew my Rashan and his friends."

"I am a volunteer worker at the Salvation Army, as I mentioned before," Kimberly sat up and looked at Martha. "I was walking around, inviting homeless people to our soup kitchen for a meal. That is when I saw the three boys sitting on a corner. They looked tired and lost. I could tell they were running from something, but I was not sure what. So, I asked if they had homes, and they said that they needed a place to stay. I invited them to come and stay at one of our shelters. It wasn't permanent, but at least they'd have a bed for the night. I was going to try to keep them there as long as I could in order to help them, but even I knew that they could not stay there forever. Unfortunately, there are too many people in this city without a place to sleep, and we don't have enough beds to accommodate them all. The boys must have run off to find someplace else to stay. That's all I know. I'm so sorry. I wish I could have done more."

Martha couldn't help but cry. Kimberly walked over to her and held her in her arms, giving Martha a feeling of security, a feeling of love. That was something Martha had not felt since Rashan passed away.

"My boy was my whole world. He was all that I had. Life is funny like that — all the good things get taken away. Sometimes sooner than you think. But don't be sorry, dear child. You did everything you could for my boy and his friends, and for that I am grateful. No one made them run off. They did that themselves," Martha said with a great deal of strength in her voice.

"I wish I could do more," Kimberly said.

"There's nothing more you can really do," Martha reached out to hold Kimberly's hand. "You coming here is good enough. Thank you. But it's gonna take some time for me to get back in the swing of things. Rashan was all that I had left. And with him gone, now, I have nothing."

"You still have your life to live. Rashan would want you to keep going on. His life here may have been cut short, but I know his spirit is still alive and well. He's happy where he is, and wants you to be happy too. Don't let this be an end — let it be a beginning. You still have many years in front of you. You don't have to be alone anymore, you have me now. I'll do anything I can to help you."

"Thank you so much. It really means a lot to me, you coming here and doing all of this. I feel much more at ease, but the pain is still there. It will be for a good while," Martha said graciously.

"Yes, but eventually time will heal the wounds as it does with all things.

"That's what they say. Real pain never seems to go away — it just has it's way of hiding from time to time, but it always comes back when you least suspect it."

"I hate to ask this, but what happened to Rashan's father?" Kimberly looked down as she inquired.

"He was a deadbeat, never around when he should be. He used to hit me and Rashan when he would come home, stinkin' of booze. He was no good," Martha said angrily. " I told him to leave, and to stay away from me and Rashan. We eventually got a divorce, and I haven't seen him or his child-support in years."

"That's a real shame," Kimberly interjected.

"Hey, it's no skin off my teeth. I'm way past that. Don't worry about it, dear." Martha's words showed no concern, but her eyes painted a different picture. There was still an unpleasantness in her soul over the situation. "It's a good thing that Lyles was around for those boys. He really went out of his way to be a strong male role model for my son and his friends. And after everything he did, they still never learned too well. I guess you always have to learn from your own mistakes," Martha's eyes began to tear again, and Kimberly reached out one more time. "It's a pity that they are fingering him as the killer of those boys and good ole Mr. Reynolds. Lyles wanted nothing more than to help them. He would never do something like that."

"Lyles — is that the man in the paper, the one that they arrested for the death of the preacher and the three boys? You know him?" Kimberly said very surprised.

"Yes, he is very close to all the people in this neighborhood. He is a good man. I guess it's true that bad things happen to good people."

"Well, is anyone going to help him, at least speak up for him in court? If he is found guilty, they'll probably give him the death penalty. We can't let an innocent man die."

"But what can I do? I'm just a poor woman from Harlem. No one cares about me or what I think, especially no judge." Martha stated an obvious case.

"I work at a law firm that specializes in criminal law. I might only be a paralegal, but I can see if I can convince someone to help. I'll do anything I can. I am always willing to help those in need. And I've never seen anyone more in need than your friend."

"That's sweet of you. I really hope you can help out Lyles. The man is innocent and should be free." Joy now filled Martha's heart.

"I'll keep in touch and see what I can do. I should probably get going now. I still have to see the other boys' families," Kimberly said as she got up from her seat.

"It might not be such a good idea to contact the other families," Martha got up with her, and started to walk Kimberly to the door. "Well, Kenny's would be the only family you could contact. Josh's parents are both deceased. They died in a plane crash years ago. Josh lived with his grandmother, but the poor lady dropped dead of a heart attack when she found out what happened to the boys. The Williams family, that would be Kenny's family, is getting ready to move to Westchester. They don't want their daughters to end up with the same fate as their son. It's sad for all of us. This neighborhood is full of too much tragedy — everyone is better off getting out while they can. But like you said, you have to keep going on."

"Forget the neighborhood — it's this world that is full of too much tragedy. Everyone is too busy worrying about themselves and not about the rest of the planet," Kimberly agreed with Martha. "If you feel that it is better for me to leave the Williams family be, I will. But if you talk to them, let them know what I told you and that I give them my condolences as well. Thank you for letting me talk to you. I feel better now. The tea was delicious by the way; that was awfully sweet of you."

"Please, come back and visit sometime. I could really use the company. It's been lonely you know."

"Sure, I'd love to come back and visit. I enjoyed the company too. It's good to have someone to talk to. It helps relieve some of the worries," she responded in a warm tone to help cheer up Martha's saddened heart.

Martha opened the door for Kimberly. The two embraced and said their good-byes. The door closed as Martha went back into her apartment, and Kimberly walked down the stairs and out of the building. With a true sense of pride, Kimberly headed on her way. She was happy that she was able to touch at least one person that day.

# Part IV

## Envy

Children are wise to fear the dark; they know what we forget as we grow older; they see what we no longer can. Temptation was forged in the darkness, giving birth to sin and death. Its minions lie waiting in the shadows, ready to unleash the iniquity hidden within. The darkness is real. It is the true essence of evil, the power bound by the gates of the Abyss. The stars give off light to hold back the darkness, but even the heavenly bodies can fall. One of the gravest sins woven in the darkness is envy. The first star fell

70

because of this very sin, and pulled many down with it. Since that moment that very same fallen one has struck all of us with the same desire that he had. Even the earliest stories of our first parents tell of this sin. For they listened to that cunning snake when he told them to eat the fruit, for if they did they would be like God. But all is not lost, for God receives no pleasure in the pain of His children. Therefore, He sent His Son into the world to suffer and die along with us, not only just to share in our pain, but to free us from it. For with His death came life in the resurrection. And with this life a way to end all evil, so that one day goodness can reign again across all of creation.

In an alley in the East Village, the air was thick with blood. An old bum tried his best to sleep the night away and forget the hard life that he had to live day in and day out. He had no food, no money, no shelter, and worst of all — no love. He was despised and looked down upon for being homeless. Yet what did he do wrong? He had a great career at one time, he was a corporate vice president. The company unfortunately went bankrupt. He lost his job and with it his confidence. Depressed, he grew addicted to the medication that his psychiatrist had prescribed for him, and the addiction caused him to fall even deeper into the pit. His family and friends gave up on him — they tried to help as much as they could, but nothing worked. Life was full of twists and turns, just like the one that this man was about to witness.

A woman sat up against the wall next to the old bum. She was covered in newspaper to keep her warm. It was dark. The old-timer could not make out her face, but he knew her pain. He felt it too. He sat back and let her be. *Some rest would be nice,* he thought to himself. The old man felt rain drops hit his balding scalp. He held out his worn callused palms to collect some of the rain, which peculiarly felt quite warm. He looked down at his hands to see that the crimson liquid running through his fingers was not rain, and instantaneously looked up to see what was dripping onto him. Six skinless bodies were hanging from a fire escape above him. All of them hanged by one single chain noose, bound together around their fleshless throats. The blood continued to drip, running like a river on the ground. Puddles formed like red lakes, thick and deep. Afraid, the man went to warn the poor girl. But when he removed the newspaper from her, he noticed that it was too late. She too was a victim of this heinous massacre. Her soft silken body was mutilated. Blood trickled from her lips, and her stomach was cut open exposing all of her intestines, which were lying on the ground. Her legs were practically broken off like the pieces of a wishbone, bent far back behind her. The sight of this disgusted the old bum and he emptied the few contents of his stomach onto the alley floor. Wiping his mouth, the poor old man looked at the wall. He knew who the dead men were — the Children of the Dragon, a local gang who dabbled in black magic and devil worship. They were known for cluttering the walls of the Village in apocalyptic graffiti, mostly from Revelation. Everyone in the area was aware of the gang and their occult practices. The reason that old man was so certain about who these men were was because the leader's tattooed skin was hung on the wall, held up by two sharp hooked blades that were driven through the brick. It was like seeing a work of art hung at a museum. It was quite ironic that these men, who sacrificed many to their false god, were now sacrifices themselves to this very same dark lord that was sworn to protect them. Then, the old bum looked down. Something was written on the ground in the blood of the six dead men. It said, "He who kills by the sword, by the sword he must be killed — Rev. 13:10." At the sight of such bloodshed, the old man fled from the alley, without looking back.

# Part V

## Gluttony

"I knew he was guilty from the start. He always knew what was going on, yet he saw nothing. I tell you dar a smmm si papl oot dar," Officer Rogers babbled as he stuffed his face with a doughnut.

"I couldn't hear you behind your breakfast. What was that last thing you said?" asked the sergeant, who was sitting at his desk, while officer Rogers stood by the file cabinets trying to get down the last piece of doughnut.

"All I said was that there are some sick people out there. I mean to kill an old man and some kids. Sheesh."

"And, Rogers, if you could wait to swallow next time. You made a mess," the sergeant said. "The one thing I don't get is why? There is still no motive. Maybe he's just some deranged psycho, like something out of one of those movies. "

"Or maybe, he's innocent." The sergeant looked up to see Detective Johnson, who was now hovering over his desk. He reiterated, "I still think the boy didn't do it."

"Yeah, and I bet you're one of them that thought OJ didn't do it either," Officer Rogers snapped from across the room. "I don't know about you, but I don't want to see any more killers walking the streets. That's why I became a cop. To make the streets safe for everyone."

"You would fry an innocent man just to feel safer? Take away his life, so that you can pretend that the problem is solved? We have rights in this country. And one of them states that we are *innocent until proven guilty*! You got that!" the detective ripped into the officer with his statement.

Johnson slammed the door as he left the sergeant's office.

"Johnson is off his rocker, Sarge. How can he stick up for a cold-blooded killer?" Rogers questioned.

"He's right, though. We have no hard evidence on this guy. Johnson really believes that this man is innocent. You saw how defiantly he preached the boy's case. This may sound stupid, but Johnson is usually right. He can tell the innocent from the guilty just by looking them in the eyes."

"Well, who cares, we'll see who's innocent or guilty at the trial next week. And that reminds me, shouldn't we move the guy to a higher security prison. We need the room for some of the lesser scumbags that we pick up on our nightly rounds."

Lyles stood, leaning his head against the steel vines which kept him from his freedom. Jack crouched in the corner. The two men dreamed of a better place — a place where there was no evil, where everyone lived in peace, and where everyone was free.

"One day hasn't even passed and I'm already sick of this place," Lyles said under his breath, as he yearned for relief.

"Well, you don't have to worry about that any longer. You leave tomorrow," Detective Johnson's voice rang loud and clear in Lyles' ears.

"What?" Lyles was startled. "I leave tomorrow?"

"Yeah, you're being moved to another prison." Johnson answered.

"Why? Jack here has been in this prison for years!"

"Jack who? There's no one there. Are you feeling okay?"

"What do you mean? He's right over—" Lyles paused in shock, for his friend was gone. "He was here a minute ago. I swear."

"I'm sorry, Lyles, but you must have been seeing things. You've been going through a lot lately — it's understandable. Well, I gave you the news, so I'll be going now. See you later. And I hope that you feel better. Maybe you need some sleep," Detective Johnson's words faded as he walked away.

"Hey, why on such a downer, Lyles, my boy? Good ole Jack will bring you back from the world of gloom, of dreary black. Come on, give us a grin," that raspy voice filled Lyles' ears as he turned to see his jovial friend sitting in the corner once again.

"Ah, stop this nonsense. I know you're just a figment of my imagination, so just leave my head!" Lyles put his hands over his ears and closed his eyes hoping that the little man would disappear.

The apparition, still lingering, touched Lyles on the shoulder and said, "How many hallucinations can hold another person. You feel the warmth of my hand, yet you believe it not to be real. Okay, so mortal I may not be, and my story stranger than you had thought, but real I am. Trust me, good friend, for I am here for a purpose."

Lyles opened his eyes and uncovered his ears, giving in to the short skinny man, believing his tale and wishing it to be true. A friend was all Lyles needed; he did not care what kind, just as long as it was a friend. He turned, and looked at Jack, zooming in on his honest face, and trusting eyes, feeling a sense of security. Salty drops rained from Lyles' eyes, and he rested his head on Jack's warm shoulder, hoping, wishing to be free.

"There, there, buddy boy. There'll be no unnecessary tear-shedding here, for I bring you hope. Believe me when I say

74

you will be free again, as will I," the little man said softly as he vanished, leaving Lyles alone.

Lyles fell to the ground crying, hoping for freedom. His tears were then cut short by the remembrance of Jack's last words, once again giving him hope for salvation. Like gluttons we devour every bit of our freedom, so much, so quickly that we don't even know how free we are. We should savor every bit of it, for one day we may not have it any longer, and we will die of hunger.

# Part VI
## Sloth

A child slept in her bed, warm and comfortable, while a woman slept on the street, cold and in pain. The dark man watched her from across the street, disgusted at the sight of her filthy body. He thought about all the pleasures of life that she was missing. But it did not matter because he would allow her the greatest pleasure of all — his pleasure. The woman opened her eyes to see the shadowy man hovering over her. Fear tingled through her body as the dark figure grabbed her by the throat and lifted her into the air. She tried to scream, but his grip was too tight, suffocating her. What a painful experience suffocation is, indeed one of the worst ways to die. Spasmodically, the woman convulsed. She tried to breathe, but he tightened his grip. Blood flowed up and out of her mouth as the homeless woman found a home in the afterlife. Radix dropped the body and passed a grin across his thin disturbing lips. The blood, still warm on his hands, filled him with joy. Then to complete his sinful deed, he wiped some of the blood onto his lower lip and tasted its pureness.

Kneeling on the floor of his prison cell, Lyles sent pleas up to Heaven and longed for an answer, "Dear God, I hope you're out there listening. I know I don't call on You often or go to church regularly but, God, I need You now. Only You can help me. I've been falsely accused of something I didn't do. It's not fair. They might even kill me. I don't want to die, not now. Please God, help me. Give me a sign that I'll be okay, so I don't have to worry all day and night." Lyles stopped and sighed, "Oh, what am I doing? You don't understand. You can't understand. You're God. Things like this don't happen to you. Of course You won't help me."

That line struck the walls of Heaven harder than the others, and an answer was given — an answer Lyles was not quite ready for.

"Peace, my brother. Why so upset?" a gentle voice was heard from Lyles' prison walls.

Out from the wall walked a man. He stood before Lyles glowing like the sun. He was handsome with dark flowing hair, and a well-groomed beard. His robe looked soft and light, almost as if he were clothed in clouds.

"I know what you are going through, Lyles," the man continued. "Or have you forgotten how I suffered and died."

Lyles just stared in shock as he realized who the man before him was.

Christ began to speak again, "Prayer is the first step toward faith. But if you truly believed in the power of God, you would not worry so. I am always here, whether you know it or not. Suffering is a part of everyone's life, as it was a part of mine. Do not lose hope because you suffer, but instead allow that suffering to strengthen you and help build your spirit. The more you endure, the stronger you will become. You are a key component in a great plan. So fear not, for you will not perish. You are blessed and will help bring an end to the most evil man on this Earth, thwarting one of Satan's greatest schemes and holding back the darkness that is craving to enter this world. This vision of me will leave you now, but I will remain always in your heart," the Lord faded away as He finished giving His message to Lyles.

"I've definitely been in here too long," Lyles sighed as confusion filled his mind.

What had he just witnessed — a revelation perhaps, or just a figment of his imagination? Lyles decided to get some rest, for tomorrow he would be transferred. But it would not be that easy for the young man to get some sleep, for three other visitors would be arriving shortly.

Lyles' cell was dark. Drops of condensation fell from the ceiling onto the ground. The noise of the drops hitting the cement floor made Lyles toss and turn. He was still confused by what he had witnessed. Why him? He was never very religious. What made him so important? The answer came at that moment.

"Lyles, Lyles," three youthful voices were picked up by his ears.

"Who's there?" Lyles asked.

The three voices rang louder, "Lyles, you forgotten us already."

Lyles looked up and was mortified as he saw ghostly images of his three young friends — Rashan, Josh, and Kenny — floating in the air.

"How is this possible? You are all dead. Why are you haunting me? Isn't it enough that I'm taking the rap for your murders?"

"That's why we're here — to help you," the voices spoke in unison. "We know who killed us, and we are here to let *you* know so you can help take him down."

"What am I suppose to do behind these bars?"

"You'll be outta here soon. Just listen as we tell you what you gotta do. The guy who killed us was named Radix. He is pure evil and has caused serious destruction for the past two thousand years, killing millions. And, as you know by now, he can't be killed. But he can be beat. You gotta avenge us and all the lives he has ruined."

"How am I supposed to stop someone who can't be killed? Why doesn't God just destroy him? Isn't He supposed to be all-powerful? I just met Jesus, and He walked through the wall. That's proof enough for me. Send Him."

"God will help in His own way, but you gotta do this."

"If this guy is so powerful, what am I supposed to do anyway? I can't take him on. I'm just a man."

"You gotta find a guy named Nathaniel Salvatore. He'll know what to do. That is all you need to know."

"Where and how do I find this Nathaniel character?" Lyles inquired in utter confusion about the matter at hand. "Once again, I am behind bars."

"You'll know when it's time. Don't forget us, Lyles, and thanks for everything." As did Christ, the three apparitions faded away with their final words.

"Come back. I have more questions. Please!" Lyles pleaded.

Silence entered his cell, and Lyles clung to the cold steel bars again. He was desperate for answers, but none were given. All Lyles could feel now was the lifelessness of the bars. His cell was cold and dark, just like Radix's heart. How would Lyles ever defeat him?

The city was full of darkness that night, more so than ever before. In the shadows lurked a monster, ready to kill. That monster was Radix, and the shadows cloaked him well. It was almost as if he were one with the darkness. His eyes began to focus. He saw an old bum trudging through the street before him. He was Radix's messenger, and he would bring a message of death. It was a shame that the old man did not know that he was being used in the Devil's plot. He just wanted to inform the police of what he saw. Fortunately for Radix, that was exactly what he wanted too.

All stopped and turned as the doors to police headquarters flew open to reveal the homeless man. He looked lost and nervous. Most considered it a side effect from his massive liquor intake, yet one man saw it differently.

"Sir, can I help you with something?" Detective Johnson politely inquired.

"Yes, you can, officer," the man panted. "I saw their bodies hanging in the alley. No skin, except the patch hanging from the wall."

"What are you talking about?" Johnson asked in total confusion.

"I'll tell you what he's talkin' about. He's piss drunk and delusional, that's what. If you ask me, I say we lock him up," Officer Rogers jumped in.

"Nobody asked you, Rogers. This might actually be very important. So, I say we let the guy catch his breath, and then ask him a few questions. What do you say, sir; will you come with me for a second, and we can talk this whole thing out?" the detective spoke in a gentle voice.

"Sure, officer. But let's hurry; we don't have much time."

Detective Johnson led the old man into the same room where Lyles was questioned, and sat him down. The old man's face was pale from fright, and he shook with nervousness. In all his years on the streets, he had never seen such a grotesque sight. As usual, the room was dimly lit. Johnson stood across from the man.

"So, you got a name?" the detective asked.

"It's Bob."

"So, Bob, what frightened you so much?"

"Well, like I was trying to say before I got cut off by my loss of breath — the members of a local gang, the Children of the Dragon, were killed, skinned, and hanged in an alley. I figured that I ought to tell you people, so you could do something about it. Plus, I was too scared to stick around. I might have been next."

"Are you sure you didn't have a little too much sauce today? Your breath tells me a lot right now."

"I might have hit hard times and the bottle as well, but as you can see, I am not a stupid man — just a poor one. My drunkenness has nothing to do with this. I saw their bodies and felt their blood. Do you see the stains on my clothes? And worst of all — I saw her — she was a mess. I don't know who would do such a thing. Please, I'm telling the truth. Go see for yourself."

"Okay, I'll check it out, but you stay here and wait for me to come back. I might have some more questions. Just stay away from Officer Rogers. He can be a real ball-breaker." Detective Johnson smiled to set the man at ease. "So, before I venture off, where exactly did you witness this incident?"

The moon stood alone in the night sky, shining down with great power from its fullness. It shed enough light for the detective and his men to see the work of a creature far more corrupt than any demon. The dead masses of tissue dripped with their last drops of blood, giving off a foul stench of rot. These brave men venture out every day to only see death after horrid death, yet never before had they bore witness to such horrors as they have seen this past month. First it was the three boys, and now this atrocity. What they saw before them may not have been as heartbreaking as seeing the three youths crucified on the alley wall, but it was more unpleasant to look at, and the stench was far worse. The blood-written passage from Revelation caught the eye of the detective. Something about it reminded him of the pentagram that was scrawled in blood over the young teenagers. He knew that Lyles was innocent, and now he had some evidence. This was indeed the same man who slaughtered those boys.

The bodies were taken down and bagged, and the piece of tattooed flesh was also removed. When the men took it from the wall, they noticed that something was seared into the other side. Detective Johnson was immediately called over to read the inscription. Now he definitely knew that Lyles was innocent, and soon he would meet the man who was truly guilty. The note read, "You cling to your flesh, when it is your death. I have liberated these men of their flesh just as I had liberated those three young lads. This is a gift I have been giving people for many years. Soon enough I will liberate all. But for now I seek information, and in seeking I will find. No door can be locked that I cannot open, and no wall can be built that I cannot tear down. Your fortress will be overtaken, and the knowledge that I seek will be mine. Once more, I will spill the blood of the innocent and set them free."

"Oh, my God—he's nuts! We've got to get back to headquarters! That is where he is heading! Come on men, let's move!" Detective Johnson ordered. The team jumped in their cars and took off.

Radix threw open the doors, and stood in the entrance of police headquarters, still as a glass of water. The entire station dropped what they were doing and stared at this ghastly being. He walked over to the front desk, slammed his palms on top of it, and leaned forward, towering over the receptionist. Her heart jumped, for she could see the evil in his eyes.

"I'll make this easy for you," Radix said to the woman. "Give me what I ask and I will make your death as quick and painless as possible. If not, I will make you suffer long torment. Afterward, I will proceed to kill as many as it takes until I get what I want, and then kill the rest for good measure. So, do we have a deal?"

"Umm," stumbling over her words, "What kind of information do you want, sir?"

"I admire your respect, but formalities are not required. As for the information, it is simple. I just need the home address of one of your city's residents, Nathaniel Salvatore. Let's just say he's not listed in the phone book."

"I'm, um, sorry but that kind of, um, information cannot just be given to anyone. It is confidential."

"I ask for a simple thing. Just one address!" Radix grew angry. "Do I have to repeat myself? You must really enjoy suffering. Do as I say, and everything will go smoothly." Radix grabbed her by the arm.

"Back off, now! Or else I'll be forced to shoot you!" one of the officers shouted, pointing his gun at Radix.

Radix paid no attention to the officer, for the only thing he was concerned about was obtaining the information he needed.

"I'm warning you to step away from her," the officer said sternly, still pointing the gun. "That's it — I warned you!"

The officer shot Radix, only to see the dark figure laugh as the wound instantly healed. Radix turned and approached the officer. Frightened, he kept on firing at the approaching monster. The only thing he accomplished was unloading his gun.

"You little nothing. You cannot kill me with your stupid weapons. Many have tried, and all have failed. I will take special enjoyment in killing you."

Radix grabbed the officer's head with both of his hands, squeezing it as he lifted the man off of the ground. Like a pumpkin in a vice, the man's head shattered with pieces of his brain and skull flying across the room.

"Is anyone else going to cross me?" Radix asked with a chuckle. "Now tell me," once again addressing the receptionist, "where are your files?"

"You can access them on the computers in there," she said pointing to a room off to the left. "But you'll need the code. And I, um, don't have it."

"That is quite all right, for I am an expert at cryptography. You know I was there when they invented the first computer. Since then I have studied the machine, like I have studied all of man's devices, perfecting my skills. I will have no problem in cracking the code. And I know what you are thinking right now. Why break into here and put all of your pointless lives at risk, when I could have just hacked into your system? Well, the answer is that this is just so much more fun."

No one in the entire station dared to stop the dark man, for they all knew that they would fail. Radix ripped the door off its hinges and entered. In the room were some PCs, all networked with criminal records and information on the residents of the city. He sat at one of the computers and began to type. In no time he had cracked the system.

"I have it, finally!" Radix shouted as he started to print out the information.

At that instant the station doors were thrown open once more. Detective Johnson and about twenty highly armed SWAT team members rushed in.

"Where is he?" Johnson asked as he entered.

"He's in the computer room," answered the receptionist. "But you can't go in. He'll kill you!"

"I don't care — he must be stopped. Let's move men!" he shouted as the SWAT team members charged the room.

"But detective you don't understand. He can't die," she warned.

"He's just a man, and all men can die."

"But Officer Daniels shot him, and it had no effect."

"He's probably wearing a protective vest. Don't worry — my men are armed with special bullets that can go through anything."

"But that's just it. The bullet did go through him, but the wound healed instantly. And can't you see, what he did to Daniels after that. It was horrible."

A multitude of gunshots were heard from the computer room, and Johnson said, "See, my men are already making quick work of him. This should all be over now."

The halls of the prison screamed the word "death" as sounds of gunfire blared. The noise made Lyles curl up tightly on his cot, looking for security and sanity. He had just had four strange visitors, and now it sounded as if a war were going on just past his walls. Darkness had overcome every inch of the cell block, and Lyles could not see through the black haze. He just closed his eyes and prayed that the dream would end and all was still safe.

With the sound of the gunshots silenced, the detective decided to check the room. "So, boys, did you get — him?" The detective's voice dropped as he saw all of his men lying on the floor, dismembered.

"These fools were supposed to stop me. Don't make me laugh," Radix said.

Detective Johnson looked up to see the shadowy figure standing before him, with a grin from ear to ear.

"I have my information, so I'll be on my way," Radix said as he neared the doorway.

"You're not going anywhere!" ordered the detective, and he pulled out his gun.

"After all that I have done, do you think you can kill me with that little toy?"

Standing tall and proud, the detective stared right at the face of the man who had defeated countless armies in the past and just dismembered an armed SWAT team.

"Fine, have it your way," Radix said, and in a flash he thrust his hand right through the detective's throat.

*Ring, ring, ring!* It was three in the morning when the phone rang at the house of the police commissioner, waking him from a very restful sleep.

"Hello," the commissioner yawned.

"Commish, it's me, Officer Rogers. I have some bad news for ya."

"This better be pretty bad for you to call me at this hour," the commissioner responded as he looked at the clock on his nightstand.

"Well, let's just say that about fifty or so of our best officers were murdered, twenty of which were SWAT team members," Rogers said.

The commissioner had no response. He dropped the phone, and stared blankly into the darkness.

Bob's body lay lifeless with the bodies of the fallen officers. Radix's use for him had come to an end. And like all life to Radix, he was expendable. Some may have referred to him as a bum, accusing him of the sin of sloth. But this man committed no such sin; his life was long and hard. He tried his best to get through, but he failed. He had proven his worthiness in the eyes of God. For this night he showed great bravery by not only informing the police of Radix's evil crime, but also by facing death fearlessly. His reward would be great in heaven.

# Part VII
## Wrath

Death was back on Earth and looking for Radix. He could sense that the beast was near. The smell of the blood that he had spilled filled the air. Too much death had stemmed from this man, and it was time that it all stopped. But Death was not fueled by emotion or pity for Radix's victims. Rather, it was his own hunger that consumed him. The shadows that surrounded Death grew blacker as the darkness spread out more and more. Slowly, Radix emerged from the darkness to confront Death.

He spoke, "Ah, so we meet again, Death. Don't you just love how we always seem to cross paths? I wonder why?"

"You know exactly why, and your game has gone too far. You're nothing but a machine, killing one after the other. You have no feeling or compassion—"

"Not much different than you, eh, Death," Radix played with his words. "We have more in common than you think. We could make a great team — I kill them, and you collect them."

"We have nothing in common. I would rather be destroyed than be associated with you and your dark ways."

"Fine, have it your way," Radix smirked. "You were never any fun."

"Playing with people's lives is not a game. And I am sick of you destroying the lives of so many good people. You think you are a god and can pass the death sentence onto anyone. You feel powerful by hurting those weaker than you. Why is that? Is it because you were preyed on as a child? Weak and helpless, you were unable to stop your family from dying. You think that you have found some sort of sick and twisted revenge. You have only gained hubris, nothing more. You are nothing!" Death yelled.

In a valiant attempt he sent a blast of energy from his hand, hitting Radix on the shoulder. The dark man's clothing ripped, but his body remained unscathed.

"Ha! That tickled," Radix bantered. "You think that you can kill me. Not even your God can kill me!"

"Once again, I note your hubris. I do indeed possess the power to kill you, for I am Death. But in doing so, I would destroy myself, casting the world into utter chaos. I cannot endure my hunger any longer. I sought God for help and He turned His back on me. So, I will turn my back on Him. Your soul has been absent from me for too long, and the hunger is forming into famine. I say let this entire creation be taken with me into nothingness. For not existing is far better than existing in pain!"

At that moment a great power surged through Death's entire being. It was a dark power that began to take total control over him, making him want to destroy Radix, and all that was in his path.

"No, you can't be serious. You cannot kill me! Think long and hard about what you are doing!" Radix shouted.

"Yes, I am powerful, I will destroy him. I will defy God, and destroy Radix! I will destroy everything!" Death exclaimed.

For the first time in his existence, Death had an emotion — pure hatred. He brought forth his mystical box of the dead and held it up to the now bleeding moon. The dark power began to fill him. Inside Death knew this was wrong, and he began to fight back the darkness that was consuming him with every ounce of energy he could muster. The battle inside the mystical being was of cosmic proportions. Radix watched Death convulse before him as the being fought to regain control. Then, Death let out a thunderous cry, and the sky lit up with a surge of immense power.

Death woke up feeling empty and weak. He had failed, and Radix had escaped. It was time to move on. Radix would be brought to an end one day. But it would not be tonight, for wrath was not the answer. This much Death had learned. Now, once again, he had to go collect the souls of Radix's victims, and they were many.

# CHAPTER V
## GOD GRANTS US A SAVIOR

Nathan and John walked out of the gym and headed down the street to their favorite diner to grab a bite to eat. They had just worked out harder than ever and were famished. This was their routine three days a week, and they would never give it up for anything. These late morning workouts were perfect. Neither of them had an office to go to — John was a real estate agent, and Nathan was a freelance illustrator. Also, it gave them an excuse to hang out. The two friends laughed and reminisced, as they gobbled down their lunch. John, the larger of the two by almost ten inches and sixty-five pounds, complimented Nathan on the new record that he had set at the gym today. The five-foot six-inch one-hundred-and-eighty-five pound dynamo benchpressed five-hundred pounds for ten reps. The most amazing part of this feat was that just a few years back, Nathan had been in a car accident and injured his right shoulder so badly that he had to abandon a very successful boxing career and was told by the doctor that he would never be able to lift weights again. Nathan's heart was stronger than his muscles, and he drove himself to do the impossible. The Lord had blessed Nathan from the time of his birth, and kept him close all of his days. Now it was time for his mission to be revealed to him, for God's plan to unfold.

# Part I

## A Hero Is Born

It was the spring of 1968; and Maria Ciccone, a high school dropout, was starting to think about her life and the path that she was heading down. She feared that the world would destroy itself with all the war that it spewed, and that she had never found purpose in her existence. In a struggle to find herself, she found God. Sure, she had known of God before; she was raised in the Catholic faith. But it was hard for her to truly believe in the concept of an ultimately infallible and supreme being. Especially, one so powerful that He could create everything in the entire universe and beyond. Infinity was a hard concept for her finite brain. All of this changed one day, when she was lost for answers. One night while she slept, she had a vision of a beautiful man, whose body shone with radiance greater than a star. He stood before her with His long woolly-soft hair flowing slightly below His shoulders. She wanted to embrace Him and feel His soft beard caress her cheek. A strong feeling of love came over her. It was a love like she had never felt before, a sort of pure spiritual love. He told her not to be afraid of all the evil in the world, and that He would always be there to protect her. Then, He asked her to come and serve Him. She knew the man was Christ. His love filled her completely. She wanted nothing more than to do as He requested. She wanted to serve Him, but she did not know how. He simply told her to follow her heart.

Days, weeks, and even months passed by as Maria contemplated the apparition of Christ that had come to her in her restless sleep. In late September as Maria walked down the lonely streets of her town, she heard an alluring tune. She followed the sweet melody. When she drew closer, she discovered that it was coming from the local church. The anticipation of who could be making such illustrious music captivated her so much that she went in, only to find a group of Salesian Sisters singing psalms. She quietly tiptoed into one of the pews and slowly took a seat. Her eyes gazed up at the choir of nuns appearing to her as a choir of angels. A rush of joy consumed Maria, and then she heard a voice in the back of her head. The voice was like a whisper, soft and calm. It spoke in a reassuring tone and told her to join these sisters and sing the praises of the Lord. What a strange idea, yet it was spectacular. All these years, Maria lived in fear of a destroyed world and a life of being nothing. But now, she saw a purpose; now for the first time, she felt peace and joy; and she finally had a glimpse of infinity. Her faith would be her reason to live, her salvation from this scary world. It was apparent at this time how she would serve Christ, her Lord and Savior.

The sound of machine-gun fire was all that these soldiers heard day and night. The year was 1968, and the United States had sent many of its young men to a jungle to die in a war that many felt should not have been fought. It was a warm August night, and Joey lay quietly in his bunk. He had no cot to sleep in, just a sleeping bag on the hard dirt floor. The war was fierce in Vietnam, and rest was a scarce thing. But all that Joey cared about was to be able to close his eyes and dream of a place far from where he was. As hard as he tried, he could not close his eyes because he was afraid that he would never wake up again. Your enemy could be anywhere or anyone. Giuseppe Salvatore, Joey for short, was a private in the United States Army and had not been stationed in Vietnam very long. Though the young man had just turned the ripe age of eighteen only six months ago, he already knew the casualties of war. It was painful for him to see his fellow soldiers being used as cannon fodder. Because of this he kept much to himself and tried not to get too close to anyone. It was hard to go on fighting while you watched your friends die, and even harder to use one of their dead bodies as a shield to save yourself. But no matter how hard Joey tried to separate himself, his troop became like his family — all of them brothers. As the days passed, his fear increased. Joey and some others had been away from camp scouting out a nearby village. When they returned, they were greeted with carnage. Vietnamese soldiers had raided their camp and slaughtered everyone. That night, the tiny band of courageous men decided to devise a counterattack on the mercenaries who killed their brothers. Earlier, Joey had spotted some enemy soldiers in the nearby village. The small band decided that that village would be their target. But the mission would not be easy. They were few, and anyone could be the enemy — even the women and children. This was guerrilla warfare. There were no rules. Therefore, no matter what, they would have to kill everyone in sight. They did not have the liberty to take chances. It was not easy for Joey to shoot all in his path just on the assumption that they might do the same to him. But he had to. It was kill or be killed, and he was not ready to die.

A couple of hours before the set attack, Joey decided to rest. For the first time in a long time, he had no trouble closing his eyes. A strange force took over him, and Joey witnessed a vision. A beautiful angel stood before him.

The angel said, "Giuseppe, listen to my every word, for what I speak unto you is a message from the Most High. The Almighty and Ever-Loving God wants you to vanquish all of your fear, for you will be returning home soon. He will not let you die in this brutal battle. You have been chosen to perform a task for the Lord. All He asks of you is to follow Him. And when the time is right, you will know your task."

Joey awoke from his dream. It was time to attack. As he strapped on his gear, he thought about what the angel had told him in his dream and wondered if it meant anything. But there was no time to think about it now — there was a war to be fought. The group of young men made their way through the thick foliage of the jungle, using their anger to push them further. Sweating and filthy, they emerged on top of a hill and gazed down at the village that they were about to attack. All of their superiors were dead. The battalion had no orders, just to kill everyone and everything in their line of vision. The young inexperienced band amassed to about twenty men, none older than twenty-three. They knew that they probably would not succeed, seeing that they had very little knowledge of guerrilla war tactics. Their enemies, on the other hand, were bred on it and outnumbered them. Joey took a deep breath and prayed to the same God who led the Israelites against the Philistines, the Assyrians, the Ammonites, and many others; the same God who gave the weak defenseless boy, David, victory over the powerful giant, Goliath; and the same God whom he was told to follow. He prayed, but Joey could not find God. Amid all the bloodshed, he only found the Devil. Then, at that very moment, one of the twenty sounded the charge. Like a herd of bison, the soldiers stampeded down the hill toward the town. But to their shame, their surprise attack was no good. Somehow, the mercenaries knew they were coming, and they were waiting. Within seconds, bullets shot across the sky and found their marks in some of the American boys — killing them instantly. Blood blanketed the streets as more bullets flew through the hot, thick air. Joey hid behind a building to dodge the bullets. He watched his squad being massacred. Fear came over him. Then, another feeling entered his body, one of valiant strength. He exploded from the corner and started to blast away, at least he could die with dignity. The tables began to turn — Joey's rampage initiated confidence in his comrades that still lived. Together the inexperienced boys began to shred through the enemy soldiers. The adrenaline pumped, and the will to survive broke through. One by one, the mercenaries fell to the barrage of lead. The bullets stopped, and all grew silent. Joey and his remaining brothers — they were now six in total — looked around. They saw the evil monsters that murdered their family lying on the ground, nothing more than lifeless piles of bloody tissue.

Just as the young men were about to celebrate their victory, a dark figure emerged from one of the buildings. He did not seem to be with the group of mercenaries that Joey and his battalion just slew. But they somehow knew he was their enemy. Instantly, the air shifted from sizzling hot to bitter cold. The slender man was pale and stood at about six and a half feet tall. He wore all black and did not hide his face like the Vietnamese soldiers did. The band of six shot desperately at the mysterious man, taking no chances. He was down. It was over, or so they thought. The man got up and dusted off his clothing that was now spotted with bullet holes. His blood evaporated, and his wounds closed before their eyes. Seeing this, the troops turned and ran off toward the jungle. That is all except for Joey, who hid in an abandoned shack nearby. As the soldiers ran, the dark shadowy man appeared in front of them. He smiled as he ripped their bodies apart with his bare hands.

Joey hid under a table, the only piece of furniture in the entire shack, praying to live. But as he did, he heard the beast crash through the door. He lay as still as he could, staring at the long dark shadow being cast by the even darker man. Joey held his gun firmly, his finger on the trigger. The young soldier knew it was useless, but it was all that he had.

"You might as well come out and get this over with," the phantasmal being said. He looked down to see Joey cringing under the table. "Ah, there you are. What are you so afraid of? I'm only here to kill you. Trust me — it won't be so bad. I'm an old pro. Just go outside and see for yourself. Your friends didn't put up much of a fight. Well, no one ever really does."

"Why are you doing this?" Joey cried.

"Simply because I can." A broad smile stretched across the man's face. "Think of it this way — I'm really helping you. I can

91

tell that you don't want to be here; and trust me, Hell is a much nicer place."

Joey trembled as he pointed his gun at the man's face. Within no time the sinister man snatched Joey's weapon and pointed it back at him.

"You know, boy, you shouldn't play with guns; you'll shoot your eye out. And by the way, *tag*, you're *it!*" That was the last thing Joey heard as everything went black.

It was now February of 1973, and Maria was on her way to becoming Sister Mary. She shortened her name in honor of the Blessed Virgin. As she prepared to make her vows, Maria volunteered to help some of her fellow sisters at a Salesian hospital in Manhattan. At that time it was housing some of those injured in the Vietnam War. Maria helped as an orderly. And while she was there, she also learned some nursing skills. She felt sad during her time at the hospital because it was full of tragedy, yet it gave her a purpose — helping those wounded and ill. This was why she stood. The worst case that Maria knew of was a young man by the name of Giuseppe Salvatore. He had been in a coma since 1968, after he was shot in the stomach in Vietnam. He was found by another American soldier and sent back to the States with others who had been injured in the war. God watched over Giuseppe. As Maria was offering up some prayers to the Lord, she felt a strange energy enter her body. She had a sudden urge to check on Giuseppe. As she entered his room he began to sit up, and Maria cried and thanked God. She ran over to the young soldier and embraced him, for she had definitely witnessed a miracle. Giuseppe, on the other hand, was full of confusion. He was in a strange place with a strange person.

"Are you an angel?" he asked.

"I'm afraid not. I'm Sister Mary, or at least I will be soon," Maria said in a shy voice.

"You're a nun? You're too pretty to be a nun," Giuseppe said as his voice faded in and out.

"Well, I'm flattered; but I had to respond to the Lord's calling."

"Maybe the connection was bad," the young soldier tried to smile through the pain. "By the way, where am I? And how did

I get here? The last thing that I remember is being shot in a small village in Vietnam."

"Mr. Salvatore—"

"Please, call me Joey."

"Okay, Joey, you are at a Salesian hospital in New York City. You were brought here after being found unconscious and losing massive amounts of blood. This hospital has been devoting itself to helping war victims like you. That is why you are here," Maria said in a soft, sweet tone.

"That's a story for the grandkids. That is, if I ever have any," Joey said in jest, as he smirked and let out a little laughter.

"Don't you worry, Joey, you'll have grandchildren plenty, a man as handsome and brave as you. You'll have a long and happy life. Trust me, God is watching you," Maria consoled Joey as she watched him doze off. He fell right to sleep. Maria was not worried because this time she knew that Joey would wake up again.

Maria always wondered why Joey had no visitors. As she spent more and more time with the war hero — that was how she saw him — she found out the sad truth about his life. Joey had been an orphan. He spent many of his years on the streets and in foster homes. He actually volunteered to fight in the war the moment that he turned eighteen; he wanted to feel important. Maria had some family problems of her own. When she decided to join the sisterhood, her parents disowned her. They wondered how their only daughter, and only child for that matter, could betray them like that. Her mother and father wanted her to get married to a rich man, be a housewife, and raise children; but now that dream was over. Maria and Joey built a strong friendship. It was hard for her when it was time for him to leave the hospital. But he recovered, and he had to move on.

A couple of months passed by, and Maria was close to making her final vows. That was when the dreams started again. She had many dreams about angels and demons fighting over the world; and like before, she was in the presence of Christ. He told her that something was about to change, and that no matter what she must serve him and follow her heart. Maria was very confused. One night while she was cleaning up, she heard a knock at the main door. At first, she was startled, but her curiosity drove her to answer it. Standing in the cold rain of the night was a sight for sore eyes — Joey. She hugged her long lost companion with such joy on her face. He was just as ecstatic to see her, maybe even more so.

"Maria," Joey's voice cracked as he let go of her. "I can't let you do this."

"Do what?" Maria wondered.

"Become a nun!"

"But, Joey, it's my calling; and you know how close I am to God."

"I know, Maria, but you're going about your life all wrong. Just because you love God and want to serve Him, does not mean you have to be a recluse. I'm sorry, that didn't come out right," Joey stumbled trying to find the right words. "I just mean that there are other ways to serve God."

"How? What other ways?" Maria asked even more confused now.

"You see, I've been having these dreams. They started out with an angel, and now they're about you — I mean us. Don't you see? We were destined to meet and to be together."

"Joey, please don't do this. I care about you a lot, but not like that. I've been promised to God. I can't go back on my word," Maria backed up and stared at Joey, pushing him away.

"Maria, I'm not trying to make you go back on your word. I'm just trying to help you clarify your purpose. Let me show you another way to serve God."

"How?"

"Marry me."

"What?" Maria cried. "How can you ask me that now, at this time?"

"Because I love you, and I know that you love me. Just follow your heart," Joey paused and took Maria by the hand. He repeated, "Follow your heart. That's all God wants you to do."

Hearing Joey's words echo those of Christ's in her dream, Maria embraced him, and they kissed.

In June of 1973 Maria Ciccone and Giuseppe Salvatore were married at Divine Body Church in Sawport, New York. The

94

wedding was beautiful. Maria's parents were even there. They were happy to see their daughter finally getting married. Most of those who attended were from her side, for Joey never knew his real family, and his brothers were all slaughtered in Vietnam. There were a few vets from the war who attended, including his best man — Private Mitch Donnellson, the man who had found Joey in the shack back in Vietnam and brought him to safety. For Maria and Joey, the ceremony was the beginning of a wonderful life together. One year later, exactly at midnight on Christmas Day, they had a son, and they named him Nathaniel.

# Part II

## Scripture Says

Two years after Nathan was born, Maria and Joey had another bundle of joy — a little girl. They were unsure what to name her at first. But once Maria held her little sprite — a pet name Maria and Joey had for their little girl — in her arms, she decided to call her Esmeralda after the elfish gypsy in Victor Hugo's classic *The Hunchback of Notre Dame.* Her eyes sparkled like little green emeralds. Her stare was so clear that you could gaze straight into her pure and innocent soul. She was gifted with a cheerful head of red hair, making everyone around her smile. Esmeralda, like her namesake, was vivacious and full of energy. She even took to dancing at quite a young age. She moved with the grace of an angel. Maria and Joey were so proud of their little sprite.

Nathan and Esmeralda were far different from each other. It was hard to tell that they were siblings at all. Unlike his sister, Nathan had dark brown hair, with eyes to match. He did not have the good looks that she acquired either. It's not that he was an ugly duckling; it's just that he was average. His arms were long, and his hands and feet were a little big for his short frame. This made him clumsy as a child. Nathan may not have been as graceful as his sister, but he was not lacking in his own talents. He was very strong, which helped him to fend off the bullies who usually preyed on smaller children. The only problem with his strength was that he broke nearly everything around him.

Nathan was also very creative and loved to write and draw. But even with these gifts, he never felt complete. He always knew that there was something bigger that he was destined for. Nathan's first memory was a dream that he had when he was a toddler. The dream felt very real, and in it he was fully grown and completely lost. Fear took over his body as darkness surrounded him. Monstrous stone walls towered over him, trapping him on all sides except one. There was no escape, for coming from the opening was something beyond human and demon — a being soaked through with pure evil. As Nathan stared into the twisted smile that glimmered in the darkness and gazed into those empty eyes, he knew that the being was the darkness that surrounded him, and he had nowhere to go. Just as he felt his life about to end, he awoke in his bed crying, for at that age, he knew of nothing else to do.

Joey and Maria were devout Catholics and made sure that their children were raised the same. Every Sunday, they would go to church as a family, never missing a service. Even though Maria had almost taken her vows to join the sisterhood, she never seemed to profess her faith as much as Joey. All the answers to life's questions were in the Good Book, he would proclaim, always trying to win arguments with Bible quotes. Of course when it was time, both children went to Catholic school from kindergarten to eighth grade. Nathan was more affected by the conditioning of the school than his sister, leading him to be strong in his faith. Esmeralda did not see the purpose of burdening her life with religion and its consequences, and she decided to just live and let the chips fall as they may. It was not that she totally abandoned her faith. She had strong morals and stood by them. But she felt that man, not God, made a lot of the Church's laws. The one thing that the siblings had in common was their concern for their studies. Both Nathan and Esmeralda would finish top in their classes throughout their schooling. Pastor John Wesley wanted to see Nathan continue his studies at a Catholic high school, but after much deliberating, Maria and Joey decided to send Nathan to a public school. Even with the thousand-dollar scholarship, they could not afford the price tag of a private education. Going to a public school did not change Nathan's devotion toward his Heavenly Father. In a way, it actually brought him closer to God, and proved to be a valuable learning experience. The Catholic school that he had attended previously was not the most culturally enriched place to be, and therefore he was not used to being around so many different types of people. He now had the opportunity to experience the real world, filled with all walks of life. As Nathan got his first glimpse of his new school, he felt uncomfortable. He was surrounded by strangers and had no friends in sight.

The school building was old and falling apart. The bathrooms were worn down and barely functional, the paint on the walls was chipped away, and the PA system hissed like a choking snake. These were just some of the many problems at the school. One of the others was the staff. Most of the teachers did not care where these kids ended up in life. They were mostly concerned about their paychecks and their pensions. Walking into his first class, Nathan hung his head low and rushed to grab a seat all the way in the back. He was trying not to draw any attention to himself. As he sat down his desk creaked. With every movement of his body, his desk made another sound. All seemed lost. Nathan tried his best not to move in order to save himself from any more embarrassment. But throughout class, his desk kept on squeaking no matter what he did, giving way to assumptions from his classmates. His cheeks reddened, and he tried to hide his face in his hands. This only caused the desk to make even louder sounds. The students turned into a wild pack of hyenas, laughing their heads off. But Nathan stuck it out and kept his cool. For the remainder of that year, he was known as the human sound system. But no matter how many times he was mocked, shunned, and laughed at, Nathan tried his best to stay positive. By the end of freshmen year, Nathan finally began to build up some confidence. Now, having been at the school for some time, he started to settle in and decided to join a sport team the following fall. He was not really a great athlete growing up, being clumsy, but he was strong and quick. Therefore, he decided to play football. Tryouts were in August, prior to the school year, followed by Hell Week — a week of intense practicing that would weed out the real men from the boys. Anyone who did not survive Hell Week would be ridiculed for the rest of his years at high school, and maybe even further. Nathan was determined to make the team.

It was a blazing August morning, nearly a hundred degrees. The boys lined up. They tried to be men, or rather, warriors. Without expression, they stood, as the coach walked up and down like a drill sergeant.

"Football is war!" he shouted at the boys.

Nathan was nervous. He had never played football, except in gym class, and he was not very good, especially at catching. He had hands of stone — not referring to their toughness, but rather to their stiffness. He wasn't very big either; and that drew the attention of the coach, who decided to walk over to him.

"Hey, boy!" the coach shouted in his face. Nathan just looked straight ahead keeping his lips stiff, and his eyes opened as the coach went on, "So, what's your name, boy?"

"N-n-nathan S-s-salvatore, umm, s-sir," Nathan stuttered.

"You're a little small to be playin' football, boy! Tell me why I should put you on the team!" The coach shouted even louder.

"I'm not quite sure. But I will try my best, umm, sir," Nathan said even more nervous now.

"You hear that men?" Now speaking as if he were talking to a baby, "He'll try his best." He began to shout again, spit from his lips sprayed in Nathan's face, "Well maybe your best isn't good enough! I don't want you to try your best. I want you to destroy your enemy! You hear me, boy?"

"Yes, sir!" Nathan said sternly.

After an intense practice, the boys hit the showers. Nathan began to have second thoughts about playing football. He never knew the seriousness of the game. All he wanted was to have a little fun and make a few new friends, but instead he was gearing up for war. Four of Nathan's fellow teammates were huddled next to a locker whispering to each other, all the while looking over at Nathan and smiling. He grew curious and decided to check out the conversation. Slowly, Nathan approached the group of boys.

One of the boys turned around, looked down at Nathan, and said"Hey, how's it goin', runt? Me and the other guys were just talking about you. You see, you're one of us now. So, you're gonna have to start looking like one of us."

"I don't quite understand," Nathan said with hesitation.

"You gotta start pumpin' iron, you know, liftin' weights. Add some meat on your bones," another boy jumped in.

"We have somethin' that will make it even easier to add on the bulk," a third boy said as he opened his hand in Nathan's face, showing him a needle. "We all do it."

"I really don't want to put that crap in my body, and honestly I don't like needles much, anyway," commented Nathan.

"Come on, Nate, take it. It's free. And like Frank said, we all do it."

"Not all of us," a new voice thundered. It was very deep for a teenager, and Nathan saw why. In front of him stood the biggest guy he had ever seen. It was hard for Nathan to believe that this kid was the same age as he was. The black youth towered over the four others just as they had towered over Nathan, and to match his astonishing height was his all-over massiveness. "I never did that junk, and I can trounce any one of you fools. So don't you try to give your poison to the kid over here, or I swear, I will severely injure every last one of you."

At that, the boys dispersed, leaving Nathan and the large boy alone. Nathan looked up at the mountain before him, not knowing what to say.

"Umm, thanks," was all Nathan could think of at the moment.

"Hey, no prob — I don't like those punks," the oversized adolescent responded. "By the way, name's Donald Winslow."

"I'm Nathan Salvatore."

"Well, Nathan, I think we'll have a good time playing together this year." Donald said with a smile.

Things began to change come the school year. Nathan started working out. His rapid muscle growth put shock in the eyes of his fellow students, who previously shunned him for his scrawniness. The other huge factor of change was that Donald and Nathan were close friends now. And not only did Nathan finally find a true friend to rely on through it all, but with Donald's friendship also came respect from the entire student body. This of course was because everyone feared the monstrous teenager. In time, Nathan learned that for a guy with so much power, Donald was quite peaceful and actually did not like fighting. The new school year also brought new students. One in particular was a transfer student, who had moved from a nearby town, named John Russell. No one knew why he left his other school, though many believed that he was kicked out. John was avoided at every cost, the payoff for being the new kid. Everyone figured him to be a loner. That was until one day, when Nathan approached him.

"Hi, I'm Nathan. You're new here, right?"

The slender six-foot-tall boy looked down at Nathan and replied, "Yeah, I'm John." He held out his hand to shake Nathan's. That was all it took for John to finally make a friend.

The school year flew by, and John grew closer to Nathan and Donald. They were like the Three Musketeers. But that summer, things would once again change. Donald's younger brother, Jared, got into some trouble with a local gang of boys. He owed them some money but was unable to pay back his debt. Donald was very disappointed in his brother, but he cared for him deeply and vowed to help rectify the situation. He decided to go with his brother to meet with this gang and clear things up. The unruly group of boys laughed at Donald's suggestion of forgiving his brother's debts and went as far as threatening to kill Jared if he did not pay up. Filled with rage, the large teen began to unleash his fury onto the gang, beating them bloody. Jared's hopes began to rise, seeing how his brother was making quick work of the miscreants. But matters took a turn for the worst, when one of the boys pulled out a gun and shot both Donald and Jared. It was a double funeral. As Mrs. Winslow stared at the caskets, she raised her eyes to Heaven. She prayed to the Lord to forgive her sons for their foolishness, and she begged God to allow them both into Heaven to be united with her again one day. Nathan was shaken up as well, and so was John. They lost their best friend, and it just did not make any sense. It was like some sick dream, a crazy nightmare. But it was real, and that is what made it so difficult.

The next school year would be different for Nathan, for now his best friend would no longer be strolling the halls with him. He tried his best to keep his head up and to remember that Donald was in Heaven with God. He was always told that the Lord worked in mysterious ways, but Nathan found it hard to believe that Donald's death would reap any benefits. John was also confused with the loss of his friend, and the fear of his own death stared him in the face. Unlike Nathan, he was not sure that God existed. Death was the end for John, so he decided to live life to the fullest. Time moved forward and the two friends decided to dedicate that football season to Donald. Nathan's parents made a big decision of their own. Maria and Joey decided to send Esmeralda to the same school as Nathan. They had originally feared that decision, thinking that the school would be too dangerous for their tiny sprite. But they could not afford a Catholic high school, and Nathan would be there her first two years to protect her. And protect her he did, maybe a little too much.

The football team finished another long practice and swarmed into the locker room to hit the showers. After changing, Nathan sat to rest for a moment. John was across the way talking to some other members of the team, the same kids who tried to push steroids on Nathan when he had first started. Nathan knew that the seedy group was once again trying to sell their poison to another sucker. He got up and started to walk over to them, but they dispersed before he could get there. John did not move, and Nathan did not like what he just saw.

"John, what do you think you are doing? I know what they gave you. Why didn't you refuse it? You know that stuff is poison!" Nathan lectured.

"What's up with you? You think you're my father or something. Anyway, I'm just gonna do one cycle. Then, I'm gonna quit. You know, just enough to gain some bulk and have something to work with it."

"That's how it starts. Then you get addicted and can't live without it. That crap does more bad than good. John, as your friend, I'm telling you not to ruin your life."

"If you were my friend, you would understand! Now, get away from me! I don't like being told what to do! So leave me alone!" John shouted and walked off.

Esmeralda took to her new environment much better than her brother had his first year. Her beauty and great personality made Esmeralda very popular from the moment that she arrived, especially with the boys. This upset Nathan, for he knew how

101

high school boys were. He was one of them. The thought of what those guys wanted to do to his sister burned him up inside. With what happened to Donald and now to John, Nathan was afraid that he would lose his sister as well. But there was not much he could do, not without destroying her social life. So, Esmeralda's big brother stayed off her case for some time.

It was late, and Nathan stood alone on the sands of an unfamiliar beach. He looked out at the water and watched the waves crash against the immovable rocks. The sand was cool in the dark night, and the moon sat above the raging waters, almost close enough for Nathan to reach out his hand and grab it. The sky was clear, and the stars sparkled like the angels in heaven. As Nathan began to draw a smile on his saddened face, something tugged on his shoulder. He turned around, not knowing what to find. Shock consumed the boy as he saw his deceased friend, decaying right in front him. Donald stood there as if he had just crawled from his grave, dirty and covered with parasites. Too stunned to scream, Nathan just gave a gaping stare as millions of others just like Donald came walking toward him. He did not run from the gruesome crowd. Instead, he felt as if he was destined to hear their plea. But he could not hear anything because all their mouths, including Donald's, were stitched shut. The young man did not know what to do. Then, Donald scratched into the sand, carving out letters with his bony fingers. The message that Nathan read confused him more, for it said, "Help my friends."

"Help them how?" Nathan asked as millions of decomposing bodies stared at him with need, looking for hope. "How? How can I help? What must I do?" Nathan began to shout at Donald.

The boy who had saved Nathan two years prior, now looked to Nathan for salvation. Once again he began to write. The new message made less sense to the confused teenager. It read, "Radix." Nathan did not know what it meant, but he swore to help these people. And as he did, he woke up. It was all a dream. Nathan had been having strange dreams since he was a mere toddler; all of them left him puzzled. Most people would just ignore their dreams and continue with their lives, but Nathan could not do that. For some reason, he felt that these dreams were telling him something. It was almost as if they were signs of what was to come. This last dream bothered him most of all.

Spring came, the football season was now over, and surprisingly they had won the state championship. This helped John, who was the quarterback, to make All-American. Nathan was happy with their success, but he and John were still not speaking. John was now hooked on steroids. His mass astonishingly increased. In some eyes this made him a better football player. Nathan was very disappointed in his friend, and the decision that he had made. He too had gained muscle mass, but without the aid of drugs. As strong and determined as Nathan was, he had lost much of his fight. He felt very alone. Donald was gone, and now John had drifted away. He decided to confront John in school one day. Nathan slowly approached John's locker, trying to be as stealthy as he could. But this was impossible for him, for he was anything but quiet. John turned to see his former friend.

"Can we talk?" Nathan asked politely.

"Why, so you can lecture me again?" John responded.

"Come on, just give me five minutes. We were best friends once, at least you could hear me out."

"Okay, just five minutes, no longer."

The two boys strolled out to the steps near the teachers' parking lot. They sat down and looked at each other, not with hate, but rather, wondering how it all happened.

"John, you were one of my best friends, and I still care about you," Nathan started slowly. "I don't mean to breathe down your neck, but I'm afraid that you are going to kill yourself with all that junk you're putting in your body."

"I thought we had this conversation already," John spoke with a slight bit of sarcasm. "Nathan, why don't you listen to my side of the story for once. I'm gonna get off the 'roids soon. Don't worry. I just need them a little longer. Just to get a little bigger. You don't understand how much they've helped me. If it wasn't for the 'roids, I wouldn't have become All-American, or even brought us to the states. Don't you see how important they are to me and my future?"

"Don't you see yourself? You're delusional. You don't need anything. Sure you packed on the muscle a little faster, big whoop; let's see that muscle when you're older. It'll be like water. Plus, it makes you more violent. You lash out at people now for no reason, and you are always getting into fights over nothing. Just the other day, you nearly took that kid's head off just for looking at you funny. Look at your new friends, a bunch of posers. They don't care about you. All your girls are tramps, and you're struggling in all of your classes. Where is the upside? Show me!" Nathan screamed in anger.

That speech did show John a lot, and Nathan's points indeed struck hard at the heart of his former friend. But curing a disease, which was exactly what John had, was not an easy thing to do. Nathan had to do more than just show John where he went wrong. He had to get through John's pride as well, and John had plenty.

"Go to hell!" John shouted, and he walked off.

All the boys' eyes were on Nathan's baby sister, and he did not like that one bit. He was always very protective of Esmeralda, feeling that she was too weak to defend herself. Now she was turning heads, and Nathan was biting his tongue.

"Hey, big bro," a high-pitched voice squeaked from behind Nathan.

"Yes, my darling little sister," he said, as he put some books into his locker.

"I just wanted you to tell Mom that I'm going to be home a little late today. I have cheerleading practice, and then my friends and I are going to get something to eat. Okay?" she said in her sweet and innocent voice.

"All right, I'll tell her," Nathan responded.

"Bye-ee," Esmeralda squeaked.

"Hey, Nathan," another voice came over his shoulder, this time a boy's. "Your sister is slammin'. I'd like to get me a piece of that."

"Oh would you? Well, how about settling for a piece of this," Nathan said as he turned and belted the boy in the stomach with his right hand.

The teenager had fallen to the ground from the impact and was unable to catch his breath. He just wondered in amazement why Nathan had struck him.

"Don't ever talk about my sister like that. Ever!"

That night, Nathan could hear Esmeralda crying in her room.

He knocked on her door and said in a soft tone, "Ezzie, Ezzie, are you okay?"

She shouted back, "Leave me alone!"

Jiggling the knob of the locked door, Nathan continued to ask her, "Are you sure everything is okay? I just want to help you. I care about you, sis."

"I said leave me alone! And if you cared so much about me, why did you ruin my life?"

"What are you talking about? What did I do?" Nathan questioned as he crashed open the door with his shoulder.

Esmeralda, in her cheerleading outfit, sat on her bed in shock, "Look at what you did, you animal? Wait till Mom and Dad get home. You're gonna be dead!"

"You wouldn't let me in, so I let myself in! Now what did I do to you, anyway?"

"You ruined my social life, that's what you did! No boy in the school will talk to me because they're afraid that you're going to beat them up!"

"What?"

"You knocked the wind out of Jim Ramsey today, just because he said something about me! And look at what you did to the door! You're a beast!" Esmeralda fled from her room and ran out of the house.

"Stop! Ezzie, stop!" Nathan shouted as his sister ran off.

Nathan did not know where she had gone, so he went to his room to think. Posters of cars, women, and comic book characters decorated the walls. He went over to his weight bench in the corner next to his bed. Lying down, Nathan started to lift the heavy iron bar and plates. As he lifted, he thought. His parents would have his head when they got home. First he broke down Esmeralda's door, and then he caused her to run away. Up and down the bar went, and Nathan's mind grew more and more cluttered. He started to think of John again, and Donald's death. All of this throwing logs into the fire that was set ablaze in his head. He put down the bar and in pure rage put his hand through one of his walls.

The doorbell rang. Nathan calmed himself down and went to answer it. He prayed that it was Esmeralda, and not his parents. He was worried about his baby sister. She meant the world to him. Nathan opened the door to find neither his sister, nor his parents. It was John — and Nathan was surprised.

"Can we talk?" John asked.

"Sure," Nathan replied in a low tone.

"It's not easy for me to say this, but you were right. I'm gonna get off the juice. You really shook me up with your speech at school today. I know it's gonna be hard, and I'm gonna need help. I just hope you'll be there to get me through this."

"Of course, you're like my brother," Nathan said.

This was the first good news Nathan had heard that day. He embraced his friend, and things felt as if they would instantly go back to the way they had once been. At that moment, the phone rang. Nathan ran to grab it.

"Hello?" Nathan answered.

"Give me Mom or Dad!" Esmeralda's voice shouted over the phone.

"They haven't come home yet." Nathan tried to stay calm. "Where are you? I'll come pick you up."

"No! Don't you dare come anywhere near me! Not ever again!" she slammed down the phone with her last breath, leaving Nathan with nothing more than a dial tone.

He hung up the phone and told John that he should go home. He needed some time alone with his thoughts. Two hours flew by, and it was half past midnight. The doorknob began to jiggle and then turn. Nathan looked at the front door and watched his parents walk inside the house. Esmeralda still had not come home, and it was his fault. He always reacted without thinking, run by his emotions and not his logic.

"Nathan, where's your sister?" Maria asked sternly.

"Um, um, I think she's at one of her friends' houses," he replied.

"You think?" his father jumped in.

"Which friend — she has so many?" Maria jumped back in with another question.

"I'm not sure. She wouldn't tell me."

Joey gave Nathan a deep stare, "Okay, son. What really happened? She never stays out this late. Something must have happened!"

"Nothing happened. She just ran out. I don't know. She sounded angry or something." Nathan paused for a moment. "She called me about two hours ago, but she wouldn't tell me where she was."

"I don't know what happened. All I do know is that something isn't right, and somehow it's your fault. So, go to your room until your sister comes home and explains this mess to me! And you better pray that she comes home soon."

Nathan slowly ascended the stairs and went to his room. Once again, he picked up his weights and began to lift.

The phone rang, and Maria answered it, "Hello?"

"Mom, it's me," Esmeralda said.

"Where are you, baby? I was so worried about you."

"Don't worry, I'm fine. I'm over at Lauren's house. Her mom said I could spend the night. Is that okay?"

"That's fine with me, but stay safe. I don't want anything to ever happen to you."

"Bye, Mom."

"Bye bye, baby."

"Was that Ezzie?" Joey asked as Maria hung up the phone.

"Yes, she's at Lauren's house," she answered.

"Did she say what happened?" Joey wondered.

"No, she didn't, and I didn't want to upset her."

"Well, then I'm going to go upstairs and have a chat with Nathan," he sighed and began to walk up the stairs.

Nathan heard someone knocking on his bedroom door. He did not want to unlock it, but he figured that he was already in enough trouble. He got up off his bench and let his father into the room. Joey walked in slowly and gave Nathan an unyielding stare.

"Son, I think we should talk. First about your sister, then about her bedroom door — and your wall," Joey tried to stay calm as he noticed the hole in the wall behind Nathan.

"Yeah, the door and the wall, I'll get to that," Nathan said, his voice cracking. "About Ezzie, it's all my fault why she left.

She said that I was scaring away the boys, making them afraid to talk to her because I might beat them up," he confessed, looking down the whole time, too afraid to look into his father's eyes.

# Part III

## Ulterior Motives

"Nine, ten— you're *out!*" The referee counted out a boxer, who lay bloody and motionless on the floor of the ring. The ref held up the other boxer's hand, shouting, "Winner by knock out, Nathaniel Salvator-r-re!"

Nathan stood there celebrating. He looked out at the crowd and into the eyes of his parents, who were at ringside. Now at the age of twenty-one, he was a professional boxer with a record of 15-and-0, all by knockout. But things were not as good as they seemed. Sure, he was on the road to success, but something was still wrong. These victories seemed vain; they lacked meaning. As a boy, he always dreamed of doing something great, something that mattered. People looked up to him, but for what, because he could knock out a guy a head taller than himself? This meant nothing to Nathan — this was not what God had destined for him.

A slightly taller man with a brown suit entered the ring to shake Nathan's hand, "Nate, that was beautiful. You're at the top of your game. Next week is the title match. Think of it, Nathaniel Salvatore, 'Light Heavyweight Champion of the World.' Has a nice ring to it, am I right?"

"I guess so, Frank," Nathan replied unenthusiastically.

"What do you mean, you guess so? It's what we've been waiting for. It's our big break."

"Can we discuss this later? All I want to do right now is get out of this ring and shower."

"Fine. I'll meet you later for the victory party. Same place as usual, okay, Nate, my boy?"

"Sure, see you there."

Shouts and screams of laughter roared from inside the small pub on the Bowery. The night was cool. The slight chill in the air was broken by the doors of the bar flying open. Nathan staggered out and tried to gain his footing. He held the bar door open as he heard Frank call from inside the bar.

"Yo, Nate!" Frank shouted. "You gonna be okay going home? You seem a little tipsy."

"I'll be okay, Frank, It's only a couple of blocks away," he responded.

"Well, then, I guess it's good night for now. Just call me tomorrow, and we'll discuss your big title fight! You're gonna be champ. I can feel it, kid!"

"Okay, talk to you tomorrow. G'night." Nathan concluded as he shut the bar door. "Champ? Yeah, that'll be the day," he murmured to himself with a smirk.

The streets were filled with the muffled sounds of passing cars and the 2 a.m. regulars hanging out on the streets. As Nathan stumbled home, he thought that his mind was playing tricks on him because when he looked over at these hopeless souls they started to morph before his eyes into grotesque monstrosities. Their skin began to bubble; extra sets of mouths opened from each cheek; and their eyes began to take on different shades of color, going from white to red to solid black. Nathan stared at these hideous beings that used to be human, as they began to babble at him. Their words were inconceivable, as if they were speaking in tongues. It must have been the effects of the alcohol, Nathan was sure. He quickened his pace in a hurry to get home. Moving faster and faster, he neared the steps of his apartment building. Caught in the moment, he bumped into someone. As Nathan went to apologize for his clumsiness, he was taken aback. The man in front of him was even more decrepit than the others. His eyes took on a pale green shade, and in addition to the extra mouths on his cheeks another opened on his forehead. Nathan jumped out of the way, but as he did he heard a voice coming from the mouth atop the man's brow.

"Help them. Help my friends," the stranger uttered, his voice low and raspy. "Radix!"

Nathan ran up his steps, and struggled to get his key in the door. He turned around while entering his building and noticed that all the people were gone. As he looked down, he saw an old bum sitting at the base of the stairs. He was wearing some torn dirty rags and was using a newspaper to keep warm from the night breeze.

"Hey, mister, don't I know you? You're that boxer guy," the man insisted. "Yeah, Nathaniel Salvatore. You have a title shot coming up, right?"

"Yeah, I do," Nathan replied. "Not to sound rude, but I really have to get going."

"That's, okay — just one thing," the man sounded very stern. "Beware the man in the ring. His motives are not your own. The fight for him will be something more, as will the man."

"All right, old timer, good night," Nathan said and entered his apartment building. He closed the door firmly, trying to put aside all the strangeness of that night.

The roar of the crowd was louder than it had ever been; yet Nathan could only think about the night after his last fight. Had he been hallucinating, or was there really something special about his competitor? Nathan's thoughts were broken up by the sound of the ring announcer, and his focus went back to the fight at hand.

"Ladies and gentlemen, tonight on the eve of October 12th, nineteen-hundred and ninety-five, we will witness a battle for the light heavyweight championship of the world!" the ring announcer's voice boomed. "In this corner, we have the challenger, wearing his signature green trunks, and weighing in at one hundred and eighty-five pounds, Nathaniel Salvator-r-e! And in the other corner, wearing the black trunks, and weighing in at two hundred pounds, the undisputed light heavyweight champion of the wor-r-rld, Jer-r-ome Lawr-r-rence!"

The two fighters entered the ring and were told the rules by the referee. Nathan felt an eerie sensation run through his body as the two boxers touched gloves. The bell rang and the fight began. The two men went back and forth, blow for blow, like a couple of wild animals. Every round seemed to last longer and longer, and Nathan was exhausted after each and every one.

The eighth round came to an end at the sound of the bell. The excitement in the arena almost blew the roof off. Neither fighter showed an advantage, and no falls or knock-downs had taken place. Nathan sat in his corner, catching his breath. He peered over at the other corner, staring into Lawrence's eyes, which seemed to be pitch black. Nathan lowered his head to realize something else peculiar about Lawrence. His shadow was demonic with two great horns growing from his temples. Nathan blew this off as just something behind him casting a double shadow. The bell rang, and the ninth round began.

As the boxers jumped back into the center of the ring, Lawrence smirked at Nathan and whispered to him, "I hope you know, I've been holding back. Sometimes, I like to play with my prey."

Nathan looked at him puzzled, and the blows flew once again. Then, all at once, something odd happened. Lawrence began to dodge all of Nathan's blows. Nathan felt as if he were moving in slow motion and fatigue started to come over him. The harder he tried, the more energy he wasted. Lawrence's big pitch black eyes dug into his own, as the round came to an end. The tenth round was about to start, and Nathan could hardly move. The young dynamo, mister undefeated, was about to have his first defeat handed to him on a silver platter by this monster of a fighter. He knew Jerome Lawrence was good — he was the champ; but this guy seemed to be inhuman. The tapes of Lawrence's previous matches that Nathan watched in preparation for this bout showed a totally different fighter. The speed and skill of this man in the ring far surpassed anything Nathan saw on any of those tapes. Maybe that old bum knew what he was talking about after all.

The tenth round went like the ninth. Nathan struggled to land a blow, and Lawrence dodged everything. Now with only two rounds to go, the challenger began to get nervous and flew into the eleventh round swinging.

As Lawrence avoided Nathan's heavy hands, he whispered, "Now, we play it my way." At that Lawrence blocked Nathan's jab, and struck him across the face. This knocked Nathan to the ground.

The world began to move slower and slower, as Nathan lay on the floor feeling numb. Blurred images were all he could see, fading to black. The noise of the crowd, as loud as it was, sounded almost silent. All he could hear was the referee counting, and a hideous laughter like that of the Devil himself coming from the mouth of Lawrence. In the blackness, Nathan began to see grim images flashing before him — people being slaughtered, children being ripped apart, men and women with their flesh melting like wax, crucifixions — nothing but death flooded Nathan's mind. Like before, in a childhood dream, he saw his friend Donald decaying before his eyes. He reached toward Nathan as if he were looking for salvation. Using the nail on his right index finger, Donald began to carve something into his own skull. He carved a word into his decaying flesh, a word written in blood. The word was "Radix." Nathan read the word, forming the syllables on his lips. Then, he saw a face filled with the same laughter as Lawrence's, with evil eyes as black as coal. Nathan knew that he had to win not only this fight, but also something even grander.

Jerome Lawrence stood over Nathan's motionless body with a booming laughter, as the referee continued to count. At the count of nine, things changed. Nathan shot up from the ground, looking quite lively and refreshed for a man who was nearly in a coma a few seconds before. He plunged toward Lawrence with a right hook. Caught off guard, Lawrence was thrown by the punch but did not go down; instead, he just rubbed his chin. The fighters locked eyes and once again that familiar bell tolled, ending the round. Both men sat in their respective corners brooding. Their eyes were still locked, and their faces were rigid like stone. A woman wearing a provocative fiery-red dress walked over to Lawrence during the break. She whispered something to him. A look of anger was on his face as Lawrence nodded his head and glanced at Nathan. She walked away and faded into nothingness. Nathan shook his head and looked down. Once again he took notice of Lawrence's shadow. It seemed to lose its demonic shape.

With the ringing of the final bell, the two fighters came into the ring for the last time that night. It was time to settle this epic battle and crown a champion. Lawrence looked a little lackadaisical. Nathan saw his opportunity and gathered up the last of his strength. He charged at Lawrence, throwing a combination of lefts and rights. The frenzy of punches ended with a final uppercut, sending Lawrence crashing to the ground for a ten count. The dragon was slain. Nathan was the champion. As his friends and family rushed into the ring, Nathan fell to his knees and thanked God for the victory.

# Part IV

## The Hunt Is Over

Five years passed by, and while some things had changed, others had not. But the biggest change in Nathan's life was about to occur, one that he was definitely not ready for.

"*Beep* — Hi, Nate, it's Ezzie. Just calling to see how you're doing. By the way, don't forget, Lent started last Wednesday. So, no sweets. And Mom and Dad are expecting you to come over for Easter, as usual. Maybe you can even help us color some eggs this year. See you — *Beep*."

"*Beep* — Hi, Nathan, hon. I know things ended rough, but I hope we can still be friends. Please call me — *Beep*."

*Friends, yeah right. She would be lucky if I ever talked to her again.* Nathan thought and continued to listen for the next message.

"*Beep* — Help my friends — *Beep*."

He was unable to make out the message, so he turned up the volume and played it again.

"*Beep*— Help my friends — *Beep*."

"What the—" Nathan yelled.

The words were too familiar, and Nathan wondered what was going on. A loud knock came from the door, startling him. He walked over and looked through the peephole, but no one was there. Then, he heard another even louder knock. Someone was playing a joke on him, or so he thought. Nathan threw open the door, and in front of him stood a tall and solemn man shrouded in a long black coat. The unexpected visitor stared at Nathan with his soulless eyes.

"Nathaniel Salvatore, I presume," the grim man said.

"Yes, and what can I do for you?" Nathan questioned.

"Nothing much. Just — *die!*" The man answered and then punched Nathan on the left cheek, knocking him back.

Times had been tough lately for the freelance artist. He was between jobs and his girlfriend had just left him for another man. But these things were trivial, especially in light of what just transpired. Now Nathan had a real problem to contend with — he was about to be killed by the most sinister and evil man to ever walk the planet. There was no escaping him. Radix had never missed a target, for no one could stop him. But Nathan would not go out so easily. His faith was in the Lord, and he believed that he could put up a fight. Though, he was not sure exactly who or what he was fighting. The former boxing champion did his best to dodge the blows that Radix threw at him, and then snuck in a few of his own. None of his punches seemed to even faze the dark man, and Nathan found it hard to move around his cramped apartment. He did not know what to do.

"You fool — enough playing around," the demonic man said, as he pinned Nathan to the ground. "Do you think you can match strength with me? Do you know who I am, boy? I am Radix. I am evil personified."

Nathan had heard that name before in dreams since he was young. Fear crept over him for he felt death knocking at his door. His fear turned into rage, and Nathan grabbed the intruder. With a power not his own, he flipped Radix off of him and sent his assailant crashing through a window to the sidewalk five stories below. A sharp pain ran through Nathan's right shoulder, thanks to the tussle he just had. Rubbing his hurting arm, he stood and looked down from the broken window. All he could see was glass on the sidewalk and some people looking up at him. Confused, Nathan ran and locked his door.

After doing so, he felt the presence of someone behind him and heard a voice say, "Do you really think that that will keep him out? This is no ordinary man you face."

Nathan turned to see a shining figure, a man shrouded in a white robe with large feathery wings of emanating light. Intense as the light was, it was soothing to Nathan's eyes.

"Who are you, and what do you want with me?" he asked the luminescent being.

"There is no time for questions. That evil man will be back soon, and you are not strong enough to stop him. You must come with me," the angelic man spoke. "Take my hand, and I will explain everything."

Nathan reluctantly took his hand, and the two vanished. At the moment of their departure, the door flew off of its hinges and crashed to the floor. Radix stood in the doorway with a look of pure antagonism. He was focused on one thing — destroying that inferior being who just hurled him from a fifth-story window. He looked around but found no one in the apartment. Enraged, Radix started to ransack the place. He was so angry that he punched through one of the walls, revealing the apartment next door. The occupants stared at the beast in terror.

"Oh, look, it's the neighbors. Can I borrow some sugar?" Radix asked in a very polite yet sarcastic tone. Then in the same tone, he continued, "Sorry to disturb you, but you really should know that you are going to die."

As he started to make his way through the crumbled wall, a strong hand grabbed his shoulder and tossed him backward. A large glowing angelic figure hovered over Radix. The angel was cloaked in intricate armor laced in gold, and he had wings glowing from his back more exotic than those of a peacock.

"Ah, Michael. Long time, my good angel," Radix bantered.

"It's always the same with you, Radix," Michael said as he punched him across the left side of his face, drawing blood.

"And like you could stop me," Radix said as he wiped the blood with his hand. "You can't do a damn thing as long as my contract is good. Not like your powers are any better than mine, anyway. Well, there is one power that you have that I don't."

"And what would that be?" the angel replied.

"The power to lose," Radix said with a smile.

Right before the archangel's eyes, the deranged Radix morphed into a large black raven with a beak as red as blood and flew off into the sky. Michael looked on with disgust, clenching his fist. As he stood there, he heard sirens and saw cop cars pulling up. Just as the cops came bursting into the now destroyed apartment, Michael faded into the cold March air.

# Part V

## Transfiguration

The date was March 14, 2000 AD, and Nathaniel Salvatore's life had just come to a major crossroad. Not too long ago, he stood in his apartment in Manhattan living a normal life. That was until he was attacked by a torrent of the Dark One. Now, he was thousands of miles away in a land rich in history and holiness. Nathan stood about seventy-five hundred feet above the ground atop the same place where Moses spoke to YHWH, the God of the Jews — Mount Sinai. The first thing that he noticed was that his shoulder no longer hurt. Actually, it felt completely healed. That shoulder had been a burden to Nathan for quite some time. Shortly after he won the world light heavyweight championship from Jerome Lawrence, the shoulder was shattered in a car accident, causing him to forfeit his title and hang up his gloves for good. Since then, Nathan had pursued his real love — art — as a freelance illustrator. But with that came a lot of struggling. Work was not so easy to find. But Nathan did well. He always seemed to get by. Plus, he had a good amount of money saved from his days as a prizefighter. The question now was where would he go from here?

"I think you will no longer have any trouble with that right shoulder. You will need all the strength that you can muster for the task that will be asked of you. I am Gabriel, the messenger of the Lord," the angel spoke with grace. "Nathaniel, I have brought you here by the will of God. We are atop Mount Sinai. This is the place where your forefather Moses received the Ten Commandments from the Most High."

"Thanks for the doctoring. My shoulder feels great. But what does this all have to do with me?" Nathan inquired.

"You were chosen by God. And as you know God works in mysterious ways," the angel said.

"What kind of answer is that? Chosen, mysterious ways, this all sounds like a bad movie or something," Nathan snapped back at the angel.

The angel did not speak any further, but rather pointed to the sky. Nathan averted his bewildered eyes up to the heavens. It was cloudy, and the mountain air was sharp and cold. Then, before the mortal eyes of Nathaniel Salvatore came a divine image. A blinding light from up high parted the clouds, and from above them descended two men. A light was emitted from these men so radiant that Nathan could not look upon them, for they shone more than the sun. Their raiment also was glistening and could not be described. He looked and knew that he could not find anything in this world to compare to what he was seeing. The two men floated down until they were about seven feet above Nathan's head. He turned to Gabriel, and noticed that the angel now also shone as bright as the men before him. The brightness no longer hurt his eyes. The angel, Gabriel, rose to join the other two men. All three now hovered in the air.

"Oh, gracious child of the Lord, listen to our message. It is from the Holiest of Holies," one of the men spoke in an ancient Hebrew tongue, yet Nathan understood all that he said. "I am Enoch, the one whom the Lord loved so much that he raised me body and soul up to Heaven to live amongst the angels in the perfect way that was fashioned for mankind from the beginning."

"I am the great prophet of our Lord, Elijah," the other man spoke in the same tongue, and Nathan understood him as well. "I too was raised up to Heaven to live amongst the angels in the way that all men and women would live if they followed the Lord's commands. Listen to our message, young warrior. You must do the will of God, or many more lives will be at risk."

"Lives at risk — what about my life?" Nathan remarked. "I was having a fine time being a normal person living in the real world. That is until, I was jumped by some comic book villain reject. He barged into my home for starters, and then he fell out my window and bounced off the concrete like it was a safety net. And you tell me that lives are at risk. Well, first, tell me what is going on, and what it has to do with me?"

"Such anger. You will never succeed with that attitude, young warrior," Enoch spoke.

"Succeed at what? I want a say in all this. I never asked to be shown anything. And why are you calling me young warrior?"

"Because you are just that. Chosen to be a warrior of the Light, Nathaniel Salvatore," Elijah countered. "Now, if you would just stop your ranting and listen, all of this will be cleared up shortly."

Enoch began, "Nathaniel, you were chosen by God, the Most High, YHWH, before you were even born. A hero was needed to stop an evil that has plagued the Earth, and that hero is to be you. But remember that just because you were chosen does not guarantee that you will succeed. This war that you have stumbled into began long ago, even before my greatest grandfather — the father of all men on Earth, Adam — was created. It began when there was no time or space. There was just heaven, God, and the angels. That is when the morning star fell and with him many others, allowing evil to take form and cast its dark shadow over God's creation. Thus, it gave birth to Sin and Death. The battle that you will fight is one that is as much mental and spiritual as it is physical. You must be ready for great hardships and loss."

"But what if I don't want to fight your battle? I don't remember enlisting. I just want to be normal again and live a long peaceful life!" Nathan exclaimed.

"You don't understand. You have no choice. You are on his list. He will kill you, regardless of your actions. The point is merely to keep yourself alive," Enoch continued.

"Keep myself alive," Nathan interrupted. "And now there's a list. Who is this guy I'm fighting — Santa Claus? Next thing I know you're going to take me to the Island of Misfit Toys or something. I don't like the sound of this at all."

"Nathaniel, did you ever wonder why your mother left being a nun to marry your father, or why your father never died in Vietnam, or why you were plagued with all those dreams and visions? It all led up to this. You must let go of the world that you know, what you call real, and grasp what is truly real. You, Nathaniel Salvatore, were sent from God as a gift — a savior — to save the people of this world from Radix," Enoch stopped.

Elijah continued on, "Yes, Nathaniel, Radix — the name you always knew but never put a face to, until earlier today. We are here to tell you about Radix. To let you know who he really is, in hope that it will help you to defeat him."

# CHAPTER VI
## THE ROOT OF EVIL

"The man you face possesses a great evil power within him, one that exceeds that of any other man throughout time," Elijah professed. "Radix Malorum, like his name, is the root of all evil, or at least most of the evil on Earth. His ominous presence can be traced back to just about every heinous deed in the last two thousand years, from the death of God's beloved Son to the Holocaust. Nathan, you are the one who must end Radix's reign of terror. But before you go out to try and accomplish a task that even the greatest heroes have failed to do, you must prepare yourself. Let me start you off with a story. It is one of corruption, of a timid boy who grew to be the most fearless and feared creature to roam the green Earth."

# Part I
## The Tale Begins

In the year that you would deem 1 AD, a short time after the birth of our Savior and Lord Jesus Christ, another man was born into this plane, a man whose existence wrought the opposite of everything that Jesus stood for. Radix was the eldest child and only son of a wealthy farm owner and philosopher, Demetrius, and his wife, Astraea, who was said to be as beautiful as the stars in the sky. His name, which is Latin for "root," represented the root of Demetrius and Astraea's love for each other and their new family. They lived in a beautiful villa, which surrounded the courtyard where Astraea would sit and watch Radix play with his younger sisters, Althea and Andrea. The slaves tilled the fields that yielded many types of crops including olives, figs, and grapes. They even had some goats for milk, cheese, and occasionally meat. Most of Demetrius' income came from the selling of his produce to markets and traders. To make sure that their crops would be rich and plentiful, the family visited the temples often, paying homage to their pagan gods. Family was top priority to Demetrius. He even wore a pendent around his neck that had the names of his wife and children inscribed around its outer edges. Life was good and simple, until tragedy struck.

When he was still young, Radix had gone to the Olympic Games with his father. His mother and sisters were left at home. The excitement of the games was destroyed, when Radix and his father came back to find his mother and sisters deathly ill. There was nothing that the doctors could do for them, so Radix was sent to stay with his aunt and uncle for a short time. The house had been quarantined and Demetrius remained behind to care for them. One month later, Radix's mother and sisters died from their illness. Demetrius was struck with such grief from witnessing their painful deaths that he gouged out his own eyes. After doing so, he walked into the forest never to be seen again.

When Radix came of age, he was granted possession of his father's property. So, he left his aunt and uncle to return to the house that he grew up in. He looked around the abandoned villa. The crops were overgrown, the animals were dead, and the slaves were gone. He had nothing but an empty house. Memories of his family came back to him — playing in the courtyard with his sisters, his mother laughing, and his father taking him to the Olympic Games. His aunt and uncle told Radix how his mother and sisters died, but he was not there to see it or to protect them. He could not understand why he was spared, and this made him feel very guilty. He also did not know what had happened to his father, and wondered if he too died from the same sickness. Regardless, his family was gone, and he was all alone. As the heir and sole survivor of his family, Radix tried to rebuild his life, but he failed. The pain grew worse and so did his anger, leading to great hatred. The winter passed, and then came the spring. Devastated, the young man became a wanderer. One evening when he grew quite weary, Radix was drawn to rest up against an old petrified oak. The young man just sat there, lost in thought and confused. Then, he began to hear a very low voice.

"Radix," the strange voice called. "Radix, you've been cheated. What wrong have you committed to deserve such misery? You've lived a good and humble life. So, why are you punished to suffer this pain and poverty? Why do the gods hate you so?" The voice stopped, giving Radix time to think.

"That's right. I don't deserve this torment. I have done no wrong." The young man jumped to his feet and screamed toward the heavens. "Why am I cursed? Why have the gods chosen to play their sick games with me? I shouldn't have to take this! To Hades with all the gods, and their vicious tricks! A pox on all the gods!"

At that instant, a man with skin as black as pitch crawled out from behind the tree and slithered over to Radix.

"So, you wish to damn the gods themselves," the dark man said. "Well, let me tell you one thing, child. In actuality, there is but one God, and He does not love you. For if He did, you would not be living so miserably. But I, on the other hand, have a great plan for you. I could make you like a god and give you great power. Together we could do wonderful things. I can see into your soul, and taste your vigor. It is quite refreshing. I know this must all be very confusing to you at the moment. There is no rush for you to decide. Just take this," the Devil said and handed Radix a large and very strange book. It was bound in what seemed to be tanned leather and was kept shut with a golden lock, in the shape of a human skull. Radix accepted the gift without fear, and the man continued. "The book will open when you are ready. It contains great secrets and spells. There is one in particular that I know you will find quite amusing. Do what you wish, but I know that you will make the right decision. Already, I can sense your fearless nature, for I did not even startle you. You are the one I need. Think about it. And if you so choose, I will return."

With that, the dark shadow-like man disappeared into the old oak tree as if he had never existed. Radix, still very tired, decided to take a rest for a while. He fell into the deepest of sleeps, so deep, it was as if he was dead. That was when the dream began, the one that changed this man's life for all eternity. It began dark and mysterious. Clouds of smoke and mist surrounded him like a great fog. There was nothing else to be seen, except for nothingness itself. He walked through the clouded space. Behind all the curtains of mist sat a man. The man was young, about the same age as Radix, and handsome. And though he was slender, Radix could tell that he was strong. Atop the man's head was a crown. The crown was not of gold, silver, or precious jewels.

123

It was a crown of thorns, yet the young man sat joyously atop his wooden throne. Radix was confused. How could a man be happy and blissful as this one, when he wielded such power, yet wore a crown of thorns and sat atop a wooden throne? Where were his riches? He seemed to be in poverty and pain, yet no misery could be found on his face. Radix stared at him. The man's gentle skin and soft beard pierced his eyes. Then the image changed.

Now, Radix saw another man atop another throne. But this man was different. He was not as young and not as handsome, yet Radix could feel intense power flowing from him as well. The power was different, but in what way, he did not know. The man's skin was coarse and had a reddish hue. No hair was atop his head. Instead, two monstrous horns grew from his skull, and a magnificent golden crown filled with gems and jewels of all sorts sat atop his brow. His ears came to a point, as did his devilish beard. Nails as sharp as daggers grew from his fingers, and his legs were those of a goat with hoofed feet. Even though his appearance was disturbing, his riches were bountiful and glistened. His throne was solid gold with a cushion that was plush and wrapped in velvet. Radix was even more baffled than before. First he saw a man who had nothing, yet he sat serenely and shone with such beauty. Then here was another who was not as beautiful or composed, yet sat proudly atop great wealth and riches. Radix was being given a choice, but he was confused and did not know which path was right.

The dream had ended. Radix got up, and realized that he was still in the forest. He did not remember exactly what had happened to him or how he had gotten there. After he stretched his muscles a bit, Radix looked down and saw the book lying at his feet. The eyes of the skull lock stared into his own. It all began to come back to him — the dark man, the book, and the dream. They all were connected. Something great was about to happen in Radix's life, but what? That is when the book opened.

# Part II
## The Word Made Flesh

Not fear, but rather utter amazement filled Radix as he turned each and every sinful page of the ancient codex that was soaked with dark magic and demonology. He was even more surprised to see that it was written in his native language, for he was certain that such an ancient text would have been written in some old forgotten tongue. What he did not know was that the writing in the book was as magical as the book itself. It could translate itself into any language understood by the reader. The mystical inscriptions enclosed in the codex could fulfill all of man's desires, most of which were achieved through pacts with demons including Satan, himself. Radix closed the book not knowing what to think. He had been taught the evils of dark magic and demons from his mother since he was a babe, yet all of his dreams and hopes could be granted so easily. He was a poor wanderer. Everything that he ever cared about was taken away from him. He had nothing else to lose, or so he thought. Therefore, he decided to take another look inside the book. He opened it to somewhere nearing the middle, page 666. The spell on this page was more powerful than any other, it was the hardest to cast, and it was very tempting. It claimed that it would grant the caster eternal life, rendering this person un-killable in every aspect of the word. The person would also remain young and healthy for all eternity — never to grow old, never to get sick, and to heal from any wound. If Radix could pull off the spell, no god would have power over him ever again. He might even have power enough to take back all that was taken from him and gain the vengeance that he sought. Now came the hard part, making this work. He read off the list of items that he would need:

1. *Three sticks about two palm-lengths each.*
2. *Oil.*
3. *Flint.*
4. *The eyes of a holy man.*

5.  *The skull of a young virgin girl.*
6.  *The blood of the caster, to be poured into the skull.*

"How will I obtain these things?" Radix asked himself.

"Worry not, Radix," a whisper carried through the wind. "I will tell you how."

"Who said that?" Radix inquired. "Why should I listen to you?"

"Just do as I say," The voice answered. "All of the items that you need can be found in a small village about one mile south of here. Go at night so as not to be noticed, and be sure to mark your path. When you reach the village, you will see a burial ground for the town's people. There will be a small grave there, the smallest of them all. It belongs to a four-year-old girl. That is where you will obtain the skull. Then, go to the house were a raven crows three times. There will be some flint and oil in that house to light the fire. While you are there take some bread, you will need it."

"Bread, why bread?" Radix wondered.

"To cast this spell, you can not do so on an empty stomach."

"Okay, and where do I find the eyes of a holy man?"

"On a holy man of course." The voice faded with a laugh.

Radix yelled out, "Tell me where!"

All Radix heard was silence as he waited for an answer.

Night fell, and Radix headed on his journey, carrying only a large purse that he had slung over his shoulder to hold the items that he would obtain. Southbound, he walked through the forest and cut into the trees with a jagged rock to mark his path. It took some time, but he finally reached the village. It was quiet. Everyone was fast asleep. Not even one soldier kept watch, which seemed strange to Radix. The Romans, who ruled all the land, never kept any town or city unguarded. Trying not to wake anyone, the prowler crept into the small village like a snake through the grass. Over at the far end, he spotted the cemetery. It was surrounded by a rusted iron fence, and looked very grim. Radix slipped through the gates, and began to look around for the smallest plot of dirt, which is where he was suppose to find the girl buried. Sure enough, he found the grave and started to dig. Finally, he reached the tiny casket and opened it with a cringe. The

126

sight of the bones and the smell of decay made the grave robber grow quite sick to his stomach. He bent over and vomited. While his head hung down, he noticed a ring on the girl's bony thumb. The ring was crafted from the most sparkling gold, and it had a six pointed star on it as well as the letters YHWH. Radix looked at the ring and was about to take it. *What a prize*, he thought. But as he lifted the skull from the child's body, he thought for a moment. His heart had not been filled with darkness yet, and he decided to leave the ring so as to not further disgrace the poor girl. He took one last look at the petite skull in his palm, and then slipped it into the purse that he had slung over his shoulder.

Radix pulled himself up out of the grave, and looked around. He hoped that there might be a holy man buried at the cemetery, as well. If so, he could get the eyes without having to take them from a living person. Stumbling through the dark ghostly graveyard, he tripped over a stone and fell head first into a fresh open grave. Six feet under and choking on a cloud of dirt, he pushed himself up and opened his eyes. As they began to focus, Radix jumped back in horror. Under him was a corpse. As much as it made his stomach churn, he looked closely at the body before him. It was an elderly man dressed in what seemed to be ritualistic garments, and he was adorned with many trinkets and jewelry. This was indeed a holy man. Taking a deep breath, Radix stuck out his middle and index fingers and went hesitantly for the eyes. He squinted and quickly pulled back, letting out a breathless sigh. Once again, he would have to confront his fears. The loss of his family had made Radix uneasy with death. It was hard for him to be so close to dead bodies, and even harder to have to remove parts of them. But as he had performed his first task of taking the skull, he would find the strength to perform this next task and remove the holy man's eyes. Readjusting himself, Radix went for the eyes one more time, but pulled back again. This was too much for him, all this death, all in one night. Thoughts of his dead family filled his head, as he became a scared boy once again. He imagined his parents' and sisters' rotting corpses coming at him like a band of zombies. Trying to get hold of himself, Radix looked into the night sky, which seemed darker than before. There was no moon and no stars, only darkness. And forming from this darkness was a demon, as if from the nethermost edges of Tartarus. Its wings engulfed the night sky, and its claws ripped the entire fabric of reality. The creature swooped down toward Radix, ready to tear his heart from his chest. Seeing this terror approaching him, Radix threw himself on top of the dead priest's body and put his arms over his head. The winged beast swooped lower, but instead of attacking Radix, it ripped the eyes out of the priest's head and dropped them in front of the fearful man. The monster flew back up, perching itself atop one of the nearby houses. Radix put his arms down and reluctantly collected the eyes. Then, he looked up at the demon, realizing that it was not a demon after all, but rather, a large black raven with a blood-red beak. As if hypnotized, Radix stared at the big black bird, only to be awakened from this trance by the sound of it crowing three times. Radix knew what to do next, but taking the items from this house would prove to be more difficult than even robbing the graves. This time the inhabitants would be alive, and Radix would have to sneak in without waking them. Luckily, he was a slim man and was able to slip in through a window. As soon as he entered, he found a jar of oil, and two pieces flint on a table. Grabbing these items, Radix put them in his purse. But before he could slip back out the window, he heard the raven crow once again. Looking down at the windowsill, he noticed a loaf of bread set out to cool. He remembered what the voice told him about not casting the spell on an empty stomach, so he took the bread and tucked it under his arm. Off he went out of the window, out of the town, and back through the woods following the marks he had made on the trees. He was safe, back to where he started, and he did it without causing even the slightest disturbance. Now, the only thing that he still needed was the three sticks, which he took from a tree and cut down to size.

Radix was ready to cast the spell. He followed all the instructions. First he made a triangle with the sticks and poured the oil on them. Second, using the flint, he sparked a fire. Then, he placed the eyes of the holy man in the sockets of the skull, and turning it upside-down so it could act as a bowl, Radix put it in the middle of the triangle of fire. After all of this, he ate the bread so he would not have an empty stomach.

He chanted from the book,

*"Darkness,*
*My soul gone,*
*Life everlasting.*
*Blood,*
*To bring me life.*
*Death,*
*So I may not die."*

As he chanted, Radix slit his wrist with the knife and filled the skull with his very blood. Then he drank the blood, and his heart stopped beating. Lightning crashed to the ground turning entire sections of the forest to dust. Rain, sleet, snow, and hail pelted down from the dark sky. Every being on the planet, in the heavens, and in the bowels of Hell could hear the ear-shattering screams of the Earth. It knew what was to come. A man had just sacrificed everything, all for a nothing gift full of sin that would one day be taken away from him as well. Only one creature smiled that night, only one being showed signs of joy as all others wept. That being was the one called Satan, for he saw his plan unfolding before his very eyes.

The next day Radix awoke from what had transpired the night before, and he gazed up at the sky, which was now clear and sunny. It was all over, yet he felt no different than before. He did notice that his wound was gone, and his heart was now beating once again in his chest. *What had happened,* he thought to himself. Dizziness was his only symptom; he felt drunk, in a way. Looking around, he noticed that the book had disappeared. Though he was disoriented, Radix decided to get moving and started through the woods. As night fell, he realized that he was not hungry or tired. Regardless, he decided to lay down under a tree for the night, for he knew of nothing else to do. The night passed and with it many dreams. One in particular stuck in the young man's mind. There inside the walls of a city stood an enormous crowd lined up on each side of the street, waiting with much anticipation. But the silence of the waiting crowd came to an end as a young man rode through the city's gates atop a donkey, followed by many other people. The crowd cheered him on, waving palm branches, and laying them down before this kingly peasant. As they exalted the arrival of the man, Radix noticed that one of the followers seemed different from the others, almost possessed. He carried in his hand a bag filled with silver pieces, and he stopped to count them every once in a while. The dream took a turn, and changed. Now Radix saw the same kingly peasant on a cross, dying; and the crowd that once shouted his praises was now mocking and slandering him. The man with the bag of silver was the only one not present. Radix wondered where he might be and was answered with another grave image. Before him was a withered old tree. From that tree hung a man. A serpent was wrapped around his neck like a noose. It licked the man's face with its tongue to taste his bitter tears, sweat, and blood. Radix felt as if this noose was strangling him, too. And with this pain, he awoke. He stood up and looked at the sun, which just peeked above the hillside. It was daybreak, and a chill went down his spine as he thought about the night before and the dream he had. Believing that it was all just a grave nightmare, he started to walk. Coming to a road, Radix decided to travel on the smooth pavement. The image of the man that he had seen on the cross in his dream was plastered in his mind. Every thought in his brain pounded with delight as he saw the man suffering like no human should. He smiled. While walking, Radix noticed the silhouettes of nine men on the horizon. Eight of them were standing, and one was on horseback. As he got closer, Radix noticed that the men were Roman soldiers. They stood tall and were heavily clad in armor with swords at their sides. Radix approached the band of soldiers with caution, his palms sweaty from nervousness.

"Halt!" the soldier on horseback called out to Radix.

"Sorry, sir, but have I done something wrong?" Radix politely asked.

"Not that I know of," The soldier gave a hardy chuckle. "But you are walking on Caesar's road, and if you intend to pass, you must pay tribute to Caesar."

"I would happily give Caesar tribute, but I have not a coin," as Radix said this, a gold coin appeared in his hand adorned with the face of Caesar. Radix looked at it in bewilderment, turned to the soldier, and said, "Well, actually, sir, it seems that I do have tribute. I must have forgotten about this coin that was in my pocket. Will this do?"

The soldier took the coin, and smiled, "Yes, Caesar will be happy. Please, carry on. Have a good day, and be careful. I hear that there have been robbers in the area. Not that you have much for them to take, but be careful still." The soldier gave Radix a suspicious stare, creating a feeling of uneasiness in Radix's belly.

Relieved to be on his way, Radix trekked on, and as he walked down the road another Roman soldier rode by him on a horse heading toward the other soldiers. Radix turned to see what was transpiring. The two soldiers greeted each other and words were exchanged. The one soldier examined the coin that Radix had given him and looked over in his direction. Turning away and moving forward, Radix hurried along.

"Halt!" the soldier shouted again. "Go no further!"

Fearful that he might be killed, Radix stopped, and waited as the soldier road up to him. "Yes, sir, is there something troubling you?"

"Just tell me where you acquired this coin? For I am looking at you and wondering how someone in rags could have such a gold coin in their possession."

"It was all that I had left, and I was afraid to spend it." Sweat poured down his face, as the soldier looked deep into his eyes.

"I fear that you are lying to me. Last night, robbers hit a village, and some gold coins such as this were taken. Do you know anything of that?"

Out of fear and sheer stupidity, Radix turned and ran from the soldier. Pulling his reins and kicking his steed, the man rode up next to Radix and knocked him down with his foot. After doing so, he dismounted and walked over to the fallen man.

"If you are not guilty, why are you running?" the soldier asked.

"Please, do not kill me. I'll do anything." Radix panicked.

"Where did you get this coin?"

"It appeared out of nowhere, into my hand. I swear, I really don't know where it came from. Please, I am telling the truth."

"Liar," the soldier said as he drew his sword and pierced Radix's heart.

The world went black, and Radix fell into a deep sleep. All that he could see or feel was nothingness. Coming to, he was afraid to open his eyes. The sun was now sinking into the Earth, and darkness was creeping over the land. He pushed himself up a bit and hesitantly looked down at his chest where the stab wound should have been. Confused, he pulled his torn shirt to the side and noticed that there was no wound, not even a scratch. Radix got up in a state of shock, and brushed off some dirt that was piled on him. The soldier had placed the soil on top of Radix, to bury his body — this was an ancient superstition that even the Romans followed. Many questions now arose in Radix's head.

"Allow me to answer your questions, my boy," proclaimed a man in a low dark tone. His skin was tan, and he was dressed in a white suit with a snakeskin tie to match his snakeskin boots.

"What do you want of me, sir, and why are you wearing those strange garments?"

"Do not worry about my garb," the man spoke. "I am a friend, the only friend you have. And it is because of me that you still live."

"It's you, the one who gave me the book," Radix realized. "You look different, but I know it's you."

"Yes, you are right. I am the same man who gave you the book, but I am not here to hurt you. I am here to talk to you about our contract. You have been granted eternal life my boy, and powers beyond your dreams. But, you do not get these powers without a price."

"I don't have anything. Do I have to go through this again? Why won't you people understand that I have nothing?"

"It's not what you have — it's what you must do. You must bring an end to lives. You must become a harbinger of death, if you will. One day, the Earth will be covered in the blood that you will shed." Flames came forth from the strange man's mouth as he spoke.

"Why should I? I hate violence, and I can't stand the sight of blood."

"Why should you? Ha! The real question is, why should you not? What has God done for you, my boy? He has taken everything away from you. But me, I am giving you anew. I am rebuilding you and making you greater then any man that God has ever created. So you hate violence, and you cannot stand the sight of blood? Don't be so weak, boy. Your weaknesses have led to you losing everything. Now take hold. It is not about the violence and the bloodshed, but what they bring forth. The world needs to be cleansed of all this humanity, and you can help me do that. Look at how the men of this world treat you, like a dog. Now I will make you unlike them, superior to them. But in order to do this, you must embrace violence and bloodshed. It is because of God and his followers that your life is like this. Take revenge and use what I will give you," the man said. His white suit reflected the red light of the flames that now surrounded them. He held out his hand toward Radix and said, "Come, there is much to be spoken of. Follow me."

Radix hesitantly followed the devilish man. Confused and scared as he was, he had nowhere else to go. He hoped that the strange man would lead him to an inn and maybe feed him, even though he was not hungry or tired. In actuality, Radix felt quit energized.

"What exactly did you do to me?" he asked the man as they walked on. "I'm not hungry, yet I haven't eaten in days. I'm not tired, yet I've been walking for miles. And I was stabbed in the heart, yet I still live."

"Relax, my good man. You should be happy. Look, you no longer hunger, you no longer grow weary, and you do not die by the sword — what more could a man want. With what I have given you, you could rule the nations. You could be the most exalted man in the world. Look at the power you possess. You're practically a god," the crafty snake said.

"But I don't care about these things you speak of. I do not want to rule, or kill, or anything. I just want my life back, my family. That or just die and let all this be over with."

"You are so foolish, Radix. You have what men dream of. I gave you more than God has given any man, and you spit on it. You put a pox on the gods, and I gave you the means to be your own. What else could you want?" The Devil paused, but Radix just stared, hypnotized by his eyes. "I see your hesitation. But by the end of this night, you will indeed see things my way.

I guarantee it. You will carry on what I began long before there was time. You are like I was, scared and confused. Now, you have great power, but you don't know what to do with it? Choose. Have a mind of your own. Do not serve a God who gives you limitations. Do not serve anything, except your own desires. Give in to your instincts, your lust, your greed, your hatred. Let go of your fears. You have already put a pox on the gods. Whose laws, then, are you afraid to break? Just let go and give in to the temptation, give in to me."

The demon kept his eyes fixed on Radix's. Flames shot up around them as before, and burned brighter with each passing moment. The two men began to levitate. Radix's body was stiff as a board. A dark mist formed around them, thick with sin, swirling faster and faster. The darkness penetrated Radix, taking hold of his heart. The man kept on speaking to him, but Radix did not know what he was being told. It was almost as if he were watching the whole thing from outside himself. Ideas began to sink into his head, as he gave in to the temptation of the Devil before him. The mist covered them completely. Radix felt a sharp pain and immense heat, and then he saw the hellish beast for what he really was. Both pity and fear filled him as he gazed in awe. The demon's eyes were like those of a venomous snake, his ears were like those of a jackal, and his nose was long and gnarled. His putrid, diseased flesh burned red. The monster's teeth were stained with blood. Radix went into shock at the unexplainable iniquity that he was witness to, and then he collapsed. The darkness had taken over. Even the Devil performing the ritual did not know what was transpiring. He only knew that Radix would wake up transformed. Now just like Satan, he would have evil intent — the one thing not from God. All went dark, and a red haze blurred Radix's vision from that point on. Over time, the blood lust would take complete control of him, making him an addict to that crimson liquor. His name would be changed from Radix son of Demetrius, to Radix Malorum, "the Root of All Evil."

# CHAPTER VII
## FORTY DAYS AND FORTY NIGHTS

"Now you know the beast that you must battle. You cannot defeat him with any weapon, for even the blades of the angels cannot end his life. Your mission is simply to survive," Elijah commanded Nathan.

"That was a nice story you told me, but I don't know what it has to do with anything. As far as I can see, it's just another case of a man steered wrong by the Devil," Nathan interjected.

"Radix, as all men, chose his own path. Do not feel sorry for him, for he is pure evil. Yes, he was a man at one time; but now, he is only a monster. Remember that. We only told you of his past so that you might gain some understanding of who he was and now is. But all that you should concern yourself with is the fact that he is an unstoppable killing machine. He does not care about anything except executing his prey. So, be wary and stay strong," Enoch added.

"Well, there's one thing I don't understand," Nathan interrupted once more. "Why didn't Satan build an army of soldiers like Radix? Why just him?"

"That is because the spell cast by Radix cannot be recreated, and once cast it vanished from the pages of the *Necronomicon* for all time. The creation of a monster such as Radix was a one-time event and, thankfully, will never be reproduced. But there is a far worse evil than Radix out there, and you should prepare well. For in time you will face things the like of which you have never even dreamed. Your test will begin now. We have done all that we can for you. Keep safe, and may the Lord of all send His blessings upon you, young man," Elijah said as he and Enoch disappeared.

"So now what do I do?" Nathan spoke to the angel that still remained hovering over him in brilliance.

"You must descend this mountain and enter the desert. There you will be safe from Radix for now. But you cannot stay there forever. The desert will test you and prepare you to succeed in your mission. Just always remember that God is with you," and with that the angel disappeared as well.

Nathan was all alone, and not happy with the task at hand.

"Hello?" Esmeralda answered the phone.

"Ezzie, it's me," Maria responded. "We have to talk."

"Is everything okay, Mom? What did Nathan do this time?"

"You're brother didn't do anything, I think. But something might have happened to him."

"What do you mean something happened? Is he hurt? "

"The cops called and said that his apartment was broken into, that the whole place was ransacked, and there was no sign of Nathan. I haven't heard from him in days," Maria answered.

Silence came over both mother and daughter, as they thought about what could have happened to their beloved son and brother. Maria did not like crying. She preferred to pray. And pray they both did without the other knowing. Esmeralda shed some silent tears. She did not want her mother to hear her cry.

"Mom, I'm gonna go to the city tomorrow and check out his apartment. Maybe see some of his friends, and see if they know what's going on."

"Thank you, my little sprite. Call me and let me know if you find out anything."

"I will, Mom, just stay strong. I have a feeling that Nathan is okay."

# Part I

## Long Way Down

Nathan understood the mission that was set before him and the sacrifices that he would have to make, but the young man was still very lost. All of a sudden, everything that he had read about in the Bible had become more real to him than he had ever imagined. It was as if his own life was now part of the continuing story of God's people. But what concerned him most at the moment was the fact that he was stranded on a mountaintop in the middle of a dessert that seemed to go on forever. The only thing he could do at this point was climb down the mountain and go forward from there. Nathan was a little scared, for he had never scaled a mountain before. At first, he tried to rely on his athleticism and his instincts, but he soon realized that the only thing he could truly rely on was the Lord. Only through God's grace could he get out of this safely and accomplish the task that was given to him. There was no way that he could hope to win his battle with Radix on his own. Nathan knew this and humbled himself before his Heavenly Father, seeking His help. After a few hours had passed, he finally reached a flat ledge and decided to take a rest. Not too far away was a small but shady olive tree. He walked over and took a seat. Leaning up against the tree, Nathan stretched out his legs. In no time, he was fast asleep.

The hot air became cold, and Nathan opened his eyes to see that the sun was still in the sky. This confused him. At that moment a black cloud spread out and blocked the sun's light. The dark haze grew and covered the entire sky. Inside the darkness, Nathan saw people trying to escape. They cried out for freedom in a multitude of tongues, yet he understood them all. Then, the cries for freedom turned into shrieks of pain and agony, as beasts devoured those same people whole. The darkness began to close in on Nathan. The closer it came, the more empty he felt inside. It tried its best to make the young man fall before its evil will, but he stood his ground and fought back. A beam of light shot out from inside the darkness. It was the sun's rays, which began to shine brighter and brighter, until they diminished the darkness completely. Before Nathan's eyes, the sun transformed and became the shining face of Jesus. Christ opened His mouth and out of it sprang a double-edged sword. The blade flew down toward Nathan, who just closed his eyes and steadied himself. With great precision the sword sliced through his chest and pierced his heart. The young man fell to his knees and grabbed the handle of the sword. He felt no pain, but rather was filled with the Word. Courage surged through Nathan as he opened his eyes. It was nighttime. The air was indeed cold, but there was no sword in his chest. Nathan knew that it was not just a dream — it was a revelation. But he did not try to analyze it for he was tired and it was still dark. He closed his eyes again and fell back to sleep, completely at peace.

The next morning, Nathan awoke, feeling fully rested and ready to tackle the mountain. As he stretched out his arms, he heard the sound of crowing from the olive tree above him. Looking up into its branches, he saw a swarm of large gray birds. These strange fowl began to crow louder than before and flapped their wings aggressively. Noticing the spying man below, the creatures left their perch and swooped down at him. Nathan ducked as they tried to rip apart his flesh with their sharp talons and beaks. Every time they missed, they would just turn back around and come at him again. Cornered, Nathan needed to fight back. Just then, he noticed a ring-shaped bronze disk on the ground. It was about the size of a Frisbee and had strange markings on it. Not knowing or even caring what it was, Nathan picked up the disk and began to slash away at his attackers. But it did not scare them off. They started to attack with more ferocity than before. One of the monstrous birds grabbed hold of the disk with both of its feet and a tug of war pursued between man and beast. Then, as they both pulled with all their might, the disk broke in half. Suddenly, the winged terrors stopped their attack and flew back to their perch in the olive tree. All was quiet until, with an ear-shattering call, the birds rose back up to the sky. Nathan listened closely, as their crowing turned into a screeching song. Anguish began to swarm in his skull, eating away at his brain, as thousands of demonic voices sang the hymn of the birds. Covering his ears and praying that the voices would stop, Nathan crouched down to the ground in pain. He slammed his fist on the rock below. Sweat poured from his skin, the skies turned a grayish black, and blood rained down. Now the birds swarmed around him in a cyclone pattern, crowing louder the same chant as before.

Nathan looked up to the heavens, and mimicking the chant that swelled in his ears, he screamed out, "Legion!"

The voices were now quiet, as was the lost man. Nathan sat up and got a grip on himself, rubbing his aching skull. He had no time to lose and his route was still a long way down; so, he got up and began to descend the rocky slopes. Time seemed endless as the sun sat high above his head. The rocks felt like Jell-o on his numb hands. He had been climbing for too long; and with nothing to eat or drink, his body was starting to shut down. The more it hurt, the faster Nathan moved. The only way home was down that mountain, and this New Yorker was not about to give up and die out in the desert. The sky began to spin; and Nathan began to lose his balance, as vertigo overtook him. He refused to look down. He would not stop. He would not let go. But the pressure was too strong, and he could not fight it forever. In his head, Nathan turned his thoughts toward God.

"Lord, have mercy," Nathan said as he lost his grip and fell.

But his fall was not very long, and it was not very hard, for the Lord indeed had mercy upon Nathaniel Salvatore. He fell about fifteen feet and landed in a small patch of bushes. His back was a little sore, but for the most part the fall had no effect on him. Getting up and dusting himself off, he realized that he was on an old, weathered path that seemed to lead to the bottom of the mountain. Lucky for Nathan that he landed where he did, for had he landed just a few more feet to the right, his fall would have been much further and fatal. This would have made Radix's mission a very easy one.

There was yet another surprise for Nathan. The bush that he had fallen into was full of ripened berries. Unconcerned if they were edible or not, Nathan dug in and feasted on the juicy treats. To his amazement, they were the sweetest and most delicious berries he had ever eaten. After eating his full, he tore off a piece of his shirt and wrapped up some berries for later. Walking down the path was much easier than scaling down the mountainside. A couple of hours passed, and the tired man took a seat on the rocky trail. He opened the pouch that he made and ate some of his spoils from earlier on. The berries tasted just as sweet, even though they were not as fresh as before. Nathan was sure that the heat would have fried them, but God was with him.

As he sat enjoying his meal, he noticed a shadow cast over him — that of a man. Wondering who was casting the shadow, he turned. No one was there, and the shadow disappeared. Nathan got up and began to walk down the trail, very suspicious of his surroundings. Then with a thump, he fell to the ground. It was as if he had walked into a sequoia. The shadow was now once again cast over him, but this time he saw what was casting the shadow. A man stood before him about seven feet tall, large in stature, and dressed in a dusty robe with nothing to cover his large feet. Nathan could not make out his face for the little sun that was left in the sky seemed to strangely block it out. He tried to get up, but the man shoved him back down. Once more, he went to stand and he was thrown again to the rocky floor. Enraged, Nathan pounced and grabbed the man's wrists, making it impossible for the man to push him back to the ground. The two began to wrestle, and for hours this match of strength continued until the sun was almost completely set over the desert sand.

As the sun dropped out of sight, the man stopped fighting, so Nathan let go and decided to finally ask some questions. But as soon as he relaxed his grip, the man struck at Nathan's side. Thanks to his keen reflexes, Nathan was able to dodge the blow and the man disappeared with the sun. That battle took every last bit of energy Nathan had left, and there were no more berries for him to eat. As night came, Nathan's weary body collapsed to the now cold, rocky ground. The sky was full with an infinite number of stars, stretching across on this ever-so-clear night. Out from the clear sky, clean sparkling rain began to fall. The cold drops fell upon Nathan's body, waking him from his dead sleep. He turned over on his back, his body soaked. The rain felt so refreshing on his battered body that he did not notice that there were no clouds in the sky. He just lay there and tasted the wonderful rain.

# Part II

## The City That Never Sleeps

It was early morning, and the sound of clopping steps woke Lyles from his restless sleep. The sound grew louder and closer, as the lights of the prison hall turned on in procession. Before Lyles could even get up, someone opened his cell door.

"Mr. Washington," Officer Rogers said in an uncharacteristic, somber tone. "As much as I hate to say this, your trial has been canceled. We have some knowledge about the identity of the killer, and we are certain that it is not you. Unfortunately, the evidence came with a high price. The man, or rather the monster, shed some more blood last night. He took out many of our best officers. Regretfully, I feel that I should tell you that one of them was your friend, Detective Johnson. I cannot disclose any more information about the case at this time. I just thought you should know this, and that I'm — sorry. Sorry, for all the crap I put you through. Johnson was right — you were innocent. He was good like that. He was a good cop, a great one; and he'll be missed."

Lyles was too stunned to answer. Officer Rogers figured as much, so he quietly stood still with his head down. That must have been the noise that Lyles heard last night through his walls. The news of the detective's death outweighed his joy of being freed, so much so, that he sat back down on his bed and hung his head low. The only man in that entire station who believed in him and fought for him was dead. Friends just seemed to come and go in and out of Lyles' life.

"I heard the shots last night. Did the cameras in the station get any footage of the killer?" Lyles asked, not knowing what else to say.

"No, all the images came up like blurry shadows. But we have a couple of people who escaped the slaughter who were able to provide us with a description of the man. I really shouldn't say more. I've told you too much already," the officer considered his words. "Why don't you get your stuff and go home. I'm sure you can't wait to get a good taste of the free air again."

"Yeah, that sounds like a good idea," Lyles said as he rose from his bed, and he was escorted out of his cell by Officer Rogers.

As Lyles left the prison he thanked God that his stay was short. But attached to the joy of his freedom was the sorrow that he had for the detective who lost his life. With all good things come bad. Before leaving the station, Lyles caught a glimpse of a drawing of a man's face posted on the stationhouse wall. The eyes in the drawing were soulless and the lips thin and sinister. Lyles saw much darkness in the man's soul, even though it was only a sketch. It was the killer — Lyles just knew it — and the likeness captured every dark trait. Now, he walked down the street a free man, or so it seemed. Something strange happened to him behind those cold lifeless bars. He became stronger. He would have to be. The name Nathaniel Salvatore echoed in his head, as did the name Radix, and the picture of the monster he saw with the soulless eyes.

"Kimberly, would you like some more tea?" Martha asked the young woman on a lovely Saturday morning.

"Yes, please," her response was as sweet as her disposition.

"I really appreciate you making all this time for this lonely woman. I can't thank you enough."

"Don't go calling yourself lonely. You have a friend right here."

"You're right. I'm not lonely. Not anymore. "

The two women sat enjoying each other's company when they heard a buzz.

"Hang on, dear. I'll be right back," Martha got up to answer the intercom. "Yes, who is it?"

"It's Lyles, Mrs. Jones."

"Oh, my dear, get on up here!" Martha was pleasantly surprised as she buzzed open the door downstairs.

They could hear the sound of Lyles flying up the stairs. Martha got up and unlocked the door in anticipation of seeing the young man, a good friend of her late son. As soon as she opened the door, Lyles swept Martha into a big hug.

"Mrs. Jones, I'm free, I'm free!" he exclaimed in great joy.

"That was a fast trial," Martha said almost sarcastically.

"I was released," Lyles said as he slowly unwrapped his arms from Martha, noticing Kimberly behind her. "I'm sorry, Mrs. Jones, I didn't know you had company."

"Don't be silly. Come join us. We were just having some tea," Martha responded.

"So, this is the Lyles Washington that you've spoken so well of," Kimberly interrupted.

"And you are?" Lyles asked, fascinated by Kimberly's beauty.

"I'm Kimberly Jackson, a friend of Martha's," her eyes went up and down as she smiled, noticing that Lyles was quite attractive himself.

Martha interjected, "Why don't we all just sit down and get acquainted, and then Lyles can tell us all about his good news."

"Well, not all of it is good."

The three sat down around the coffee table, Martha in her chair, and Lyles and Kimberly sat next to each other on the couch, with some awkwardness.

"Would you like some tea, Lyles?" Martha asked.

144

"No, thank you, I'm fine."

"You know, Kimberly here knew Rashan, Kenny, and Josh. She is a volunteer for the Salvation Army and helped them when they ran away. Thanks to her they at least had a place to sleep for one night." Martha said trying to stay strong, as memories of her lost son filled her every thought. "She was the last person to see them. I just wish I could have seen Rashan's darling face one more time. And to think they blamed you, Lyles. You were their role model. They loved you as much as you loved them."

Lyles got up to console the woman, who at times was a mother to him. Lyles knew she was a strong woman, but losing a child is pain enough to make any mother weep.

"Don't worry, Mrs. Jones. The man who did this to the boys will be stopped, trust me. I just know he will. The only good news that I have is that some cops have seen him. That is why I'm free. But it took blood to prove my innocence. That takes me to the bad news. The killer showed up at the police headquarters and killed a lot of the cops. I could hear the gunfire from my cell. Scary."

"That's horrible," Kimberly spoke up. "This world can be cruel. For a man to just go around slaughtering people like that — especially children."

"I wouldn't quite call him a man, not after all he's done. He's more like a demon. His heart can only be full of darkness," Lyles' words were very true. Darkness did lie in the heart of Radix.

"What's a real shame is that even the good guys like you are treated like garbage by this society," Martha patted Lyles' hand while she spoke. "They turned you into a monster, when you've never shown to have a vicious bone in your body. A scapegoat was all that you were to them, a quick solution to their mystery, just to make their jobs a little easier. What ever happened to 'innocent until proven guilty'? This whole country is going to Hell, and the Devil is playing puppeteer with everyone in power. No matter how small a role, he seems to have them all."

"Hey, that's not true," Lyles spoke up. "There was one man who had my back the whole time — Detective Johnson. He believed in me. It was because of him that I was released. But he was killed in that massacre at the precinct. All cops should be as good as him."

"Well, amen to that, my son, and God rest his soul. I'm sure he's in heaven with the angels, my dear," Martha pronounced.

"I know he is," Lyles said with a smirk. "I can just feel it."

Kimberly stood up and stretched her legs. "I'm sorry to do this, but I have to get going, Martha."

"That's okay, hon. It was nice seeing you again."

"Yes, it was. And it was a pleasure to meet you, Lyles," she put her hand out to shake his.

Casually, Lyles took her hand and kissed it softly, "It was a pleasure indeed. I hope to see you again soon."

After she left, Martha turned to Lyles and just smiled. He knew what she was thinking because he was thinking the same thing. But right now he had more pressing matters to attend to, like figuring out who Nathaniel Salvatore was and how he was going to help him to stop Radix.

It was nightfall, and rain beat down from above. The streetlights flickered, lightning crashed, and thunder roared in the sky. Down on Canal Street, an old shopkeeper began to close up, tired and ready to go home. This man, an immigrant from China, was a good family man. He had only come here to make a better life for his children, who now were all grown and had families of their own. A shadow drifted down the street. The people walking did not notice it in the darkness, but they felt a chill as it passed by. The shopkeeper finished cleaning up and went to lock the door behind him as he left. Before he could turn the key, the shadow grabbed his arm, stopping him.

"I need something. If you give it to me, your death will be painless," A harsh whisper came from the shadow that held the shopkeeper's arm.

"I am but a humble man. There is nothing that I have that you could possibly need, my friend."

"Oh, but you are wrong, Wang Sheng. You see, you have something I need, and you know exactly what it is." The voice seemed to make the thunder roar louder.

Wang Sheng opened the door, and they entered the shop. The shadow took the form of a man. His complexion was pale, and he was cloaked in black.

146

"I see you have found me after all this time," Wang Sheng spoke to the man. "You really don't change. Maybe the clothes, to go with the latest style, but you, you're still the same, Radix."

"I don't change. And if you remember me well enough, I don't hold lightly to my threats. So, give me what I have come for, or your suffering will be severe."

"Please, kill me. I have everything that I have wanted from life. I need live no longer. You tracked me down for nothing. I don't have the ring."

"You lie, fool. No one would give up a prize like that. Give me the ring. For if you do not, I will kill you first and look for it myself. It has to be here somewhere. So what will it be? My patience is running short."

"I told you, I don't have it. And what would you do with the ring. Is your power not enough? You could have done so much good if you had only chosen the other path when you reached the fork in the road. But you chose the dark path. Blind, you have become."

"I did not come to hear some Confucius fortune-cookie crap. It is not about the power the ring will give me, and you know that all too well. It is the power that someone wielding the ring might gain over me, imbecile. You had that power once. What did you do with it?"

"I gave it to a priest years ago, right before I came to this country. He seemed very interested in keeping it away from you, which was exactly my own intention."

"You fool!" Radix's voice crashed with the lightning as the storm came flooding down on the city.

The lights in the shop flashed, and Radix disappeared into the shadows again. Like all who crossed paths with the beast, Wang Sheng lay lifeless on the floor. He lived a good long life, and he was finally at rest.

The rain kept falling on the city, thunder boomed, and lightning crashed. The shadow moved once again into the night, looking for blood to appease his pain. He wanted to destroy the world, but even he could not do so. If he could, he would have done so more than a millennium ago. He pretended that he had a choice in the matter, and that it would be no fun if there were no more people to kill. But that was not it. He simply could not. Something, more powerful than he, kept him on a leash. It controlled his every move, his thoughts, and his emotions. Finding an alley, the shadow fell to the ground and lay in the rain to cool off his burning brain. No matter how much power he had received, it was not enough. He was still weak and a slave to the darkness.

Radix sat with his thoughts, letting the rain soak his body. Not in centuries had he had such a challenge from one of his victims as he was experiencing now. *This Nathaniel Salvatore must be something important to God*, Radix thought. His thoughts then drifted off to the treasure that he was searching for earlier — the Ring of Solomon. It could be helpful for him to find it. For if Nathaniel Salvatore could get his hands on it, Radix might have more of a challenge than he had bargained for. The ring dated back to King Solomon and held many mystical powers, especially when used against creatures of darkness. Radix had the chance to swipe the ring from a dead girl's corpse about two millennia ago. But that was before the darkness took hold of his heart and before he knew that the ring could have been of importance. Now, Radix just sat and looked up at the sky thinking of what was, is, and was to come. The whole time Radix did not notice that even though it was raining, there were no clouds in the sky.

*August 18, 1960*

*—My ministry has been very effective, and I have the Lord to Thank for this. He has granted me with the gift to help people realize the power of His word, and with that gift I have been able to bring many to Christ. Our church is still small in numbers, but the energy is immense; and I know that more and more will fill up our walls soon enough. We have been lucky to be able to hold our gatherings at the old YMCA, in a small room that they lend to us, free of charge. I have even been able to reach some youths of the community. This is a blessing within itself. The younger they turn to God, the stronger they can become. I have now even started counseling people who need someone to talk to, and help guide them to the light of Christ. God has strengthened me like his prophets in the days of old, giving me the gift to preach, and to not only be heard but also understood. My only desire is to help who I can—*

Sitting on his bed, Lyles read Mr. Reynolds' diary. He never forgot about the special book, while he was in prison; for he knew that it held some answer, some secret waiting to be discovered. Patience was a virtue, and for some reason it was granted to Lyles at this time. He read each page slowly to get everything out of it that he could, not skipping a word.

*September 1, 1960*

*—I felt something strange in my heart today, like it skipped a beat. In my whole life, I have never felt this. I have tried to keep my life simple. I follow a straight path to God with no distractions, only focusing on His Word. But today, I felt different. I met a woman. Her name is Andromeda Houston, like the street not the city. She came to me for counseling. She was afraid of something, so afraid that she looked over her shoulder every second; as if she expected someone to come and grab her. She would not tell me what was exactly wrong; just that she needed someone to talk to, and she was told that I was a good listener. We met at the old YMCA, where our Sunday services are held; and we talked for a couple of hours. I did not get much personal information from her except that she was an actress, her name a stage name. She never told me her real name, but she did tell me that she left her family down in North Carolina to move to New York and become a big star. I hope to see her again soon. It is strange these feelings that I am having, they seem wrong; and at the same time, they feel amazing. Can this be love?—*

Lyles chuckled, "You old dog. Sounds like cupid pricked you with one of his finest."

Then, Lyles rubbed his eyes and looked at the clock. It was three in the morning, and he was very tired. The rain hitting his windowsill played a sweet melody, so he decided to stick his head out the window to feel the beat of the cool crisp drops. He had been confined in a prison, not for a very long period of time, but long enough for him to appreciate his freedom. *Nothing is freer than being able to feel the rain,* thought Lyles as he looked up at the sky, noticing something quite odd. Rain was indeed falling, yet there were no clouds above. Was this possible? After everything Lyles had seen lately, anything seemed possible.

"John, thanks for coming with me to the apartment."

"No problem, Ezzie. I'm worried about your brother too."

"I know, John. You've always been his closest friend."

John and Esmeralda walked around the trashed apartment in complete awe. They had never seen such destruction in their lives.

"What could have done this? It looks like a steamroller came through here," Esmeralda said, dumbstruck.

"Seriously, Ezzie, this all seems a little surreal," John added as a chill ran down his spine.

"The people who lived next door, in that place," she said as she pointed to the living room on the other side of the gaping hole in Nathan's wall. "They moved out yesterday. They said they saw nothing."

"The cops said that they found some of Nathan's blood on the floor, right?"

"Yeah, but it was too little to really tell much of anything. Do you think he was kidnapped?"

"Anything is possible," John said, and then put his arm around Esmeralda. "Don't be worried. He'll come back — he's too tough not to."

She smiled, and looked toward the window. Stuck on the sill was a large black feather. She went over and picked it up, and then gazed out the window.

"What do we have here?" a voice whispered from the shadows on top of a nearby building. "A pretty one. Who can she be?"

Radix watched the apartment from the shadows. He stared at Esmeralda as she looked out of the battered window; and then he moved his focus to John, who was snooping around.

"And a gentleman. Maybe those two can lead me to my prey. I will let them live for now," Radix keenly said.

"Well, there's nothing we can do here. Maybe we should go," Esmeralda said, wanting to get as far away from the apartment as possible, for it only made her worry more about her lost brother.

"Okay, let's go."

Esmeralda let go of the feather and watched it float down to the sidewalk. Just as she backed away from the window, a large black bird with a red beak flew by, startling her.

"You okay?" John asked.

"Yeah, I'm fine, just a bird. Probably the one who that feather belonged to," she responded in a coy manner.

Radix kept his eye on the two friends as they left the apartment and walked down to a nearby diner to grab a bite to eat.

"Did you talk to anyone about Nathan?" Esmeralda asked John.

"I spoke to some of the guys at the gym and to some of his neighbors, but no one seemed to know a thing. He doesn't talk to many people."

"I guess not," she said as she dropped her head. "I don't know what to do. I'm scared. Even though we've always had our differences, I love my brother more than anyone else. He's always been there, even when I didn't want him around. But he was always there. You can't say that about too many people, you know."

"I know what you mean. He can be a pain sometimes, but he never let's you down."

A fly brushed against Esmeralda's nose. She swatted it away, and it buzzed out the door as another customer entered the diner. Outside in an alley, the fly found a shadow and set down on the shadow's shoulder.

"So, his sister—." The shadow rubbed his chin. "This is very good. No better way to attack a man than through his own family. Follow her home and let me know where that is. I'll be around."

The fly went off as the shadow faded into nothingness.

The room was dark. Lyles lay in his bed, looking up at the ceiling. His mind was on Kimberly. He was thinking about how beautiful she was, and how much he wanted to call her. *But it is too soon*, he thought. Plus, he had much to accomplish. How could he be thinking about this woman, when he had a world to save? He had not even started to look for Nathaniel Salvatore, nor did he even know how to find him. He dared not even try to look for Radix, the monster that he was told to help stop. Lyles did not know what to do. He figured that things would unfold as they were supposed to, and that he should not rush into anything — just let it happen. For some strange reason, he was calm. He turned the light on, went over to his dresser, and picked up Reverend Reynolds' diary. Once again, he began to read, looking for some answers.

*October 18, 1960*

*—Andromeda came to see me again. This time, I decided to take some initiative and asked her out for some dinner. I told her that it would be nice to have a change of scenery. But what am I doing? I cannot throw myself at a woman like this. I am a man of God and have many obligations. My whole life, I have felt as if I am to do something great, something that will help people find hope in the Lord. But lately all of my thoughts have been focused on this woman and spending my life with her. Could I do this — perform God's will and have a family? Could I spread myself out enough to handle both jobs? I just hope that I have helped my sweet Andromeda in any way. She can be very vague and beats around the bush a lot. I'm not even so sure why she came to me in the first place. We have talked a lot about little things — her childhood, her dreams, but not what is troubling her. I hope tonight at dinner I can show her that I am a true friend and want to help her. But the only way I can is if she opens up to me. Well, I must go now and get ready. This should be an interesting evening—*

*—I should have guessed that I was coming on too strong. Andromeda never showed tonight. She probably got nervous because I asked her out. She must think that I'm looking for only one thing, and I don't mean her friendship. But I did not have any ill intentions, I really just wanted to have a nice dinner and talk. Yes, I have strong feelings for her, but I am an honest and good man, or try to be. I would never try to do anything ungentlemanly. I just hope I see her again. I tried to call her, but there was no answer. I'll try again tomorrow. I'm just going to go to bed. Maybe this is my answer from God. I guess a man with a mission such as mine cannot balance that and a normal life—*

Lyles kept on reading. The next few entries were short and about how much the Reverend missed Andromeda. Lyles felt for the poor man, and his dilemma. He too knew what it was like to meet someone so special and have other obligations that could affect ever really knowing that person the way you would like to.

152

*—Three weeks have gone by and still no sign from Andromeda. I feel as if I should just give up hope. If I am destined to see her again, then so be it. But seek her further, I will not. I will let her come to me—*

*—I woke up from quite a disturbing dream. I have had many in my life, but this one was like no other. I felt my heart stop just before I awoke and caught my breath. I can only describe my vision as that of complete and utter darkness. I was surrounded by this darkness. I could feel its cold emptiness. The thing that scared me the most was that I could not feel God. I have always been able to feel His presence and hear His voice inside of me. But how could something be without God, for He is in everything, even those who do not know Him and push Him aside. Life cannot exist without God. But this thing was alive, it did exist, and it had no part of God anywhere within it. I could feel its empty evil thoughts and its tremendous evil power trying to devour me. My heart stopped as I saw an image of Andromeda being sucked into this darkness, destroyed right there before my eyes. What could this thing be — A force that can destroy that is not God? I was able to escape this nightmare by some miracle of my eyes opening and air once again filling my lungs. The dream felt too real, but it was impossible; nothing like that could exist. I should just leave it as it was, just another nightmare, a dream, not reality—*

Lyles stopped reading and rubbed his eyes. Scratching his head, he thought for a moment about this darkness that he just read about. Could it be possible for something to exist without God? Then Lyles thought about Radix, and his mercilessness. In Radix, he saw potential for such a thing. Maybe that was what Mr. Reynolds was dreaming about. Maybe he knew of Radix, and that is why he was killed. Lyles decided to read on, noticing that the next entry was almost three months later. Up until then, all the entries were no more than two or three days apart. Lyles knew this would be important.

*January 1, 1961*

*—It is a new year, and with it, a new outlook on life. I finally know what it is I must do, and it took losing someone that I loved to teach me what love really is all about. I have not written in almost three months,*

which is bizarre for me. I like to write every day if I can. It is like therapy for me, a way to help me to understand myself and everything around me better.

Andromeda finally came back to me in late October. I was home reading the Bible, still trying to make sense of the darkness that I had envisioned. At that moment, I heard a knock at the door. It was Andromeda. She was soaking wet from the rain that had been overcasting the city for a week. I let her dry off and change into one of my robes. She sat on the bed and began to cry. As I held her, I told her that I was willing to help her if she wanted, that I felt that I was meant to help her. There was something more to her than just a lost and confused girl trying to make it in the city, something darker. But I told her if she wanted my help, she would have to tell me everything. And tell me everything she did. I was not ready for what she was about to unleash. I figured that she was going to tell me that she got mixed up with the wrong guy and was beat, or even that the mob was after her, or her pimp; but it wasn't anything like that. It was supernatural. I already knew Andromeda lived on a plantation in North Carolina, her father being one of the few black plantation owners down there. She had a nice life. Nothing strange, and she really did not need anything for her father was quite wealthy. But since she was a child she always aspired to do something great, something spectacular, something on her own. She had fantasies of moving to the big city and making it on Broadway, being loved and adored by many. But she had no experience and no real training. She had to find a way to make herself famous. She wept with every word that she spoke. Fear shook her voice as she told me her dark secret. Apparently, she had found a local witch, who helped her to make a pact with the Devil — a pact made with blood, binding and unbreakable. I had only read about such Faustian tales, never had I met someone who actually sold their soul to Satan; that was until now.

Lyles dropped the diary. He did not believe what he was reading. He picked the book back up and read it again. Deals with the Devil, what kind of life did Old Mr. Reynolds really live? He read on, relating all that he was going through right then with what the preacher had already experienced. He would be a hypocrite to say this was all a fantasy.

I was not sure what to say next. She continued telling me how she came to New York and changed her name to "Andromeda Houston," and right off the bat she was in a show on Broadway. She seemed to be doing really well. Her acting career blossomed more each day. She slowly lost contact with her family and now had not heard from them in at least two years. But like all deals with the Dark Prince this one turned sour. Her play went under, lost all of its funding, and she was without a gig. She looked and looked but could not find anything, and slowly her money began to run dry. She did not know what to do except go back home, but she just couldn't. She had too much pride. Luckily, she was smart enough to stay away from the drug and prostitution scene. She was raised Baptist, a good Christian girl. I couldn't understand why she was so quick to turn to Satan in her time of need, instead of the Lord. But she was smart enough to find me. She said that she heard about me at the local soup kitchen, where she had been getting her meals. I asked why she left those months ago and did not return until now. She said she was afraid of what she had done and felt that she did not deserve my help. Now that more time had passed, she said that she had no other option but to come to me. I was the only one that ever listened to her, that ever cared. She looked to me for salvation. I was to be her savior. But could I, a humble man, break a blood pact that someone had with the most evil demon to live? How could I battle such power? Unlike her, I turned to God at this point and asked for strength, the strength to save her life. I told her that I would help her, she would have to trust me completely and do everything that I tell her. She stayed the night in my bed. I slept on the couch. But before I went to bed, I prayed to God harder than I had ever prayed in my life. My night's sleep was restless, full of nightmares and no answers.

The next day, Andromeda stayed in my apartment as I went to the corner store to get some groceries. On my way back, a tall gentleman tapped me on the shoulder and handed me some sort of medal, insisting that I had dropped it. I knew it was not mine, but for some strange reason, I was compelled to take it. After I got back to my place, I put the groceries on the table, and I took the medal out of my pocket to examine it. It was a medal of St. Michael slaying the Devil. I did not know what to do with it, but something told me it was important so I went to my bedroom and put it in one of my drawers under some clothes. Andromeda had not seen me walk in. She was passed out on the couch. That night,

I sat up and thought long and hard about how I should help this girl. Turning to God, I prayed once again.

A couple of days passed, and then I came to a solution. We would go down to North Carolina, to her hometown, and find this witch that got her into this mess. Maybe she knew how to reverse all of this. Just before we left, I grabbed the medal of St. Michael and put it in my pocket. Something told me that I might need it. I spent every dime that I had at the time on train tickets for the both of us to North Carolina. It was worth it, she was worth it. The whole ride down, all that I thought about was how much I loved Andromeda and how I wanted to spend the rest of my life with her in my arms. To experience love was the true reason to live. That is all God really wants us to do — love. Things got a little funny once we got down South. For starters, I was completely lost. Everything was so open. I was used to the clutter of the big city. But that was not the half of it. Andromeda seemed different, confused almost. I just figured that it felt strange for her to be back home after everything. I did find it odd how easily I believed in this girl, venturing all the way down to North Carolina to help break a deal with the Devil. You do not get much more bizarre than that. But my faith was strong; and the supernatural was always so real to me, since I was young. I did not even give it much thought. It almost felt natural. She told me that we should go to her father's plantation so I could meet her family. Then after that, we would take care of business. She said that she really missed them, and with me there, she might be able to find the courage to confront them. We took a cab, and as soon as we got out, I noticed something was quite odd. The place looked completely abandoned. There was not even a door on the house, and the windows were boarded as if it had been unoccupied for years. The sun was starting to set on the horizon, and the wind began to pick up. I looked out at the overgrown fields behind the house that seemed to go on forever. Like a zombie, Andromeda began to walk toward the fields. I followed her, not knowing what to do. About halfway out, she told me that we were almost there — where she sold her soul.

Tobacco plants and other crops surrounded me. It seemed as if it was one endless maze of vegetation, until we finally came to a clearing. She told me that this was the place. The clearing was circular with about a ten foot diameter. On the ground were some sticks standing up in the dirt making another circle. In the center were some stones and rotting animal parts. The smell was atrocious.

The wind grew violent, as the sun completely set over the horizon. Then, clouds began to fill the sky, blocking the stars and moon. It was pitch black. My only security was my faith in God Almighty. I held Andromeda's warm hands, which began to grow cold. Fire shot up from the center of the circle — a fire so bright, so hot that the entire field was set ablaze around us. Then the fire went out just as it came, leaving us surprisingly unharmed. There was no natural or scientific explanation for this. Then, what I saw left my mind certain that the laws of nature were not at work. The circle we were standing in was illuminated by a red glow. The glow provided enough light to see a hideous demon standing before us. He stood about 10 feet tall. His skin was even more pitch black than the sky, and his build was unnaturally muscular. He was completely naked yet stood proud. His two curved horns atop his head stood erect. As I looked up in awe, I said a prayer for strength and courage; for I knew this could be it for me, my final stand. But at the same time this might be my chance to save Andromeda's life. I had to make this a good one.

The demon spoke to me, calling me Good Reverend. He asked if I were here on account to save the soul of my dear Andromeda. But he refuted by telling me that on the contrary he was there to collect it. He told me that I was standing in front of the fallen morning star, and that this was only one of his many forms. I asked him what it would take to save her from damnation. Then he smiled; his teeth lit up the black sky. And without further ado, he asked for my soul in her place. I did not know what else to do; I was here to save people, and who better to save than the woman that I loved. For love, I gave up my soul. I signed the contract in my blood. The fire shot up again, his black skin turned red as did the sky, and the only sound that I heard was thundering laughter. At that moment, my dear Andromeda morphed before my eyes. And what a hideous form she took. Her skin blistered and sprouted feathers; wings shot out from her back, looking halfway between a chicken and a bat's; and fur covered her chest. Her legs seemed goat like, and a long tail grew from her backside like a lizard. Then, I knew that I was tricked; lied to, deceived. I was strong in the Word of God, but even I was not strong enough for the Devil's games. He beat me, and I had no way to get back my only true possession — my soul.

I held my head in shame, as the succubus that used to be my dear Andromeda moved in on me. The laughter boomed louder and louder as the fire got hotter and brighter. And then at that very moment, I reached into my pocket, rubbed the medal of St. Michael with my thumb, and asked God for forgiveness.

A ray of clear light shot through the red haze, and the wind calmed down. The fire was extinguished, and the laughter stopped. I lifted my head up to see what was happening. There between the Devil and me stood a man as tall as the beast. He shone like a perfect diamond, standing like a true soldier, with no fear. His wings were enormous and beautiful like those of a peacock, and his armor was magnificent and exquisitely detailed. I had never seen such a sight in my life. The succubus advanced. As she did, his sword — like a hot knife through butter — sliced her head clean off and sent it rolling to the ground. Her body was then engulfed in a stream of light that he shot from his hand, disintegrating it. With that evil wench taken care of, the victorious angel asked to have the contract. The beast refused to hand over the contract for it was final, but the angel said otherwise. He forced the Devil to comply. Then, he spoke in a language that I could not understand, and the Devil vanished. The angel destroyed the contract and looked down at me as he shrank to my size. He told me that the contract was no more and not to worry. He also told me that my faith was strong. The fact that I signed over my soul for love made it impossible for the contract to hold. For such a selfless act could not be punished. He then told me that I was special and God had an important mission for me. He told me to be strong, that I would live for a good number of years; but then be killed for what I knew. He also told me that soon I would be given a revelation, something powerful that would change lives. Then a great light filled the sky, and I awoke in my bed safe from harm.

I was unable to write down these happenings when they first occurred for it was all too much for me to face. But now enough time has passed and the words just seem to be flowing naturally —

"Okay, Rogers, since we are short on men, I'm putting you in charge of one of the teams that will be searching for this madman. You have a group of rookies, so good luck," the chief explained. The two walked through the precinct station to a room where twenty rookie cops were waiting for orders. Once again the chief spoke, "Oh yeah, and, Rogers, don't screw this up."

"I'll do my best, sir," Rogers replied.

"That's what I'm afraid of."

The group of young men and women waited for the officer's instructions, as he stood before them. It was his first time leading a group on an investigation. If he pulled this off, he could be looking at a big promotion, maybe even detective.

"Okay, children, we are on a manhunt, or rather, a monster hunt," Officer Rogers spoke firmly. "This thing we are looking for is a killing machine. We are not sure how, but he seems to be almost indestructible. Proceed with much caution, but more importantly take this man down. He probably has some high tech armor, so you've all been equipped with the strongest armor piercing bullets available. Now go out there and make me proud. I want to see this monster's blood spilled all over the streets for all the good lives that he took, especially our brothers and sisters who were slain. Let's move out!"

Before the officers left, one of them raised his hand. He was young, maybe twenty. His spiked brown hair, long side burns, and earring showed off his rebel spirit.

"Yes, can I help you, officer?" Rogers asked.

"Sir, if a whole SWAT team could not put this man down, what are we suppose to do?" the rebel rookie asked.

"First rule of policing, don't ask stupid questions," Rogers responded.

"I don't think it's a stupid question," the rookie stated back.

"Did I ask you to think?" Officer Rogers was fuming. "What is your name, officer?"

"Sil, Jay Sil, sir."

"Well, Sil, Jay Sil, don't be such a wiseass. No one likes a wiseass."

"Yes, sir," Jay answered, though he had a much better answer in mind.

At that Officer Rogers walked away and began to lead the youthful team out onto the streets for their first manhunt.

"Yes, Mom, I'll be coming over for Easter as I do every year. You know how much I love to color eggs, plus all the yummy food and desserts. What else am I going to do anyway, being single and all. It'll be good to be with you and Dad during this time.

159

I'm getting scared," Esmeralda's voice dropped as she thought about her lost brother. She began to slouch down on the couch and almost dropped the phone. "I wish I knew where Nathan is. When I think of the apartment, the wreck it was in. Oh my God, Mom, I don't even know anymore if he *is* alive. But deep down inside, I have a feeling that he'll come back. That he's okay."

Maria spoke from the other line. "Everything is going to be okay, hon, just keep on praying. God will get us through this."

"I know, Mom, I'm praying right now. I've been. It's just it seems so unreal." Esmeralda dimmed the light in the living room of her townhouse in Stamford, Connecticut. "I'm going to go, Mom. I promised John I would call him when I got home."

"Okay, hon. I love you. Have a good night."

"You too, Mom. I love you."

Esmeralda sat up and dialed John's number. No one answered. She tried again, but with the same result. All the time she did not know that on the roof of the house across from hers was a peeping tom, a disciple of darkness watching her every move and listening to her conversations.

"It'll only keep on ringing. Your pathetic friend cannot answer his phone, for he is no more than a bloody pile on the floor, my little dear," Radix thought. "So Easter with the fam. That should be fun. I'll make sure to come in time to help with the egg coloring as you put it. I think I'll color mine my favorite color — blood red."

# Part III
## Dust and Bones

"That was a good show you put on last night," a calm voice awoke Nathan.

"Huh?" Nathan said as he stumbled to get to his feet.

It had poured rain the whole night in the desert; yet everything was dry, including Nathan himself. He rubbed his eyes to see who was talking to him.

"Sorry to wake you, but I am here to bring you a message," the voice spoke again.

Nathan looked to see a glorious angel before him. The heaven-sent being glowed with a pure light, just as Gabriel had. Looking deeper to see the angel's face, Nathan could not. The light was too bright.

"Okay, you people have to stop this, really." Nathan spoke. "What are you, like Jehovah's Witnesses or something? You keep coming uninvited, and never know when to leave."

"Well, I have born witness to Jehovah. His love fills my spirit as He fills all things. As for being uninvited — you should ask yourself if I am needed here or not," the angel carried on. "Nathan, I agree that it must be hard for you to take so much in at one time. To see such presences as you have seen, and to face what you have faced is unimaginable by man these days. But I am not here to sell you anything or be of harassment. I am here only to help guide you; much like my brother Gabriel did a few days ago. I am here to take you to the next step. My name is Raphael, the Healer; an angel of the Lord."

Cracking his neck and stretching, Nathan calmed down, and decided to listen to what the angel had to say.

"I apologize for my sharpness. I am just very tired," Nathan responded.

"It is understandable. Do not worry, I was not offended. I have been watching you for some time, Nathaniel Salvatore. We all have. And I must say that all of us are well pleased with you. Your tongue can be a little sharp, as you put it. But you have done all that you have been asked thus far, which is more than most men. Your strength also proved to be very admirable last night when you wrestled the angel of God to a standstill; a task only accomplished once before you by Jacob, called Israel. That is with one exception. I had to heal Jacob's hip after his encounter with the angel. You finished the battle unscathed."

Raphael quieted his tongue, and listened to the desert wind. Nathan stared at the angel, bewildered.

"You look troubled," Raphael spoke again. "I am listening to the cries of the desert. This desert is a place of torment; much pain lies in these sands and rocks. The Son spent forty days and forty nights walking these lands. During this time, He was tempted and attacked by all sorts of demons and ill-tempered spirits, as you will be. Just be careful not to listen to all that you hear. Deceit lies on the tongues of these creatures. Follow your heart and do not lose your faith. When you have survived this place you will be ready to do what God needs of you. And let me give you one piece of advice for the future. Yes, you are a man, and sin comes with the flesh; but the flesh can also be glorified. Pride leads a lot of great men to their downfall. Not only must you humble yourself before God, but also you must do so before all things that He created. Even the Son came as a servant. When you learn this you will be that much stronger."

Nathan began to hear unpleasant screams in the distance. Cries of excruciating pain drowned his ears.

"I see you hear their screams. Do not fear. You will win. Know that, and it will be made true. I must depart from you now. But before I leave, let me tell you one more thing. When you leave this place victorious, you will receive a gift — a powerful gift that I bestowed upon a mortal thousands of years ago. A man holds it now, waiting for you. This gift will help you in your battle with the one called Radix. God bless."

Nathan watched as the angel vanished in a flash of light. He sat down on the dusty ground, the heat of the sun beating on his brow. After thinking over his talk with Raphael, Nathan realized that thirst was coming over him. So the brave hero stood up and began his quest for water. Then, it would be time for him to figure out how to get out of this barren wasteland.

The winds began to pick up, and the sand blew vigorously. Nathan had never experienced the desert before; and he knew nothing of its conditions, or how to avoid its hazards. A desert storm could swallow a man, and swallow Nathan it would. The winds grew more violent every minute, and he had no way to block the sand that was blowing in his face. It irritated his eyes and filled his mouth, causing him to choke. The walls of sand shut out the sun, and Nathan could hear the screams and cries that he heard earlier when he was speaking with Raphael. The cries grew stronger and more severe, his eardrums bled from the desperate sounds. Like a raging sea, the sand lifted Nathan from the ground and tossed him about as if he were a leaf blowing in the wind. He reached out for something to grab, something to hold onto, to anchor him; but there was nothing, and the storm grew even more violent, as did the screams. All seemed lost as the world went black, and Nathan's body was buried deep within the desert floor. Calm came over the desert, and our hero was nowhere to be found.

"Can feel you," a scratchy voice was carried over the desert wind. "Can smell your blood — rich with holiness."

Then, a multitude of demonic voices spoke at once, "Smell the Spirit in your blood, we all do, Godchild." The voices grew louder, "Chosen, you are, for a meal. Our home, you are in. Not safe to be alone. Feast on your flesh, and drink of your blood, we will. Ours, you are, now. Your God, nowhere to be found. Only us, the keepers of this desert. Darkness, we worship. Iblis our king."

Nathan could hear the voices from below the desert sand as he struggled to make his way to the surface. But the more he struggled, the more helpless it seemed. His strength began to fade, his lungs were filling with sand, and he felt his life coming to an end.

The whole time the unholy voices kept screaming out, "Godchild!"

Then, a host of clawed hands pulled Nathan from his sandy grave and threw him onto the surface. It was nighttime, and he had been under the sand all day. Surprised to still be breathing, he tried to move. His muscles were too sore, and he just collapsed back to the ground. The hands came back out of the sand, grabbed him once again, held him down, and covered his mouth. Nathan could not even move an inch. All he could do was wait and watch. And watch he did as fire spewed from the ground. The fire was strange; it was smokeless. The flames began to manifest into form, and Nathan looked closely to see exactly what it had become. The hairy creature was short, maybe three and a half feet tall, and looked almost human. It stood naked. And even though its musculature seemed to be male, it had no gender. Its face was a cross between a boar and a man. It had a short snout, and two fairly large tusks protruded from its lower lip. The most peculiar feature was by far its eyes. They were very human-like, except for one trait; they were vertical, which was very odd indeed.

It walked over to Nathan. When it got to him, it crouched down and looked deeply into his eyes. Nathan could see flames in its eyes, almost as if he were looking into Hell itself.

"Yes, Godchild, he is" the creature squealed. A thousand voices could then be heard echoing what the creature just said. "My brothers, they have been watching you. We have. Down the mountain, you came victorious. Even wrestled the angel of God. Strong, you are, yes. So what secret do you hold, Godchild?"

The hand that was covering Nathan's mouth released its grip and went back into the sand below. Nathan coughed and spit out some sand that was in his dry mouth.

"Who are you, and why are you calling me Godchild?" Nathan shouted and spat in the demon's face.

A long fat tongue came from the demon's mouth, and it licked up Nathan's spit with a grin.

"What anger, you have. Quite strange for a Godchild to speak so harsh. Djinn, we are; and home, this desert is to us. From smokeless fire we were formed. Angels, we were not. Only demons, we have been for all time, made to tempt and torture. A Djinni, every man they say has one. Maybe yours I am, maybe not. Many tales, there are. Which are true and which are false, one can never tell."

"That's really great to know, vodka boy, or is it gin. I'm sorry, but it's really hard to make out anything that you say, especially with your Dr. Seuss speech about foxes in boxes, or whatever it was you were saying. Honestly, I don't care who or what you are. All I care about is getting out of here and away from this madness. So, get these filthy paws off me, you damn dirty ape!"

"Mock us, you do. Toy with us, do not. Cut you from end to end, we will, and make stew of your innards," as the Djinni spoke it took one of its claws and dug into Nathan's forehead. The monster then licked the open wound to taste his blood. "M-m-m, like aged wine. Your blood boils in my body. Godchild, you are indeed. I can taste it. God loves you, yes. Hate you, we do. Kill you, we will. But first tested, you will be. After the test, only, can we eat of your yummy flesh."

"What test? I'm not in school. I'm not taking any test! And I'm getting sick of these games! How about you let me go, and we'll see who eats whose flesh! And once again, what is a Godchild? I don't know if you've noticed, but I'm no Jesus."

"No, the Christ you are not, but Godchild you are. Your blood burns. Only anointed blood burns. Yes, anointed you are, chosen to save. Do great things, you will; or at least you were to. Change that, I with my brothers will. Corrupt you, and make a meal out of you; a good one, yes."

The clawed hands of the Djinn, which still had Nathan pinned to the desert sand, burst into roaring flames. They seared Nathan's skin and made his flesh bubble. The Djinni that spoke to him began to grin. It held its head high, and its tusks pointed to the sky. The demon, then, gave off a squealing laugh. Nathan screamed in agony.

The sun came up over the horizon. The eyes of our tormented hero began to open to see dawn's first light. What a beautiful image it was. Colors unimaginable blanketed the desert sand in the distant horizon. Nathan's body ached worse than the day before, and he could barely hold his head up. As the sun rose a little higher, he felt some strength come back. The rays warmed his body.

"Where are the burns, I thought I was — I felt the flames," Nathan said to himself as he inspected his body in the daylight. "It must have been another dream. I can't tell the difference anymore between dream and reality." Nathan sat himself up and stretched. "I need water, I must be dehydrating. That would account for all of these illusions. But then what about the angels, and the man I wrestled." Then he screamed out to the open desert, "What is *real*?"

There was no response, not even an echo. The day before, the path to water was thwarted by a vicious desert storm that almost completely swallowed Nathan, and now, he was not only unsure about where he was but also *when* it was. With no navigational tools or chronological indicators, he decided to rely on the sun, moon, and stars to lead him the rest of the way and help him tell time. A Boy Scout he was not; he had never gone camping or done anything even remotely rustic. Nathan was not someone who knew how to survive alone, out in the open with no food or water. God had blessed him with good instincts, though, and he was a quick learner. So putting these things into practice, Nathan trekked on.

He walked through the coarse desert sand until he could walk no further. Unable to carry on without some form of nourishment, Nathan collapsed. Standing before him was a large rock that was split in the middle. Grabbing onto the rock to reposition himself, the worn out man noticed that the rock was smooth in some places. It seemed to be eroded somehow. *Erosion is caused by water*, thought Nathan; and he sat himself up against the rock. But how could this rock have signs of erosion out here in the middle of the desert.

"Strike the rock," a voice in Nathan's head said.

So with no energy to stand, Nathan threw his fist back over his head and hit the rock behind him. With a sigh his hand dropped to his side, his eyes almost completely shut from exhaustion. A few seconds passed. Then, miraculously out of the rock gushed a fountain of water. It sprayed Nathan, and poured out into the desert. The water, sparkling and pure, tickled Nathan's parched lips. He threw his head back to lap up as much of the refreshing drink as he could. *It is a miracle*, he thought, as he felt his strength being restored. Nathan thanked God for this wonderful gift, dancing in the rushing tide, much like the children he would see playing in front of an opened fire hydrant on a hot day in the city. Nathan shouted his praise to the Lord. And at that moment, he remembered that Moses was told by God to strike a rock in the desert to get water. This must have been that very rock. That would explain the erosion. He was truly following the path of the great prophets and holy men of God. Nathan stopped thinking for a moment and just enjoyed the fresh, abundant water, which was bestowed upon him. After rejoicing and playing like a child in the spurting stream, Nathan saw that the water had stopped flowing. Nathan knew that this was a sign to continue forward. He knelt down to thank God for the water and for returning his strength. His only regret was that he did not have a vessel to store some of the water in for his journey. But thinking it over, Nathan realized that God would provide. He did not need to worry about food or water, but only surviving the tests that would come as he traveled deeper and deeper into the seemingly endless desert.

# Part IV

## Tests

"I'm telling you, Kimberly, he's a good man."

"I'll have to test him out myself, before I can give a fair verdict. But in all honesty, Martha, from what I have seen and heard, he doesn't sound like any man from this planet," Kimberly commented as she sat with Martha drinking some tea, a common activity for the two on a Sunday afternoon.

"I'm not saying he's perfect, or anything like that. Just that despite his rough life, he was brought up right. The man has always been a positive role model for the boys in this neighborhood. And except for recently — under false accusations, I might add — he's one of the few who has never had a run in with the police, not even a parking violation. Mind you, he doesn't own a car, but that's beside the point," Martha said with a chuckle.

"Yeah, but I'm still nervous. I haven't dated in so long. I have to say, I'm a little scared."

"You scared — no, please. You're gorgeous, you're sweet, and you're great company. There is nothing more a man could want in a woman."

"You seem so confident about the whole thing. I know that you've known him for a while, but I just met him; and just because he's great doesn't mean everything is going to work out. How about we just take it one step at a time," Kimberly smiled in reaction to the grin on Martha's face.

Martha could tell that Kimberly was happy, and really liked Lyles. She also knew that Lyles felt much the same for Kimberly. The future seemed bright as Martha put the cup of tea to her lips.

"What was I thinking calling her and asking her out on a date? I don't have time to date," Lyles said out loud. "Not only that, but I'm not even in the right mind-set."

He panicked as he looked through his closet for something to wear. It was six o'clock in the evening, and he was supposed to meet Kimberly at her place at eight. Not only did he have to finish getting ready, but he also still had to endure the subway ride to 59th Street. Then, at that very moment, it dawned on Lyles. He had been so busy thinking about finding Nathaniel Salvatore, and getting to the bottom of this whole Radix thing, that he never took the time to think about where he was going to take Kimberly on their date. He was done for — nothing but one disaster right after another.

"This is what I get for trying to go out and have a good time, when I know the world is in danger. What on Earth are we going to do this last minute?" Lyles brooded and brooded as he rummaged through his closet some more, grabbing a pair of slacks and a button down shirt. "See, life is nothing but a test, and I'm in jeopardy of failing big time. It figures that I have to be chosen to help sort out this biblical mess, like I have nothing better to do. And during all of this, I decide to go out on a date — damn libido."

*Ring, ring, ring* — Lyles dashed to get the phone thinking that it was Kimberly.

"Hello?"

"Hi, Lyles, dear. It's Mrs. Jones."

"Hi, Mrs. Jones. How's everything? I was just getting ready to pick up your lovely friend, Kimberly. She is a sweet girl. I appreciate you introducing us."

"Don't worry about it, hon. It'll be good for you to get out of the house. And you're right, Kimberly is a sweet girl. Might make a good wife one day. You never know."

"Don't get too far ahead now. We hardly know each other, but she is really nice. Do you need anything, or are you just calling to inquire about Kimberly and what I think about her."

"Well, I was actually calling to tell you something. Knowing you like I would know my own son, I figured that you did not have any definite plans for tonight. I also figured that you would like to do something nice with her, so I took the liberty of getting the two of you tickets to see *Cats*."

"That musical with those people prancing around in cat suits like Heathcliff on crack?"

"Hey now, be nice. I didn't have to do this for you. Plus *Cats* happens to be Kimberly's favorite musical. She's been dying to see it again, and by the summer it will no longer be on Broadway. I hear they are closing the show. So, I would prefer a thank-you."

"Thank you, Mrs. Jones. I really appreciate your looking out for me like that. And actually, you were right, I didn't have anything planned for tonight."

"Well, you do now, sweetie. The tickets are paid for and are being held at the box office under your name, so everything is all set, okay?"

"Yes, Ma'am."

"Okay, then, have fun, and come by and visit me with details when you get a chance."

"I will, Mrs. Jones, and thanks again. You really didn't have to do this."

"Yes, I did. You and Kimberly deserve to be happy. Life is too short. Now, have fun."

Martha hung up the phone, and Lyles went back to getting dressed. He felt a little less stressed than he was before; but in the back of his mind, he still could not shake the thought of that madman running around the city, ready to kill at any moment. Further research into that situation would have to wait for tomorrow. Lyles had a big date, and he did not want to be late.

"I'll be right down," Kimberly's voice came over the intercom.

Lyles waited patiently outside of her apartment building, knowing that when a woman says she'll be right down that means another fifteen minutes — at least. Knowing that she would be worth the wait, he tried his best to keep his composure, as he glanced at his watch from time to time. About fifteen minutes later, just as he suspected, Kimberly came through the lobby to the front door. Lyles' eyes nearly popped out of his skull as he gazed at the beautiful woman before him. Lyles was dressed very nicely and looked quite handsome, but Kimberly was like a goddess before him.

"You look amazing," Lyles said as he looked into Kimberly's eyes.

"And you look very *GQ*," Kimberly responded as Lyles took her hand, gave it a gentle kiss, and proceeded to walk her down the steps. "Quite the gentleman."

"How could I be anything else in the presence of a lady as lovely as you?"

"Wow, Martha was right, you're not like any guy I have ever met," she said with a smile.

Lyles was so happy to be with such a beautiful woman, so much so that he completely forgot about the evil that was lurking in the shadows.

"Okay boys and girls!" Officer Rogers shouted. "We have been unsuccessful in tracking down our prey, and I am very disappointed! It is our job to protect this city, to keep it safe from all harm. So what are we doing? We are sitting around with our thumbs up our backsides, while a killing machine is out there ready to shed massive amounts of blood at any moment. Not even one lead! You are supposed to be New York's finest. More like New York's finest pieces of crap!"

"But, sir, we are trying our best. He is one man in a city full of millions, not to mention that he could be out of our boundaries by now. Plus, we have no positive ID on him. He killed all those officers, used our computer system, and left not a fingerprint on the whole scene. We really have nothing to go by except for a composite sketch and a description that fits about half the people who live here — tall, white male wearing all black," one of the young officers shouted back to Officer Rogers.

"Listen here you whiny milksop, stop sniveling about positive IDs and start finding this man. The longer we wait, the longer the trail of blood will be. I don't want it to lead to that. I want him now, before he can kill again! You hear me? Now *go!*"

Like soldiers, the officers marched out of the station and into their vehicles. The entire investigation was to remain on the hush. They did not want anyone in the city or the rest of the world to know of the threat that roamed the streets. All of the officers involved agreed in writing to keep the secret and did their best to be as discreet as possible. But the media's eyes are wide and have a way of seeing everything. One particular reporter, trying to get her break into the business, stood and watched the officers as they headed out. Judy Ramirez was a rookie reporter at Channel 13 News. When the Commissioner tried to cover the massive slaughter at police headquarters as a gang related crime, she did not buy it. She knew that a gang could not do that, no matter how well equipped they were. The crime seemed too over-the-top, fantastic in a way, and possibly supernatural. Patiently, she waited in her silver Beetle for all of the cops to drive away. Her video camera was in the seat next to her, ready to record the breaking story whenever it would hit. When the last vehicle left, she started her engine and began to follow. This scoop would be hers, and hers alone, with a big fat promotion to go along with it. The savvy reporter was bent on making a name in the industry for herself, no matter what the risk.

"I can't believe you got tickets for *Cats*!" Kimberly cheered. "You know that in June they are going to close the show, which stinks because it is my absolute favorite musical of all time. I am so excited that you got tickets! I've been meaning to see it again but I could never find anyone to go with. We are going to have so much fun!"

"I love it, too. There's something about cat-people that just grabs me. Definitely an amazing show."

"You've seen *Cats* before? I didn't know that."

"Well, I never saw it *per se*. But from the commercials, I knew it was a masterpiece," Lyles said. He then held his head down like a shy little boy and admitted, "Honestly, Mrs. Jones told me that it was your favorite musical."

"I think that is so sweet. You actually bothered to find out what I was interested in. You are something else, Lyles."

"Hey, like I said, a lady like you really brings it out in me."

The two were lost in each other's eyes as they walked into the theater.

Death sat in the shadows of a now empty room. Though, just a few days ago, it was filled with the blood of many good men and women, who had fought to protect the people of this city. The thoughts of the grim being swirled around in his head as he tried to make sense of Radix's recent motives. The dark mercenary of the Devil seemed to be more reckless, especially with the incident that had taken place here at police headquarters. Something was indeed afoot, and Death wanted to know what it was. He stopped his wondering when he overheard a conversation going on in one of the other rooms. He fazed through the walls and entered the office unbeknownst to its inhabitants.

"Officer Rogers, I have some important information," a nerdy man spoke to the overweight officer seated at his desk.

"Well, spill it!" Officer Rogers replied.

The man continued, "We were finally able to go into the system and retrieve the information that was downloaded by the criminal suspect—"

"Criminal suspect — he's a *monster*!" Rogers yelled.

"Sorry, sir. Well, it seems that the monster was looking up information on a man named Nathaniel Salvatore."

"Wait a second. Nathaniel Salvatore, isn't that the guy whose apartment we investigated recently, the one that was totally demolished."

Death found this conversation very intriguing. Could this Nathaniel Salvatore in fact be the man that Radix was looking for?

"Good work, Pete," Officer Rogers said as he stood up.

"The name is Steve, sir."

"Steve, Pete, same thing. Go tell the Commissioner what you just told me, pronto. This Nathaniel character might just be the lead that we need. I'm going to his apartment now and reinvestigate the crime scene. Maybe there is something that we overlooked."

"Yes, sir. Right away, sir."

"Good boy, Frank," Officer Rogers said as he left his office with Death following close behind.

"It's Steve."

Outside, the streets were swarming with cops, who were trying to do a job that no one had ever been able to accomplish before. They were looking for the source of great evil, an evil that they could not fathom. But they did not know this; all that they knew was that there was a killer, that he needed to be stopped, and that under no circumstances could they let the public know that he even existed. The job was not easy, but all of them had known this from the time they first put on their badges. Yes, these young men and woman were willing to stake their lives. But they wondered if all of it was in vain.

Two officers sat in a patrol car looking for any clues that could help them bring justice to a world in desperate need of some.

One of the officers turned to his partner and asked, "So, Jay, what do you think about this craziness that's been going on lately? Do you think we have a Charles Manson on our hands or what?"

"I don't know what to think," Jay said. "All I know is there have been some seriously sick murders lately, definitely of the serial killer variety; and with all this, still people know nothing! This is a serious threat, and people should know about it."

"Well, I'm not so sure I agree with you. I think it's better they stay calm, and know as little as possible. Their lives are at risk living in this godforsaken city, no matter what; so, why cause extra alarm? Look at all the publicity that these criminal types get, how they feed off it, and use it for their own glory. If we publicize this thing, we'll only make this guy want to kill more."

"I don't know. To me, being a cop means being a man of the people. And this game of secrets, in my opinion, is not in the people's best interest."

The two young rookie cops drove around, patrolling the city for any clues that might lead them to a monster who was ready to kill. Jay Sil and Edwin Suarez had no idea who they were hunting. All they had to go on was a sketch and a vague description given to them by Officer Rogers. They knew that they would not find this man. There seemed to be no motive; the killings were sporadic and unrelated. The only link lay in certain cult-like rituals that had been used in two of the killings. The Children of the Dragon had been strung up, their skin peeled off; those boys had been crucified; but the cops, the SWAT team, they had been slaughtered. It just did not match. The two continued to drive, not realizing there was a small, silver Beetle following them.

"Are these guys ever going to find anything? This is just boring. I was hoping for some action, a story. I need a story," Judy Ramirez complained, as she drove behind the two cops.

173

Jay Sil flipped on the sirens and began to race down the street.

"Yes, it's about time!" Judy exclaimed, as she put her car into high gear and followed the officers' lead.

Death did his own investigation of Nathan's apartment, as Officer Rogers struggled for clues. But no clues were found, only destruction.

"I can't believe this crap. In all of this mess, not one clue. The only fingerprints belong to the victim. The same for the blood found at the scene. Yet there is no body, and no note from the kidnapper. Nothing. This guy's apartment was torn apart, then he disappeared, and now we find out that that monster pulled his information off of our system just prior to this. There has to be some connection we're missing," Rogers talked to himself as he looked at some pictures of Nathan and his family on the wall. He focused on a picture of Nathan with his title belt on the night that he had won it.

"You fool, you are not hunting a man. He cannot be tracked like your usual criminals. And even if you find him, then what would you do? You cannot stop him. No one can," Death threw his words into the wind for no one to hear, or so he thought.

"Death, what are you doing here?" a voice asked.

"Who's there? Who called my name?" Death inquired.

The response that followed was too big for words. Before Death in a cloud of light, Gabriel appeared in all of the glory bestowed to him by the Creator.

"Gabriel, the question should be what are *you* doing here?" Death asked.

"Touché, my friend."

"So, what happened here? I'm sure you know. It was Radix, wasn't it?"

"Death, you know the answer to that already. Must I say a word," Gabriel spoke curtly.

"The man, Nathaniel Salvatore, I know he still lives because I did not collect his soul. He must be Radix's next victim. His last kill for the century."

"Once again, I need not say a word. I am but here to give you a message."

174

"You are here to give me a message? Since when has God decided to inform me of anything?"

"Oh, God did not ask me to deliver this message, but rather one of my fellow brothers. Someone you know well — Azrael."

"Azrael?" Death was quite curious to hear this name.

"He wanted to know if you could pay him a visit at the Hall of Records, right away."

"What could he possibly have to tell me? And God is okay with this? Because I'm sure the Omniscient One knows all about this, just like He knows everything else."

"Of course God knows; and if He wanted to stop it, He would have stopped it already. He does not hate you like you think, Death. It is just that His ways are not our ways, and we must understand that."

"All I understand is that all of this is a sick game, and I'm tired of playing. But I am interested in what Azrael has to tell me. I have a feeling I know what it's about."

As Death gave those final words, he disappeared with Gabriel in a flash of light.

Officer Rogers felt a ghostly chill and then sprang up as his walkie-talkie went off.

"Yeah, what is it?" he said as he held the receiver to his mouth.

A voice came back over the receiver saying, "There's been another murder."

"Hello, this is Judy Ramirez, reporting for Channel 13 News," the young reporter said, holding her video camera as she filmed both herself and the building behind her. "I am standing in front of an apartment building on West 28th Street, after following a police vehicle here to uncover clues to the strange murders that have been plaguing our city. The police have thus far blamed the murders on gang warfare to keep the people from knowing the truth. I am going to move inside to get a better view of what in fact is going on at this particular scene. My guess is that we have another murder on our hands."

Judy turned off the camera, put it in a carrying bag, and threw it over her shoulder. She knew that the building was heavily guarded with police officers, including the two she had followed there, who were now standing at the front door. With no other option, Judy moved around to the other side of the building to find another way in. It seemed hopeless, unless she could somehow get onto the roof. There was a door on the roof that was wide open. It was just the invitation that she was looking for, and she knew exactly how to get there. Stealthily, Judy entered an adjacent apartment building as someone was leaving, and began to charge up the stairs. It was not the most ingenious plan, but it was good enough. This story would be hers, finally. Just as quickly as she entered the building she exited on the roof, and quietly made her way toward the opposite roof. She climbed over the ledge that connected the two buildings, and made her way to the door. As she entered the building, her shoes clopped on the stairs. She did not want to blow her cover. Therefore, the soon to be star reporter removed her shoes, placed them in her bag, and continued forward.

"Okay, how long has this guy been dead?" Officer Rogers asked as he pointed to John Russell's body, which was still where Radix left him — on the floor in front of his favorite chair, cut from his head down to his groin.

"I'd say about three days, give or take," one of the forensics officers responded. "I can get you a more exact figure after the autopsy."

"Okay, did someone call the Commissioner about this?" Rogers asked.

"Yes, he was radioed and will be here shortly," another officer quickly answered, and walked away.

"Good, let's get this investigation under way. I want results, and no press. You got that. All I need is some media scandal," Rogers paused and walked over to the body. "Something tells me this is linked to that psycho that shot up headquarters."

Still barefoot, Judy continued down the stairs checking each hallway that she passed. The halls were empty. The people were most likely told to stay inside their apartments, she figured, so as not to get in the way of the investigation. She also figured that news reporters would soon swarm the building, and she was determined to get first dibs on the story. Judy peeked around the corner as she came onto the sixth floor, and noticed that four cops stood in front of one of the doors. They were like an impenetrable wall, there to stop anyone from getting inside. How was she going to get her story? She was in no shape to get by those officers let alone the ones inside. There had to be a way around. She studied the hall but could not think of anything. It was not like she could just turn invisible, walk by the guards, and enter the room. She had to think of another plan. But it was too late.

"Excuse me, miss, can I help you?" a voice came from behind her.

Judy turned around to see Jay Sil, one of the police officers that she had followed before. Now what could she do? She was trapped by this intimidating, yet cute, police officer.

"Umm, no. I was just going to my apartment," she responded. "Just wanted to see what was going on here. See, I'm not even wearing my shoes."

"Well, can I see some ID?" Jay asked, arching his right eyebrow.

"I don't have it on me," Judy said with a cheesy smile. She was a horrible liar.

"I'm not buying this, lady. What's in the bag?"

"There's nothing in there, just makeup and girly things, you know."

"Real cute. Open the bag — now."

Judy opened her bag to reveal her camera. Jay Sil looked at it, and looked back up at her.

"So were you planning on making a submission to America's Funniest Home Videos, or do you always carry a video camera with you?" His sarcasm was thick. "Or how about you're a reporter. Sorry, but this scene is closed to the press. You'll have to wait like everyone else for the commissioner to give his briefing on the situation. Now come with me, or I'll drag you out of here."

As they walked down the stairs, Judy tried another approach.

"You're too cute and nice to be a cop. What brings you to this dirty business?" she asked.

"Not all cops are dirty — some of us shower."

"Ha, and did I mention funny."

"Flattery won't work on me. I was given orders to let no one in the building, unless they could present identification that they lived here. And you obviously don't, so out you go. It's simple."

Judy had no other options. This story was too important for her, she would do anything to get it, even get arrested. So in a moment of final desperation, she lifted her shirt and flashed the rookie cop. Jay Sil was dazed as he took a good long look at Judy's perfect, full breasts. Her plan worked, and she was off and running.

"Get back here! You can't flash an officer and run. It's illegal! — I think?" Jay yelled as he chased Judy down the hall.

He was fast, but so was she. Judy turned the corner on the second floor and in one more desperate maneuver, began to bang on one of the doors.

"Let me in, police!" she yelled.

"You're no cop!" a man's voice yelled back from the other side of the door as he peered through his peephole. "But you are kinda cute."

The man on the other side quickly opened the door, let her in, and locked the door behind him. Judy was out of breath panting, as she looked at the old man standing in front of her only in his boxers. His old wrinkly skin was sagging, which made her sick to her stomach. This story meant a lot to her, and she was definitely paying the price.

"So, baby, what brings you over this way, my little Latina cupcake," the old man said as he licked his lips.

"E-e-w, I am not your cupcake," she said as she clobbered him with her camera bag, knocking him out cold. "I am desperate for this story but not that desperate."

Then a loud series of knocks came at the door.

"Open up — it's the police!" Jay's voice came from the other side of the door.

This time it really was the police, and Judy did not know where to go or what to do. She looked out one of the windows and saw a fire escape. Bingo! It was her ticket out. She climbed out the window, onto the fire escape, and began to climb up. Lucky for her, the cops below were too busy conversing and stuffing their faces with doughnuts to even notice her. After climbing up two floors, she realized that she was just outside the room that the cops were guarding on the sixth floor. Jay Sil busted down the door to the apartment.

178

"Okay, come out, and I'll go easy on you," he said with his gun gripped tightly in his hand.

The rookie entered and saw the old man knocked out on the floor. He squatted down, and checked the man's pulse. He was alive. Jay walked around the apartment, kicking open all the doors. No one was there. He wondered where the reporter could have gone. Then, he turned to see the open window.

"This is Judy Ramirez reporting again. I am now looking into the apartment where the police are investigating a crime scene, to uncover the true plot behind these recent murders. Let's see what we find inside the apartment," she reported as she crouched down on the fire escape, holding the camera lens to the corner of the window.

Judy did not want to be seen by the officers inside. As she scanned the room, she got a glimpse of John's dead body on the floor, and zoomed in.

"Just as I thought — another murder. Will this string of tragedies ever end?" she continued to report.

"Freeze! Put down the camera!" Jay yelled from the fifth floor fire escape, pointing his gun up at Judy.

The cops below dropped their doughnuts, looked up, and drew their guns as well. Hearing the commotion outside, the officers inside the apartment looked at the window to see Judy now standing outside with her hands raised in the air.

"Somebody go to that window and place that girl under arrest!" screamed Officer Rogers.

Judy now sat in the back seat of the police cruiser that she had been following earlier, and her driver was the rookie who she had harassed in the building.

"So, are you really going to lock up little ole me?" Judy asked from the back.

"Yep, breaking and entering is a crime; as is lying to an officer of the law, attempted escape, and assault on that poor old guy. Need I go on," Jay responded. "Oh yeah, I forgot, indecent exposure. Nice boobs, though."

"Great, this just sucks. I finally get my chance to test my mettle, and I fail. Just great," Judy whispered to herself.

"Now, this is the real test. If I can sit through the rest of this godforsaken musical, I can truly face this Radix guy head on. This is worse than Ice Capades," Lyles deliberated, while sliding ever lower into his seat.

"So, how are you enjoying the show?" Kimberly said and turned to Lyles, squeezing his arm.

"I simply love it — it's everything I expected and more," he replied with a big grin, as he fixed himself in his seat.

"Ooo, this is my favorite part!" she squealed and squeezed his arm tighter.

"Dear God, have mercy on my soul," Lyles said under his breath as a frighteningly flashy dance number began.

Time dragged, the minutes felt like hours, but eventually the curtain dropped and the lights came back on; and Lyles' skin color, which had become a shade of green, began to return. The two got up, put on their coats, and exchanged smiles as their eyes met again. Lyles was grateful for one thing — that he actually went the evening without worrying about Radix and the end of the world. Leaning in to sneak a taste of each other's lips, Lyles and Kimberly were stopped by the crowd that pushed them out of the aisle. They proceeded to walk out of the theater, both giggling about what just happened.

"I guess this means we should be heading home," Kimberly said softly, looking into Lyles' eyes again.

Lyles gently placed his hands on her arms and said, "Yeah, it is getting late. I'll walk you home and then catch the subway back from there."

The two began to walk back to Kimberly's apartment, holding hands. But as they journeyed further, they ended up in each other's arms. It was as if they had been together for years, laughing all the way. There was joy amid all the sorrow. Once the couple reached their destination, they said their good-byes and thanked each other for a lovely evening. Both agreed to do it again soon. But as Kimberly was about to enter her apartment building, Lyles could no longer resist. He took her by the hand, brought her to him, and in an instant their lips locked. Passion consumed them. Then at that moment, Lyles realized that he might be making a big mistake. He was falling for this woman, while he should be hunting a killer. With those thoughts the kiss ended, and Kimberly walked inside with a big smile. Lyles had a smile on the outside too, but inside he was afraid — afraid of the monster roaming the streets and of losing someone that he loved yet again. There was no way that he could stop this beast, and the most frightening thing was that Radix was close by and ready to kill anyone and everyone in his path.

The train was surprisingly empty. Lyles had never been on a subway where he was the only one in the car. It was peculiar, yet relaxing. He spread his body out comfortably in the seat, his legs stretched out in front of him. It must have been a slow night in the city. Lyles looked at his watch; it was already midnight. How time just seemed to fly by. The subway stopped, and the doors opened. He peered out as he saw some police officers wearing armored vests and carrying heavy firepower. One of the cops came to the subway car and stopped at the window to talk to the engineer.

An announcement came over the loudspeaker. "There will be a delay. Remain where you are. Police will be searching all cars."

Two male officers walked into the car that Lyles was in and stood over him.

"Excuse me, sir," one of the officer's said to Lyles.

"Can I help you, officer?" Lyles responded.

"We were just wondering if you saw anything suspicious tonight?" The other officer continued.

"Not really, officers, except for that fat guy in the cat suit, he looked like Garfield ate James Earl Jones. I didn't like the way he looked at me — scary," Lyles smirked at his own joke.

"Ha, ha, real funny, guy. No, we are looking for something else. But keep clean, okay," the first officer spoke again.

"Well, can I ask what exactly you are looking for?"

"Sorry, sir, but we cannot divulge that information. Just giving a routine check, that's all. Have a good evening," the second officer answered.

The two officers exited the car and flagged the train to leave the station, which it did. Lyles watched as they marched out of the station. *They must be looking for Radix*, he thought. That must have been why they would not say what they were looking for.

But he knew the truth; he knew that the cops were scared to let the people know what he knew. In a way, Lyles understood and agreed with that decision. The people of this city would never be the same if they knew the truth. But the sad part was that the cops did not even know the truth because if they did they would not even bother hunting this beast.

*Why hunt what you cannot kill?* Lyles thought as he rode the rest of the way home.

The lights went out in the subway car. When they came back on, Lyles was not alone. A shadowy man was standing in front of him. He was tall, and his pale skin stood out against his black attire. Radix had come, and Lyles was not ready. In fact, Lyles was petrified, unable to move a muscle. The beast lifted him over his head. Then in one swift motion, he threw Lyles into a metal pole in the middle of the car, denting it. Lyles could not move from the impact. The demonic villain grabbed him again and sent him crashing into the door in the back of the car. The car began to shake, and everything became a blur. Smoke came up from all around and Lyles just sank lower on the floor, dizzy from the beating he took. In horror film style, Radix slowly walked over to the young man and grabbed him by the throat. He lifted Lyles up again, slammed him into the wall of the car, and began to squeeze the life out of him. The beast just smiled, his teeth whiter than his face, and put his hand through Lyles' chest. Lyles screamed as he woke up. It was all a bad dream.

He looked out the window as the train was leaving another station. His stop was next so he got up and stood by the door. The car was still empty; Lyles was still alone and scared, more scared than he ever had been. That dream was more than just a dream. It was exactly what would happen if he were to face Radix. He must find some answers. There had to be some way to stop this monster. The key might be with that Nathaniel Salvatore guy that he was told to find. Lyles would have to try harder to find this man. The fate of the world depended on it.

Back in John Russell's apartment, Officer Rogers sat alone. The evidence had been carted away along with the remains of John's body. In the fashion of his curious self, he decided to have a look around. Maybe he could find a clue and indeed he did. On the mantle in the living room was a photograph in a wooden frame. This photo would be the first link in this case. It was a picture of John standing next to Nathaniel Salvatore, like they were old friends. Maybe, Nathaniel Salvatore was not kidnapped; maybe he was dead, just like John — another victim in this whole charade.

Nathan began to feel a change within himself, as his time in the desert grew longer. Things that seemed so important to him when he was back home in New York just did not seem to bear as much weight as they did before. The only thing that was important, now, was surviving. As he walked further on the rocky, sandy desert terrain, he started to think about life and its meaning. God was more real to him now than ever before, and so was the Devil. Life seemed to be one big tug of war between the righteous and the damned. The desires that he had as a man were all creations of his mortality, his prison of flesh. These desires held no merit outside the physical world; nothing was really to be gained from any of it. Nathan was not only growing physically and mentally from the challenges that he was facing, but he was also growing spiritually. The body and the mind are very important, but so is the soul. All three must be worked hard and made strong. Nathan truly felt himself changing. The path God chose for him was a difficult one, and now he finally began to see that it was righteous for him to do all that he was asked. His epiphany at this moment would be his guiding light on the rest of his journey through the harsh desert sands, for he was now to be tested, and these tests would not be easy. The Djinn were not to be taken lightly; their power was ancient and strong, and beyond that of any mortal. Fortunately for Nathan, he was not alone. Someone was guiding him along this journey, walking along side him, holding his hand, and even carrying him at points. God loved Nathan and was with him. This journey was not a punishment. It was a blessing.

The wind began to pick up again. The sun sat up high overhead, laughing down as it burned Nathan with its rays of light. This was expected by the young hero, who was becoming accustomed to the ways of the desert — the weather, the mirages, the miracles, and the demons within. The wind howled louder, and dust began to fly at Nathan's face. Another sand storm began to brew. Stronger and stronger the wind blew, until it formed a cyclone and came charging at Nathan with full force. *Another test,* he thought, *another trick.* His body was sucked inside the storm and thrown about. Spinning around in the funnel of sand and wind, he was unable to do a thing, just watch and hope for the best.

"Have you, we do, Godchild," cried a familiar voice. Then, it was joined by numerous others. Like a demonic choir, they chanted, "Your tests, now, will begin. Yummy, you will be. A feast for us. The taste of a Godchild, so sweet, so succulent."

The whirlwind stopped, and Nathan crashed to the ground. He looked up, dizzy and beaten. Walls of sand surrounded him like a prison of some sort. He was trapped. Nathan rolled himself over onto his stomach, and struggled to get up. Feeling nauseous from that cyclone ride, he could barely stand. He stumbled over to one of the walls of sand and pushed up against it. It was as solid as stone, and so was the ground below him. Unable to go through or under the walls, Nathan tried to go over the walls. But they were too smooth; there was nothing for him to grab onto to help him climb.

"Trapped, you are," the voices of the Djinn echoed from all around. But Nathan could not see anything except the walls and the sun in the sky, which slowly sank out of his view. Night began to fall upon the desert, and the voices cried out again, "Find your way from here, you must. But easy, it will not be, no. At the end, meet you, we will, Godchild. That is if the end, you make it to. If Godchild, you are, find your way, you will. But remember once a Godchild does not mean always a Godchild. Like your virginity, your right to sanctity, you can lose."

The voices faded, and the sky was now dark. Nathan was cold once again, and thankfully his nausea was leaving him. Sitting for the first time in what seemed to be days, he realized how long he had been away from home. His hair was growing longer, and he was starting to sprout a beard. It was funny how he was called Godchild; and now he was starting to look the part. As he stroked the fuzz on his face, the wall in front of him collapsed into the desert sand and became one with the ground. Freedom at last, or so it appeared. He got up and approached the opening. As Nathan stuck his head through the clearing, he saw nothing but more walls. Like a laboratory rat, he had to now face the labyrinth before him. The testing had only begun, and Nathan knew this as he took his first step into the maze. *Should I go right or left?* he wondered. Not knowing what else to do, he decided to follow the voice in his heart and went right. Continuing down the long twisted corridor, he did not know where he was heading. The moon was out, but it was still very dark. Nathan put his hands to the wall next to him to help him find his way. The wall felt damp to the touch. This was odd indeed because of the dry desert climate, but not impossible. It had rained not too long ago, though Nathan was not sure how long ago that really was, nor for how long he had even been in the desert. It already felt like months had passed.

The wall grew more and more damp the further he went along, until eventually, a warm thick liquid began to pour down the walls. Nathan put his hand to his face and smelled the liquid that appeared red in the moonlight. It was blood. The crimson liquid began to drip faster and more furiously from the walls, until it was streaming down. Nathan began to run as fast as could, trying to escape the flood. It was already up to his ankles and rising. The faster he ran, the more it flowed, slowing him down as it went passed his waist. The current became too strong. Before he knew it, the river of blood was over his head and carried him downstream. He tried his best to keep his mouth closed and hold his breath, as he fought his way to the surface. His head came crashing out of the bloody waves, and he gasped for air. He could taste the blood in his mouth. It seemed familiar in a way, like something he tasted before. Then, Nathan bit his lip really hard and drank some of his own red juice. Yes, that was it. The blood that he was swimming in was somehow his own, but how could this be. These Djinn were no joke. Just then something grabbed Nathan's legs and began to pull him under. Blood began to fill his lungs as he fought his hardest to get free. He was drowning in his own life force. Something had to be done, and fast, but he had no options — he was surely doomed. With no other option, Nathan stopped struggling and turned his thoughts from the outside situation inward toward God. This was merely a test. The blood was his own. He was fighting himself. In a way, the struggle was truly within. So within is where Nathan decided to fight this battle. Clearing his mind, he looked deep inside to see his true self. He saw the strength and wisdom that God had given him. Many obstacles have been thrown at him, and all have been overcome. His faith would be his salvation. He was no longer choking, breathing was not an issue, and soon whatever it was that was dragging him down had stopped. The blood began to drain, until there was nothing left of it but stains on the ground. Nathan just lay there, his faith stronger than before. He had faced his inner demons, faced sure death and won. But this was only the first test. His life was still in danger. How much longer could he fight death? He spat out some blood on the floor, as he caught his breath.

It was time to move on. The sun was now out, and its warm rays dried the remnants of blood on both Nathan's body and the ground. He went around a corner, coming to another intersection. This time, he went left. Now that there was daylight again, Nathan could easily see where he was going. Things were much calmer than they were last night, almost as if the Djinn's powers came from the dark of night. Moving around the twists and turns of the maze, Nathan grew weary and decided to take a short rest. He sat up against one of the walls and began to fall asleep. With nothing to eat or drink, he was weak, and the nap that he took gave him some strength back. The stars and the moon were now in the sky as he awoke. It was night again, and Nathan knew that it was best for him to keep up his guard. The Djinn were watching him from all around. He could feel their dark presence as he carried on. The sound of the cold night air whistled through the long corridors of the labyrinth. Something was growing from the ground. Kneeling down, Nathan saw that it was a withered flower, dry and dead like the rest of the desert. On a whim, he took the flower from the ground and put it in his pants pocket. In a way, he identified with the flower, remembering how much he dreaded to be alone. Ahead of him, he could see a strange blue light. Following the light, he came to a beautiful garden, green and full of colorful flora. In the center of the garden was a blue rose, which shone with a light that seemed to give the garden life. This was very bizarre. But nothing was ever as it seemed.

Nathan approached the rose to bask in its odd blue luminescence. The scent was sweeter than that of any flower Nathan had ever smelled. The whole garden smelled fresh and new, like spring in the country — not what one would think to find in the middle of a desert. Nathan's curiosity got the better of him as he touched a petal of the rose. With this one simple touch, everything around him fell dead. The entire garden withered to nothing, and the beautiful blue light was no longer shining. What had he done? He killed this garden. It was all his fault. Nathan sat with his thoughts, until he felt a tap on his shoulder. The solemn man turned to see who it was. His jaw dropped as he saw his dead friend, Donald, looking much how Nathan had seen him in his dream all those years ago; the same dream where he first heard the name Radix. Donald's flesh decayed more and more each minute, as he reached and ripped off the stitches that had covered his mouth. Nathan just looked on in fright.

Donald spoke, "Nathan, they will all die, just like this garden. All of them because of you."

Nathan listened to what Donald had to say, and then responded, "Because of me? What did I do?"

"What did you do? You were born. Your family and your friends will all suffer because of you, just like me."

"But I had nothing to do with your death."

"Yes, you did. You had everything to do with it. I only died because I was too close to you. Anyone who is close to you will die. You have been marked, a curse to all who you love. Radix will kill them all, and then he will kill you. If you were never born, none of this would be happening."

"Radix? This is about Radix? He barely knows who I am. Yes, he is after me; but only me, not them. It's my fight, and I will make sure that it stays that way."

"That's where you are wrong, Nathan. It is not your fight. When Radix comes for you, he comes for everyone and everything around you, until you are no more. He will kill everyone in his way, including your mother, your father, and even your sister," the corpse carried on.

"That's ridiculous!" Nathan shouted.

"Oh, is it? Why don't you ask our good friend, John," Donald said and stepped to the side as John Russell came from the shadows.

John was even more grotesque than Donald. He was split in half, and his legs were broken. Hunched over, he hobbled toward Nathan like a zombie. This all felt unreal. John could not be dead. Nathan did not even get to say good-bye to him. But it was true; while he was gone, John had been killed by Radix, as were many others. Nathan now felt that this was truly his fault.

"John, *no*! This can't be true!" he cried out as he looked at his long-time friend. "No, this is a dream, a test. Yes, all to get me to give up."

Somehow, Nathan knew in his heart that John was in fact dead — another victim of the relentless killer, Radix. But what he did not know was what he could do to stop all of this. And with that thought came an answer.

"Join us," Donald said to Nathan. "If you want to make things right, join us. It'll be like old times, the three musketeers reunited."

"What do you mean? I can't just join you — I have a mission," Nathan responded.

"Is your mission worth all of this death, all of this misery? He will kill again. Your family will be next. Let go, Nathan. Radix only wants you dead. Once you die, then your family and friends will be safe again. Come on, join us. Join us. Join us," Donald repeated over and over again, and John joined in the chant.

"*No*! Go away, you demons! You are not my friends! My friends would not tell me to lay my life down and die! Yes, Radix is evil, and he will kill again; but I will make sure when I return home that his killing spree comes to an end. I must go on, the world is depending on me. If I die, Radix will only go after another, and another, and then there may never be an end to his torment. I have not gone this far to give up. I am sorry. I love you all, but I have to fight. I have to continue. It is my destiny, my choice."

The wind howled as Nathan's two old-time friends disappeared. He just sat alone in the now dead garden, like the withered flower that he picked up just outside of here. Nathan reached into his pocket and took out the flower. He planted it in the dry sandy ground, then laid his head next to it, and fell asleep with some sadness in his heart. Would Radix kill his family — his mother, his father, and his sister? They were all in danger, and Nathan knew it. He had never really thought about it, until now. Yes, he chose to live and fight; but the thought of letting himself go, the thought of ending his own life to save theirs was still in his mind. Strangely, his dreams were peaceful that night. He dreamt about playing football with his old friends back in high school, when everything was so simple and fun.

Lifting his head and opening his eyes, Nathan stretched as his dreaming was now over. He looked down to where he had planted the dried up flower in the desert sand the previous night. Miraculously, the flower was in full bloom, beautiful and white. The sun watched over him and the flower. It was now mid-afternoon. Nathan figured that it would be a good time to get started on his walk, and to try to get through as much of this maze while it was still light out. Some days passed without any deadly pranks; only voices shrieking in the night along with the sounds of banging and scratching from beyond the walls that loomed over Nathan. The time seemed to come and go as the sun and moon rose and set more times than he could count. The twists and turns became sharper, and Nathan met countless dead ends, after which he had to turn around and find another way to go. There were even a few small pits in the ground that he had to jump over in order to proceed.

The night once again held its shadow over Nathan's head. He looked up to the moon, wondering what this night would hold for him. After walking a good distance, he came to the entrance of a cave and hesitantly entered. It was dark and musty, and the walls and floor were solid granite. He could hear demonic laughter echoing through the cavern, a sound that was becoming very familiar to him. It was strange to not see the sky above him. He had been outside in the desert for weeks already, and now that he was inside this cave, he would not be able to tell time — not without the sun and the moon. The cave was strangely warm and comfortable, giving him a break from the cold desert nights.

But Nathan did not know what kept the cave warm, or where it ended; as far as he could see there was no exit close by. The Djinn were still testing him, and he was still inside their deadly labyrinth. Without knowing when night was falling, Nathan would not know when he would be attacked. All he knew was that it was night now. About a hundred feet ahead of him, he saw a small light coming from the wall. Though it might not have been such a good idea, he fearlessly approached the light. To his amazement he found that the light was actually a torch hanging from the wall. Nathan took the torch down and used it to guide himself through the darkness. It was good to finally be able to see. There was one odd thing about the flame of the torch; it had no smoke much like the fire that the Djinni appeared from. Regardless of this discovery, Nathan held onto the torch for he had no other means to see where he was going. He was tired of walking around blind. Miles and miles he walked; and the torch was still lit as bright as when he took it from the wall. This was indeed no ordinary torch; hopefully, it would last him for the extent of his time inside the giant granite cavern. His feet ached from all the walking, and he needed to sit down for a spell; though, he did not know what to do with the torch in his hand. There was conveniently a good-sized crack in the ground next to him. He managed to wedge the torch into the crack, so it could stand firmly while he rested.

A rustling noise startled Nathan, forcing him to get up. The sound continued to get louder as if it were moving toward him. It almost sounded like little feet marching, and now he could also hear a low chirping. He grabbed the torch to see what was making this noise. Off in the distance, it appeared as if the floor was moving. Nathan walked ahead to get a better look. But when he did, he wished that he had not. A stampede of scarabs, beetles thought to be sacred by the Egyptian people, were charging toward him. And though Nathan knew little of these creatures, he could tell one thing — they were hungry and looking for food. Not wanting to be the meal, he dug deep into his days on the football field and sprinted faster than ever before. The innumerable army of insects sped close behind, swarming the floor and walls. No matter how fast and far he ran, the horde of bugs always seemed to be getting closer and closer. Almost out of breath and very malnourished, Nathan could not go on much longer. It seemed as if he would indeed become food for these hungry beetles. With a sudden burst of energy, he dashed forward to gain some ground; and he was now a good hundred feet in front of the raging scarab sea that followed him. Nathan stopped. His energy was spent, and there was a huge chasm in front of him. It was at least twenty feet to the other side, and it seemed to go down for miles. He held his torch out to look down, but he could not see the bottom, only darkness — a great abyss. There was nothing he could do, so he ran back and waved his torch in hopes of scaring away the oncoming insects. But the fire did not scare them. They just kept moving ahead. Nathan had no other option, so he threw his torch at the beetles. A good number of them caught on fire, delaying the army slightly. Taking this opportunity he turned, ran, and leaped over the chasm. His body glided in the air as his adrenaline pumped. When in danger, people can do amazing things; or so it has been said. In fact, Nathan did clear the twenty-foot chasm, barely. As his feet reached the other side, the rocky ground under them gave way and crumbled. Fortunately, his fall was thwarted. He was able to grab the ledge and pull himself up.

Nathan tried to sit and catch his breath, but he could not for his plan was flawed. He had forgotten about the walls and ceiling, which were still moving toward him. Once again he would have to run, no matter how tired he was. And to make matters worse, he no longer had his torch. Lucky for Nathan, the path in front of him was straight. But not lucky enough — for just then, Nathan's ears picked up the sound of rushing water, and it was coming from the direction that he was heading. *Not again,* he thought as he heard the huge waves roll toward him. They crashed against the cavern walls. He was trapped between two rampant rivers, one of water and the other of bloodthirsty insects. Drowning seemed better than being eaten alive, and he had already survived the river of blood earlier. So, Nathan decided to take his chances with the rolling stream. With no hope of fighting the current alone, he grabbed tightly to the wall. The waves wrapped around his body and engulfed him. The current was stronger than he had planned, and his grip was not tight enough. The waves pulled him from the wall and dragged him away. His destination was certain, and he was too weak to struggle further. He was just happy that the scarabs would not eat him, and that he was in water this time, not blood. The water carried Nathan, and came crashing to the bottom of the chasm, where it filtered into a large underground sea.

The waves of the sea splashed over Nathan's head, as he flowed with the current. The depleted man was happy to be alive, though he was barely conscious. The stream that he was trapped in had helped to cushion his fall, and insured that he broke no bones. With dear life, he grabbed onto a wooden plank that floated by. He was blessed indeed. Sluggishly, he slid his chest on top of the plank and lay over it to help him float. The ocean waves quieted down, and the water became still as Nathan calmly floated by. Unappetizing as it was, he had no other choice but to drink up some of the seawater. He needed something to hydrate himself, and that was all he had. This of course made him ill. Holding his face to the water, he threw up the little that he had in his stomach. Beaten and battered, his body could not last much longer in these conditions; but his inner strength was growing, and he refused to let himself be defeated. Like a true hero, Nathan would not give up. He would not die. Still lying on the board, he floated for about three or four days. It was a miracle that he was still alive. Everything was dark around him. He could not tell where he was, or if there was any land in sight. All he could see was the board and the water around him.

The water began to ripple, and some bubbles came to the surface. Something was in the murky sea, and Nathan could feel it coming right for him. The board rocked as more bubbles came up and the ripples grew larger. Out of the ocean sprang a gigantic fish, straight into the air with mouth opened wide. Nathan stared as everything slowed down. The fish seemed to be suspended in mid-air, its teeth, bigger than a house, sharp, and jagged. The eyes were completely white. The scales were like shields, strong and hard. The blade-like fins cut the air as it swooped down toward Nathan, and in one big gulp swallowed him whole.

The foul smell inside the fish caused Nathan to vomit some more. This time he spat out blood for that was all he had left inside of him. The trapped hero had to find a way out, for he knew that he would not last very long inside this beast's belly. Nathan tried to pull himself up toward the front of the mouth, but the giant tongue of the creature pulled him back. As the mammoth fish swam through the ocean, Nathan found it harder to hold onto its squishy insides. He began to slip further down and was nearing the stomach. If he fell into the gastric juices, the acidic fluid would digest him with the rest of the food, and he would leave as excrement. At that moment, the fish changed its course and started to swim up toward the surface. Nathan dangled, holding on as tight as he could, and prayed with all of his heart, praying to be saved. Then, he got an idea. Climbing a little higher in the throat area of the fish, he began to tickle it roughly. The young man from New York did not know much about fish, but he did know that if he had a tickle in his throat he would cough. Hopefully, the fish would have the same reaction and cough him out. It was simple, but it was a plan. Just as Nathan had perceived, the fish began to cough a little. So, he tickled its throat even more. Once it reached the top of the water, it gave one big cough and spat Nathan out onto dry land. Not only was he free from that leviathan, but he was also out of the water, hopefully for good this time. Covered in mucous, Nathan crawled along the shore, until he felt that he was far enough from the ocean; and he once again laid down his head to rest. Any man would have died by now. But Nathan was blessed, and his spirit pushed on. As he rested, God gave him back his strength because it would be needed in order to escape both the abyss that he had fallen into and the bloodthirsty Djinn. Nathan did not know it, but he was just outside the secret city of those crafty desert demons. He would have to be careful if he wanted to make it out alive.

Feeling strong and healthy, Nathan woke from his rest and saw a light coming from a tunnel just ahead of him. After a short walk, he reached the tunnel and entered it. The light seemed to be coming from the other end and got brighter as he drew nearer. He reached the end and stepped out to find himself on a cliff, overlooking a vast city of gold. The light that he saw was being reflected from the glittering golden buildings, all beautifully designed. The city had the appearance of an ancient Egyptian city with temples, pyramids, and gargantuan statues, all of which looked hideously demonic. Nathan thought about climbing down to get a better look. That was until he heard a voice scream out—

"*Godchild!*"

The sound echoed, the walls shook from all around, and out of the city poured a host of Djinn that were even greater in number than the scarabs that had chased Nathan earlier. They ran for the cliff and began to climb. The entire ground below was blanketed with the ferocious demons, giving Nathan little choice but to get out and fast. He looked around and saw another tunnel that led upward, maybe to the surface, he hoped. With that in mind, he ran and climbed his way up the tunnel, which got steeper and steeper as he continued. The host of Djinn were not far behind. Like a pack of hungry wolves, they kept on after their prey, ready to make a feast of Nathan's flesh. As he reached the end of the tunnel, he realized that the granite was now sand. He clawed his way through the sand. And before he knew it, he had reached the surface of the desert. But as he lifted his head above the sand, the Djinn had caught up; and a couple of them reached out and grabbed his ankles. Nathan kicked as their talons dug into his skin. He tried with all of his might to get them off and get his body to the surface. Then from the sand all around him, more and more Djinn began to sprout up — like zombies exiting their graves. Nathan felt a strange rush of strength as he pulled free of the talons that were holding him down, making it to the surface. The tests were finally over, but the Djinn were angry and continued to chase Nathan through the desert. Cries of "Godchild" sprang from all around, and he knew that he could not outrun these devils. As he gave a quick glance behind, Nathan tripped and hit the ground hard. It was over. The Djinn surrounded him and were ready to feast. The leader of the pack, the one that had spoken to Nathan when he first crossed their path, appeared once again from smokeless fire in front of the group.

It spoke to Nathan, "Godchild, escape us, you cannot. A feast, you will become. Very impressed by you, we are. Passed all of our tests, you did, indeed. Sweet, very sweet, your blood will be. Toyed with you, we have, Godchild. All for show, that chase was. Snatched you up at any time, we could have. But with chase, your blood even sweeter, it grew. A privilege, it will be to devour your flesh. First cut, mine it will be — your succulent heart."

As the Djinni moved closer, Nathan just remained still on the ground. It stepped right in front of him, and all at once its foot began to sizzle like an egg on a frying pan. The demon squealed in pain and jumped back. Nathan was very confused and intrigued by this. Was he on some sort of holy ground? The Djinni spoke to the others in a strange tongue that Nathan did not understand. They all moved back and sat down on the desert sand, watching their prey and nothing more. This was odd but good for the tired young man. He reached out and grabbed some of the sand that he was lying on. It felt strange and was covered in a crusty sediment. Curious, Nathan smelled it and tasted it. It was salt. Some of the seawater from underground must have evaporated and rose to the surface, letting the salt settle on the sand, creating a salt flat. The science lesson that Nathan just processed still did not give him the answer to why salt would have any effect on demons such as the Djinn.

"Yes, Godchild, salt," the Djinni once again addressed Nathan. "Loathe salt, we, Djinn do. Safe, you may feel; but sit there forever, you cannot. Die, you will. Leave that spot, and our feast, you will be; no more games. Over, it is, Godchild. Won, we have. Wait all you like; and wait, we will as well. Being Djinn, die, we do not."

It stopped talking, and all grew quiet. Nathan just sat and waited as night turned into day and day into night. The Djinn sat there all the while. The power that they possessed seemed to be stronger at night, since that was the only time that they had attacked. But he did not want to chance anything, even during the day. If he was caught, he would be no more than a meal. So, he tried to devise another plan. But no ideas came. Five days had passed, and the Djinn were still sitting, watching Nathan. He was now beyond famished and almost completely dehydrated, but he would rather die of starvation than let those monsters feed on his flesh. His body grew rigid, and he was unable to move. He could not even sit up. The desert grew dim and blurry, as his heartbeat became fainter and fainter. The vicious monsters licked their lips as Nathan lay there with almost no life left in his body. No, they might not be able to eat of his flesh as they had desired,

195

but at least they could watch the Godchild die. A Godchild such as Nathan was a threat to all things evil, including the Djinn. When a Godchild passed away, the Djinn and all demons were very pleased; for a piece of the light was diminished and was replaced with darkness.

As they waited for Nathan's heart to collapse and for his body to expire, an ear-deafening screech came from all around. The sound was loud and penetrating. It drilled into the eardrums of the Djinn, stabbing them like needles. Not only do they loathe salt, but they are also scared away by loud noises. This particular one frightened away the desert demons, causing them to return to their city below the sand. Nathan was now alone and seconds away from death.

It was Good Friday, and the Salvatore family had more on their minds than just the death and resurrection of Jesus Christ. Their son and brother was lost. The police had just called and informed them that with new evidence there was a possibility that Nathan might be dead, another victim of a heartless killer. But Nathan was not dead. He was in the desert, barely holding onto the last bit of life in his body. His parents and sister thought the worst as they stood in church, the same church that Maria and Joey were married in. They held each other as the priest walked through the mystery of the Passion of Christ by following the Stations of the Cross, which were represented by beautiful marble reliefs on the walls around the church. This was the first time that they had come together to this church in years. The last time, Nathan was with them. It was just before he went to college. The Salvatores sent a prayer up to God, hoping that Nathan might still be alive. The holiday would be solemn for this family. They exited the church saddened as if leaving a funeral, and they drove back to the house. Esmeralda had decided to stay with her parents for the weekend to give them some needed strength during this difficult time. Nathan had been gone for more than a month now. Hope was slowly fading.

The next day, the Salvatore family prepared for Easter Sunday. Esmeralda helped her mother bake, and then the family sat down to color the hard-boiled eggs. She remembered when Nathan and she were younger, and they used to tear the house apart looking for the eggs that the "Easter Bunny" hid. The family laughed as they shared these memories of the past. The entire time, they were being watched, stalked by a creature that knew that Nathan was indeed still living — a monster that wanted to make sure that he did in fact die. Tomorrow, this monster would pay a visit to the Salvatores, just before their Easter supper.

The doorbell rang. Easter had come, and the Salvatore family was just getting ready to eat. Joey went to the door to answer it, wondering who it might be. He opened the door to see no one. Joey figured that it was probably some neighborhood kids playing a joke. He went back into the dining room to sit down with his family. A man was standing at the other end of the table, his arms wrapped tightly around both Maria's and Esmeralda's necks.

"What are you doing?" Joey screamed at the man, afraid for the lives of his wife and daughter.

"Relax, old man. I'm only here to spread some holiday cheer on this dismal Easter. I must say, your wife and daughter are quite lovely," Radix said and stuck out his tongue, slowly licking Maria and then Esmeralda from their necks to their lips. "And they taste good, too."

Joey grabbed the carving knife that was next to the baked ham, and began to move toward the evil man, enraged.

"Let go of them, or I will cut you to pieces!" Joey yelled.

"Drop the knife, tough guy, or I'll have to make this visit a quick one."

Joey proceeded to approach the sinister intruder. In an instant Radix threw Maria and Esmeralda to the floor. Then, he grabbed Joey and turned the knife around, causing Joey to stab himself in the gut.

"See what you made me do?" Radix bantered.

"Joey, no!" Maria cried.

"Daddy!" Esmeralda joined in. "You, monster!" she screamed as she grabbed Radix's legs and tried to pull him to the floor.

With unbridled strength, he kicked her off his leg and sent her flying into the wall. Esmeralda lay on the floor, unable to move and bleeding internally. The blood poured out of her mouth, and she just stared at Radix as he broke her mother's neck. He looked like a shadow with his long black coat, and his movements were quick and powerful. Then, he hovered over Joey, the knife still in his stomach. Joey was breathing ever so slightly. Through the blur, he could see Radix, his bloody child, and his dead wife on the floor. He looked up at the monster before him, and at that moment, he made a connection. He had seen this man before, in a similar situation back in Vietnam.

"You, it was you back in 'Nam," Joey sputtered. "You killed my brothers, and you almost killed me."

"Well, I'm glad I was able to finally finish the job," Radix proclaimed, and he stepped on the knife that was still planted in Joey's abdomen, sending it out his back.

Joey and Maria would be together again in heaven. The only one left alive was Esmeralda, but for some reason Radix did not want to kill her. No, he would do something far worse than kill this girl. He threw her on top of the table and ripped off her clothes. She could not move as he raped her. This act gave him a sick sense of pleasure as thoughts of killing Nathan surged through his head. Blood flowed from Esmeralda's body. Her internal injuries were uncountable. Radix was gladly stained with her blood, as he completed this sinful act.

Nathan felt the cold touch of water on his lips. He was still lying on the salt flat in the desert. His tongue involuntarily moved, helping his mouth to catch as many of the cool drops as it could. Another Heaven-sent gift, he believed, as he began to regain consciousness. The water stopped pouring down, and Nathan's eyes began to focus little by little. He saw a blurred outline of a person standing over him. After some time, he could see that it was a woman; and she was holding a water jug in her arms. Nathan could not see her face behind the veil that she was wearing, but her shape was very pleasing to the eye. She was adorned with jewels from head to foot and wore a skimpy silk top that showed off her sensual bosom. A lovely silk skirt hung low from her shapely hips, which danced in the desert wind. She was indeed a sight to see for the weary man, and Nathan could not help but find her very appealing. *Yes, indeed, Heaven-*

*sent*, he thought. He sat up a little, as much as he could, for he still did not have all of his strength back. She knelt down and put her arms around him, held his head up to her voluptuous bosom, and caressed his scalp. Nathan enjoyed the sensation of her fingers running through his hair, and she smelled like a field of fresh flowers. Her scent was like an aphrodisiac, making him a slave to her will. The woman advanced further as she laid him on his back and took off her top, throwing it behind her. Nathan just stared aimlessly at her beautiful breasts; he had never seen the likes on any woman before. Then, she continued by removing her dress in a very provocative manner. Her naked body stood before him, perfect and breathtakingly beautiful. She danced for the tired man. His energy raised the more that she moved, his blood pumped, and his heartbeat sped up. All that she wore was her veil, and Nathan was very curious to see what he imagined to be the most stunning face on the planet to go with such a body. She persisted further by removing Nathan's shirt, ripping it off, and she rubbed her hands on his chest. Finally, she made her way down and unbuckled his pants. At this point, Nathan realized what was transpiring, as if he was being awakened from a dream. Who was this woman, and why was she here? It all seemed very obvious to the fooled man. This was another test, something to get him to stray.

"Get off me!" Nathan yelled and threw the woman off of him.

"What, you do not find me appealing? I do not quench your libido?" her words were more seductive than her shape. "Look at my body — perfect, naked, and willing to satisfy all of your desires."

"You can't fool me, skank," Nathan said in reply, fighting off the temptation as best he could.

"You will not refuse me. No man can refuse me!" she wailed.

"Well, sorry, toots, I'm refusing you. So get lost!" Nathan shouted back.

Utter contempt took over the woman, who finally removed her veil, exposing the most hideous face Nathan had ever seen. This woman was not sent from Heaven — far from it. And she was, by no means, an ordinary woman. She was a succubus. But not just any succubus, she was Lilith — the bride of Satan. Her jaw was long and separated like a serpent. Her teeth were small and sharp, and she had two long fangs coming from the top that oozed with deadly venom. Her dragon-like tongue slithered from her mouth and flapped around as the rest of her body transformed. Nathan fell back to the ground. The monstrous wench grew large bat-like wings from her back, her legs and feet were like those of a hen, and her body grew camel-like hair. Soaring into the sky and then swooping down, she went for Nathan's throat. He took some of the salt from the ground and threw it at her eyes.

"You fool, there is no escaping me. Salt cannot hurt Lilith, mother of all demons!" she wailed.

Nathan turned over and tried to run, but he could not. There was no place to go; for every time he moved, Lilith was in front of him. She was too quick for the mortal.

"Enough with the games. You did not want to taste of my body when it was sweet and attractive, so now it is my turn to taste of yours. I will tear your flesh from your bones. You might have escaped the Djinn, but you cannot escape me, human!" the demoness wailed again.

"Back down, wench!" a voice boomed around the desert wind. It bounced off the mountains and came back, hitting the sand.

Lilith stopped, looked at Nathan and said, "You are lucky, Godchild, someone else is interested in you. I will have to make a snack of you some other time. Good-bye for now."

She disappeared as if she was never there. The salt and sand below Nathan's feet began to rise and swirl. *Another storm*, he thought, but not this time. The funnel of salt and sand turned to smoke. The smoke faded, and before Nathan stood a gentleman in a white suit with a red tie. He had black hair and a black beard. His skin was nicely tanned. The Devil had now come to tempt Nathan. This would be the last of the tests.

Esmeralda was still conscious and bleeding on the dining room table. The man who had killed her mother and father and defiled her was standing over her. He had moved her parents' bodies out of the dining room, but she did not know to where. She was terrified, but she could not move, and she could not cry.

"You're lucky, little girl. You get to live," Radix said to her.

Esmeralda noticed that his black coat was splattered with blood, matching the deep red silk shirt that he wore.

"Looks like I'll need a change of clothes. Too bad, I think red is a good color for me. How about you?"

Esmeralda could not answer him; all that she could do was try to think about something else, anything else. But all that she could think about was being raped, her dead parents, and her missing brother, perhaps dead as well.

"Oh, by the way, Nathaniel is not dead. Just thought you'd like to know. You see, I let you live, so you can give him a message when he gets back home. Tell him to give up. Tell him to let me kill him. Because if he doesn't, I will give him no reason to live; and I will take his life regardless, just as I have taken the life of your parents. I know God has been helping him. Tell him that not even God can save him from the Root of All Evil, Radix Malorum."

The cynical man walked out of the house and disappeared into the shadows of the night. At that moment, a blinding light came to Esmeralda. She could see a beautiful face in the light.

"Do not be afraid, Esmeralda. Your parents will be safe with our Lord. Your wounds will be healed, and you will wake up in a safe place," the face spoke to her.

The light grew even brighter, and then, everything went black.

# Part V

## The Hall of Records

Escorted by the magnificent Gabriel, Death arrived at the Hall of Records. This was one of the most prestigious planes in Heaven, for here was kept in countless volumes all the accounts of every being and event going as far back as the dawn of time. The keeper of this vast library was Azrael, who was known by many as the Angel of Death. Because of this title, the angel knew his grim visitor very well. Throughout time they had had many disputes over jurisdiction, for both beings monitored the death of mortals. Azrael though, also monitored life. Gabriel left, and Death was lost amid the colossal bookcases and random stacks of texts laid about the ground. The Hall of Records had no walls, it was a plane within itself, and walls were not necessary. The bookshelves just seemed to stretch out into infinity, going in all directions. Death wandered about the massive volumes, reading the spines every now and then. He stopped when he noticed that he was in the evil section. Right in front of him was an entire set of shelves dedicated to Radix, and all the torment that he had caused.

"Death, I see you have arrived safely," a voice called out.

"Azrael, stop these games and show yourself already. I still do not understand why you like to sneak up on people."

"It gets boring up here, you know," Azrael spoke back as he appeared point blank in front of Death, nose to nose.

Azrael was not in his true form. No one had seen that in ages, not since the times of great wars and punishment. Azrael preferred to take on various shapes now. One which he preferred more than others was that of a man, and this was the form that he chose to appear in now. The Angel of Death had been studying humankind far more than any other creature and found them to be a very fascinating species. The other angels, when manifesting themselves, also took on human-like appearances, yet always kept an angelic look to them; while Azrael was simple in his choice of form — no glowing light, no wings, no frills. He stood there before Death; his long blond hair was tied back in a ponytail; his eyes were as blue as the morning sky, though they had a tendency to change with his moods; his skin was as white as milk; and unlike the other angels, he wore a long black robe.

"You were always one for dramatics, Azrael," Death said in an easy tone. "Last time we spoke, you were in a much more hostile mood. You're not still angry about the whole thing are you?"

"You over-stepped your bounds, but now I understand why. Death, if anything, I know you have good judgment. You have proven this. And these days, I have been a better judge of character," Azrael spoke with the same easy tone as Death.

"That's good. I would rather be your friend, than your enemy."

"I agree. But the reason I called you here was to talk about that man," Azrael said as he pointed to one of the books on Radix.

"Yes, you more than anyone know how Radix has been a thorn in my side."

"Yes, Death, I do know, and I feel the same as you. This

creature has to be put to rest. That is why I am willing to give you some information. I would have helped years ago, but there never really was an opportunity to stop Radix. The others were all missing something. The only one that could have ended all of this was Christ himself, but His death was inevitable. He had to take away the darkness, by saving men from their own sin," the Angel of Death paused. "But Nathaniel Salvatore, he has something special about him. It is deep in his soul. I listened to the Djinn. They called him Godchild. They can smell it in his blood."

"Djinn?" Death interrupted. "Then, he is in the Arabian Desert. I must go find him now."

"Wait, Death, do not leave yet. There is nothing you can do. He is a mortal; you know you cannot speak with mortal men and women. Nathaniel has already been informed of his mission, thanks to Gabriel and some others. But I fear that will not be enough. He will need help. And I hate to say this, but there is someone in the desert who *can* help Nathaniel."

"Ravenblade?" Death interjected. "But he will kill Nathaniel if he finds him, putting him in even more danger than before."

"No, Raven will not kill Nathaniel if you relay to him the situation. You see, the one person Raven hates even more than me is Radix. Radix is the most evil being to ever walk the Earth. We both know that. It is a shot to Raven's pride. He wants to destroy Radix, so that he will be the most feared and evil man on Earth, again. But he will not listen to me. You know that. But he might listen to you. You have never been a threat to him. I think he actually likes you, being Death and all."

"I see what you mean. Then, I will seek out Ravenblade in the Arabian Desert, and I will try my best to convince that vicious savage into helping Nathaniel Salvatore stay alive."

"Thank you, Death."

"No. Thank you, friend," Death said as he vanished.

# Part VI

## The Temptation of Nathan

"Nathaniel Salvatore, it is a pleasure to meet you, son," the Devil spoke with a forked tongue.

"I am not your son, old man. Who are you anyway? I mean you appear out of nowhere, right after a disgustingly hideous succubus tries to devour me; and you are wearing that tacky white suite with a red tie. What's up with that?" Nathan remarked.

"Ah, a sense of humor — now that is refreshing. The rest of them rarely cracked a smile. Ah, but you are different. I can sense it."

"I'm glad you are sensing all this. Maybe you can sense a way out of here. I've been in this desert too long, and I'm getting tired of all this sand."

"You have been here for forty days, and tonight will make forty nights. I have been watching you, child. I must say, I am very impressed. You are a clever one, and durable too. But the worst is not over yet. That is, unless you would like me to help you out a bit?" the demon of demons offered.

"I don't know if I should trust you, old man. I don't know you. And after being out here, I've learned not to trust anyone," Nathan wisely said.

"You're right — you should not trust anyone. Anyone, that is, except me. Look, sit down, and have a bite to eat, maybe something to drink."

As Satan spoke he clapped his hands, and a banquet appeared on the desert sand. Nathan looked shockingly at the table full of rich, hearty food, and there was plenty of water and wine to drink. The Lord of Hell gestured for Nathan to sit down. Nathan's stomach begged him to fill it; his throat pleaded for a drink. But he was too smart for this crafty snake. This was merely another test. Nathan knew exactly what was going on.

So in similar fashion to Jesus, he quickly responded, "Man does not live on food alone, but by every word that comes form the mouth of God."

"Nice, so you've read your scriptures. Isn't that special," the snake spoke with contempt behind the smile on his face.

He clapped his hands and the banquet was gone as instantly as it had appeared.

"I was merely trying to feed your hunger, child. There was no malice in my gift. Would God condemn one of his children for eating food that they were offered?" the Devil said cunningly. "That might not have been to your liking. Well, I have another gift for you."

"That's okay, you can keep your gifts to yourself. I do not believe your lying tongue, Devil."

"Such harsh words. I am only here to help you, child."

"You keep saying that, but I don't think it's me you want to help, but rather yourself."

"Before you set judgment, just look at what I have to offer," Satan said as he clapped his hands once again.

The desert began to warp and shift. The world around Nathan transformed before his very eyes. He was high atop a tower. He could see out over a vast kingdom adorned with more gold, silver, and precious gems than he had ever seen. It sparkled even more than the city of the Djinn.

"This is the kingdom that I will build one day on this Earth. The kingdom that I will rule over with a just hand."

"I'm sure of that," Nathan cleverly insulted.

"You have quite the repartee, don't you, child? If you are so great and know so much about your God, then jump from this tower. For wouldn't your God send His angels down to catch you and bear you up on their hands, so you would not even dash your foot against a stone? How important do you think you are to Him?"

"It says, 'Do not put the Lord, your God to the test!'" Nathan avowed.

"I would make you a place in my kingdom by my side. They would all call your name, and bow down to you, as they do me. Can you hear them praising you?" The Devil's eyes grew a fiery red as he looked at Nathan. Shouts of praise along with chants of Nathan's name came from the vast city below him. "All you have to do is join me, worship me. Only I can save you."

"You save me? You cannot save me. It says 'Worship the Lord your God, and serve only Him.' I would never serve the likes of you, Satan!" Nathan screamed in the face of the Devil.

The Prince of Darkness was now enraged. This man was denying him without even blinking an eye. This was unheard of. It was an outrage. Grabbing Nathan by the throat, the Devil transformed into a scarlet monster, large and muscular. He had legs like an ox, and horns to match. Satan held him over the side of the tower. Once again caught in peril, Nathan fought for his very breath, as his feet dangled thousands of feet above the ground.

"I will no longer take your tongue, boy," Satan's voice shook the city. "You will worship me or die! Your parents have already been slaughtered by Radix. Your sister raped and bleeding, barely alive."

In one quick movement the monster threw Nathan onto the floor. A sword then appeared in his hand; and the beast threw it at the young frightened man; it landed inches away from Nathan.

"It's not true! These are more lies! Lies, *lies*!" Nathan cried as he gasped for breath.

"I speak no lies. Look for yourself," The scarlet beast said, and the air in front of him swirled until a picture formed.

Nathan watched in horror as images of Radix torturing both his parents and his sister were shown to him.

"Take that sword and kill yourself. There is no longer any reason for you to live. Your God has abandoned you!"

Nathan picked up the sword, and held the point to his chest as he stared at the images before him.


"Radix." The voice came from smokeless fire. The fire manifested into a Djinni before Radix, as he left the Salvatore house.

"Yes, what is it? Can't you see that I am working tonight," Radix said back to the Djinni.

"A message, I have for you, I do. In the desert, our home, the Godchild is. Tried to eat him, we did; but Satan's whore stole him for her own food."

"So wait, — he is dead now? But that cannot be. I would have known if that had happened."

"Dead, he is not. Satan, himself, has interest in the Godchild. Tempting the boy, he is."

"Tempting him? Whose side is he on?" Radix angrily questioned. "Thank you. Have an egg."

Radix threw the Djinni a hardboiled egg that had already been peeled of its shell. The Djinni graciously caught it. But its gratitude turned into disdain, as its hands began to burn.

"Salt! Curse you, Radix! Curse you to Hell!" the Djinni scolded. He left then, in the same smokeless fire in which he had appeared.

"So, Scratch is tempting the boy," Radix thought. "He must think he is really clever. Hmm. Now, I know where the boy is; and I will kill him. I do not have time to go all the way to the Arabian Desert. But I know something that will do the job for me. It will find Nathaniel Salvatore and strike him down."

Radix put his palms up, and into his hands appeared the sinful *Necronomicon*, the same book that Radix used to become the monster he was today. He had just recently recaptured this text in order to help him perform his dark work. It opened, and the page read across the top, "Conjuring a Mamu."

The sword was starting to dig into Nathan's flesh; he could not bear the pain and all of the suffering that his own family had faced because of him. It was just as Donald had told him.

The city shook with every breath Satan took, as he declared, "Do it, do it now, boy. Kill yourself and join me! I will save you! Join me!"

"No, I will not kill myself! Not for you! Not for anyone!" Nathan cried with all his might. "Away with you, Satan!"

With this decision, Satan was gone. Nathan was back on the desert sand. It was that simple — deny the Devil, and he could not harm you. Whatever had happened would have come to pass regardless of Nathan's decision, and if he gave up now only more people would suffer. Nathan knew this deep in his heart; and he vowed to go home and take down Radix, one way or another. But there was one thing that Nathan did not understand. He had already spent forty days and forty nights in the desert, yet he looked around and saw civilization nowhere. He was sad that night, but he felt strong and was proud of his ability to resist the temptations that were thrown at him. Touching his chin, he realized that his beard was now full, and the hair on his head was long. With thoughts lifted up to God, Nathan lay down to rest.

# Part VII

## Escape from the Desert

It was the morning after Easter. A lone figure stood atop a cliff, looking down into his territory at a man who was sleeping. The menacing garb of the figure was obscured behind its worn and weathered appearance. The trials of the desert climate and the many battles that he had waged had left their marks. His tanned leather boots came up to his knees, where they met a set of kneepads made of the same tanned leather. A rough brown fabric clothed his body, and a dark brown hood and cape sat atop his head and shoulders. From the darkness that masked his face, his piercing eyes penetrated all that met them. A blade was slung over his back concealed by its sheath. The cape of the lone stranger blew in the wind. He watched the trespasser with the eyes of a hawk, waiting to strike.

"Do no harm to that man, Ravenblade."

"Death, what is it to you if I kill a man who crosses my path?" The lone man in the cape responded to the cloaked figure that now stood before him.

"There is a good reason why you should let that man live," Death answered.

"You know," Ravenblade said, "you are lucky that I like you. I'll listen to your reason, but it better be good."

"He is the next victim that Radix is set to kill. If you kill this man, Radix will benefit and live another hundred years. I know how you feel about Radix. Would you have him best you again?"

"Radix has never bested me. I am still here, still standing. He will always just be a man to me. I am immortal. And why should I care if Radix lives another hundred years? It'll give me more time to prove that I am his supierior."

"As long as Radix meets his quota you cannot kill him. He is just as immortal as you are right now, maybe even more so. But if that man lives until the end of the year; then Radix will perish, as will your competition."

"Radix is no threat to me. What has he done, killed a few people? There was a day when I destroyed entire civilizations."

"Do not lie to me, Ravenblade. I know you better than you think. You are not the same being that did all those things in the past. You are only part of what you once were. And thank goodness for that. Or we all would be in trouble. But you do indeed hold a grudge toward Radix for not falling to you in battle, and for the reputation that he has built as 'the Root of All Evil.'"

"I hear you, Death, and you may have a point. But if I let this man live, then I will show weakness; I will show myself as being soft. That would hurt my reputation more than anything."

"No, it wouldn't. Not if you had a hand in taking down Radix. Then you would be the one who did what no one else could do. As infamous as you are now, you would only be more so."

Ravenblade chuckled as he thought over what Death had said.

"If letting this man live will end the life of Radix Malorum, then I will see to it that this man lives. But the second that Radix perishes — thanks to me, I might add — this man's life will be mine to take, and yours to collect. Understand, my friend?" The uncaring stranger spoke, using the term "friend" very loosely, for Death knew this man had no friends.

"Yes, that suits me just fine. I never thought that I would see the day when you would be wearing a shade lighter than your other half. Though there was a day when you wore white. But that was a long time ago. And it is still not as peculiar as why, out of everything that you despise — which is indeed everything that I know of — why you would not despise me?"

"You are Death. I like to kill. So without you, I cannot do what I love best," Ravenblade said very seriously.

"Good enough," Death responded, and he disappeared.

Nathan opened his eyes, oblivious to the man who was watching him from afar. Though, the young man had far more to be concerned about, for at that very moment the desert sand began to rise again, and from beneath it came a behemoth. Most of Nathan's demonic encounters had been at night, but this was in clear daylight. Radix had used the *Necronomicon* to conjure up a Mamu — a flesh-eating demon of the desert — usually not common to Arabia, but rather to Australia. The obviously male creature stood naked, tall, and large in frame — the size of a small house. Its head was pointy, and it had long bloody fangs. In its right hand, it wielded a mighty club that could easily crush all of Nathan's bones in one blow. The Mamu roared and beat the sand with its weapon. Nathan knew what to expect next, but he was tired of running. So, he just stood up and looked at the ogre.

"This guy has to be crazy," Ravenblade thought to himself, as he watched Nathan stand face to face with the behemoth. "It might actually be some work keeping this kid alive."

The angry Mamu swung its club at Nathan, who jumped to the side, barely dodging the blow. Without a second thought, Ravenblade leaped from the cliff and landed on the monster's back. It moved and shook, trying to knock off the fearless immortal. In one swooshing motion, Ravenblade unsheathed his sword — a beautiful double blade, sharp from one end to the other — and cut off the demon's head. Nathan was stunned. He watched the huge creature's body collapse to the desert sand, as its head rolled past him; blood was everywhere. The unlikely savior jumped from the back of the fallen Mamu and landed in front of Nathan. Ravenblade removed his hood to reveal his face. He was handsome, rugged, and had long reddish-brown hair. His skin was tanned from the desert sun. He looked at Nathan with his cold brown eyes.

"You're lucky I showed up, kid," he said to Nathan. "I'll guide you from here."

"Why should I trust you? I'll find my own way."

"Listen here. I just saved your hide, and consider it lucky that I didn't take your head with that filthy Mamu's. No, you shouldn't trust me. I'm the last person you should ever trust. But if you want to live, then come with me. You really don't have a choice."

"Like I said, I'll lead myself. I've gotten this far on my own," Nathan said, and he began to walk off.

"You're heading the wrong way. The city is in that direction," the immortal corrected him and pointed to the west.

Nathan turned and began to walk west. Ravenblade slowly followed behind.

"Stop following me!" Nathan snapped.

"I go where I please. You are in my territory, so watch your mouth. Remember, I'm the one with the sword here."

Nathan stopped and turned around, saying, "You think that sword makes you so tough. I've been out here for forty days and forty nights with no food, no water, and no weapons. I survived countless numbers of demon attacks, I was swallowed by a fish, and I even matched wits with the Devil himself. I think that says enough. Thank you."

"Forty days and forty nights — I thought you looked a little like Yeshua," Ravenblade made a rare joke. "Kid, I've been in this desert for thousands of years. No food, no water, only my sword. And if I did not have my sword, you would have been Mamu chow."

"God would have saved me."

"Well guess what, *He* didn't. I did. So shut your mouth and walk behind me. I'll show you to the city, and you can go from there on your own. But be warned — Radix is not one to take lightly. You'll be wishing you had my sword when you face him."

"How do you know about Radix?"

"That's not your concern. Just walk."

"You have no manners, you know that?"

The agitated nomad just looked at Nathan with a piercing glance, and the two continued forward. Nathan was very hungry, and the city was still a few hours walk from where they were. They decided to sit for a rest. As Nathan sat down, he looked to his side and noticed a fine flaky substance on the ground.

"What is this?" he inquired.

Curious Ravenblade walked over, looked down, and said, "Manna, bread sent down from heaven. *He* really must like you."

"Manna, you mean like the stuff that the Israelites ate when they were in the desert?"

"You got it, kid. You said you were hungry, so eat up."

Nathan did just that. The more he ate the more there was, until he was full.

"Now that you have had your fill, maybe we should start heading out. The city is still four hours away. The sooner I get you out of here the better. Let's move."

211

The pair set out and did not stop until they reached the city. The city, it turned out, was more like a small town. The buildings were simple, and close together. The streets were not paved, and there were many small market stalls. Most of the people walked or rode bicycles. The townsfolk were poverty-stricken, their clothing minimal and dirty. Nathan was far from home, but he was happy to finally reach civilization — so much so that he let out a joyous cheer, and gave his guide a giant bear hug, lifting him from the ground.

"I should kill you for that," Ravenblade said with disgust. "I will be leaving now. But before I go, one piece of advice — stay alive."

The desert wanderer turned at that point and walked off. Nathan ran into the city. The people all looked at him confoundedly, wondering where on Earth he had come from. He tried to speak with some of the locals but none of them knew English, except for one man. Approaching him from the front was an older gentleman with gray hair, clean-shaven, and a black Catholic priest's robe. He was using a finely sculpted wooden cane to walk.

The priest stuck out his hand and greeted Nathan with a thick Irish brogue, "Nathaniel Salvatore, I presume."

As they shook, Nathan asked, "How do you know my name?"

"My name is Father Dan Reilly, and I have heard a lot about you, son."

"Sorry, if I'm a little confused. It seems that everyone knows who I am these days."

"That's because you are special. Come with me to my church. I have something for you, and we can talk about your adventures."

"I don't know? I really have to get home. Is there an airport around here?"

"Not for miles. Why do you have to leave so soon?"

"My parents — I think they were killed, and my sister badly injured. I have to find her and make sure she is okay," Nathan sadly said.

"I am sorry about your family. It was indeed a tragedy. But your sister, she is in a safe place; and you will see her soon enough. You are not ready to return home."

"How do you know all of this?" Nathan questioned. "Why is it that everyone seems to know what is going on, except me?"

Nathan hung his head low as the priest placed his hand on his shoulder.

"Don't worry, son, just come this way. We can talk over supper."

Nathan felt that this was a good man, and he knew that he could trust him. The sun began to set, and Father Dan Reilly and Nathan walked off. In the distance, the mysterious Ravenblade watched the two. He told Nathan that he would leave him, but the immortal was too proud to let Radix remain alive. It was time for him to finally have his victory and win back his crown as the most evil being to walk the Earth.

# CHAPTER VIII
## WAR ON THE HOMEFRONT

The light was beautiful and pure, completely encompassing. The innocent young woman knelt in its glow, tickled by the warm sensation of the rays touching her cheeks.

"Greetings, Esmeralda," an angel of the Lord spoke from the light. "Do not be afraid, the Lord is with you. He loves you and has found favor with you."

Esmeralda was in awe as she gazed up at the winged being, who radiated before her. Then instantly, she felt a strange sensation inside of her womb.

"You are with child. One, whom will grow to do marvelous and wonderful things," the angel joyously sang.

Esmeralda could not speak. She was afraid. To bear a child from that heinous act would only remind her every day of the nightmare that she lived through. The pain, the suffering, and the humiliation had already been too much to bear on their own.

"The Lord understands your pain and misery. It is true that your life will not be easy from this day forward, but no holy life ever is. If you bear this child, love it, and nurture it, the blessings that you will receive from on high will be without end. For even though this child was conceived from darkness, it will be born and baptized in the eternal light. God has a special plan for this babe that is growing within you."

Esmeralda finally obtained the ability to speak and said, "But how could one like me bear something such as this? I am no one special. I am still grieving the death of my parents, and my brother is still nowhere to be found. My frame of mind is not in a place to raise a child. Why must I hurt any longer? Why does God punish me so?" Tears came from her eyes but were evaporated by the light, wiping away all of her sorrow.

"The death of your parents was indeed a tragedy, but they are at peace now. As for Nathaniel, your brother, he is safe and will return to you shortly," the angel foretold. "Do you feel the light? That is the Holy Spirit. The Spirit will fill you and give you the strength to go through all that God asks of you. God will bear your pain and make it light; He will carry you all the way through the struggles. All you have to do is accept this gift."

Esmeralda looked at the angel who grew more beautiful with each passing moment. She felt the gentle and loving power of God filling her. Her heart answered for her and said, "Yes," accepting the gift of the child. The Holy Spirit filled Esmeralda and she was made pure in His light. And in that light she awoke as from a dream.

# Part I
## The Spilling of Blood

"Finally, you are awake, Esmeralda," a familiar voice spoke to the waking girl as she focused her eyes.

"Sister Elizabeth? What are you doing—how did I—?"

Esmeralda was lost for words. She had awakened in a strange bed in a small quaint room, looking at her second grade teacher. The young woman had not seen Sister Elizabeth in some years, but the friendly nun looked just the same. She was short with big thick glasses, her white hair hidden under her black habit. Everything seemed so bizarre to Esmeralda, like she was in a fairy tale.

"Child, I watched you grow, and I always knew that you would be special," the nun said as she patted Esmeralda on the hand. "The angel of the Lord brought you here to stay in my care. We are at the convent just across the street from where you attended my class all those years ago."

"But, sister," Esmeralda sat up, "you know about the angel that sent me here? Then, you also know what happened to my family and me? It just seems strange — like a dream. And I just don't know what's real except for the pain."

The tears could no longer be held back; she was confused and scared. Just a day ago, her family was killed and her brother was thought to be dead. But now she knew that he was alive; and she had suffered not only bodily violation but also countless internal wounds, which were all miraculously healed.

"There, there, my sweet child, everything will be okay. The Lord will provide for you. You will see," Sister Elizabeth comforted Esmeralda as she put her arms around her.

216

"Sister, it's complicated, though. I'm pregnant, and the angel told me to keep the baby. I said yes. It seemed like the right thing to say at the time, but I can't take care of a child. And the child will always remind me of what happened," Esmeralda sobbed in the arms of the caring sister.

"I know everything that happened. I know that you suffered hard, and that the child you carry was not of your choosing. But I also know that the child has to be born, and that you must mother it. For God has graced you so. I will do anything that I can to help you in your pregnancy and afterward, too. The angel came to me as well and told me your story. I vowed that I would do all that is in my power to help. And I will."

The two held each other as Esmeralda cried both tears of sorrow and joy. Despite all the pain that was in her heart right then, she knew she had a friend.

"Thank you, Father, I feel much better," Nathan said as he walked out of the bathroom wearing new clothes and drying his hair.

"Nothing like a shave and a shower to make a man feel refreshed," Father Reilly responded. "Now let's sit down for some supper and talk."

Nathan, who had now cut his hair to a more comfortable length and shaved his beard, took a seat at a small wooden table in the priest's humble quarters. He was at a tiny Catholic church in a small town in Jordan. Father Reilly lived there alone in a small apartment attached to the back of the church. Nathan was sitting in the dining area, which was not too far from the stove that Father Reilly was cooking on. A grin came over the young man's face, as he smelled the hearty stew that his new friend placed in front of him.

"It smells great, Father."

"Eat up, son, there is plenty for the both of us," Father Reilly said as he took a seat at the table as well.

The two ate and chatted. Nathan told the priest of his hardships in the desert and all that he had survived. The good father then told him of how he long awaited his arrival. That an angel came and told him that Nathan would come needing his aid.

"So, you see, Father, I have to go home. I have to face Radix, man to man, and avenge all that he did to my family and those innocents throughout the ages. And of course, I need to find my sister and make sure she is safe."

"My boy, your sister is safe for now. I told you this. She is at a convent back in New York, at the parish of Divine Body."

"Divine Body? That's the parish I grew up in. It's not too far from my parent's home. How could she be safe there?"

"God is watching over her, as are His angels. Plus, she has been filled with the Holy Spirit. Harm will not come to her. But if you go to your sister, then Radix will follow you; and what will you gain then. Your only concern at this time should be the one called Radix. He is crafty and very powerful. I know, I have seen his dirty work firsthand."

"When?"

"He wiped out my village back in Ireland, years ago, when I was a small boy. I watched him burn the bodies of my family and friends. Only by the grace of God was I saved. An angel of the Lord appeared to me, and led me to safety. Before he departed, he told me to follow God and serve Him always. That was why I became a priest."

"It seems that we have much in common, then. Both of our lives changed because of the evil sowed by Radix. That monster has destroyed too many lives, and I cannot let him live any longer."

"You cannot fight him either. He cannot die. Your best strategy is to hide."

"Hide and let him kill more innocents. No, not anymore. I'm sick of hiding. I'm tired of thinking I am too weak to do anything."

"How are you going to battle a man who is literally a million times stronger than you, and craftier than a serpent? Plus, from what I can tell, he has the *Necronomicon* once again. Satan handed that book over to Radix almost two millennia ago; but thanks to the efforts of a priest in the Middle Ages, it was taken from him. Now it has somehow found its way back into Radix's hands. With it comes great evil power, making Radix even harder to stop. He sent that Mamu after you, most likely conjured up from that sinful book. I've been studying that wicked fiend, my whole

218

life and I vowed that I would see the day when he would fall and wither into dust. You can make that happen, but only if you remain alive."

"Don't worry, Father. Death will not take me, not yet. I will face Radix, and I will end his bloody reign. No more will people cry at night in fear of that beast. God is with me. I know He is. Please, Father, understand why I cannot just lie in a hole and wait this out."

"I knew what your answer would be, and the angel was right. You will face Radix then, but you will need assistance. I have a gift for you as I told you when we met. Come with me."

The two got up from their seats, and Father Reilly led Nathan into his bedroom. From under the bed, he took out a lead box and opened it. Inside was a golden ring. Engraved on the face of the ring was the Star of David encircled by some Hebrew characters.

Father Reilly gave Nathan the ring and said, "This is the mystical Ring of Solomon. It holds great power for the one who wields it, especially when used against the forces of darkness. This ring was given to the wisest of all men, King Solomon, and it has been used by many wise men after him. Not just anyone can wield this sacred ring; only those who are wise in heart, mind, and spirit; as well as strong in character. The ring has been used in the past to thwart Radix, giving its holder the strength to battle him. Plus, it can help you to locate your foe, for it can sense the presence of evil."

"This little ring does all that."

"Yes, indeed, and I was told to give it to you," Father Reilly insisted as he handed the ring to Nathan, who placed it on his right ring finger.

"I can already feel the power in my veins."

"Be careful, young Nathan, that you do not become overtaken by the power. For it can corrupt a soul as easily as it can strengthen one," the wise priest advised.

"I will be careful, Father, and thank you. Now, tell me how I can get home from here."

"Stay here the night and rest. In the morning, we will go to the airport in Amman. I have a friend who can drive us, and I've already made arrangements for your flight back to New York."

"You really did have everything planned out. Didn't you, Father?"

"Always be prepared, for you never know the hour or the day."

It was out of desperation alone that Lyles came here. The buildings were all run down, covered with graffiti and boarded up. The only people who dwelled here were criminals as far as Lyles was concerned. He knew that he was lucky to have made it this far, yet he was unafraid. It was late, dark, and he was unarmed unlike the man who stood before him. The tall black man was carrying a loaded nine-millimeter. He had long snake-like dreadlocks that crept from his head halfway down his back, and he wore a leather jacket with a falcon on one sleeve and a hooked sword on the other. Lyles knew this man. His name was James Clark, and Lyles and he were like brothers once. With time, James changed, as did his name. He was known as Pharaoh now, and he led a very feared and ruthless gang called the Scimitars. Entering their territory could mean sudden death for any man, but Lyles had no other choice — there was something far more powerful and scarier than these cutthroats on the streets — a beast known as Radix. The man called Pharaoh was his only resort right now, his only place to turn, for war was inevitable.

"Lyles Washington. I never thought I'd see you around here. I always figured you were too good for a place like this," Pharaoh greeted his old friend.

"Things change, James," Lyles spoke up and courageously stood eye to eye with the man.

"I can see. By the way, they call me Pharaoh now; and I would like you to do the same."

"Pharaoh it is then," Lyles said boldly.

"Yes, things do change. You seem to have a backbone these days. You're not even twitching. I commend your courage. Most men beg me for their lives."

"Well, I've been through a lot lately, and whatever doesn't kill you makes you stronger."

"I heard you did a little time behind bars, very little it seems. Plus, I hear your record is still clean. I wish I could say the same for mine. So, like I asked you before, why have you come here? I don't let most people who walk through here uninvited live for long. When I heard you were coming, well, I had to see it for myself. You were always such a good boy, and now you are here in my kingdom."

"This is not easy for me to say but I need your help."

"My help?" Pharaoh inquired as he rubbed his chin.

"Yes, your help. You see, this is going to sound crazy, but I have to stop someone from destroying the world; and I have no means to take on this monster."

"It seems that your short time in prison screwed up your mind real good. This isn't a comic book, and I don't have time for games. Just quietly leave, and we'll forget this ever happened. Though, I find it ironic that the man who tried to help me keep clean, now, wants my help."

"Laugh, make your jokes, but I'm not playing any games," Lyles said as he looked more serious than before. "I came to you because I need some heavy firepower; anything to hold off this guy, until I can figure out how to stop him."

"First, you insult my intelligence, and then you ask me to just give you expensive hardware," Pharaoh grabbed Lyles by the face and pulled him close as he took his nine-millimeter from his belt and put it right between Lyles' eyes. "If you don't leave, I will have to kill you. You might have some bravado these days, but my bullet is stronger than your stupidity."

Lyles' eyes stared straight at Pharaoh without a blink. He was full of the Spirit, and he knew that he would not die this night. Without moving anything but his lips, he spoke once again, trying to reach the angered gang lord.

"When your mother died in your arms, who was there to give you strength? When your father beat you halfway to death, who let you hide out in his room for a month? And when everyone had given up on you, when you were nothing more than a pathetic junky; who tried to get you clean? Who found a place at the center for you to live, even though you chose to run away instead?"

Lyles stopped talking. The tough angry eyes of Pharaoh began to soften, and he lowered his gun. The man born James Clark took his hand from Lyles' face and placed it on his friend's shoulder.

"I tried so hard to help you. I never thought you were crazy, and I never ran away. I need you now, like you needed me then. And if you help me, I will help you; because it is never too late for any of us to come home," Lyles said as the wisdom of the Spirit spoke through him, his words woven from gold.

"You win, Lyles. I don't know why, but your words hit me harder than any bullet. It's like when we were kids all over again. Funny, how you get lost in your ego. I figured I was dead to all emotions. But when you spoke just now — if you laugh, I *will* kill you — I felt something move inside. I think it was my soul coming back to life," Pharaoh laughed. "I will give you whatever you need, but you must tell me more of this supervillain. And please call me James."

In his mind, Lyles sent up a quick thank-you to God for giving him the strength to not back down. Pharaoh then led him to what appeared to be an abandoned building. Two men stood outside, guarding it with fully loaded automatic weapons. They were as still as statues and kept a watchful eye on Lyles as he walked in. The building that seemed to be abandoned was actually quite crowded. As he looked around, Lyles wondered if he had come to the right place. He was surrounded by drugs, thugs, and loose women. The Scimitars' empire was built on the selling of various contraband, especially weapons. This young man was in a house of sin, looking for help with a holy mission. Actually, it was much more like a holy war. And if it was indeed a war that he would have to wage, then he was in the right place. Four flights of stairs and past many an unconscious body, Lyles was led into Pharaoh's private chamber. The room was dimly lit, and the walls and ceiling were completely covered in mirrors. There was a large king-size bed against the back wall covered with leopard print silk sheets and pillows, as well as an actual leopard skin lying on top. On the wall above the bed hung two scimitars that crossed each other. There was also a small card table in the corner with four wooden chairs.

"Please have a seat," Pharaoh said as he and Lyles sat down at the table. "You were like a brother to me, growing up. Too bad it couldn't have stayed that way. But let us pretend that it is old times and talk. So, tell me exactly what's going on."

"Well, the whole thing started when Mr. Reynolds, the old preacher, was shot and killed by some creep. Three boys that I knew saw the killer and followed him to an alley, where they shot him in vengeance for what he had done. But apparently the man didn't die. The boys had run away in fear of the law, and were brutally murdered by the monster that they thought they killed. The only description that I have of this devil is that he is tall, white, and wears all black."

"Yeah, I've heard some talk about this. They thought it was you at first. I knew they were wrong about that; you're not the killing type. Though, now, it seems you might be," Pharaoh rebutted. "The pigs have been coming down hard on the gangs, blaming us for these wild murders. A lot of my men have been harassed lately. I'm not saying that we are blameless. We are far from that. But these sick ritualistic killings — that's not our thing. All thanks to some cracker. Only white people are that crazy."

"He's not just some crazy white fool. He is supernatural. He can't die. Not from bullets or anything. He dismembered an entire SWAT team with his bare hands. That's why I'm not behind bars any longer. I am not sure how to stop him. All that I know is that I must."

"See, I don't buy that whole supernatural thing. I've met a lot of guys who claimed to be invincible, and I watched them all fall to the bullets in my gun. If you can get me to this guy, I'll show you how quickly he can be put to rest."

"James, I'm not joking around. We are dealing with something beyond our comprehension. I just need to get some hardware to keep me alive, until I find some guy named Nathaniel Salvatore. He is supposed to be the one who can help stop this beast."

"What, another white guy? Please. We don't need to be dealing with any white people. They only mess things up, and you know it. Look here, I'll help you kill this crazy white devil. Me and some of my men — no charge. Think of it as a favor for old times' sake. You don't need to be getting this Nathaniel Wonder Bread in the way. And don't you worry, we will kill this sucka. We'll kill him good. Trust me."

"I'm not sure — that's not what I originally had in mind. I don't want to put your life in jeopardy."

"My life is in jeopardy every day, so don't worry about it. You'll stay here tonight, and we'll discuss the battle plans in the morning. I'll show you to your room."

Pharaoh brought Lyles to a very nice guest bedroom. It was strange to see such luxury inside a building that seemed to be falling apart on the outside. *Never judge a book by its cover*, thought Lyles, as he sat on the very soft and comfortable bed.

"I was just thinking about Old Man Reynolds. How he was killed and all. I feel kinda bad," Pharaoh said with his eyes downcast. "You see, I stole this medal from him a long time ago, right before I left the neighborhood."

Lyles looked with awe as Pharaoh showed him the medal that was hanging around his neck. It was the same St. Michael medal that he had read about in the good reverend's diary.

"It's kinda been a good-luck charm for me, in a strange way," Pharaoh concluded and walked away, leaving Lyles alone to rest for the night.

"Hello?" Martha answered the phone.

"Hi, Martha, it's Kimberly."

"Hey, sweetie, how is everything?"

"I'm okay. I'm just a little worried about Lyles."

"Why's that? He seemed to be okay when I last saw him."

"Well, I talked to him the other night. He sounded very disturbed about something, but he wouldn't tell me what was wrong. Then, he told me that he was going away for a little while and wasn't sure when he'd be back. I know I haven't known him long, but I'm still concerned. I was really starting to like him."

"Don't worry, darling, I'm sure he's fine. He's probably still upset about the boys and Mr. Reynolds. He just needs some time alone to think, and maybe getting away is good for him right now. He'll be back, don't you worry."

"I know. I just want him to know that if he needs me, I'm here for him."

"He knows that, but he's also a man. You know how they are about their feelings. I'm sure wherever he is, Lyles is safe and sound."

*Click* — Lyles woke up to the touch of cold steel against his forehead. He almost forgot where he was for a second, but that quickly came back to him as he stared straight into the barrel of a gun. He had stayed the night at Pharaoh's Palace, or so the place was called; and now he was receiving a rude awakening from an adolescent boy with a loaded pistol. Lyles could tell the boy was still inexperienced in the ways of the street; he seemed nervous. But the kid still held the power; he had the gun, and Lyles was anything but bulletproof.

"Explain yourself, fool!" the boy shouted.

"I'm a friend of Pharaoh, and—" Lyles said in as calm a manner as he could, the Spirit keeping him strong.

"Pharaoh ain't got no friends!" the boy yelled back, ready to fire.

"That's enough, Toni. Back off — right now!" Pharaoh's voice boomed from the doorway of the room.

The kid put down his gun and slipped it into the front of his pants.

"You know this fool?"

"This fool is my friend," Pharaoh answered. "So you better get steppin', or you might catch the tail end of one of my bullets."

Lyles sat up and rubbed his head. "Thanks, James."

"No problem. That's my nephew, Anthony. He's only been here for a few days now. He still needs to learn the ropes. I guess I should've told him that you were here. He seems to be a little quick on the draw, though he hasn't shot anyone yet. Doesn't have the guts."

"Guess not," Lyles reaffirmed.

"But we shall see if you do — have the guts, that is. Let me show you around, and we can discuss our battle plan."

Things were beginning to move rather quickly, and Lyles was very unsure of what he was doing. He knew that he needed to stop Radix, but he never really expected to make such a big production. Deep inside, he still knew that he needed to find Nathaniel Salvatore; but something assured him that Nathaniel would in fact find him, instead. Pharaoh led Lyles to a garage just outside of his palace. Inside were housed weapons that Lyles had only seen in movies. Such firepower seemed unimaginable.

How Pharaoh was ever able to gather such a force and obtain such high-tech weaponry, he could not figure out; but Lyles felt more secure now that he would have a way to defend himself, if that was even possible. The only thing left for Lyles to do was to find Radix. This task seemed almost as impossible as killing him. But James assured Lyles that with his resources, he would not just find Radix; he would lure the beast right into his own kingdom to be slaughtered by Pharaoh's unstoppable army.

Before Nathan knew it, he had arrived at the Amman Airport; and he was relieved to know that he would be home shortly. The airport was not what he had expected at all. He figured that he was going to be flown back to the States in a small biplane that was going to lift off from the desert sand. But much to his surprise, the airport was quite modern, and he would be able to fly home comfortably in a commercial jet. Nathan and Father Reilly stood inside the airport saying their good-byes, while the priest's friend waited outside in the truck.

"Here is your passport, your tickets, and some money," Father Reilly said as he handed an envelope to Nathan.

Nathan reached into the envelope and pulled out ten thousand dollars in cash.

"Thank you," he said. "But you didn't have to give me any money. Please, take it back."

"No, I refuse to take back a gift. My parish may be small, but the Catholic Church has more than enough to spare. Let's just say that I called in a few favors for you back at the Vatican. How do you think I got that passport so quickly, and the tickets? You see, Nathan, I knew you were coming, and the council knew as well. We have been waiting for you for a long time; for God to grant us with the gift of a savior from the evil that is Radix. You will end his reign of terror. I just know you will. Now, Nathan, my boy, remember all that I taught you about that ring. It can be very powerful, if used wisely; but also very harmful, if used for evil. Good luck on your journey home, and please come back and visit some day," the good father advised the young man.

"I will make sure to complete my task; and, as you put it, end this reign of terror for once and for all, Father. You have been great to me in my stay here, and I could never repay you. I will write to you as soon as I get a chance; and after all of this is over, I will come back, so we can celebrate together."

"Very good, now get going and fight the good fight. But remember, let your sister be where she is. If you go to her, you will only bring Radix with you; and then once again, you will put her life in danger. I will call the convent, and tell Sister Elizabeth to let your sister know that you are safe. But you keep your distance and make no contact with her. You hear me?"

"I will do my best, but it will be hard to not go to her. I feel as if she needs me."

"What she needs is to stay alive, and you are a hazard right now. You will only bring danger wherever you go. Good-bye, and good luck. And don't forget, if you need anything else along your journey, just let me know. Ask and it will be granted," Father Reilly said as he embraced Nathan before parting.

Nathan began to walk toward his gate where he was to board shortly. Just before he reached his destination, he felt a tingling sensation surge through him. It was the ring. There was an evil presence very close by. He turned to find Ravenblade standing there with a cold, dead stare in his eyes, looking down at him.

"Come to say good-bye, have you?" Nathan said in jest.

"I'm in no mood for jokes," Ravenblade said with a snarl. "You are about to go and face Radix. I cannot afford for you to die, so I have a proposition for you. Find him and bring him back here, to the desert where we met. I will take care of him from there, and I will assure you that you will live."

"The last thing that I want to do is go back to the desert."

"So you would rather put all those people's lives in jeopardy. At least if you bring him back here, no one will get in the way. The desert is very big, and a man can be lost there for many years."

"I know how big the desert is. Remember, I spent forty days there. You do make a good point, though. No one else would get hurt. I'll think about it. Right now, I'm only worried about finding him; then I'll see how I'll deal with him."

"He won't be hard to find, not with that charm you are wearing. The same feeling that you just felt from me, you will feel from him. Follow that feeling. Just be careful that he doesn't find you first. More importantly, bring him here as I have asked; and he will finally be slain. Trust me on that."

"We shall see," Nathan said as he turned and walked to his gate.

"Yes, we shall see. And when I am through with Radix, I will take care of you, Godchild. Oh, yes, and I will be most feared, once again," Ravenblade said quietly to himself as he watched Nathan board his plane.

"Okay, gentlemen, let's all have a seat and discuss our plan of attack," Pharaoh commanded as a general would over his army.

Twenty large African-American men, all physical dynamos, sat around a large circular table. Lyles was having second thoughts about what he had gotten involved in as he sat next to Pharaoh who was standing at the head of the table.

"Men," Pharaoh spoke again with vigor. "We have a mission to undertake, and I need all of you to play your part. This man that we are after is no ordinary man. He is very strong, and very tough. But we have taken out some major players before, and we can do it again. The target is a white man. He is roughly six and a half feet tall and likes to wear the color black. He goes by the name Radix. Now, there is a lot of mumbo-jumbo that goes along with this cat. They say he is immortal, that he cannot die, and that he has been around for two thousand years. But I think it's all a bunch of bull. He is a man, and we will kill him. But first, we will lead him here. Remember, men, we cannot under any circumstances have the police get wind of any of this. I have run this operation for many years, and we have worked under the noses of the law the whole time — never to be found. Many of us, including myself, have gone to prison for what we do; but none of us have ever let on about our organization. That is why the Scimitars have been so successful. No one knows who we are, or if we really even exist. Let's keep it that way, and with it the loyalty we have for the family."

"But, Pharaoh," one of the men spoke.

"Yes, my brother, Deevon?"

"Why are we helping this outsider? Like you said — we have to keep loyal to the family, the tribe. This man is not one of us."

"Yeah!" the rest of the group shouted in agreement.

"Listen, this man is a part of *my* family and has been for most of my life. When no one else believed in me, this man — Lyles Washington — believed in me. Now he needs someone to believe in him, and I will do whatever I can for this man. To me, he is blood, and he will always be blood. Just as I would sacrifice myself for any of you, I would for him. And I expect you to do the same."

"Well, I still think it's too risky," Deevon said boldly, shaking his head. "But I have sworn loyalty to the family, so I'll do this."

"Thank you for your honest words," Pharaoh commended. "Now, let us take guard. I will have a few of you scout the city for this Radix; while the rest of us take up position here, ready to strike if he comes our way. If any of the scouts finds him, they will lead him back here as well. No killing will be done out of our territory, just to keep it safe. But I assure you that this man will die," Pharaoh turned to Lyles and smiled. "Victory will indeed be ours."

The men got up and left the room to prepare for battle. They expected this to be quick and easy, but they did not understand the man that they were about to face. An army, they might be; but much larger armies had fallen to Radix. Strength does not necessarily come in numbers, but rather in spirit. Lyles knew this and was certain that these men would not complete their task.

As one of the men walked away from the group and headed out onto the street, his shadow slipped away and crawled into an alley. It was now dark; and the shadow moved through the darkness of the night to its master, Radix. He had sent out many demons around the city to watch for Nathaniel Salvatore's return. Radix waited under the Brooklyn Bridge, deep in thought. The demon crawled from the shadow, showing its true form. Its head was large in proportion to its impish body, which was scrawny and colorless. Its eyes were wide and red, and its nose was gnarled and crooked. It had small pin-like teeth in its gaping mouth, and its ears were like those of a bat.

"Master Radix, I bring some news," the demon spoke.

"Yes, has the boy come back so soon? I'm still upset because that jealous fool, Ravenblade, had to interfere by killing the

Mamu that I had sent after young Nathaniel. He has always tried to one-up me. But that is fine — I will kill the boy myself, if I have to. So where is he?"

"I have not found the one called Nathaniel Salvatore, but there are some people looking for you."

"And why should I care? Men have tried to stop me time and time again, and none have ever accomplished the task. You were suppose to find me Nathaniel Salvatore," Radix said intently as he grabbed the demon by the throat. "Do not waste my time, or you will have none left."

"But, master," the demon gasped for words. "One of the men there was looking for Nathaniel Salvatore as well. I could read it in his eyes. I could smell the touch of the angels on his flesh. If you get to him, he might lead you to the one you seek."

Radix threw the demon to the ground and dusted his hands.

"Very well, then. Nathaniel might not be out of my sights yet. Now, where exactly did you see this man?" Radix questioned the imp, as he hauntingly looked down at the creature. "Tell me everything."

Lyles sat at the edge of the bed that he had been sleeping in. He wondered if the soldiers that Pharaoh sent out would find Radix, or if he even wanted them to. Lost in his thoughts, he sat alone, wondering what he would do if that madman did show up. He was told to find Nathaniel Salvatore, that he could help him stop Radix; but Lyles did not know how any man could help him with this mission. It all seemed very hopeless to him. His whole life, he faced adversity; he battled his own demons and moved forward, never giving in to the darkness around him. But now, he had to actually fight a real demon, or a man who was as close to a demon as any man could be. Lyles was so overwhelmed that he just laughed out loud.

"What's so funny," Pharaoh's voice came from the doorway.

"Nothing — just thinking about this crazy mess," Lyles responded.

"It is indeed crazy, my friend; but it'll be over soon."

"Are you absolutely sure of that? Don't take lightly what I told you. This Radix is a monster. He can rip you apart with his bare hands."

"He'll never get close enough. If the guns don't take him down, the explosives will. I have more firepower than that man can stand up to. Don't worry. I will show you that he can die like anyone else. And then, we will celebrate."

"I hope so."

"I know so," Pharaoh said with a smile. "By the way, I just wanted to update you on everything. My men have found squat. Sure they came across a few freaks in the village that fit the description, but none of them were this Radix. But I'm sure we'll get him."

"Oh ,yeah, I wanted to ask you, where did Toni go off to? I haven't seen him since that day he tried to shoot me."

"I sent him to stay with some of his family on his father's side. This is no place for a kid like him. He might turn out as screwed up as me."

"That's good to see that you knew to get him out of here. You've come a long way, James."

"That I have, and so have you."

"Excuse me, Pharaoh, sir." One of Pharaoh's men came up next to him. "We just spotted a white male fitting the description that you gave us heading this way."

"Is anyone with him?" Pharaoh sounded intrigued.

"No, sir, he is alone; and he seems very confident."

"Tell the boys to get ready, we're gonna bag ourselves a white devil tonight."

Pharaoh gathered his men on the roof of his palace, all of them heavily armed including Pharaoh himself. With a wave of Pharaoh's hand, one of his men flipped a switch, shining some spotlights down below; and they all watched as Radix proudly walked into the light.

"Okay, men, get ready to fire when I say so," Pharaoh boldly commanded. He then proceeded to shout below, "Listen up, down there! Yeah, I'm talking to you, white devil!"

Radix responded, "Who me? My name is Radix. I'm not sure what you think you're going to do, but I would think it to be wise if you just handed over the man who knows about Nathaniel Salvatore. Not that I will spare any of you, it'll just save me some time. Time is a precious commodity, you know."

231

"Fire!" Pharaoh sounded the war cry, and the bullets began to fly at Radix.

The evil man was unable to move due to the barrage of bullets that were piercing every inch of his body. Pharaoh's soldiers kept pumping round after round into Radix, who was now on the ground in a pool of his own blood.

"Ha, ha, we did it, men. We did it!" Pharaoh screamed in joy. "Long live the Scimitars!"

Lyles could hear the men cheering from the roof as he still sat on the bed. In his hands, he held a loaded shotgun. What good would it do him? He heard the shouts of joy, but he did not believe any of them. They would not last. And just as he thought, Pharaoh's men's cheers turned into silence. The blood under Radix's body dissolved, and he stood back up to his feet, completely healed.

"That hurt. But the pain that I will cause you will be far worse and more permanent!" Radix shouted to the men on the roof.

"What?" Pharaoh exclaimed. "Lyles was not kidding when he told us about this cracker. Okay, men, we're gonna have to hit him harder. This time hit him again with the AK47s and M16s. When he starts to go down, Deevon, I want you to use the M72 A2. Launch some rockets at that crazy devil, and see how he likes it. Also, I want you five to go down on the ground with me. Grab the biggest guns you can carry. I'll be bringing old faithful," Pharaoh pulled out a near mint-condition Smith and Wesson Schofield model from 1873. "We'll do this like Jessie James, if need be."

Lyles listened as he could hear Pharaoh and the five other men that he selected run down the stairs. This was his battle not theirs. Sitting on a bed with a shotgun was not going to solve anything. Radix was here now, and it was only right that he join the fight. Gathering his courage, Lyles stood up and charged down the stairs after Pharaoh and the other soldiers.

As they exited the building, Pharaoh stopped and walked over to Lyles and said, "We're going to get through this, don't worry. But before we go any further, I just wanted to give you something."

Pharaoh grabbed the St. Michael medal that he took from Mr. Reynolds years ago and handed it to Lyles.

"Please take this. It has always brought me luck; and right now, you need it more than I do. You have given me so many second chances, and now you give me another chance — a chance to help you fight evil, instead of creating it. You deserve this medal. Wear it proudly," Pharaoh said to Lyles, and then he turned and cried out, "Attack!"

Lyles put the medal around his neck and held it tightly as the men on the roof and the men on the ground fired again at Radix. Pharaoh stood back, holding his Smith and Wesson, waiting patiently for his men to finish off their prey. Radix's body convulsed as he was hit again and again.

"Okay, Deevon, now!" Pharaoh shouted.

Hearing his cue, Deevon fired a rocket straight at the heart of Radix. The rocket found its mark and completely blew out Radix's chest. The five men on the ground surrounded him at that time and fired a few more rounds into his body for good measure. They were being much more careful before celebrating this time. Lyles still stood back hoping that it was finally over; but he knew in his heart, as he did before, that it was not. Killing Radix could not be that easy. And once again, Lyles was right. Just as quickly as the men ceased fire so did Radix's wounds heal, and he was back up. Before the men could reopen fire, all five were dismembered. Pharaoh angrily cocked his Smith and Wesson and fired a bullet into Radix's heart, sending him to his knees. Radix's chest sizzled as he held his wound in pain.

"I have all my bullets blessed, just in case. So, who's laughing now?" retorted Pharaoh as he walked over to Radix and put his gun to his head.

"Me!" Radix yelled. He grabbed Pharaoh's right hand, which was holding the gun, and twisted it around so that Pharaoh shot himself in the gut. "You think some holy bullet can kill me?" Radix said. "Granted, it hurt like hell; but nothing can kill me."

Conjuring up his dark powers, Radix spread out into the shadows, disappearing from sight. The remaining members of the Scimitars stood on the roof still looking down at their fallen king, who was dead on the ground below. Lyles held the St. Michael medal that Pharaoh bestowed upon him tighter now. He mourned the death of his friend; praying that James Clark's soul would go to heaven, and his sins be forgiven. It was time for Lyles to finally take action. James lost his life for him. Now, Lyles had decided that he would put his life on the line, too. Die if he would, he would fight Radix until the end.

The ground began to shake, causing Lyles to fall down as he fumbled the shotgun in his hand, almost pulling the trigger. Large gaping cracks spread along the street. Lyles could hear the sound of chanting coming from all around, growing louder every second. It was as if someone were casting a spell. The words that were being chanted shook the ground with such a force that Pharaoh's palace began to sway. Two enormous scaly tentacles burst from the asphalt and wrapped firmly around the building. They rocked the building back and forth as they began to squeeze. The bricks cracked, and the steel frame twisted. The tentacles' grasp grew stronger and stronger, until the whole building — Pharaoh's great palace — came crashing to the ground in a pile of rubble. The chanting stopped, the tentacles slithered back to beneath the surface, and they disappeared into the netherworld. Lyles looked on, fearful of the pain that he brought to this place. Everyone was dead. Blood was everywhere. Those in Pharaoh's army were not saints by any means, but even this ungodly gang did not deserve the fate they were dealt. As far as Lyles was concerned, all of this blood was on his hands. Cocking his shotgun, he stood tall; he was ready to die like the rest of the brave souls that stood next to him a few moments ago.

"Come and get me! I'm the one you want!" Lyles screamed.

Just as he stopped screaming, a mist appeared before him that formed into Radix. The beast stood there confidently. The only thing that Radix wanted was to extract whatever information that he could from Lyles, and then add another body to the pile of corpses on the ground.

"Where is he?" Radix questioned. "Where is the one called Nathaniel Salvatore?"

Lyles cocked the gun again, pointed it straight at Radix's throat, and said, "I don't know where he is. I don't even know who he is. All I do know is that he is the one who will stop you. I'm just hoping that I can hold you off long enough for him to find you. Even if I have to die in the process."

"Well, then, it looks like you are of no use to me," Radix said as he grabbed the shotgun and kicked Lyles in the stomach, knocking him to the floor. "So, start saying your prayers because you're about to meet your Maker."

Radix aimed the shotgun at Lyles' head and prepared to fire. But the young man heeded the heathen's warning and said his prayers, and they were indeed answered. Just as Radix pulled the trigger, he was tackled out of the way. The shot hit the ground, missing Lyles by an inch. The gun flew from Radix's hand and slid away from him on the ground. Angry he looked up to see who attacked him. It was dark, but Radix could see him clearly as if he were standing in a white glow. It was Nathan; and he had found Radix, just as Lyles had said.

"So, the prodigal son has returned," Radix said as he stood to his feet. "I hope you don't mind; but while you were gone, I spent some time with your family. Your parents really seemed to like me; I knocked them dead. Your sister, on the other hand, I just knocked her up."

"I know what you did to my family, you monster. You will pay dearly for that and everything that you have done throughout your existence. No more will you prey on the weak, for your days are numbered; and they will pass, as will you," Nathan spoke.

"Strong words for such a little boy. What makes you think you can do what no man has been able to do? What makes you think you can stop me?"

"God has heard the cries of His people, and it is His will that your reign ends. I know that He is with me, and He will not let me fall at your hands." Nathan said, and he held out his fist.

Radix got a good look at the ring on Nathan's hand and inquired, "How did you get that ring?"

"It was a gift. I know it has been used against you before, among other weapons. I know this will not be easy, but I am ready to use everything that I can to destroy you."

"You think just because you have a little faith and that ring you can defeat me. You must be crazy. Even with all the faith in the world and the wisdom to use that ring at full capacity — I still cannot die, but you can. So, if it's a fight you want, a fight you will get. Let's see what you got, boy."

Nathan cracked his knuckles, and the two combatants prepared to lock up. They were ready to battle to the end. Feeling like he was back in his prize-fighting days, Nathan could hear the sound of the bell; and he came at Radix with a left and a right jab. The miscreant dodged both hits and threw a couple of his own. Nathan countered as well. The two went back and forth for a while. Neither of them landed a hit, until Nathan tricked Radix with a little stick-and-move, connecting with a nice right hook to his jaw that sent the vile beast down.

"Not bad — I actually felt that. Your faith must be greater than I thought," Radix said as he rubbed his cheek and got back up. "It's funny. Now, I remember where I know your name from. I never forget a right hook. Though last time, it didn't even make me budge. October 12th, 1995. Light-heavyweight championship. You were pretty good. Too bad, I had to go that night. I could have finished you off then."

"What are you talking about? I was fighting Jerome Lawrence, not you." Nathan was baffled.

"That night, I *was* Jerome Lawrence. I used him to kill his wife and unborn baby girl. The little girl was going to be something like a modern-day Joan of Arc. So, she found herself on my list. You see, sometimes I like to make the game interesting; so, I possess bodies and call upon demons, among many other tricks I can conjure up thanks to my alliance with the Dark Prince."

"You're a monster! I heard that his wife was killed, didn't know she was pregnant. You are sick. And to use him to do it. Luckily he was never even fingered in the case. But I still don't get why you stayed to fight me?"

"It had nothing to do with you. You weren't on my list yet, boy. I just thought it would be fun to jump in the ring and have a little boxing match, that's all. Unfortunately, I was needed elsewhere and had to leave the match before I got to kill you. But don't worry, I'm here now; and you have my undivided attention. I'll make sure that I finish the job this time."

Radix did not hesitate after finishing his sentence and went straight for Nathan's jaw, knocking him back. Nathan got up, lunged forward, and the fight ensued. He landed a left and a right, followed by an uppercut. Radix flew into the rubble on the ground but got back up very quickly. The time for words was over, and the two warriors were fully engaged with the fight at hand. Nathan was furious. He thought of his parents and his sister, and how they suffered at that wicked creature's hands. The energy level rose in his soul, strengthening him further; and it was multiplied by the power from the ring. But Nathan did not know how to harness this power; all that he knew now was rage. Radix was holding back. He wanted to get a feel for Nathan's potential, and from what he could tell, it was not much at this stage.

Lyles watched the two men exchange blows. After bearing witness to the bloody massacre that had previously taken place, he could not believe that any man could stand next to Radix for as long as Nathan was with just a set of fists. The Ring of Solomon was a powerful weapon in the hand of someone with great faith, for it had the ability to increase one's power based on their spiritual energy. Lyles crept up to his feet. Yes, Nathan was doing well against Radix, but Lyles knew that it would not last. He knew that Nathan could not win this fight, and that the two of them should try to escape as soon as they had the chance. With this in mind, he slowly made his way to the shotgun on the ground. There was one shell still in his pocket, a gift from Pharaoh just in case the one in the gun did not do the trick. Reaching the weapon, he picked it up and loaded it. Just as he did, the fight began to change hands. Blocking a left hook, Radix grabbed Nathan's wrist and swept his legs from under him.

"Too slow that time," Radix chuckled. "You have spunk, but I've been around too long. Your skill with the ring is only mediocre. If you had more practice with it, you might have actually had a chance of equaling me in battle. But, boy, you will never win. I've seen men bear that ring before. All of them were better than you, and all of them are dead. Yes, they all gave me quite a fight; and some wielded the ring with such precision, that it was not until they no longer possessed the ring that I was able to get to them. But get to them, I did. Your blood will be shed today, for you are weak."

Nathan got up, but this time he landed no punches. The speed of Radix's blows increased, as did their strength. The only thing keeping Nathan from having every bone in his body broken was the power he received from the ring, but it was not infinitely powerful. Even though it made his body stronger, it did not make it invincible. If Radix continued with his assault, Nathan would surely die; and Radix would live on for another hundred years. With a crashing hit to the jaw Nathan collapsed onto the asphalt below, unable to get up this time. Looming over him was the arrogant Radix, ready to finish him. Or so he thought, for behind him stood Lyles, shotgun loaded and ready to fire. This time, Lyles pulled the trigger and blew Radix's head clean off. The boiling blood of the beast splattered on the street as his body crashed to the floor. Lyles ran over to Nathan and helped him to his feet.

"We have to get out of here, now!" Lyles ordered Nathan.

"But I have to defeat him," Nathan responded.

"You 're in no condition to win. He'll kill you once he heals. I've bought us a few minutes. This is our only chance, so let's move."

Lyles threw Nathan's arm over his shoulder and helped the battered man escape. The two ran as fast as they could down a few blocks and turned around a building where they sat down on some steps.

"Okay, I think I can make it on my own from here," Nathan said to Lyles.

"No way, man, I've been looking for you for too long. I'm in this too deep. We do this together."

"I don't even know who you are. How do you know who I am?"

"Long story. I'll have to tell you later. All we have to worry about now is getting far away from that monster."

"Fine, let's head toward the 125th Street station, there should be a train heading toward Westchester in a few minutes. You think we can make it on time."

"Positive, just follow me."

With no more words exchanged, they made a mad dash for the train station. Back over at Pharaoh's fallen kingdom, many lay dead; and as in all cases such as this, Death had now come to collect the souls of those who had passed. His timing was perfect;

238

for as soon as he arrived, Radix had finally been restored and was ready to hunt again. Noticing this, Death quickly went over to Radix to hold him back for as long as he could.

"Where do you think you are going, Radix?" he solemnly spoke as he stood nose to nose with the evil man.

"Get out of my way. I have a job to do, just as you do here."

"My job can wait as can yours. They are long gone by now, Radix, and you will not get them tonight. It's nice to see a couple of men give you a challenge. Quite refreshing, actually."

"Real funny, bones. Those boys will feel my wrath soon enough; and when this world passes, you will feel it as well."

"Strong words. I have heard them before. But it seems that you've been around for two thousand years. Shouldn't you have wiped out this planet by now?"

"How I go about my business is none of your concern. I work as I choose."

"Are you sure it's your choice?"

Fed up with Death's banter, Radix changed form once again to that of a large black bird with a beak as red as the sea of blood that was on the street below; and he took flight into the night, tracking the scent of the two men who escaped him. Death turned to administer to the dead who lay on the street. He was unsure what would happen to the souls of these men, who gave up there lives to fight the evil that was Radix. Only God could know.

# Part II

## Speak of the Devil

Radix's tolerance of Satan had been wearing thin lately. It was almost as if the Devil was changing the game on him. They were supposed to be a team, or so the man thought. But he also knew that Lucifer could be sneaky, with hidden agendas and ulterior motives. Radix never really trusted his employer, though he was grateful for all that had been given to him. It just seemed that the Devil was working against him now. And that he could not tolerate. But why would Satan want one of his own mercenaries to fail? Could this Nathaniel Salvatore be that special? Radix needed to know what was really going on, and that was why he had come here and called forth that which had made him into this beast.

The evil man stood alone in an abandoned subway station, waiting for the demon of demons to arrive. There was no light, yet the darkness grew even dimmer as the sinful Prince approached. His red eyes glowed in the shadows and looked into Radix's.

"Why have you called me here?" the Devil asked.

"I am not here to answer questions, but to ask them," Radix responded.

"Your will becomes stronger with your days. I remember a time when you were a very fearful lad. Now you speak as if you are my superior."

"Pardon my bluntness, but I am a little disturbed about your recent motives."

"And what would those motives be? My business is my own. You work for me, remember."

"I do what I must, and I do it well. But what business do you have with the boy that I have been trying to kill — Nathaniel Salvatore?"

"Why do you ask?"

"Let's just say, I heard that you were off in the desert tempting the young man. Why waste your time on someone who won't be here much longer? Are you trying to get rid of me?"

"Never. You have always been an intricate part of my plan, and you still are. I would never try to end something that has worked so perfectly. I just wanted to see what this one was made of, and why the Man upstairs thinks so highly of him. You've seen him. He's not much, but he seems to have potential."

"Potential for what?"

"To ruin my plans, if you don't hurry and stop him."

"Don't you worry about that. I will get to him. But you keep out of this. I don't like being made a fool of. Let me do my job, and you do yours."

"Oh, I am doing my job. Things are about to change, my son, and I have you to thank. You really don't know how important you have been to me. After this little episode is over, we can talk about it in further detail. Do what you must, and do it fast. There will be a dark day falling upon this rock, sooner than anyone thinks. The wheels are in motion, and the blood is being shed. But I must go now. I hope our talk has chased away at least some of your concerns. You might not have always been brave, but you have always been smart. You never really should trust the Devil, but I think you know that. Good-bye and good luck."

Satan was gone again, and as usual, there was more to what he said than what was on the surface. He said it himself: "Never trust the Devil." Radix contemplated the entire situation over and over again. But his mission remained the same; and as long as he did his part, he would still be alive.

"Master Radix," a ghoulish voice shrieked from the darkness.

"What is it?"

"The two men you were looking for, they have gone to a small town called Sawport to the Parish of Divine Body. The girl is there, too. Very pretty, she is."

"Yes, very pretty indeed. You have done well. Now, go. It is time for me to end this."

# CHAPTER IX
## THY KINGDOM COME

"So, what does he know, my sweet prince?" Lilith whispered into her husband's ear.

"He is still blind to the truth, and I would like to keep it that way. So, don't go wandering off this time, my beloved bride," the Devil replied.

"You have not called me that in some time."

"And when was the last time I was your sweet prince. I know you better than anyone. I helped create you, don't forget."

The Devil had returned home from another world that he felt was his to control. Earth was different than any of the other planets that existed — its energy was the greatest by far. That was why it had been fought over for so long, and why it had yet to be destroyed. Since its creation, the Devil has stained the Earth with sin, charming its people into following his evil ways over those of their Heavenly Father. He had even convinced many that God did not exist, and that there was no consequence to their actions. And this conviction gave way to heinous deeds becoming acceptable and even commonplace in society. But there was still good out there. The Holy Spirit still filled many people, and this angered Satan most of all.

"So, what really brings you here, my dear?" the Prince of Evil asked as he looked at the floor below. The image of his fall danced before him on the ground.

Lilith stepped back to give her husband space.

"The man in the desert, Nathaniel Salvatore, why did you not let me eat him?" she asked her husband.

"He is too important to be your meal," the keen prince stated.

"Then it is true, you do want him to stop Radix. But why?"

"I do not wish anything of the sort. I was just hoping to corrupt him a little before he dies, that's all."

"Why? Was not his sister the one you needed?"

"That has already been taken care of. This Nathan, he is more than just another man on the list — he is blessed."

"Yes, I smelled the scent of Godchild on him. He would have been delicious. But if you have other business for him, then he is yours."

"Thank you, my love. Leave me now to wallow in my past failures and to revel in my future endeavors," Satan said, and he waved Lilith out of his chamber.

# Part I

## On Earth as It Is in Heaven

*Our Father, who art in Heaven,*
*Hallowed be Thy Name.*

All around the world, the Lord's Prayer was heard. Souls cried out for refuge, looking for their Father to save them as they lifted their voices up to heaven. The same words were transformed into hymn by the holy choir of angels, making a sweet melody for the ears of the Lord. God heard His people cry and felt their pain, but it was not time to act.

*Thy Kingdom come;*
*Thy Will be done;*
*On Earth as it is in Heaven.*

The prayer was given to humankind almost two thousand years ago by the One who is both man and God. Jesus Christ bled and died for His people, the same people that called forth the prayer that He had given to them. But Christ had already come, died, and risen. He had already saved all men and women from their sin. It was not His time to come again — not yet.

*Give us this day our daily bread;*
*And forgive us our trespasses,*
*As we forgive those who trespass against us;*
*And lead us not into temptation,*
*But deliver us from evil.*
*Amen.*

The Spirit spread His wings and soared through all creation, filling those who cried out. But the Spirit was only there to guide and strengthen the people, not deliver them from the evil at hand. The prayers continued and would continue for times to come. An age of few miracles was upon creation, a time where God held back His mighty hand.

The Archangel Michael, in his brilliance, shone across the New York City skyline as he stumbled with his thoughts of Radix. For centuries, the Prince of Hosts had tried with all of his might to put down that incorrigible beast, but he had never been successful. His hand had always been stayed and held back by his Lord. Yes, his power was great; his strength was only matched by the One who gave it to him; but all of his power was still not enough to kill Radix and stop his evil ways. Michael perched himself on the cross just above the glorious rose window that decorated the facade of St. Patrick's Cathedral. He sat between the two sky-spearing spires, as he listened to the prayers of the people of this city — the city where Radix had recently taken up residence. He listened intently, as he had many times before, unable to do anything but pray himself.

"I did not know that angels prayed," Death spoke to Michael.

"And what brings you here, Death, besides the usual?" the Archangel asked.

"Radix, of course. How many more centuries, millennia even, do we have to endure this tragedy?"

"I feel the same as you, but God has told me time and time again that this battle is not mine, nor that of any angel; but for mankind, and mankind alone."

"A battle that they will surely lose, and once again another planet will fall and be destroyed. Earth is the final hope. Does God not know this? All of the other planets are gone, there is nothing left out there to save anymore, nothing but dust."

"Contrary to what you believe, God knows everything. And there is more out there than just dust, and you know that too. I just wish He would let me interfere a little more than I have been allowed to."

"Can you not protect the one that Radix hunts? You are an angel and are sworn to protect mankind."

"I can watch over, but I cannot stop Radix from killing his intended. I have stepped in at times, but I have never been

245

successful. Radix always seems to make his kill. My sword holds no power over him. He cannot die. It is that simple. But I am sure that mankind will find a way to stop the beast. The Lord says so, and I will keep my trust in Him."

"You are funny sometimes, you know that? You follow Him so closely, so blindly."

"I would not say blindly, for His ways are the only ways worth following. His is the only justice we have. Not being an angel, you could not understand how I see the Father. Your eyes are the ones that are blind."

"That might be so, but I do see that this is a travesty and should be put to an end. I just do not understand why it has to go on this way. God should have never created if his creation was only destined for pain and suffering."

"Through suffering, they will be cleansed and born again. That is the way of all of God's creation. Even we suffer. You have your pain and I have mine. I live to serve. I have no freedom like man does; yet I know my service is good and will lead to greater things, including my own freedom after the war is over."

"This war will never be over."

"Yes it will, trust me." Michael paused and looked at the crowds of people down below and spoke again, "It has been very pleasant speaking with you, Death, but I must go now. I need to see the Lord. There is something I must ask Him."

"What would that be?"

"That I cannot share with you, only God."

"So be it. I never get to know anything."

"You know enough," The gallant archangel said. He spread out his wings and flew up to Heaven.

The light of Heaven intensified as Michael entered its gates. At once, the entire host of angels on all the heavenly planes fell to one knee and bowed in reverence. The humble archangel paid them no mind as he passed through each and every luminescent plane, for he knew that all adoration was for the Lord alone and not himself. Finally, he reached his destination and stood before his Father's throne. This was as close to God as any being could possibly get, and only a few could stand in this place. Michael was one and the seraphim, God's angels of pure light, were the

246

others. These holiest of angels stood around the most magnificent manifestation of the Ever-Living God, as if guarding His presence with their very existence. But of course Michael, as all angels, knew that the true nature of God had no bounds and could not be contained by the infinite vastness of Heaven, let alone the plane that Michael stood on. The archangel moved as close as he could, but his bright light was still too dim to stand directly before the all encompassing Light of God, which was so bright and pure it could banish any darkness.

"Welcome, My child, ask your question and I will answer it. For nothing will I keep from you." God spoke to Michael in the tongue of the angels — a language unable to be heard or spoken by mortals, for it was far too intense and dimensional for such beings.

"If You know my question, why must I ask it? Can You not just give an answer?" Michael questioned in the same tongue.

"By now, you know why. Just because I know what you will say, as I know everything, does not mean that you should not say it. I prefer My children to personally ask things of Me, even if I see it in their hearts already. Ask and you shall receive."

"I know, Father, but I am just bothered by all that goes on outside our gates. You know that as well."

"Yes, I do."

"Father, is it my duty to protect mankind?"

"It is your privilege."

"Then why is it that when Radix hunts, I cannot protect his victims from facing death?"

"Your duty is to protect not from death but rather from destruction — the true death from the true evil."

"But if he kills all that is good, then destruction will come, and with it true evil."

"Do not worry of such things, My child. Just let things be, and all will work out according to plan."

"Yes, Father, you keep telling us this, but there must be something that I can do. I cannot just let Nathaniel Salvatore die like the others. He is different; he is blessed. I feel like I should help him. If he dies, Radix lives. What good will Nathaniel be then? What good is a champion that loses the battle?"

"Michael, I have made you the prince of angels for a reason. You are strong and bright, as well as intelligent. If he dies, he has not lost; even if Radix continues forth. Radix's treacherous reign will come to an end, regardless; even if it is not until the end of days. I have shown you how easily death can be defeated by sending a part of Myself, My own beloved Son, to die and rise again. Death is not the end, only the beginning."

"Thank You, Father, for Your precious time. I will bother You no further with my ramblings."

"Wait, before you depart, My child. Remember, there is one that you are obliged to protect. He is wearing your medal, and his life belongs to you as long as he keeps it with him. Do as you wish for this man. He is your responsibility now. I hope that answers your question."

"It does. Thank you, again, Father. You have been most gracious," Michael said and once again spread his beautifully colored wings, leaving Heaven in a brilliance of light.

# Part II

## Lead Us Not into Temptation

The torrid climate singed the flesh of those chained to the ground, as the sunless red sky sat overhead. The skin of the damned blistered and bubbled until it dripped off like fat from cooked meat, only to grow back and be subject to the same fate over and over again. These were not souls to feel sorrow for. They were not so innocent. These sinners were paying heavily for their unfortunate mistakes and wondered how a God of love could condone such torture.

The atmosphere changed, as did the climate. The dryness left, and boiling blood rained down from the sky. The blood burned all that it touched; all except for one creature, the master of all who dwelt in this Hell — Satan. The heathen of heathens roamed the land. He walked its rocky soil from end to end, moving through its changing conditions with no concern. This was his world, and he could go as he pleased. Suddenly, he stopped at his destination.

The lake of fire was the home of those who, like Satan himself, defied the Lord completely, turning their back on their Creator. These souls were drenched in darkness, much like the Devil that stood before them. The inhumane demon moved to the scorching lake and looked at its inhabitants with a grin. He looked into the flames at the folly of those roasting inside, knowing how they felt, for he was like them. He had fallen into his own pit of fire many ages ago. But his sin was far worse, as was his punishment. To the demon world, Satan was like a god, the only one of them who could come and go as he pleased — or so it seemed. Yes, he could briefly escape his prison at times, but his power outside of this land was limited and almost useless in many ways. No matter how far he traveled, his torture was inescapable. Lucifer was severely punished those eons passed, his suffering internal. He never showed anyone how much his fire blazed inside, a fire that destroyed him more and more everyday. The Devil felt his hideous face. What had he become? There was nothing more than a monster where a beautiful angel once stood. Yes, he was beautiful once, more than anything else in creation. His light had shone almost with the same intensity as the Son. But that light was taken away from him, and it was replaced with darkness; his angelic form was replaced by that of a demonic beast. He could have been a great and powerful king — he *should* have been. Now, he was a king in many respects, but not of any kingdom worth ruling. A Hell of torture, fire, and brimstone; a land of evil and ugliness was bestowed unto him to rule. Satan looked down at the men and women who fell like he did, who suffered the same defeat. But unlike them, he would rise from the fire and gain his true kingdom. One day, his pride would be restored.

"Yes, your pride," tens of thousands of voices cried out from the fiery abyss that the Prince of Darkness stared into. "Our pain is thanks to your pride. We burn; we anguish eternally for your foolish, reckless behavior. Stop the fire, stop punishing us, who only sinned on the account that we followed the path that you paved."

"You burn because you did not have vision. Your pain is nothing more than what you deserve, as all who suffer in this Hell!" he yelled back angrily. "You were all pathetic and weak, following a tune that I played before you were even a spark in the eye of God."

"What vision did you have? You were just as much a follower; you were weaker than any of us. You had everything. You even stood in the presence of the Lord, and you fell. You followed the tune of evil. You did not create the notes; they were played in your ear, and you went accordingly. You were orchestrated just as we were by you. You are the Prince of Darkness, but not the king. You will never be king," the voices called back amid their screams of pain.

"All of you know nothing! I was a revolutionary, a visionary. I commanded the first war in history; and I led many to go against that which made them, that which gave them life. I conducted the orchestra, I wrote the opus. I gave all of them and all of you something that God never did — a choice."

"What choice did you give us — the choice to suffer, to die, to not live happily in paradise? The choice was and is not yours to give. You did not create it. God gave you and all of us choice. You were just the first to choose against Him. We would do anything to stop this unbearable pain, even give up our God-given right to choose," the voices pleaded as the fire was intensified by the Devil's angry hand.

The voices in the pit sang their woes and sorrowful pain in harmony, flooding the ears of the fallen angel. Visions of the past filled his head, as he remembered a time when he happily stood before the Almighty. Now, he stood in a pit of flames and tortured the sinful to give relief to his own internal pain, making them suffer for his own sins. The voices struck him to his core. But those that he heard were not really coming from the pit of fire that he stared into below. No, they could not cry out. They could only scream in agony. The voices were coming from the darkness inside and all around him. Yes, Satan did bring evil to the masses; but Satan did not create the evil. He did not create anything. He only led those around him into the same darkness that he wandered into all those eons ago.

"Was everything in vain?" the Devil contemplated. "This fire, this brimstone, this horrific form? I truly have nothing! Is there any reason to continue this war, or should I just let myself finally get devoured and fall completely into the abyss that I stumbled into before the dawn of time?"

Shaking his head in disgust, the demon prince moved onward past the lake and past the entire plane of Hell; he headed straight for the gates themselves. He had to see the one being that walked beside him every step of his downward spiral. Sin knew Satan would be coming, and he knew there was an urgent matter to be discussed. On Earth something had just transpired that would have a major impact on the warfront. A new player was about to enter the game, and Radix was to thank for all of this.

"Lucifer, my good friend, I've been waiting for your visit. Not often do you leave your golden palace to greet me at your gates," Sin spoke with a tone of both sincerity and sarcasm.

"I only go where I absolutely must. You know that. Your job here has been superb," Satan spoke back with the same tone.

"You know why I agreed to stay at these gates? The view of the outside world is wonderful from here. I just love looking out at the vast mortal universe and seeing all of the calamity that we have caused. But what I see now pleases me even more than anything I have seen previously. The outside world is fading, Lucifer. Our time is close at hand. Earth is at the brink of falling, the last of the planets, the last of God's people. Radix has indeed done better than I could have ever imagined."

"That's where my vision far outshines yours. I knew he would do great things. I tasted his potential when I first laid eyes on him. He has indeed done everything that I could have dreamed for him to do, and he played the role of puppet well. But his role is coming to an end."

"It's a shame to see such a good run come to a close. Radix was a great champion of evil. But I see he has lost something. This Nathaniel Salvatore is putting up a very good fight," Sin stated.

"Yes, I am very pleased with the Godchild, and his soul will be mine soon enough."

"He does not seem like the others. He has much vigor."

"You are right about that. And that is exactly what makes him so desirable. His faith makes him strong, but he must be careful with how he uses it. For the brighter the light the darker the shadow. I should know. But there is more the discuss."

"Yes, soon it will be time as the mortals say, 'to pass out the cigars.' The child has been conceived, and he will have a heart of darkness."

"Yes, and many will follow him into that very darkness. That is why he must be mine. He could help us to turn the tables, give us a taste of victory. This boy will be our salvation, and Hell will follow with him. Radix has completed his mission. He has helped to spawn a child of darkness," Satan said with a smile.

Sin looked at Satan and said, "Yes, he will be great, but he will not just come to us. We must get to the child before anyone else does. Everyone, including God Himself will seek after him. We cannot let the boy escape our grasp for if God gets the child, then we will have no hope for the war."

"Simmer down — the child will be ours. I guarantee it. And I will make him a general in my army, and together we will spread evil across the universe. We will take control of all that we touch. The Kingdom of God will fall before me, and I will rise as the true king and ruler of all."

"The day of darkness is at hand, as is our day of liberation."

"Yes, Sin, we will be free again, and all will pay for our torment," Satan paused and sniffed the air. "Do you smell that aroma?"

"I do smell a strange scent, but I do not know what it is," Sin said in a curious tone.

"My wife, Lilith, but she is gone now."

"Do you think she heard us?"

"Of course she did. That crafty wench, she is always with her own devious agenda. But I cannot blame her. I made her that way. She was so sweet and innocent when I first met her; then I violated her, twisted her, corrupted her from the inside out. The mother and whore of all demons; she is yet another one of my creations, but quite treacherous at times. Why I keep her around, I'll never know. I guess I enjoy her company."

"Should you not be concerned about what she heard?"

"Concerned about her? Never. I wanted her to hear everything. She is just another part of my ingenious plan."

"How is that?" Sin questioned again, this time even more curious.

252

"She will obviously try to get the child as well, creating a diversion for me to swoop in and take him before anyone knows what happened."

"But what if she actually gets the child? Do you think she would try to overthrow you?"

"She will never get to the child. She has some vision, but her execution needs work. She is better off devouring men like the succubus she is."

"She might not be acting alone," Sin pointed out.

"Maybe, but who would she turn to for aid? She has no friends, except me."


"Lilith, what are you doing in my kingdom?" Iblis, the king of the Djinn, inquired as Satan's bride entered his chamber.

Finely woven tapestries decorated the walls of solid gold. Iblis sat on his golden jeweled throne, wearing his regal crown proudly. He was a ruler of monsters, much like Lilith's own husband. The only difference was that Iblis was no prisoner. He lived on Earth below the desert sand. He chose to stay where he was. He was not forced to be in his kingdom like Satan. Lilith silently stood before him, her luscious body exposed. Iblis could smell her intoxicating scent, but he was too strong to succumb to her seduction. The king of the Djinn had a sturdy muscular build, and his deep purple clothing was made of the finest silk. His face was not very handsome for he looked much like the Djinn that he ruled. Lilith looked into his vertical eyes, trying her best to make him prey to her will.

"Enough games, Lilith," Iblis boomed. "Speak now, or I will have you cast out. Your seductive charm has no power over me. Remember, I am the one who refused to bow to Adam. If I could defy the will of God, then how could you imagine that your will would have any hold over me."

"Fine, if my will has no hold over you, let me at least speak."

"Before you go any further, let me remind you that you are lucky enough that I have allowed you to step foot into my kingdom after you let that tasty Godchild slip away."

"I was hungry. And don't get so angry. It's not like I was able to feast on him either. Thanks to my husband's interference. And that is why I am here. You see, he took the Godchild away from both of us; just like he always takes away our glory. A time of darkness is at hand, Iblis. It is now time to act; it is time to lay claim to what we can before the war, so we can survive."

"Please, I have no interest in any war with Heaven. I fought my battles with God a long time ago. Maybe you have forgotten that I am not in Hell. I am very happy where I am."

"This world will not exist much longer. What will you have then? Nothing, just like everyone else that does not win the war. Lucifer knows about a great and powerful child that could either lead the people to good or great evil. If we could get this child before he does, then the war could be ours. Your kingdom and life will be saved, as will mine."

"Sounds intriguing, but where is this child?"

"In the womb of the Godchild's sister. And to add some intrigue to the story, Radix is the father."

"So, this child has not yet been born? A very interesting tale you tell, Lilith. Should I believe such a story from your deceitful lips? You did steal a meal from my children. And you have crossed me before."

"As you have crossed me. Neither of us is a saint. Yes, you were once an angel, but now you are a monster like me. Your kingdom is full of monsters. Look at everything around you. This whole world is crooked. But now we can work together to survive. I am not interested in ruling like my husband. I just do not want to be destroyed when everything is said and done."

"I will give what you have told me some thought. Come back when the child is born and bring me to him, so that I may see this great evil for myself. Now leave!"

"You know something, Iblis, you are very well spoken for a Djinni. How did that happen?"

"I am their king, their brains, their leader. They are not like me, just heat from the desert sand."

"You better not let them hear you say that."

"I am not concerned with what they hear. They will follow me blindly to the end of days, for I made them that way."

"What a great king you are, makes one happy they're not one of your people."

"My business is my own, not yours. Leave now, wench!"

"I am gone," Lilith said and mockingly disappeared in a puff of smoke.

Just as the succubus left King Iblis' chamber, ten of his loyal Djinn barged in, dragging one of their own. They tossed their kin toward the throne of their master. The creature had been noticeably beaten and whipped; bruises and lash marks covered its naked hide. It trembled as if cold and frightened, and it looked up at the eyes of its king in fear of what would happen next.

"What is all of this?" Iblis inquired.

From the entrance of the chamber came another Djinni, the one who tried Nathan in the desert. It was enraged as it spoke.

"Treason! Guilty this one is, yes, look at its eyes. Tell its secret, they do," the Djinni fired off.

"On what grounds did it commit treason?" Iblis asked.

"A spy, this one is; a spy for the Devil."

"How do you account for this?"

"Caught it in talks with Radix, I did. Exchanging our business with him, it was."

"Is this true? Did you speak with Satan's cohort, Radix?"

The accuser walked past the other ten, who were growling and grunting in anger over the traitorous act that took place. It looked down at the scared and intimidated creature with a frown of disapproval. The beaten Djinni looked at the ground, too ashamed to look any of them in the eyes.

"True, it is. Spoke with Radix, I did. But not of any importance were the matters. Wanting to know about the Godchild, he was. Told him how we had him in the desert, until Satan's whore took our meal. Nothing else did I speak of," the frightened Djinni said, pleading his case.

"Then, your brothers are correct in damning you of the heinous act of treason," Iblis said defiantly. "You are not to discuss any of our matters with outsiders, especially not with cohorts of the Devil. We have no friends in Hell — remember that. We are our own friends, our own family. Everyone else is our enemy!"

"Yes, guilty I am! But not free from guilt are you, master. Smell Lilith, I do. You have spoken with the whore, who stole our snack; the wife of the Devil, she is. A traitor, you are yourself."

"Infidel! What I do is my own business! If you must know, I was discussing that very matter with the wretched woman. I told her to stay out of our affairs, unless she would rather face the consequences. You on the other hand were exchanging information, and on those grounds you are banished from the tribe. You are no longer one of us, and you will have to wander the surface for the rest of your days — alone. Be gone from my kingdom, you traitor, you defiler!"

The eleven Djinn that stood there clawed at the turncoat and dragged it from the chamber and threw it out onto the desert sand.

The mediator of the group walked over to it and said, "A Djinni you are no more, one of us never again. Sold your loyalty, you did, for a salted egg. The salt of the desert, eat you up, it will. Open your eyes to your scandalous act, your pain will. No more our family. Cursed you are and all who cross you."

Then in one blaze of smokeless fire, all eleven Djinn disappeared and left the outcast alone to wander for eternity.

# CHAPTER X
## SPEAK OF WAR

"Oh, Nathan, I'm so happy you're here," Sister Elizabeth said as she greeted the young man with a warm hug. "And who is your friend?"

"I'm Lyles Washington. Nice to meet you, sister," Lyles said as he put out his hand to shake, but he was greeted by the same warm hug as Nathan.

The two men looked worn and beaten. It was not so easy to walk away from a fight with Radix; very few have. Sister Elizabeth ushered them inside, and locked the door.

"So, sister, how is Ezzie doing?" Nathan asked.

Esmeralda also survived a tangle with Radix. The only difference was that he *let* her live. The suffering that he caused her was far worse than any death that he could have dealt her. But what Radix did not know was that she was bearing his seed. Satan surely knew of this, and he was very persistent on keeping Radix in the dark.

"She is doing much better. Miraculously, all of her wounds have been healed. Though I am sorry, I could not say the same for your parents," Sister Elizabeth said, with her eyes downcast.

"Does anyone know that she is here?" Nathan wondered.

"Just you two and Fr. Reilly. I was given strict orders to keep her whereabouts a secret until you arrived."

"And who gave you these orders?" he questioned back.

"Like you don't know, Nathan. I know who you are, what you have been through, and what you will be. We need not play charades. The Lord has revealed everything to me through His angel that brought your sister here. I have taken care of Esmeralda, but I cannot watch her forever. You must take her someplace where she'll be safe. The Lord is with you, Nathan. You are our only hope right now. That is until the child is born."

"What do you mean child?"

"Your sister is pregnant — she will bear a child who will do great things. That is why you must take her somewhere safe."

"Pregnant? But how?" Nathan was puzzled. "No, it can't be. Sister, please tell me that the child was not conceived from that beast who defiled my sister."

"I'm sorry, Nathan, but that is the truth. But God has touched her, and the Spirit flows within her. It is important that the child be born."

"No. It makes no sense, all of this craziness. What have I done to my family?" Nathan screamed.

"Nathan, stop putting the blame on yourself," a familiar voice rang in Nathan's ears.

At the sound of her voice, he turned and ran to Esmeralda. Nathan fell to his knees, wrapped his arms tightly around her waist, and cried.

# Part I

## Holy Ground

Lyles did not want to intrude on the brother and sister reunion, so he asked Sister Elizabeth if he could be excused. The understanding nun felt the same and went with Lyles into the sitting room. It was a small room with a sofa, a TV, and a rocking chair. Sister Elizabeth, told him to rest on the couch and make himself comfortable, as she settled into her rocking chair.

"You can put the TV on if you like. We have cable," she said.

"Thanks, but I think I'll just sit back and relax for a while," he responded.

"Suit yourself. I think I'm going to watch Conan, then. He's a funny fellow."

Lyles chuckled to himself, as he watched the little old nun laugh hysterically at the jokes being made on the TV. He definitely felt more at ease, so he laid back and began to doze off.

Esmeralda grabbed her brother by his arms, which were still tightly wrapped around her waist, and began to pull him up to his feet. Once she managed to get him to stand, she gave him a hug and a kiss on the cheek.

"Nathan, I'm going to be fine. None of this is your fault," Esmeralda said. Looking down she noticed the ornament on his finger and asked, "Where did you get that ring?"

"A priest, Father Dan Reilly, gave it to me in Jordan. It's very sacred and will help me fight Radix."

"I hope it works. Nathan, I think we need to talk," she said as she led him into the kitchen where the two sat at a small table not too far from the refrigerator.

"I have to say you look great for all that you've been through."

"Yeah, I was lucky. I guess you can say my guardian angel saved my life."

"Have you been to a doctor yet about the baby?"

"No, I haven't left the convent. I've only been here a couple of days, and it's way too early in the pregnancy to worry about anything. I'm more concerned with what happened to Mom and Dad."

"Things aren't easy like they used to be. It's funny how your life can change in the blink of an eye. I'm just surprised that you are handling everything so well."

"I can't take the credit for that. I was given strength from God. It used to all seem like a fairy tale when we were kids, but all of it is so real. I've been having nightmares about what happened on Easter. I can see him cutting them, and the way he touched me. I don't want to think about it anymore. But that is going to be impossible with me having this baby. Every time I look at the child, I'll be reminded of how it was conceived. I promised to keep the baby, and I will. Something good has to come out of all of this."

"Well, I hope something does. I feel like things just keep getting worse. I spent forty days and forty nights in the desert. The things I went through, what I saw, what I felt; it was all surreal."

"The desert, what desert?"

"The Arabian Desert. I walked the path of Christ and many great prophets of old. It was not easy, but I survived."

"I know what you mean, about surviving that is. You do seem different now, more mature. I guess you have to be with all that's going on. But how do you know about what happened to Mom, Dad, and me? What did they do to you in the desert?"

Esmeralda's gentle hand stroked Nathan's cheek.

"A lot happened in that desert, too much for me to tell. All I can say is that I gained much wisdom. As for how I know of what happened; Satan — the Devil himself — showed me everything that Radix did to Mom, Dad, and even you."

"Everything?"

"Everything," Nathan confirmed.

"Oh, God, no. You didn't? Please, no. Don't look at me."

At the thought of someone witnessing her moment of humiliation, especially her brother, Esmeralda curled up and covered her face in shame.

"Stop this. You have no reason to be ashamed."

"Of course I do — you saw me being defiled. You saw him violate my bleeding body."

"I love you, Sis. Nothing that I saw will ever change how I see you, or how much I love you. I saw you suffer, yes. But that is what gave me the will to press on. I had to live to keep you safe. You're my baby sister, and you always will be."

"Thank you. I love you so much, Nathan," Esmeralda sobbed as she softly touched Nathan on the shoulder. She wiped her eyes and sternly looked at her brother saying, "You're going to have to stop him. You know that. You are the only one who can."

"That's what everyone tells me. But who am I to stop this beast?" he somberly asked.

"You're the former light heavyweight champion of the world, and you're my big brother. I know you can do it — the angel told me."

Nathan smiled at his sister, whose demeanor completely changed before his eyes. He was not sure if she was brave or naïve. It must have been the Spirit giving her strength.

"I'm sorry that I was not home to save Mom and Dad, and to stop that monster from doing what he did to you."

"You didn't kill them. What's done is done. I know that God has a plan in all of this."

"You're right, He does. But I still feel guilty, as if I brought this pain to them, you, and everyone else that I know."

"But you didn't choose any of this. You are a good person, and you are doing what is right. Things will turn around, just don't give up," Esmeralda assured her brother.

"I know, it's just easier to think it's my fault."

"Well, it's not."

"Thank you," Nathan quietly said, and paused. He started again on a different note, "I'm just curious about something. Does anyone know that Mom and Dad are dead? Where are they?"

"Mrs. Gardoki found them and called the police. It was all on the news. According to the report, the police are looking for the murderer, and they think that you and I were kidnapped, or possibly dead, too."

"Let's keep it that way for now. We can't let anyone know where we are."

"But what about the funeral? Don't you think we should be there?"

"No, we have to move fast. I'm going to find a place for you to hide until the end of the year, while I fight this monster. If everything goes according to plan, and I live through the New Year, Radix will be no more; and I'll be there by your side to help you when you are ready to have the baby. I won't let you go through this alone. But if we want things to go smoothly, we have to leave by tomorrow. I can't allow Radix to do any more harm to you or anyone else."

"But they were our parents. I want to be there with our family. They need us to strengthen them."

"They will be fine without us. There are more important things at hand than funerals right now. I loved Mom and Dad dearly, don't get me wrong; but they are in a better place now. We do not have time to mourn the dead, or else more will join them. I will take you to someplace safe, and then I will go on my own to fight Radix. But don't you worry," Nathan held his darling sister close, "I will come back; and everything will be fine again, once I put an end to that monster."

"I know, Nathan, I know. It's just even though I know they are in a better place, I still miss Mom and Dad so much."

"Me too, Ezzie, me too."

A moment of silence followed Nathan's words as brother and sister sat together, holding each other and praying for the world. Together they shared a vision of the future. The land was dry and pale. The sky was red and dusty. There was no sign of a sun, or moon, or any stars above. Hideous demonic creatures roamed the land, feasting upon the men and women who still lived. A dark day was at hand. Just as the sky turned from red to black, a small light shimmered from up high. It was Christ; and from his mouth

263

hurled a double-edged sword that ripped through the ground, causing great earthquakes and calamity. All of the evil, wretched demons that plagued the land were split open and burned to nothingness. From the sword came a little girl, who shown like the angels. The girl gave off a light that vanquished the darkness that was all around. The sky turned from black to bright blue, and the sun sat high at midday. The land was green, and great seas and rivers flowed abundantly with crystal clear water. Then from the ground arose the dead as new life rejuvenated them. The world had become paradise, and the sword remained in the center, giving light to all around it. Nathan and Esmeralda woke from their vision, confused.

"What do you think that was, Nathan?" Esmeralda fearfully asked.

"I'm not too sure — probably a vision of what is to come. But the future is never definite," Nathan tried to reassure his sister. "We can talk about it more in the morning. It's late, and we should get some rest."

They got up from their seats and walked quietly to the den where Lyles was fast asleep. Sister Elizabeth was still watching her program on the TV, laughing harder than before. Just at that moment, Lyles woke up startled.

"I just had the weirdest dream," he said as he rubbed his eyes. "The world was dark, and there were these demons running around killing people and eating their flesh. Then Jesus came, and a sword flew from his mouth. It hit the ground and killed all the demons. Then the really strange part was that a little girl came from the sword and everything got better. It was like paradise. Weird, huh?"

"Not really," Nathan responded.

"We had the same dream," Esmeralda added.

"Now, *that's* strange," Sister Elizabeth answered. "It was a prophecy. Two or three witnesses — you know, that's what they say. But I think you all need some good sleep. Tomorrow you can figure where you'll go from here. I'll show you to your rooms. The rest of the sisters are on retreat this weekend, thankfully. I could not have explained this to them. You can have their rooms for the night. They won't mind."

Lyles got up from the couch, and Sister Elizabeth crept up from her rocking chair. They were all very tired, and like a good hostess the kind sister showed each of them to their own rooms. The lights went out and all slept soundly.

It was a beautiful spring Saturday morning. The sun was shining in the east, and the air was warm and cheerful. Yet, not all was bright and sunny. A dark menacing shadow stretched along the street, until it reached the doors of a church. This was the very parish that Nathan and Esmeralda grew up in.

"Divine Body, strong name," Radix read the sign above the church's doors. "I do not remember the Body being that divine. Especially, hanging from that cross."

The dark enemy of God walked up the stone steps and looked above the double doors. Just over the sign that read Divine Body was a mosaic of Jesus with his arms wide open. The image of Christ beamed down with a smile as if to welcome all who entered the church. The vicious blasphemer knew he was not welcome, but he entered nonetheless. Inside the foyer, Radix noticed a wall filled with pamphlets, booklets, and other religious paraphernalia.

*More crap people don't need*, he thought to himself.

Turning to the right he saw a walkway that led to the choir loft and a small room. Inside the walkway was a full-sized and very life-like crucifix that hung from the wall, showing every ounce of blood and sweat that Christ spilled as He died for our sins. Radix walked over to the crucifix and gaped at the bloody Savior with a smile. The Son of God bore much pain that day. His suffering was intolerable. Radix knew this. He was there. The memories of a time long ago came back to the miscreant. He ventured on into the small room. A statue lay before him of Christ with his weeping mother. She was wrapping Him in a shroud, readying Him for burial. The church's main focal point was indeed the death and resurrection of Christ; and that did not sit well with the dark man, who was loitering on this holy ground. Then before him he saw a beautifully carved marble tank where baptism was administered to new members of the faith. Shoving the heavy lid to the side, Radix scooped his hands into the burning holy water.

His skin blistered as he lifted his hands out and poured some of that same water down his throat, drinking the smoldering liquid as it scared his insides.

"Nothing like a refreshing drink," Radix quipped. "I was parched."

Intoxicated by the effects of the holy water, Radix stumbled through a side door and into the main church. The statues representing the angels and saints looked down at him from all around. They watched him with disapproval. Radix's soulless eyes scanned the white walls with their gold trimming, following the Stations of the Cross around the entire church. The remarkably crafted marble scenes of affliction played out before him, as he was reinjected with memories of those days from the past. He could not escape them. Constant reminders surrounded him — from the statues, to the paintings, to the luminous stained glass windows that shined their light at Radix; all showing images of Christ in His glory. Radix felt victimized. He felt trapped. Still dizzy from the drink that he took, the evil man slowly moved down the center aisle. He proceeded past the marble columns and wooden pews, and he went up the steps leading toward the altar. Reaching the white marble altar, Radix fell to his knees. The angels and saints around him stared deeper. He turned and looked to the left side of the church, as a statue of Mary changed her smile to a frown.

"You frown at me. You turn me away. But I am no worse than any other man who sins. I am just flesh!" Radix cried out to Heaven. "Look at Your gold, Your marble, all of Your fine ornamentations. Is any of this necessary? Yeshua, You were poor, a carpenter's son; and now You have all the riches in the world. Is that what You really wanted? Those who follow You, they don't do what You want. They don't listen. They all do as they please, and pretend that they are good boys and girls when they come to Your house to worship. Some don't even come unless it's Easter or Christmas. Am I any worse than these fools? At least I know who I am and what I do. I don't pretend to believe in something that I don't. I'm not a hypocrite!"

Angry, Radix turned his eyes up past the altar. In the center of the wall was a large crucifix, luxurious and inviting, unlike the painful and bloody image of Christ that Radix witnessed earlier. Behind the crucifix was a mosaic showing a bright blue sky, some white clouds, and light shining forth, which gave glory to the icon of death.

"Do you mock me with this?" Radix asked up to Heaven. "Do you find humor in all that I see? I remember things differently. I remember them more like the cross out by the foyer. Blood poured that day. I made it so. You died, and I made it so!"

Enraged Radix smashed the altar with his fists, breaking it to pieces. Calming himself, he rose to his feet and walked toward the lectern, which was set inside a pulpit made of the same fine marble as the altar. Next to the pulpit was the Easter candle, which was lit and sat atop a beautiful tall gold candlestand. Radix blew out the candle. After that he leaned his left hand on the pulpit and thumbed through the lectionary that sat on the lectern. As he did this, a family of three walked into the church. The father was a hard worker; Radix could tell from his tired eyes, his callused hands, and the stubble on his chin. He was not as well built as he was in his younger days, but his stocky frame still showed some strength. The mother seemed very sweet and caring. She held her son tight and stroked the top of his head. The boy was young maybe nine or ten. He did not seem as sweet and innocent as his mother, though he seemed to care about her and gave her a big hug and a kiss on the cheek. There was something about the boy that Radix did not like, something strange and familiar; but he could not put his finger on it. The family seemed stunned as they looked at the smashed altar. Then they scrolled their eyes over to Radix, who was watching them from the pulpit.

"Please excuse the mess. We're remodeling," Radix said.

Believing what they just heard, the family walked slowly down the center aisle and sat in one of the pews on the same side of the church as the pulpit that Radix was standing at. The father, mother, and son knelt in unison and began to pray.

"I was just about to read some scripture from the Good Book," Radix said. "Please sit and listen."

The family got up from their kneeling positions and sat. Radix thumbed through the lectionary again. He stopped at Luke, chapter 22.

The sinful man read, "Now the festival of Unleavened Bread, which is called Passover, was near. The chief priests and the scribes were looking for a way to put Jesus to death, for they were afraid of the people. Then Satan entered into Judas called Iscariot, who was one of the Twelve; he went away and conferred with the chief priest and officers of the temple police about how he might betray him to them. They were greatly pleased and agreed to give him money. So he consented and began to look for an opportunity to betray him to them when no crowd was present."

Finished with the reading, Radix slammed the book closed and placed both hands on the pulpit. He leaned forward.

"What is wrong with this passage?" he asked. "I do not speak of the deed of selling the Son of God to the authorities. This is not a question of betrayal that I am proposing. What is wrong with this passage is that credit is not given where credit is due!"

The family began to get uncomfortable as Radix boomed from the pulpit. They stood from their seats and began to walk out.

"I am not finished!" Radix called forth.

The father turned and said, "We don't care if you are finished. We have to leave."

"So, you don't care?" Radix said as he knocked down the Easter candle. He grabbed the gold candle stand, snapped it in half to make two sharp jagged lances, and said, "Maybe, you will care about this."

He hurled one half of the candle stand at the father, spearing him like a fish — right through his throat. The man dropped dead on the floor, his wife and child covered in his very blood. The mother screamed and grabbed her son. She tried to make it through the doors but Radix hurled the other lance, spearing her through the back of her neck. The boy stood alone not knowing what to do. Both of his parents were dead; their warm red blood coated his body.

Nathan woke from his sleep with a tingling sensation. It was Radix. The ring was letting him know that evil was nearby. The sensation grew stronger as he rolled out of bed. Radix was very close, but where? Too anxious about his enemy's whereabouts, Nathan did not bother to wake his sister or Lyles from their sleep. Instead, he readied himself and rushed out the front door of the convent. He stopped and focused, letting the power of the ring guide him. Radix was inside the church; he knew this. So, he ran across the street and threw the doors open. Nathan sprang through the second set of double doors in the foyer and tackled Radix, saving the young boy from instant death. Radix's body crashed into one of the pews, and Nathan got up. He was in time to save the boy, but not his parents.

"Leave!" Nathan begged the boy. "Go now, before he does the same to you!"

"I don't care — I'm not leaving!" the boy yelled back.

Seeing that Nathan was distracted, Radix got up and struck Nathan on the jaw. He went to hit the hero again with a right, but Nathan caught his fist.

"I will not fight you here. Enough blood was spilled on this holy ground today. Let's go have this fight somewhere else," he said to Radix as he still held the evil man's right fist.

"What do you think this is, a movie? We fight where we stand. I don't care how holy the ground is," Radix retorted as he struck Nathan with a left that knocked him through both sets of doors, demolishing them.

Nathan rolled down the stone steps and crashed into the pavement below. If it were not for the ring on his finger, Nathan would have been killed on impact. Forgetting about the boy, Radix made his way over the splinters left where the doors once stood. Looking down at Nathan, who was spitting up blood on the concrete pavement below, Radix laughed heartily.

"Come down here and fight me, you monster. I am not through yet!" Nathan called to Radix.

"Very well, if I must," Radix replied as he began to make his way down the steps.

All of a sudden, the dark man fell to the ground; he was skewered from behind, blood shot from his belly. In an act of vengeance, the boy used the very same weapon that was used to murder his mother to impale the one responsible for her death. Nathan staggered to his feet, and kicked the fiend in the face. The boy walked back into the church and knelt down next to his parents' dead bodies, angry at all that took place that day. Quickly, Radix pulled the candlestand from his back and stabbed

Nathan in the shoulder. Screams of pain shot from Nathan's mouth as Radix, still holding his golden weapon, pinned him up against the black iron fence behind him. Nathan grabbed the candlestand and kicked Radix in the gut, knocking him into the fence opposite them. The pain was sharp as he pulled the spear from his shoulder. Radix had healed from his own wound, but Nathan did not have such powers, his wound was exposed and fresh. Taking advantage of the situation, Radix rammed him into the fence and began to pummel him to the floor.

Inside the convent, Lyles could hear the commotion outside. He got out of bed, still dressed in his clothes from the previous night, and scampered out of his room. In the hallway he bumped into Esmeralda, who was also still wearing what she wore last night, and Sister Elizabeth who threw on her habit and a robe. They too had been awakened by the commotion coming from outside. The three hurried out the front door of the convent to witness Nathan being severely beaten. Lyles dashed across the street to help his new friend. Radix turned to greet him with a kick to the chest. A couple of ribs were broken, as Lyles slammed onto the pavement. He could not move.

"Now it is time for me to finish the two of you. But first let me get this ring off your finger. Can't take any chances," Radix explained as he grabbed Nathan's right hand and began to pull off the Ring of Solomon.

At that very moment the medal around Lyles' neck began to glow, and the sun began to beam down brighter.

"What is going on?" Radix marveled as he looked up at the sky squinting from the brightness.

In a beam of light the Archangel Michael appeared and drew his sword on Radix.

"Let go of that ring, creature of darkness," Michael dictated.

"No!" Radix defied as he snatched the ring from Nathan's hand.

Before Radix could think, Michael sliced off the hand that was holding the ring. The wound stung more than most, for the sword that struck the evil man was forged in Heaven.

"You have no business here. My affairs are none of your concern. You cannot just meddle wherever you see fit. Does not your God have to decree you to interfere with the lives of men? Yet you always seem to do as you please, never being punished for striking your sword where it is not needed," Radix spoke.

"Things are different this time. That man over there," Michael said as he pointed to Lyles with his sword. "He is under my protection. As long as he is in danger it is my duty to do whatever it takes to keep him safe. And you are putting him in danger."

"Very well, you can have him. All I really want is this guy over here," Radix settled, speaking of Nathan.

"It is not that easy, Radix. Not this time," Michael spoke again as his sword fired up. "Back away from him and leave."

"You cannot order me around, and you cannot pry into my affairs!"

"I can, and I will!"

The princely archangel grabbed the dark shadow of a man and disappeared in a gleam of light. Esmeralda and Sister Elizabeth dashed across the street as soon as they saw it was safe. They were not the only audience. Just now they realized that people were standing on their porches and lawns, watching all that took place. People in cars and pedestrians stopped and gawked at the broken church doors and the two men who lay on the ground beaten half to death. No one knew what to believe. Most of them pretended that they saw nothing. But a couple of these people knew that they witnessed something supernatural, something on a higher level than their mundane everyday lives. The only thing that all of the spectators shared was that they decided to keep their mouths closed on this affair. Who would believe them if they spoke of what they saw?

Esmeralda knelt on the pavement and held her brother. Covered in his blood, she ripped off a piece of his shirt and wrapped up the wound on his shoulder. Nathan was thankfully still alive; she could hear him breathing.

"The ring," Nathan wheezed. "Get me the ring."

Cautiously, Esmeralda pried the ring from Radix's severed hand. She was waiting for it to jump up and grab her. Instead the hand turned to dust and blew away in the wind. Relieved, she placed the ring on her brother's finger. Nathan's body tingled as he began to feel life coming back into him. The ring had some powers of rejuvenation and revitalization of energy, though it was not made to completely heal the body, nor could it prevent its wearer from dying. But it was helpful and made Nathan strong enough to now be able to stand. The problem that remained was that, as strong as the ring made its wearer, Radix was still stronger; and he had dealt with many people who had adorned themselves with the Ring of Solomon in the past. In fact the evil mercenary killed many while they still possessed the ring, though he made sure to deal with the ones who had survived after the ring was no longer in their hands. The fact was simply that none were able to beat Radix, no matter how powerful they had become. He knew the ring's powers, as well as its limitations. Nathan did not know enough of the ring to tap into its full potential, nor was he able to tap into his own. There was a lot to be learned, both of himself and the ring. Unfortunately, there was not a lot the time. Now on his feet, Nathan leaned on Esmeralda for support as she walked with him. Sister Elizabeth helped Lyles to stand. He hunched over holding his broken ribs. Both men needed medical attention. Neither could afford to receive it. They did not have time to deal with cops but the police would surely be on their way to the church. The band of four scurried across the street as fast as they could. Sister Elizabeth led them to a garage in the back of the convent. She opened the door to reveal a silver minivan.

"Please take it," she said as she held the keys out to Esmeralda.

"Are you sure, sister?" Esmeralda asked.

"You don't have time to argue, my dear. Just take it!" Sister Elizabeth demanded.

"Ok," She accepted.

"Go to this place," the nun said as she handed Esmeralda a piece of paper. "They will help you with your pregnancy and give your brother and his friend the medical attention they need. The directions are right there. It shouldn't be hard to find. Good luck and God bless."

"Thank you for everything," Esmeralda said in reply as the two hugged one last time.

Esmeralda helped Nathan into the back and closed the door. She proceeded to take the driver's seat and started the engine as Lyles slowly made his way into the passenger seat. Sister Elizabeth watched them drive off just as three police cars arrived at the scene. She did not know how to explain what had just happened. Even worse, she did not know how to tell her fellow sisters that she had given away the minivan. The good nun signed herself as she prepared to fib. God would forgive her for her lies this time, for no one was ready to hear the truth of what took place. In a timely fashion, Sister Elizabeth walked across the street to greet the officers. They were baffled by all that they saw. The pastor of the parish came out from the rectory to see what all the uproar was about. The pleasantly round priest had slept through everything and was staggered by the chaos. Immediately, he approached Sister Elizabeth, who was being interrogated by a female officer.

"Sister Elizabeth, what happened here?" The pastor asked.

"That's exactly what I was just trying to find out myself," the policewoman remarked.

"I just finished telling this sweet young lady that I don't know anything. I woke up hearing a lot of clamor outside to find this when I got here. Look, I'm still in my robe," the not-so-honest sister told the trusting pastor.

"Well, if she says she saw nothing, she saw nothing," he reiterated, supporting his friend and colleague.

Four officers walked past the rubble where the doors once stood to find the father and mother that Radix had killed earlier. Both lay in a pool of blood, the father still with the golden lance in his throat. The boy was nowhere to be found. He had run away during Nathan's fight with Radix and was long gone. One of the officers called forensics to come down and look at the bodies, while another walked up to where the altar had previously stood. He reached into the rubble to touch some fine powder that was once solid marble, not knowing how this had happened. The entire case was piled with confusion, and no one who witnessed it would ever speak a word. Outside, more police vehicles pulled up to the church, followed by an ambulance and a couple of news vans. The church grounds had been turned into a circus as crowds gathered around.

# Part II

## Fire and Ice

The freezing wind blew hard against Radix's face, showering him with snow and ice. He had grown back the hand that he had lost at the church, and he was now thousands of miles from his intended victim. Michael had teleported the two halfway around the world to the southern-most continent of Antarctica. In royal fashion, the archangel stood; his posture was straight, and his chin was in the air. Radix was enraged for being taken away from his kill.

"There is no escape for you, Radix, for I will make it so," Michael ruled.

"You have tried to meddle in my affairs too often. My time is precious, and I will make sure that I have the time I need to do what I must. But I do have a little time to play," Radix said with a dark smile tracing his lips. "You cannot hold me here, for your powers have limits on this Earth. This is not your world. But I am of this world, and the one who sent me has more control over this planet than your God ever has."

Radix dropped his arms as his dark shadow stretched out over the frosty terrain. The shadow rooted into the ground and turned the white scenery black. Clouds moved in from all around, and the violent wind grew angrier. The mountains shook, and the icy ground before Radix's feet split wide open. From the crevice sprouted the arm of a blue snow-goblin, heavily muscled and wielding a sword of black metal. The blade was sharper than any blade forged by man, for it was forged beyond man's existence.

"The Blackblade," Radix laughed, "forged in darkness to bring chaos to the world. A weapon worthy to fell an angel."

Radix grabbed the Blackblade, and the goblin's arm receded back into the ground. The shadow that he had cast over the terrain grew blacker as did his entire person. The blade that he wielded was powerful. He had only used it once before for it was not an easy weapon to control. In fact, the Blackblade has more control over the one who wields it than the wielder has over the blade.

Whoever holds it for too long will become a slave to it, until the holder is no more. The sword can drain its possessor completely for it is tapped into the pure essence of evil.

Michael knew well of this blade for he had fought against it the last time Radix had called it forth, and times before that as well; including the time Satan first wielded the blade during the Rebellion. His sword could match the Blackblade and has. It was forged in the light of God and was made of the strongest strand of Angelmetal, a spiritual metal only found and forged in Heaven. Fire sparked from Michael's sword as his entire essence was engulfed in the white flames of the Holy Spirit. He was ready to dispel the darkness that Radix had brought to both this place and to the rest of the Earth. The light that beamed from the glorious archangel clashed with the darkness that spread from Radix's growing shadow. The ground quaked; the mountains split in half; and lightning poured down with snow, sleet, and hail. The preparation was now complete, and the two beings charged into battle. Swords met in an earth-shattering collision as both parties jockeyed for position.

"The blade gives me power to match yours," Radix boasted.

"The power it gives you is borrowed. My power was granted to me from the time of my creation. If you borrow enough power from the blade's source, you will only destroy yourself for you are not a vessel meant to hold such power. You may be immortal, but you are still a man. That very power you brag of will only lead to your demise," Michael contested.

"Say what you will, but this time I will be the victor, not you. The darkness inside my body has grown since the last time I used this sword. My control is far more advanced, as is my skill. I will strike you down and send you to the second death; and when I am done with you, I will kill Nathaniel Salvatore."

"Stop talking and fight!" Michael ordered as raging fire spewed from his eyes, knocking Radix to the ground.

The exchange of words had come to an end. Radix, now up from his fall, held his blade firmly in his hands and ferociously swung at his adversary. With a steady hand, Michael blocked Radix. Both blades sparked as they struck repeatedly, lighting up the dark and snowy Antarctica sky. Radix was matching Michael swing for swing, step for step; but the archangel was allowing this to happen. He was toying with Radix to buy as much time as he could. Knowing Radix's massive ego, the wise archangel knew that Radix would not pass up a test of strength in battle. Therefore, while the two tussled in the southernmost hemisphere, Nathan was safe and alive.

The evil fiend was not completely oblivious to the angel's game. He too was holding back. He was smart enough not to give the sword too much control. A slave to the Devil, Radix already was; he did not want to be slave to the sword as well. The battle was growing thick as the two combatants sliced the air left and right, missing their targets only to hit steel every now and then. Cleverly, Michael picked up the pace and struck swifter and surer at the sinister Radix, forcing him to do the same. Indeed Radix had many powers, but an angel did not serve the same material laws as flesh; and Radix, as immortal as he was, was still flesh. Once more the evil man swung. His dark sword passed through Michael who vanished and instantaneously appeared behind Radix, sending him crashing into a distant mountain with a kick to the spine. Bones cracked as Radix rolled down the mountainside and struck the ground hard. He was very angry. Michael was making a fool of him, and he did not like being made a fool of.

In a gallant manner, Michael hovered above the fallen Radix and said, "You have no chance. You are pathetic. Can you not see when you are beaten, or must I continue trouncing you?"

"You said to stop talking and to fight. So, practice what you preach and shut up!" Radix shouted back as he flung an ice boulder at the high-class angel.

The large chunk of ice became nothing more than snowflakes on Michael's breastplate. Incensed, Radix clenched the Blackblade and charged up his body. The sword's dark energy flowed around him as he began to chant a demonic verse. The dark power of the sword was beginning to take effect. Radix was becoming stronger but with a heavy price. Demonic voices called out to him from the depths of the great Abyss, granting him more and more power. Radix's shoulder blades broke through his skin and began to grow outward. The bones transformed into large black feathery wings like those of a raven. He looked up at the avenging angel floating above him. The gap was closing. Like Michael, Radix could now fly; and fly he did with his sword aimed straight for Michael's heart. If the Blackblade would pierce the heart of the angel, he would surely be hurled into the second death — a place where those things of a spiritual nature go when they have been drained of their spiritual energy. A shield, glowing with the same fire as Michael's sword, appeared in the left hand of the tactful angel and blocked Radix's sword from striking his heart.

"You cannot beat me, Radix," Michael assured the dark man. "My knowledge of warfare far exceeds yours for I was there from the first war. Your battles have been many, but mine have been more."

"Talk all you want; but no matter what you do to me, I will heal. I will not die. You can go to the dark place, to the second death. You can lose."

"Don't be so smug. You can lose as well. If you do not kill the man known as Nathaniel Salvatore, you will fail your mission. Your body will cease to live, and your soul will be thrown into the fires of Hell — just like your master, when he tried to conquer Heaven."

"I have no master!" Radix cried out as he attacked the angel again and again, only to be blocked each time by Michael's shield.

"You *do* have a master," the angel insisted. "Satan has controlled you from day one. But if you are not careful, that sword will control you as well."

"You do not know of what you speak."

"I know weakness when I see it," Michael said as he nicked Radix on the cheek with his fiery sword.

Blood dripped down from Radix's face, melting the ice below. He was enraged at being caught off guard and swung back at the angel with fury. The fight ensued in the sky as the warriors battled for days. Michael's plan was working, Radix was so engaged in the fight that he was losing the precious time that he needed to complete his evil mission. But the darkness grew inside of Radix as the days dragged on, and he finally began to fall slave to blade.

"You have only begun to see the dark power of my sword. How about I let you feel what it can really do," Radix haughtily said, his dark chi increasing as the blade siphoned its power into his body.

A blast of dark energy sent Michael flying backward. The Blackblade was now in full control of Radix, binding him to its will. Radix's skin turned as black as his soulless eyes, and the angel's light was now dimmed by the surrounding darkness. Michael had never felt such evil as he did now. The voices called from all around, whispering to the valiant angel. They called for him to fall, to take the throne of Heaven — a seat that was rightfully his. The temptation engulfed the chief of the heavenly host. His light was being swallowed as he felt what Lucifer felt that time long ago. Paralyzed by the tempting urges that soared through his soul, Michael remained still. Seeing this, Radix tackled him into the rocky mountainside. The two bored through mountain after mountain until Radix slammed Michael into the icy ground. The voices were still singing lies in Michael's head, driving him mad. By order of his new master, Radix grabbed the Blackblade with both hands. He raised the stygian sword to the sky and aimed it at the defenseless angel's heart. The blade would soon vanquish the angel and then devour its wielder. Fortunately, for the entranced angel, he was not as weak as the sword believed him to be. The light that his heart reflected was too pure, as was his service to the Lord. Unlike Lucifer, Michael would not fall so easily. The Blackblade's scheme was foiled as Radix received the sharp end of Michael's fiery sword through his throat. He choked on his own blood as it filled his lungs and sprayed the ice and snow. The flames of the sword seared Radix's flesh. Fully conscious, the angel used his heel to push the dark mercenary from his blade onto the snow-covered terrain. Before Radix could heal his wound, Michael sliced off his right hand, which held the sword. The Blackblade spun through the air and stuck itself into the snowy ground. The evil sword opened a dark vortex and was sucked inside. The vortex closed, and Radix was no longer possessed by the power of the Blackblade. The original pale complexion of his skin was restored. Immediately, the triumphant angel grabbed Radix by his dark locks and decapitated him. Using absolute precision the angel continued by mincing the remains of Radix's body. He then disintegrated the tiny pieces with the flame of his sword. Michael now stood on the snow-covered ground holding Radix's head, which showed no signs of consciousness. Taking the head of his fallen enemy, Michael flew to the top of an icy mountain where he found a small dead olive tree shivering in the cold wind. On that tree the angel stuck Radix's head and lit it on fire.

Looking down he said, "Heal from that," and then ascended into Heaven.

# CHAPTER XI
## THE CALM BEFORE THE STORM

The roads were long and winding. The sun shone brightly above, giving hope to those who had none. It was almost noon of the same day that Esmeralda, Nathan, and Lyles left the convent. Though the three crusaders were still awestruck by the appearance of the archangel and wondered where he had taken Radix, they were more concerned about the urgent matters of Nathan and Lyles' health. The two had taken quite a beating at the hands of Radix and had injuries that needed immediate attention. Hurrying to find help, Esmeralda drove diligently through the wooded area of northern Westchester until she came to the address that was shown on the paper that Sister Elizabeth gave her. It was an out of the way Catholic retreat facility that was run by a small group of Salesian Sisters who called themselves the Sisters of Saving Grace. The facility resembled a large cottage with a wooden cross hanging above the door. The cottage was surrounded by acres of forest and beautiful green grass. Just as the tired Esmeralda pulled into the gravel driveway, two of the sisters walked out from the front door to greet their new guests. The nun on the left was in her mid-thirties and pleasantly plump. Her round rosy cheeks hugged her smile. The other nun, to the right, was in her fifties and well conditioned for her age. She did not seem as cheerful, but she had a nice demeanor all the same.

Still traumatized from the morning's events, Esmeralda jumped out of the van and ran to the younger more cheerful sister, crying, "Please, you have to help us. My brother and his friend are badly wounded and need immediate medical attention."

"You must be Sister Elizabeth's friends. She told us you were coming. I'm Sister Suzanne. Welcome to our home," the joyful sister said. "Just go inside with Sister Catherine and we will have someone take care of your brother and his friend."

"Thank you, sister," Esmeralda said and walked over to the older nun. She began to tell her story as they entered building.

Sister Suzanne walked over to the van, still with a smile on her face. That smile disappeared once she opened the back door. Nathan was lying on a seat full of blood, and Lyle's broken ribs were sticking out of his side from under his skin. Without hesitation she bolted inside to get help. Four more sisters wearing nursing gowns came out with two stretchers, one for each man. Quickly, they hoisted the injured heroes onto the stretchers and wheeled them into the cottage. The inside of the cottage looked even bigger than it did outside, and resembled a hospital more than a house. Nathan and Lyles were rushed into what seemed to be an operating room. Two sisters walked in, both dressed in surgical attire, and began to give medical attention to the battered men. Outside the operating room, Esmeralda sat with Sister Catherine in a small living room. Together they prayed, hoping that Nathan and Lyles would be okay.

# Part I

## Time to Heal Wounds

Hours felt like days to Esmeralda as she waited, thinking the absolute worst. Her fears climaxed when one of the sisters who operated on Nathan and Lyles walked into the living room.

"Esmeralda Salvatore, I'm Sister Thomastina," the sister said.

"Hi, sister. Is everything okay?" Esmeralda responded.

"Yes. Don't be so nervous," Sister Thomastina lovingly said as she put out her hand to hold Esmeralda's. "Your brother and Mr. Washington are going to be just fine."

"Oh, thank you, Lord!" Esmeralda said as she looked up to heaven; her fear now subsided.

"It may take a couple of months for them to be back at one hundred percent, because of some severe broken bones and internal injuries, but they are stable and resting now. If you want, you can come inside and see them."

"Yes, I would like to very much, sister."

"Just follow me."

Happily, Esmeralda followed Sister Thomastina. They walked into the room that Nathan and Lyles were moved to after their operations. With the recent deaths of her parents, Esmeralda was relieved that her brother, was still alive. Nathan and Lyles were lying in hospital beds, and were now clothed in hospital gowns. Next to both of them were a couple of wooden dressers with flowers on each. A large picture window allowed light to flood in from the sun, which was now starting to set into the horizon.

"We normally remove all jewelry from the patients when operating, but I could not get your brother's ring off. It seemed to be stuck. So I left it on," Sister Thomastina explained to Esmeralda. "As for his friend, we took off his St. Michael pendant. It's sitting on the dresser next to his bed. I will leave you alone with them now. You can stay as long as you like."

"Thank you, sister."

An hour passed by and Esmeralda still stood in the same place that she did when she first entered the room. She did not want to disturb her brother or Lyles, only watch over them so she could know they were safe.

"Ezzie," Nathan said as he woke up, looking at his sister standing in the moonlight in front of the window. "Am I alive?"

"Yes, you are, and thank God for that," she replied, running to her brother and throwing her arms around him.

"How's Lyles?"

"He's actually in better shape than you. He only broke a couple of ribs and had some internal bleeding," Esmeralda confirmed. "You are lucky. If you didn't have that ring, you would have been killed."

"I know."

Some days went by, and Nathan and Lyles were finally out of their beds; even though their wounds still needed some more time to heal. The Sisters of Saving Grace were more than hospitable during their visit and offered to let Esmeralda stay for the duration of her pregnancy. This order of nuns was not any ordinary order; they dealt with those matters of great supernatural impact, and that is why they were located in such a secluded area. The facility was there for those who needed a place to hide and recover from bouts with the unnaturally evil, and the sisters who resided there were prepared for any circumstance to come their way. They already knew who Nathan was and why he was there, even before he set foot in the door. The sisters also knew that Esmeralda was carrying a very powerful child inside her and would be a target for great evil as a result. Therefore, they felt that she should stay with them, where she could receive the proper care and protection. But not even the Sisters of Saving Grace could protect her from *all* evil. A cross on the door and prayers would not scare away Radix, and that is why Nathan had to leave. He could not have Radix drawn to him and consequently drawn to his sister. The only problem was that he did not know where to go. Then a thought came to him. With his sister safely hidden, maybe he should go far away. Lyles agreed, and the two readied themselves for a trip back to Jordan. The desert was a much more fitting battleground and it would be safer for everyone else, especially Esmeralda and her unborn child.

The sisters were kind enough to make the traveling arrangements for the two heroes, and Nathan called Father Reilly to tell him the news and arrange for a pickup at the Jordan airport. Nathan told the priest of all that had taken place thus far, and of Lyles' great help. Both men were very happy to hear the other's voice, like a father and son who had not spoken to each other in years, though they had only been apart for a short time.

A week passed and it was time to leave for Jordan, but before the two left on their journey Lyles gave Esmeralda a present — his St. Michael medal. He felt that it was much more important that the great angel protect Esmeralda and her child. Lyles could sense that the baby she was carrying was very special and knew that it must live. As long as Esmeralda wore the pendant, no danger would come to her, for Michael — the Archangel and head of God's army — would fly down to her aid, just as he did for Mr. Reynolds and even for Lyles himself. With the passing of the medal, Nathan and Lyles said their good-byes and were off to Jordan. Shortly after their departure Sister Suzanne found an envelope that said "Thank You" on it. Inside was the money that Father Reilly had given to Nathan. He felt that he owed the Sisters of Saving Grace some gratitude for all that they had done for him, his sister, and Lyles. He would not need the money where he was going and he felt it was the least he could do, though he wished he could do much more. The modest man that he was, Nathan would never realize that he was indeed doing them — and all people who lived on the Earth — a great service by putting his life at stake against the evil destroyer of lives, Radix.

Back from his vicious battle with Radix, Michael entered the Hall of Records to see Azrael.

"That should take care of that cretin for now," Michael said.

"He still lives. He is not defeated yet," Azrael responded.

"It will take him at least a few months to heal, figuring that the ice and snow have already caused his ashes to freeze. This will give Nathaniel time to regroup and figure out his next steps."

"Do you think he can win?"

"I know he can. His faith is strong. Plus that boy has good strategy. He has moved into the desert. Your other half has already been acquainted with our young hero. Maybe he could lend a hand to Nathaniel, while he is out there."

"I'm sure Ravenblade will put his hand into the battle, if it is fought on the desert sand. His dislike for Radix is even greater than his dislike for me."

"Good, I was counting on that."

"But what about his sister and that which she carries in her womb?"

"Do not worry about her. She is wearing my medal. It is my duty to protect her at all costs. And as Radix has learned, as well as countless others, I perform my duties well."


The plane safely landed in Amman airport. It had not been too long ago that Nathan flew out of this very airport. Father Reilly had arranged a ride for Nathan and Lyles to his home. Nathan looked around the airport, and sure enough the same man who drove him there that short time ago was there now waiting to take him back. The drive was long, but eventually Nathan and Lyles were at Father Reilly's church. They walked around the back to the priest's living quarters. Before Nathan could knock, the door swung open. Father Reilly came out, dropped his cane, and threw his arms tightly around Nathan.

"Well, oh well, look who has come back, and so soon. I see you brought your friend with you," the priest said, as he gave Nathan some room to breathe.

Nathan picked up Father Reilly's cane and gave it to him.

"Thank you, my son. I guess, I got a little carried away there," Father Reilly pardoned himself, then turned to Lyles and shook his hand. "I heard a lot about you, son. Nathan told me that you have been a great help. God will bless you indeed."

"I can't say I've done much of anything," Lyles replied.

"Poppy-cock. Anyone who faces Radix is brave and surely deserves a hero's praise," the priest assured him.

"Well, thank you, then," Lyles said, accepting the gratitude.

Father Reilly finished his salutations and invited the men in. The three sat and began to chat. The good priest asked both men to feel at home. Lyles tried to feel comfortable, but he still felt a little out of place. He had never been so far away from home. Every day seemed more trying and bizarre than the one before, as the young man tried to grasp the last bits of reality that he could.

"Father, I don't know what else to do," Nathan said, "I have fought Radix and lost. If I continue to take the fight to him, I will fail; and the whole mission will be thrown away. His evil will continue on, for century upon century. There has to be another way to stop him."

Father Reilly took a deep breath and let out a sigh. He shook his head and then preached, "Nathan, you and your friend have fought hard, but the fight has only begun. You cannot throw in the towel now. You can and will succeed, if you believe that you can. Remember, you are not alone. God is with you, and His power is true power. You must go back to the desert, and find Ravenblade. Yes, I know of him. He will train you how to harness the power of the Spirit. The ring will help you to amplify this power to aid you greatly in your battle. You, too, Lyles, must learn these things, as you are just as important as young Nathan. The Lord is with you as well, and His Spirit flows within you. Both of you have pleased the Highest of all Powers, and your names will be with those great heroes of days past and days yet to come. You will be refined like gold one day to shine for all the nations to see. God be with you and bless you in your fight."

It was getting late, and all three men were tired. The gracious father allowed the men to stay there that night, but advised them to leave as soon as the sun rose over the horizon. When the sun came up the next morning, they were gone, just as the priest had instructed. All that they carried were some rations and water that the generous father had given to them. Lyles had heard Nathan talk of the desert heat, but the strong midday sun was far beyond what he had conceived. The two traveled through the desert sand, keeping a mindful eye for predators. Nathan knew well of the evils found in this desert, for he had faced many during his forty-day stay. Unfortunately for Lyles, he had not known of what crept in the desert sand; but by the end of his journey he would know plenty. The wind howled from all around, carrying sand with its song. The sand created a haze, blocking Nathan and Lyles' vision. They remained still, unable to see where to go. A few moments passed, and then the wind just stopped. Their sights were clear, and the sun beamed down on them.

"So, you have returned," a voice said from behind.

The two friends turned. Nathan recognized the man. It was Ravenblade. He stood straight, his sword extended toward Lyles.

"And who is he?" Ravenblade asked.

"This is Lyles Washington. He is aiding me in my fight against Radix," Nathan responded.

"And how is this? He is but a man. He will do you no good and just be a liability. I say, we kill him now and end our troubles."

"No!" Nathan exclaimed. "I need him, for he is just as much a part of this as I am. And since when have you and I become *we* anyway? I don't remember seeing your name on Radix's hit list."

"Always with the jokes. If I didn't want to destroy Radix so badly, I would kill you for your sarcasm," Ravenblade said with his sword up against Nathan's throat. "I know why you are here. You need me to train you. Radix is out of commission thanks to that sap Michael. Not like I couldn't have done the same thing. But just as all who have fought Radix, Michael did not succeed in killing him. Radix is rejuvenating as we speak, and he will return. And when he does, he will bring a war unlike any you could imagine. Your friend can live for now, but only until Radix is dealt with. We will see what kind of help he is. Just pray he is not your downfall."

"Hey, don't I have a say in any of this?" Lyles objected.

"No!" shouted Ravenblade. "Let's go. There is much to learn."

There *was* much to learn, and it would be more difficult than the young heroes had perceived — especially with the injuries they still had, courtesy of Radix. The skillful Ravenblade started with some simple self-defense techniques. As the two progressed, he moved onto weapons, emphasizing mostly on swordsmanship. Ravenblade was a master at dueling with bladed weapons; it was his passion. Nathan had a slight advantage in the beginning, given his training as a boxer. He already knew basic punches and defense maneuvers. Yet Lyles caught on quickly. Soon enough, both men were ready for the real training — learning how to tap into the Spirit to increase their power, strength, speed, stamina, durability, and skill. This was a chance for these men to show their true potentials. Not just anyone could learn what Ravenblade was about to bestow upon Nathan and Lyles. Tapping into raw spiritual power would take great faith, focus, and determination. Ravenblade only hoped that they were ready.

Lyles was still not used to the cool desert nights, and this particular night was cooler than most. Nathan and he sat by a fire eating some of the rations that their friend Father Reilly had given them. Ravenblade did not need to sit by the fire to keep warm, nor did he need to eat the food that they were devouring. Training was making the two men very hungry. The mysterious immortal laughed at their human weaknesses. To him it seemed a joke that these men were chosen to help save the world. He could take these two amateurs out in no time. How was Radix not able to kill them yet? There was something he was missing.

The fire roared. Nathan and Lyles grew weary. Their doubtful instructor walked along the sand and watched the stars, leaving them alone as they fell fast asleep. Just then, a pair of eyes caught a glimpse of Nathan and Lyles sleeping. Watching the men as if watching chickens roast, the creature began to salivate. It had not eaten in days, and it desired a bite of fresh meat. Whispering came from the creature's lips and entered Nathan and Lyles' dreams. The words sounded familiar to Nathan but were abstract to Lyles.

No longer whispering, the creature shouted, " Godchild!" and pounced onto Nathan, waking him from his deep sleep.

It tried to take a bite out of Nathan's arm but thanks to his recent training, he was able to throw the creature off of him. Lyles was awakened by the noise and rushed to help Nathan battle the creature. The light of the fire gave some shape to their adversary. Nathan recognized the creature. It was a Djinni, and it was ready to strike again. Now, the brave men were ready. Nathan cautiously moved toward the Djinni, keeping his guard up. The fire gave off enough light for the creature to notice the ring on Nathan's right hand. The pitiful demon fell to his knees and bowed.

"Please, forgive me, I did not realize you were master. Obey you, I will," the Djinni humbly stated.

"I don't understand. Why are you calling me master?" Nathan said, bewildered.

"The ring you bear, obey you I must. Just as all Djinn have for all who have bore that very ring. Your service, I am in. My apologies, I implore."

"Stop groveling and stand," Nathan insisted. "I don't care what you do, as long as you leave me and my friend alone."

"No, that I cannot do. Your servant, I am. With you, I must go, wherever you go," the Djinni implored.

"Okay, but I don't want a servant. I want some sleep."

"Then sleep. Guard you, I will."

"And you promise not to eat me or my friend?"

"Promise you, I do."

The Ring of Solomon was a very good judge of character. The mystical band revealed to Nathan that the somewhat evil spirit was being honest, so Lyles and he decided to go back to sleep. Time moved slowly that night as the two men rested under the guard of Nathan's new servant. Ravenblade was now returning from his walk. He sensed the presence of an unclean spirit at the camp. As he drew near, he caught a glimpse of the foul Djinni and readied his sword for attack. With unparalleled stealth the immortal leaped at the creature, swinging his sword with intent to kill. Luckily for the Djinni, it smelled the blood of its attacker and vanished in a flash of smokeless fire just before the blade could take its head. The Djinn were odd creatures and could do many amazing things, such as vanish at will. But this Djinni did not go far; it had a master to serve now; and it had nowhere else to go. Ravenblade watched as oddly shaped footprints appeared all over the sand.

The strange Djinni was invisible and running amok on the campsite, screaming for mercy, "Please, spare me! Only wanting to serve the master. Please, let me live."

The poor creature begged some more as Ravenblade swung his sword repeatedly wherever the footprints appeared. Soon enough, Nathan and Lyles were awakened from their sleep by the raspy cries of the Djinni.

"Stop!" Nathan screamed. "What is going on here?"

"A vile Djinni has snuck onto our camp, probably looking to make a meal out of you and your friend. Not that I normally would care, but I need you alive right now. So, I figured that I'd kill the little pest," Ravenblade explained and then began to look around for the creature again.

"You can put your sword away," Nathan commanded. "The Djinni is no threat to us. Since I wear the Ring of Solomon, his service is indebted to me. So, relax."

"That's right — Solomon's Ring. Solomon used the Djinn to help him build his palace, among other things. What a crafty man, he was. I, unlike Solomon, have no need for Djinn. They are nothing more than vermin. So, I will kill this one anyway."

"Why must you kill everything?"

"It's what I do. Unless you have forgotten, I am not one of the good guys." The immortal paused and then questioned, "But why must you make so many friends?"

"It's better to make friends than enemies. You don't have to watch over your shoulder as much."

"You do, if you have untrustworthy friends."

"Well, the only one that fits that description here is *you*."

"Fine, then train yourself, fool. I will deal with Radix in my own way," the now offended dark warrior said and walked off.

Nathan did not care. He just sat down by the fire to think. Lyles came over and sat next to him. The two remained silent. The only noise that could be heard was the cool night breeze blowing through the desert sand. A set of footprints walked over to Nathan and materialized back into the strange little creature that was now bound to him.

"Master, problems I did not mean to cause you. Please, for these mishaps, forgive me," the Djinni sputtered.

"Don't worry about it. And stop calling me master. I hate that. I am no more your master than any man. You are free to live your own life. Please call me Nathan."

"Yes, master Nathan."

"Forget it," Nathan said and shook his head with Lyles laughing behind him. "Do you have a name?"

"No, we Djinn have no names. Unlike humans, we have no use of labels. Names are meaningless, family is important. All Djinn are tied together. Stand out, we need not."

"Well, how about we give you a name." Lyles interjected. "I think the name Puck suits you, like in Shakespeare."

"Not sure, I am. Never had a name before. But no longer a Djinni, I am. Maybe a name, I need. Yes, like it, indeed. Call me Puck."

Night passed, and the sun replaced the moon in the sky. The fire was no longer burning as the light of the sun hit Nathan's eyes, waking him from his rest. Lyles opened his eyes as well. Both men were greeted by the image of the dark and eerie Ravenblade, who threw down two swords — one for each man.

"Come. We have much training to do," the grumpy instructor commanded.

"But I thought you said last night—" Lyles started.

"Forget last night. Let's go. And tell your little vermin friend to come along."

Puck, who was invisible once again in fear that Ravenblade would cut him to pieces, now slowly appeared and followed as the motley crew walked through the desert ready to start another training session. From the heavens Azrael watched the foursome, and was amazed at the strangely formed group.

"It seems that Raven is actually developing a conscience. My other half and I are finally starting to balance out. But what could this mean for the future?" Azrael contemplated.

Azrael continued to watch as days turned into weeks, which turned into months. The training got more and more intense, and the group of four grew closer together. Even though the once wicked and impervious immortal would not admit to it, Ravenblade was beginning to enjoy his new company of friends; and his black heart was slowly becoming lighter as time passed.

Calm had restored to the city of New York, or at least as close to calm as the city was before Radix began to sow his evil seed. The search for the mysterious supernatural killer had now slowed down to a whisper as no more bodies turned up. The police figured that the killer was finally dead or had moved on by now. The men in blue had returned to there normal routine. Those agents of the law that the sinister beast slew were still alive in the hearts of their families and their fellow officers, especially Detective Johnson. There are many good cops, but none were better than he. The events that took place will never be forgotten, though most will deny that they ever occurred. The truth is always hidden behind stories that are much easier to swallow. Strange phenomena are always concealed from the public eye. Once again, this was the case. It was not important if there was danger. The only important thing was that the people of New York City and the rest of the world felt safe. Their safety was produced from lies. But the sky over the world grew dark as dawn approached. The evil that is Radix had not been defeated yet. Even if his reign was brought to an end, evil itself would still flourish. As long as there is a balance, with good there will always be evil.

# Part II

## The Rising of the Storm

The doors to Satan's private chamber opened, and in came one of his subjects. The lowly demon covered his face out of reverence and made his way toward the Dark Prince's throne.

"Come forward and tell me of your news, Catal," Satan replied as he stooped in his seat, looking down at the demon.

Catal was thankful for his lord's hospitality and slowly ascended the steps that sat before Satan. He stopped and genuflected where the light from the stained glass window hit. The image of the Fall danced as the insignificant Catal looked up at his master reverently.

"Thank you, my lord, for gracing me with the ability to speak with you, and—"

"Enough!" Satan roared. "Now, tell me why you have come."

"I have brought back some news of the Godchild's sister, just as you requested. We have located her, in a Salesian retreat house in upstate New York."

"Very good, you will be rewarded for this," Satan gleamed.

"But, lord, I have some bad news. She is wearing Michael's medal. That means—"

"I know what it means, fool!" Satan thundered. The ground shook and Catal was sent rolling down the stairs to the hard floor.

Shaken by Satan's fury, Catal crawled backward toward the onyx doors and said, "I am sorry for troubling you, my lord."

"You should be. And for that you will pay a hefty sum."

The powerful Prince of Darkness held out his strong hand. From his fingertips came forth a stream of hellfire that charred the unfortunate bearer of bad news to a pile of ash, sending him to the second death. After releasing his rage, Satan relaxed himself and began to brood once again. The Archangel Michael would pose a threat, as he had many times since Lucifer first went against the Host of Heaven. The Devil did not worry too much. He had faced adversity time and time again. A plan would be formed, and the child would still be his to take. The evil despot was a master of scheming, and scheme he did as he watched all the elements of the game unfold before his very eyes.

The summer had ended, and fall had followed. The leaves had already changed to their beautiful hues, fallen off the trees, and died. Winter was here, a time of death and loneliness. Kimberly was being taken over by the lonesome mood of the desolate winter, so she decided to pay her good friend Martha a visit.

"Martha, I don't know if I'm still worried or just plain angry. I guess I thought Lyles was going to be different, you know," Kimberly expressed as she sat on Martha's comfy couch sipping some freshly brewed tea.

"Lyles *is* different. But I understand your concern. You cannot wait around forever for a knight in shining armor; they never show up," Martha explained. "I was hoping things would work out for the two of you. He is such a sweet young man, and you are indeed the sweetest girl I've ever met. I figured that you two were a match made in Heaven. I just hope he is safe. I'm very worried about him, Kimberly. And despite what you say, I know you are not really angry. You are worried, too. This isn't like him to just run away. The death of my son, his friends, and Mr. Reynolds — not to mention that short time behind bars — it all must have really affected him a lot more than he's letting on."

"I'm scared, Martha," Kimberly said as she leaned over on the armrest. "I know my time spent with Lyles was short, but you know that thing they always talk about — love at first sight. This may sound stupid; but I think from the moment that I first laid eyes on him, I fell in love with him. And I might be crazy for saying this, but I think he felt the same way."

"You're not stupid *or* crazy. Love is real, and you can fall in love at any time. There are no rules. Let's just pray that Lyles comes home safe and soon."

The Antarctic wind was cold, but the figure that sat on the icy mountain did not feel its bitter sting. Radix's head, as well as the tree it rested on, had been reduced to a pile of ash and had frozen from the icy climate. Death watched day in and day out as Radix began to reform slowly due to his frozen cells. Michael was wise to leave him in the freezing Antarctic weather. But now, regrettably, the notorious fiend was fully healed. Radix was incensed and would no longer play games with his prey. He was ready to seek and destroy as quickly and painfully as possible. Unable to do a thing, Death just watched as Radix called forth the *Necronomicon* to conjure up something to get him away from the winter prison that he was trapped in. Just then, the wind blew stronger and colder; and a most violent ice storm brewed. A loud screech bellowed in the distance, getting closer. A colossal winged beast appeared like a behemoth from the mouth of Hell. Radix jumped on its back and before Death knew it, he was gone. The evil man was heading north in search of Nathan. Death only hoped that Radix would not be able to find his prey in time.

# CHAPTER XII
## IT'S ALWAYS DARKEST BEFORE THE DAWN

As Radix soared through the open sky, one of his impish spies appeared to him and said, "Master, I have been searching for you for months."

"I was a little incapacitated, but I am feeling much better now. I pray you have come to tell me where I can find my quarry," Radix snapped.

"Well, master, a few months back, I did see the Godchild, though he has been lost to us recently. He was staying at a church in Jordan with a priest and that friend of his."

"Show me the church. I will persuade this priest to tell me where to find Nathaniel Salvatore. And I can be very persuasive," Radix snickered.

Through the sharp wind currents, the beast flew as the little imp led Radix to Father Reilly's church.

# Part I

## In the Twinkling of an Eye

It was midday. Father Reilly was sitting in his chair, catching up on some reading, when he heard the sound of his door crashing in. Baffled, the good priest picked up his walking stick and went over to see what had just happened. All that he saw were the splinters that used to be his front door scattered on the ground. No one was there. It was quiet. Just then, a shadow cast over his back and blocked out the light that was coming from the doorway. Afraid, the priest turned to see the most evil man to ever walk the Earth.

"Radix," Father Reilly said as he turned around.

"You know of me, old priest?" the dark man responded to his own name.

"Yes, you destroyed my village back in Ireland when I was a young boy. I have been waiting my whole life to watch you die!" Father Reilly cried out as he charged at Radix and carved down the left side of his adversary's face with the sharp end of his walking stick.

Radix screamed as his wound bubbled, "What is that stick made of. That really stung!"

"It was carved from the wood of Christ's true cross and was given to me as a gift a long time ago."

Radix swiped the walking stick from the priest — it burned his hand and he threw it to the side. Quick and strong, he grabbed Father Reilly and threw him up against the wall.

"You got in a good shot, I'll give you that, old priest. But it takes more than a good shot to stop me. I'm not here to play games. Tell me where Nathaniel Salvatore is. Tell me!"

"He will beat you, and I will laugh when you are no more. What a joyous day it will be."

Radix took one of the priest's arms and snapped it in half.

"I told you I am not here to play games. Now tell me!"

Trying to bear the pain, Father Reilly murmured, "He is waiting for you in the desert."

"In the desert? This whole land is a desert!"

In spite of the pain he was suffering, Father Reilly continued to speak, "He is on the Path of the Righteous. You must be familiar with that path. You have slain many men there before. Go there and you will find him. But be warned — he is not alone. They will end you and the darkness you bring to this world."

"Thank you, old priest. I know exactly where to find him, and I think I know who he is with. Now, it is time for me to finish what I did to your village in Ireland — by killing you."

Father Reilly gazed at Radix's soulless eyes as the world around him went black.

Down by a small oasis, Puck sat with Nathan and Lyles. The two men were shaving with razor sharp knives that Ravenblade had given them. The last few months had not been easy, but the training made both men much stronger than they had ever dreamed. With his new strength, the mystical Ring of Solomon, and his friends, Nathan was sure he could finally defeat his foe — Radix. Soon enough, he would be able to put his thoughts into action because Radix was moving quickly through the desert, ready to attack. At that moment, Nathan's stomach growled. Both Lyles and he were very hungry.

Puck could hear their noisy stomachs and asked, "You would like Puck to find food to fill bellies so hungry?"

"No, Puck, don't worry about it. We'll be fine," Nathan replied.

"No, master, an honor it would be to find you food, yes. Go now and return with something yummy, I will," Puck said as he vanished to look for sustenance in the barren desert.

Ravenblade stood out in the desert practicing with his blade when Death appeared to him.

"Radix is approaching from the east. He knows where you are," the grim messenger told Ravenblade, who was still practicing his sword-fighting techniques.

"Good — let him come. We are ready for him. At least I know I am," the proud immortal stated.

"I hope you are," Death said and vanished.

Ravenblade sheathed his blade and made his way over to his companions to prepare them to fight the approaching evil. After cleaning up, Nathan and Lyles were sitting back and enjoying a refreshing drink of water from the oasis. With a very serious demeanor, the immortal approached his new allies and threw each man a sword. Both of them caught their blades and stood, not knowing exactly what was going on. The weapons they now wielded may have been made from ordinary steel, but the fashion in which they were crafted was not of this Earth. Like the sword that Ravenblade held dear, these swords were forged with fire from Heaven. But they were not as strong as the immortal's sword, for the steel of his blade was not that of Earth but of Heaven as well. The sword called the Ravenblade had a different name when it was forged, though it has been forgotten by many. It was brought down to Earth by Azazel, a fallen angel, and was hidden under the desert sand. This is where the former angel who now possessed the sword found it — after being banished to the mortal plane. He named the sword Ravenblade after its sharp double bladed design that looked like a set of dark wings. Later on, that being took the name of the sword for his own, a name which he carried to this day.

"It is time," Ravenblade said with a calm blank look.

"Radix is here," Nathan knowingly stated. "I can feel his dark power."

"Yes, you are right. He is moving in from the east and is not aware that we know he is coming. It won't matter much, but it will give us a small element of surprise. So, let us go. Attack!" Ravenblade sounded the battle cry as the three men charged.

Stealthily the trio ran until they came across a grouping of sand dunes. They took positions behind the dunes in order to hide from Radix. Nathan could sense that the evil mercenary was very nearby. All three men readied their swords to strike. They could hear Radix's feet crossing the desert sand. The noise stopped. He was standing perfectly still.

"Do you really think you could catch me off guard? Now that is rich," Radix laughed at his opponents. "I could smell your blood from a mile away, especially yours, Nathaniel. It's funny how you thought to surprise me. Well, I have a surprise for you. It seems your friend the priest knew exactly where I could find you. Here, why don't you thank him for me."

Father Reilly's head rolled on the sand, past the dunes, right to Nathan's feet. Nathan could not bear to look down. He had lost so much already thanks to this war, and now another body was added to the count, leaving an empty pit in his heart.

"Don't look down, Nathan! Don't look down!" Lyles screamed from the next dune over. He then turned, sword drawn, and ran for Radix. "You beast!" he screamed as he slashed his blade at the murderous monstrosity.

Radix dodged each slash of Lyles' sword, yet did not strike back. Ravenblade joined in to help. The immortal knew Radix well for they had battled many times throughout the years. This time Ravenblade hoped to score a victory over his long-time rival. But just then, Radix moved from the defensive to the offensive by pulling out a concealed blade from his long black coat. The sword was beautifully crafted and seemed very ancient, though Ravenblade could not identify it. Radix now dueled both men, and was doing so quite well. His skills had much improved from the last time Ravenblade and he had fought.

"Nice sword — where did you find such a blade?" Ravenblade asked Radix curiously.

"I found it on my way here. The Path of the Righteous is full of dead heroes and their toys," Radix joshed back as he continued to fight. "It belonged to one of the Caesars, I believe. Not sure which one, there were so many. It was said that it was brought down from Heaven by an angel. That's a cute story, but I don't believe in that crap."

Then looking at Radix's face, Ravenblade noticed something bizarre.

"A scar?" he asked referring to the mark made by Father Reilly's cane, which was still visible across the left side of the evil man's face, "I've never known you to scar before."

Radix just shrugged off the immortal's comment. The wound was made from a relic most holy and would take a while to heal completely. Soon enough, the wound would be gone, but it would never be forgotten. The swords clashed on the desert sand as the sun moved through the sky. Radix was now gaining an advantage in the fight; and he swiftly kicked Lyles in the chin, sending him to the ground. Both amazed and angered by Radix's increased skill, Ravenblade charged fast and furious at the dark man. He would not be outmatched by Radix for he was far older and far more skilled. The tide began to turn, and Ravenblade now had the upper hand. He knocked Radix back and disarmed him. Miss followed by miss, Ravenblade's sword was dodged again and again. Radix rolled on the ground and retrieved his blade to even the odds. Lyles was now back up; and once again, it was two on one.

While the fight continued on the desert sand, Nathan looked down at his friend's bloody head. This was the final act to drive the heroic warrior over the edge. The camel's back was now broken, and the straw was scattered about. Fury came over Nathan, as rage ripped through his veins. His heart raced. Thoughts of his parents being slaughtered and his sister being raped flooded his mind, accompanied now by thoughts of the good Father Reilly — dead. It would have to end. He had survived many things from those simple pains of growing up to the loss of many lives. The torment was enhanced by the suffering he endured in the desert, his being tempted by the Devil, and the beatings he received at the hands of Radix. The wounds were opened wide, and there were no more tears to be shed. Ravenblade had taught Nathan many things in their training. One of these many things was how to tap into his innermost spirit, and through this to tap into the true Spirit of the Lord. The unorthodox immortal could no longer achieve this for he had abandoned the Spirit centuries ago. Nathan on the other hand let go; welcomed the Spirit; and focused with all of his might, with all of his strength, with all of his heart, and with all of his soul. Using the Ring of Solomon to channel this energy properly, Nathan began to go through a transformation. In a vigorous explosion, he wailed. His voice lifted to Heaven; and down from Heaven echoed a power that Nathan never thought he could experience — a righteous fury of unbridled might. The sand around his feet began to fly and shot all around as his energy grew. Electricity blasted from his body and electrified everything around him. The three combatants stopped brawling for a moment to look at the sight that was truly amazing to behold. Radix lowered his sword in shock and stared at what was to him just another man, just another kill. Nathaniel Salvatore was no longer just another man. He had done what men had not done in many, many lifetimes. He had reached a phase that Radix had never had the good fortune to witness before. Nathaniel Salvatore had now hit what men of old times called Chaos Fury, and with the fury would come a battle like no other.

Nathan turned to his sworn enemy and warned, "You keep taking away from me. What are you going to do when there is nothing left to take? What are you going to do when I have nothing left to lose? What are you going to do now?"

The sun's rays died over the distant mountains, however the sky did not grow dark for the energy that Nathan radiated lighted up the night. Awestruck, Radix blankly stared at the rays of energy that glowed from the young hero. He did not know what he was looking at, or how to approach the battle. First blood went to the side of good, as Radix's chest was sliced open by Nathan's blade. Then a backhand from his hilt sent the evil one into a sand dune. Instantly, Radix snapped out of his stupefied state and blocked Nathan's next strike. Like a great battle of the days of yore, the young hero and villain went toe to toe across the desert terrain. Ravenblade and Lyles just stood back and watched.

"This is amazing!" Lyles exclaimed. "I think Nathan can actually beat him. I didn't think this type of power existed."

"I've seen it before," Ravenblade butted in. "Though, I give your friend credit. I have never seen anyone hit Chaos Fury this quickly, especially at this magnitude. But regardless of his power, Nathan cannot beat Radix unless he survives. And he can still die, trust me."

"But how? Look at him."

"Chaos Fury is a power that is tapped into the primal nature of the universe through the power of the Spirit. Many have reached this level, but few have gone beyond it. Many of them, I killed myself. That's how I know he can still die. But his power is greater than theirs. I can feel it."

"But if you could beat men with power like this, why are you not helping him to defeat Radix now? I think we should jump in and really shake things up."

"Not yet. You see, Nathan only has Radix on the ropes right now because Radix does not know what he is fighting. Once he gets used to Nathan's new abilities, Radix will turn the tables. That's when I'll jump in."

"You know you can be real incorrigible sometimes. I don't care what you do. I'm going to help out Nathan. We need to win. This isn't about egos. And anyway, what makes you so powerful?"

"I'm an immortal, and I used to be an angel. But that's not a tale to be told right now. Go help your friend if you must. Just a word of warning — you have not reached the level that Nathan has reached, regardless of whatever power you have gained in the recent months. Radix will make quick work of you, once he gets his hands on you. But, go do what you wish. Just try not to die," Ravenblade gave Lyles his blessings. The immortal remained still and studied the brutal struggle.

Ready to sacrifice his very life, Lyles ran toward the fight. A plateau had been reached in the battle. With all the power that Nathan had gained, it seemed that Radix was equally as powerful. Nathan's power was primal and strong, but so was Radix's. The one difference was that Radix had a great deal more experience than the green hero. This experience helped him to gain the upper hand as he blocked all of Nathan's hits, caught him off guard, and slashed him across the shoulder. Blood ran down Nathan's arm as Radix blocked another of his attacks. Out of the corner of his eye,

Radix noticed Lyles coming to join the fight. He did not want to be bothered by fighting both men at once. So, Radix kicked up some sand with his foot, blinding Nathan for a moment, and clubbed him with a back hand. This sent Nathan flying fifteen feet across the desert and into a bed of rock. Immediately, Radix slit open his own wrist. He dripped his venomous blood onto the sand, and hymned a verse from the *Necronomicon*. Then, he licked Nathan's blood from his sword, rolled it on his tongue, and spit it onto the sand as well. The hot desert sand swallowed and digested the rich red plasma. It rumbled and groaned, and when it was done, the ground vomited up an army of dead men from times long past. They were heroes, much like Nathan, who had died along this path trying to achieve greatness. Radix knew many were buried below this trail. Now the thousands upon thousands of corpses were his to control, and he ordered them to kill his enemies. That is except for Nathan, for Nathan was his alone to kill. Lyles was unable to aid Nathan in his fight with Radix because now he had an army of the undead to contend with, and they were attacking him from all sides. Even though he had not reached Chaos Fury, Lyles was no weakling. Maybe a few months back, this putrefied militia would have eaten him alive. But thanks to his training with Ravenblade, he could handle himself just fine. And he did. Like a hot knife through butter, Lyles sliced his way through the zombie horde. Unable to just stand around and watch any longer, Ravenblade drew his blade and began to hack through the legion of the undead along with Lyles. Together, they daringly fought as each second more and more zombiefied corpses flooded the sands of the desert.

Meanwhile in the distance, Radix fought Nathan undistracted. The skilled dark assassin was unable to gain an advantage over the inexperienced young warrior. Radix was fighting as hard as he did against Michael, and even though Nathan was making no progress in the battle, neither was he. This upset the evil man greatly. Time was running short, and if Nathan was not killed soon, Radix would perish. His soul would belong to Satan and be tortured in Hell for all eternity. Filled with pride, Radix cringed at the thought. If only he had not wasted the Blackblade on Michael, he could have used it to destroy Nathan right at this very moment. But the sword was now lost in the darkness that it sprang from. Satan could not even retrieve the blade if he so desired, and he did. There was no more power for Radix to tap into. He had reached his peak. Nathan's power on the other hand was increasing, and soon it might even surpass the dark power that Radix possessed.

"How could this boy be so strong and fight so well?" Radix said to himself as he looked for a way to regain the advantage..

With all the thinking and contemplating Radix was doing he left himself wide open. A swift swipe of Nathan's sword cut Radix down the middle. A thrust through the beast's heart came next. Nathan did not feel the burn of the acidic blood that splattered onto his skin. He felt nothing at all and tossed Radix onto the stony ground. The night was almost over, and dawn was approaching. The battle sped up as Radix, wounds healed, was back on the offensive. Nathan had to be careful because unlike the regenerative Radix, he could not just instantly heal from his wounds. If his heart or any vital organs were punctured, it would mean certain death; and all would be lost.

Lyles and Ravenblade continued to cut through zombie after zombie, but every time they did it seemed as if they were making no progress. The undead just kept coming. There seemed to be no end to the mindless battalion of rotting flesh and bones.

"Food, must find food for Master," Puck mumbled as he scavenged through the desert.

He had been out all night looking for anything to satisfy his master's hunger. In his eyes, Nathan did not see himself as a master, or Puck as his slave. He just wanted the poor creature to be free to live as it wished, but the Djinni was too used to living a life of service. It knew no other way to live. Puck searched the desolate desert further, until he ran into one of his former kin.

"Traitor!" Puck's fellow Djinni cried. "The traitor, I see!"

"Shh. Keep down voice, hear you they will," Puck pleaded. "Traitor, I am not. My brothers, it was that betrayed me."

"A different story we hear of you, traitor. Believe king Iblis, we do," the Djinni responded. "Seen, were you not, with the Godchild in the desert of recent days?"

"What you say, I know nothing of," Puck denied.

"Rumors of the Godchild returning, a whisper from the winds told us so. But unable to find the succulent morsel, we were, for refused to guide us, the winds did. Angry is Iblis, and angry we are," the creature spoke again to Puck.

"With the Godchild you were, the winds so spoke," yet another Djinni called out as it appeared from smokeless fire.

"Already told you. Know not the Godchild, I do. Eat him I would if saw him, I did," Puck denied a second time.

Still another Djinni made itself seen and said, "But stink of him you do. Serve the Godchild, you do."

"No, lies. All lies!" Puck denied a third time, and the cock crowed signaling dawn.

The helpless Puck fled as a few hundred thousand Djinn now followed in pursuit, screaming out the word "traitor." They intended to make a quick meal of the Benedict Arnold, and chased him over the mountains and across the hot sand. Puck did not know where to go. If he led the hungry pack to his master, then they would try to make a meal of him as well. It was too late. As they darted across the desert sand, the great multitude of demons stopped and looked to the east. They could see a bright flashing light over the horizon. Staring at the light, the Djinn began to feel the energy coming from that direction.

"Godchild!" they cried out and charged to the east.

Puck realized what he had done and was very disappointed. While trying to lead them astray he led them right to his master. Now, he would have to hurry and make it to Nathan before the hungry flock did.

The frightened Djinni panicked as he appeared before Ravenblade. "Flee, approaching they are, heading this way!"

"I'm a little busy to flee at the moment, or did you not see the huge army of dead people trying to kill us?" Ravenblade said, blocking a zombie's axe that nearly took Puck's head off.

"See them, I do, but worse from the horizon is coming." Puck told the immortal.

"And what is so bad that is coming over the horizon?"

"Djinn! Hundreds of thousands of hungry, munching, and crunching Djinn!" Puck shouted in response. "They mean to

306

make a meal they do. In danger we are, especially master Nathan. Master is where?"

"Relax, we can handle some stupid Djinn — no offense. As for Nathan, see those pretty lights over there," Ravenblade pointed to the east where spots of lightning flashed and danced in the sky. "That's him."

Instantly, Puck vanished in a blaze of smokeless fire. Lyles and Ravenblade continued to fight off their decaying foes, when all of a sudden, a loud roar came over the horizon. Just as Puck had said, a multitude of Djinn raced like a pack of wild dogs toward the battling warriors. In a matter of seconds, the entire army of the undead was devoured by the blood thirsty demons; and Lyles and Ravenblade were surrounded. Calmly Ravenblade took a small pouch from under his cloak and opened it. He then sprinkled some of the contents onto the ground in front of him. It was salt. The creatures backed off as Ravenblade waved the bag at them. Lyles was confused. He did not know of the Djinn's dislike of salt. Ravenblade did his best to use the salt to keep the hungry monsters at bay, until he could think of a plan.

Over to the east, Nathan and Radix were still locked in battle. Puck tried again and again to gain his master's attention, but Nathan was too busy fighting to notice him. Taken over by the fear that his master may be in danger added to his hatred for the loathsome Radix, Puck made a brave and very dumb move and took a nice big chomp at Radix's leg. The evil man screamed, and the fighting stopped. Nathan looked down to see his friend Puck still holding onto Radix's leg with his powerful jaws. Trying to free himself of the Djinni's clenched teeth, Radix swung his sword to chop the creature from his leg. But this would not be the case, for Nathan's sword blocked Radix's. Caught off guard, Radix was handed a walloping right hand across the jaw — Nathan's signature knockout punch. For a moment, it did just that.

"Master Nathan, leave we must," Puck called from the ground.

"Why is that?" he questioned in response.

"Coming, they are, the Djinn, from all around. Feast on you, they wish. To taste the Godchild's flesh, they desire."

"Let them come — we are not going anywhere," Nathan said.

"But, master Nathan, we must," Puck insisted.

307

"You are forgetting something, my friend. I have the Ring of Solomon, and by decree all Djinn must bow before me and heed my command. They can do us no harm."

"Yes, master, I see. Sorry, about the ring, I forgot," Puck apologized. "Please, forgive Puck."

Nathan just smiled at the humble creature. Radix began to come to as the stampeding Djinn rumbled toward them. The ferocious mob crowded around, blocking their three victims from all sides.

"A pleasant treat, we have, yes," one of the Djinni spoke. "Both Radix and the Godchild, fortunate we are this day. Then, a quick meal we will make of the traitor as well. Happy, King Iblis will be to know of our feast."

"You will not feast on me or my friend today," Nathan said to the drooling horde. "For just as Solomon commanded you, I command you." Nathan spoke holding the ring up high.

In unison they bowed down including those that were surrounding Ravenblade and Lyles. Nathan informed Puck that he did not have to grovel for he was his friend not his servant. Radix grumbled and remained still, not knowing what to do.

Quickly, Nathan directed the Djinn with the exception of Puck, "And as your master, I command all of you to attack Radix!"

Unable to escape, Radix was trampled by the vicious assembly of Djinn. Nathan walked away with Puck as the monsters clawed, bit, and tore at Radix's body. The deadly harbinger of darkness was now being mutilated. Ravenblade and Lyles were awestruck for only a moment ago they were about to be eaten alive, and now the Djinn were all gone in a flash.

"The ring — Nathan must have used the Ring of Solomon," Ravenblade concluded.

"That's right. He could use the ring to control the Djinn," Lyles added.

"Yes, that is exactly what I did," Nathan said from behind.

"Nathan!" Lyles screamed as he hugged his comrade. "But how did you get here so fast?"

"Puck gave me a little help," Nathan explained as he patted his little buddy on the head. "I think Radix will be busy for a while."

"Don't be so sure," Ravenblade raised a point. "Radix is not yet beaten. He has faced armies before, including the Djinn. If anyone can get away from them, he can; and then he will try once again to kill you, Nathan. You must leave, so he cannot find you."

"No, this is almost over; and I will see it to the end," Nathan demanded. "He can't beat me. We have seen it. Even if he breaks free of the Djinn's grasp, I'll just hold him off until time runs out."

"You are being stubborn and proud," Ravenblade boldly stated.

"And you aren't?" Nathan asked back.

"Well, if you are staying, then we all are. If we all fight Radix at once, we may be able to hold him off long enough for his time to expire," Ravenblade answered.

Suddenly, Radix sprang from the limitless pile of Djinn. He swung his sword with great power, trying to slice through the hungry mob. But the creatures kept attacking, and the sadistic horde seemed to have no end as Radix was being bombarded from all sides. Running out of alternatives, Radix punctured his wrist and sprayed his venomous blood onto the creatures. The blood ate at their flesh. He then cried out ancient words to the west winds and stirred up a salty storm. The rain poured down, burning the Djinn, and caused them to flee back under the ground.

Rid of those pesky creatures, Radix was now focused again. He looked at his prey. Nathan, seeing that Radix was free from the Djinn, gripped his sword tightly and readied himself to fight as did his companions. But just as he did in Antarctica, Radix called forth that gargantuan winged beast. The flapping of the beast's wings caused a violent sand storm, blocking everyone's view; and swiftly, Radix jumped onto the back of the giant monster. The beast swooped down and opened its mouth wide, swallowing Nathan whole.

"Sorry to cut the show short," Radix called from the back of the beast. "I'm moving the scene back to New York. There are plenty of helpless people there that young Mr. Salvatore cares so dearly for. I will execute him, and then butcher the rest with my bare hands."

All seemed lost as Ravenblade felt his first feeling of sorrow in his heart, fearing he might lose his friend, Nathan. The two warriors and their Djinni companion watched as the beast soared off into the distant clouds, carrying Nathan in its belly. Matters grew worse at that moment for the rain had now stopped, and the horde of Djinn began to resurface angrier and hungrier than before. The Ring of Solomon was still on Nathan's finger, so the three would have no other choice but to fight.

# Part II

## Labor Pains

The water was dark and cloudy, and Esmeralda was about to drown. She was not sure how deep she had submerged into the murky sea, nor was she sure of how she had gotten there in the first place. All she knew was that she could not breathe, and the water was getting darker as she sank lower. Worse than even the pain of not being able to breathe was the squeezing force of the water pressure from being down so deep. The pain started in her lower back, radiated around her abdomen, and shot to her head. It was a cramping pain worse than she had ever felt or imagined to feel. She opened her mouth, but water rushed into her lungs, muffling her screams. The pain was so strong that it woke her from her dream. Esmeralda was no longer in the sea. She was safe in her bed back at the retreat house. A couple of the nuns that she was in the care of rushed into the room when they heard her screams of pain. The bed was soaked. Her water had broken; and she was now starting to get serious contractions, which were the cause of her pain. Labor had begun, even though it was nearly a month premature. One of the nuns ran to get help. Esmeralda just sat back as best she could and waited, though, her contractions were now about five minutes apart.

The pregnancy was hard; and even though she was in the care of many loving sisters, Esmeralda felt very alone and scared. Her brother was off in the desert, and her parents were gone. Plus, there was no father to speak of for the child in her belly; no one to share her pain and joy. Things became even more complex during the first trimester when they discovered that she was having twins. This assumption came to Sister Thomastina when

310

she heard two distinct heartbeats coming from the womb during one of Esmeralda's routine check-ups. Some babies had been born in this facility and the place was equipped for any medical emergency including childbirth. No technology was spared including an ultrasound machine, which the Sister used to prove her assumption that Esmeralda was in fact having twins. She was in good care, and she was now ready to release her children into the world that she so feared.

Amid the sporadic contractions, Esmeralda waited to be checked on. All she could think about was how time had passed. Christmas came and went, and with it her brother's birthday. It was now the last day of December, and a new year was approaching. She hoped that Nathan would live to see it and bring an end to Radix's evil ways. Then she prayed for a world without evil, so that her soon-to-be-born children could grow up happy, laughing, and playing. Just at that moment, Sister Thomastina came rushing in with some other nuns, who were wheeling in a stretcher.

"Esmeralda, how are you feeling?" Sister Thomastina asked.

"Okay, except for the fact that I'm wet, cold, and having shooting pains in my lower extremities," she responded in a cross manner, though she was really upset at the discomfort and not at the sister.

A couple of the sisters picked her up and placed her onto the stretcher. They began to wheel her toward the operating room. All the while, Sister Thomastina walked beside her. She held Esmeralda's hand and told her that everything was going to be just fine. Quickly, Esmeralda was placed on the same table where Nathan was treated for his injuries. Now the table had some stirrups attached to it, so that Esmeralda could keep her legs comfortably apart. She lay as still as she could and bit her tongue every time she felt a contraction.

"Now, just relax. I'm going to see how you are doing," the medically trained nun said, as she grabbed some instruments. "Your contractions are getting closer to two minutes apart, but they are still too far apart for delivery. Plus, your cervix still has not dilated to ten centimeters yet. This could take anywhere from one to twelve hours. We can be here all day for all we know.

But you are making good progress. Remember the breathing techniques that I taught you; and if you need an epidural or any meds, just let me know. You're going to be fine."

But Esmeralda did not know if she would be fine. She still did not even know what her children would be. She was told that she would have a child that would do great things, but now she was having two. Would these great things be for good or for evil? She was not the only one wondering about her soon-to-be-born babies. All of Heaven and Hell watched, as well as countless others. Even Lilith and Iblis sat, waiting for a chance to get a hold of whatever was about to be released from her womb. But Michael stood tall with his sword held firm by his side, ready to strike down any who dared to place a hand on the mother or her unborn children. Everything that the Lord had set into motion was now drawing closer to its climax. Only God, Himself, knew what the future held for all involved in this chaos that started two thousand years before when Radix was born. And just as all things do, this epic was now drawing to an end. But with every end comes a new beginning.

# CHAPTER XIII
## THE PASSION

Above the clouds that swallowed the entire island of Manhattan, the winged monstrosity flew furiously with Radix on its back and Nathan still in its belly. The city had experienced quite a snowstorm and was still blanketed with winter's white powder. Winds were strong and icy, and plows worked hard to clear the streets for that night's New Year's Eve festivities. People from all over the world would be crowding into Times Square to watch the ball drop. Radix knew this, yet Nathan did not, for he did not even know where he was being taken. All he wanted was to be freed from the tentacles that held him tight inside the beast. If not for the grace of God and his newfound strength given by the Spirit, Nathan would have died by now. But this was not the case. Nathan was still alive, and he was very angry. He stood, waiting for his chance to battle Radix again.

Behind the blanket of the clouds and violent winds, the beast descended from the sky onto the Wollman Rink in Central Park. The people ice-skating on the rink looked up with terror at the creature soaring down from above and began to scurry and scream. Like a preying lion, the beast swiftly raced down and clawed through the flesh and bones of those in its path. The warm blood from the monster's victims stained the ice on the rink. Radix enjoyed watching the beast play with the corpses like a cat would with a ball of yarn. Fortunately for the sinister killer there were still a few people for him to slay, which he did with a smile. Not too many people were left in the rest of the park, with the exception of some children sledding and having snowball fights. But they soon ran off after hearing the unbearable sounds of the beast tearing the flesh of its victims. It was dark now, and most people were home getting ready for later that night. Radix had hoped for a bigger crowd. *Maybe I should have gone to Times Square*, he thought. Soon enough he changed his mind, remembering how much he hated the busy city streets and all of the commotion. The serenity of the park was the perfect stage for him to slaughter his prey. It was enough that he was back in New York where Nathan cared for so many, and it would be great irony to spill Nathan's blood on his own soil.

Armed and ready, Radix signaled for the beast to spit out Nathan. The hero rolled from the monster's jaws covered in slimy mucus. Along with him was his sword, which slid across the ice out of reach. Nathan was weak from trying to fight his way out of the creature's belly. Knowing this, Radix instantly struck at him with his blade. Instinctively, Nathan rolled. He glided away from Radix's attack and grabbed his own sword as he passed by it on the ice. Radix glided down the ice and struck at Nathan again, before he could stand. But Nathan had learned a great deal of sword-fighting techniques under the coaching of Ravenblade. He blocked Radix's attack from the ground and slowly got up to his feet. The battle was engaged once again, but this one would prove to be their last.

# Part I

## The Garden of Gethsemane

Nathan saw the blood-stained ice and the dismembered pieces of what were once men, women, and children lying about. No matter how hard he tried to isolate his fight with the evil incarnate known as Radix Malorum, more innocent blood was spilled. The righteous anger of God burned inside of Nathan more than before and took his newfound powers to an even higher level, one that most men have never come back from.

"No more will suffer!" Nathan boomed as he radiated with energy.

The ice in the rink began to crack and split apart, and Nathan charged up his spirit more and more. Radix could no longer keep his footing on the broken, slippery surface and fell flat on his face. But before attacking his foe, Nathan shot over to the beast that was now gnawing on the head of a little girl. Disgusted, Nathan sliced the creature across the throat and gutted it down its belly. Blood and guts from the creature dripped down Nathan's brow, and he turned to Radix who had regained his footing and was coming at him from behind. Underestimating Nathan's power, Radix was caught off guard; and he was flung through the wooden terrace onto the walkway above the rink. Radix rolled through the snow, until he hit a tree. Nathan leaped to the walkway and looked around for his enemy but all that he could see was snow and trees. He began to focus and realized where he was — back in New York City in Central Park. As Nathan searched for his foe, he was caught off guard and was slashed across the back by Radix's blade. Bloody and wounded, Nathan swung his sword back around, hitting only air. His wounded back was bad, but he could not feel the pain for his focus was on the battle alone. Radix had never known a mortal man to fight with such vigor and passion. He was as much in awe as he was aggravated.

The two men battled through the snow-covered terrain, over rocks, and through trees. Nathan led Radix deeper and deeper into the park, trying to keep him from spilling more innocent blood. Radix could not believe that this man could match his swordsmanship. Ravenblade's training had proven to be very helpful in Nathan's survival. The immortal was possibly the greatest swordsman to ever live and had bested Radix plenty of times in battle, though he never was able to kill the fiend. The young hero was able to catch Radix at that moment with a powerful strike of his blade, sending the villain into a set of stone steps. Nathan walked backward up the stairs never taking his eyes off of his fallen foe. They were now at the Chess and Checkers House, an octagonal brick building surrounded by benches and concrete tables with chessboards engraved on top of them. Nathan ran to the other side of the building and rested his back against it, as Radix recovered and walked up the stairs. Radix then walked around the building but could not see where Nathan had gone. From the roof, Nathan jumped down. He sliced Radix on the left arm and rolled into one of the chess tables. In retaliation, Radix ripped up one of the concrete tables from the ground and threw it at Nathan, bashing him in the head and knocking him down another set of stairs. With a giant leap, Radix came down at Nathan with his sword pointed straight for his head. On his back and without his sword in hand, Nathan grabbed a piece of the concrete board to block the strike; but Radix's sword was too strong. It went right through the cement, stopping only an inch from Nathan's face. Lucky for Nathan, the block was thick enough to keep the blade from killing him.

Twisting the block, Nathan rolled Radix off of him and into a tall tree. Without a second thought, Nathan grabbed his sword again and made his way through a tunnel. He dragged himself along the corridor, scraping his blood along the brick wall.

He came to the Central Park Carousel, which mysteriously was running, even though the ride was supposedly closed for the winter. He watched the horses go round and round to an eerie circus tune. The painted cherubs that circled above seemed to take on the form of demons, as did the rest of the images on the walls and fences. Intrigued, Nathan walked inside. He stood, almost hypnotized by the circling steeds. Finally, he was only awakened from his daze when Radix, riding on one of the carousel horses, cut him across the arm. Nathan screamed and held the wound as Radix came around again with another slice. The ride stopped, and Nathan fell to the ground bleeding. Radix dismounted from the horse and loomed over Nathan, ready once again to deal a fatal blow.

All the fight was not out of Nathan's body yet. The power that the young man possessed was a strong power indeed; and with a burst of that power he gave Radix a double-heel kick to the abdomen, sending him flying into the motor of the carousel. Radix's blade got stuck in the engine. This caused an electrical jolt to surge through his body, frying him to a crisp. Seeing his opportunity to escape, Nathan fled north. Unfortunately, though, he had walked out into the middle of an open field and was an easy target to spot from anywhere around. In a way, Nathan was happy for he wanted nothing more than to battle Radix to the end, even though Nathan's top priority was to survive above all things. Time was inching along, and Nathan was still alive. This proved to be a problem for Radix. Slowly, Nathan walked across the Sheep Meadow. His rage was subsiding along with his strength, but he did not worry for he knew God was with him. Hidden in the black shadows of night, Radix swept over Nathan's path of footprints and blood in the snow. Longing for a rest, Nathan wished to lie down on the soft white "quilt" that covered the ground. No rest would come to him; his predator had returned and was now somehow in front of him. Nathan asked the Spirit to give him strength, courage, and fortitude in order to continue his fight with the evil man. Radix charged at Nathan but was met by his blade. The Spirit heard Nathan's prayers and gave him the power to stand and fight his wretched foe.

"Why can't you lie down and die, like all the rest?" Radix shouted, annoyed at Nathan's resilience. "You are nothing more than a man!"

"I may be just a man, but my power is not my own. It has been granted to me from One who is infinitely powerful. It is by His will, and His will alone, that I will stop you. And the world will rejoice at the sight of your death," Nathan proclaimed as he pushed up against Radix's blade with his own, looking the heartless cretin in his soulless eyes.

Blood dripped drop by drop from both men, as the unrelenting battle continued into the night. The two warriors seemed evenly matched at this time, and no advantage could be gained by either warrior. Carefully, Radix stepped backward as did Nathan, to create a space between themselves. The air was cold and bitter, but neither man felt it as it slapped their skin. They were too engrossed in the battle to notice anything else. Radix gently stuck the tip of his sword in the snow and began to whisper. Nathan knew now that the fiend was once again looking for dark magic to aid him. Before Nathan could even move, Radix spun his sword like a top. With that motion, a tornado of snow rose from the ground and swept Nathan from his feet. Radix watched with delight as Nathan was carried from the field and through the park. Trees, iron gates, and giant rocks bashed up against Nathan's body. Radix finally called for the tornado to stop as it came to the lake. The winds died down, and Nathan crashed through a canopy made of branches and vines and hit the snow covered walkway. The asphalt cracked as Nathan slammed into it.

"Had enough?" Radix laughed as he bent down over Nathan.

"No!" Nathan exclaimed.

He grabbed Radix by the shirt and flipped him into the air. As Radix hit the ice that covered the lake, it cracked and he fell into the frigid water. Up from the ground, Nathan walked out onto the ice. He had not seen Radix fall into the lake for he was on his back at the time. Suddenly, the ice under his feet broke open and a hand pulled him down into the freezing water. The harder Nathan tried to break free of Radix's hold, the deeper he was pulled under. The powers Nathan had gained could not help him to breath underwater and he was losing oxygen, which was making him weaker. Radix, on the other hand, did not have to breath and dragged Nathan down deep. With his arms wrapped around Nathan's chest, Radix tried to expel the oxygen from his prey's lungs. Mustering up every ounce of strength he could, Nathan tapped into the power of the Holy Spirit. With unbridled strength, Nathan burst from Radix's grip, and the villain was sent crashing down to the bottom of the lake. Like a torpedo, Nathan shot through the water and blasted his way to the surface, breaking through the ice as if it were peanut brittle. Upon reaching the surface, Nathan inhaled a giant gulp of the cold winter air, which filled his lungs with a chill. He breathed heavily as he pulled himself out of the water and made his way to dry land.

The snow-covered land was thick with shrubbery and trees, all barren and lifeless from winter's cold touch. Nathan used his sword to hack off branches in his way and sat down to rest under a small bridge. The bridge was made of wooden planks held together by a metal frame. Metal spikes, which were shaped like little pyramids, ran across each of the railings. Ready to move on, Nathan stood and ducked to go under the bridge. But just then, a small tree came flying from behind him, struck him square in the back, and knocked him down.

"I am not so easy to get rid of. You should have run farther and faster, boy," Radix said, grabbing Nathan and lifting him over his head.

Radix leaped into the air and slammed Nathan, back first, onto one of the railings. The spikes pierced Nathan's flesh, and the railing gave way causing Nathan to crash through the bridge. Laughing to the heavens, Radix was unprepared when Nathan whacked him in the face with a piece of the broken railing. With his enemy on the ground, Nathan quickly headed east. Radix followed close behind with sword in hand, ready to kill. The paths grew narrower, and the rocks seemed much larger. In order to distance himself from his foe, Nathan scaled some of the large rocks and cut through unmarked paths. But Radix was an excellent tracker and followed the scent of Nathan's blood. The running had come to an end as Nathan stumbled into the court of Belvedere Castle, the highest point in Central Park. The stones on the platform were cold, and the door to the small castle, to Nathan's right, was locked. He was just about to break the door down, when Radix showed up behind him and threw him into the castle wall.

"You have been running from me for too long. Now you will no longer be able to run," commanded Radix, who was now holding the *Necronomicon* once again in his hands.

He spoke some words from the sinful text, casting a spell over the entire park. Soon, thick wild vines covered with thorns sprang from the ground and surrounded the castle, caging in Nathan and Radix. Nathan tried to hack through the vines, but his blade did not even leave an impression. The vines were magical and very hard to penetrate. The two men had only a small stone stage to fight on, so fight they did. Nathan and Radix both gathered their energies and attacked vigorously. Radix swung his blade with immeasurable force at Nathan, who blocked it with an equally immeasurable force. The two warriors seemed to be frozen as time stood still. The pressure began to build as both men tested the strength of their hands and their blades. Though Nathan's hand was strong at this time, his blade was not; and it began to crack and split in half from the pressure. The reason for this was that Radix's blade was made from Angelmetal, like the Ravenblade; and no sword from Earth, even one forged with fire from Heaven, could hold in battle for long against such a weapon. With no other options Nathan flung what was left of his sword into Radix' shoulder, causing him to drop his own sword. He then kicked Radix's blade far away from him. The villain ran to retrieve his weapon. However, Nathan caught him just in time and threw him into one of the castle's walls.

"It's just us, Radix. You and me, hand to hand," Nathan said as he held Radix up against the wall. "You think you are so tough, so powerful. Let's see how tough you really are."

"Fine, I will show you my power," Radix said, kneeing Nathan in the groin and pushing him off.

Numb to the pain in his groin, Nathan charged Radix and the two rolled back and forth. As powerful as Nathan was, Radix was still stronger. Using his advantage, Radix knocked Nathan down a set of stone steps that led to a rocky cliff. The section of the rocks at the bottom of the stairs was fenced in. Nathan leaned on the black iron bars of the fence, trying to gain footing. But he could not even move. Radix pummeled Nathan with lefts and rights; and then, he lifted the hero by the neck into the air.

"It ends here, boy. Just as it did for your Savior," Radix spoke to Nathan who just dangled in his grasp, unable to fight any more.

Then, Radix raised his other hand, and from the ground grew a cross made from the same vines that surrounded the castle. He pressed the weakened hero into the cross. The thorns stabbed Nathan all over his body, and a crown of thorns grew around his head. Radix then ripped off three bars from the fence and used them to pierce Nathan's wrists and feet.

"I was just thinking," Radix said laughingly, "How funny it is that now I have nailed both you and your sister."

Radix then took the Ring of Solomon off of Nathan's right hand and placed it on his own.

"It's a good look for me, don't you think," Radix chuckled.

Nathan screamed in pain as loud as he could, for that was all he could do. He was dying, but his will would not concede. No matter how hard he fought, Nathan could not break free. Off in the distance the night watchman at the Central Park police precinct heard Nathan's screams, and he was certain that they were coming from Belvedere Castle. Using a pair of binoculars, he looked over toward the castle. He could not see much for the castle was far and the night was dark. But he knew something was wrong and radioed for backup.

"Rogers, we got a call from Central Park," the police commissioner transmitted over Officer Rogers' walkie-talkie. "You have to send some guys over there. But make it very discrete. The ball is about to drop, and we don't want to spoil the party."

"Gotcha, Commish. Rogers, over," Officer Rogers signed off from the heart of Times Square, making sure the city was safe for this festive night.

The crowd was huge, larger than any the officer had seen, and they were quite boisterous as well. It was a party greater than any, and all waited for the coming of the true new millennium. As quietly and secretively as he could, Officer Rogers dispatched four cars to Central Park to check out the disturbance.

Back in the park, the night watchman decided to look around. He grabbed his gun, loaded it, and set off toward Belvedere Castle. The vines that surrounded the castle were still growing and were now spreading throughout the park. As he began to make his way around the Great Lawn, the watchman felt something grab his leg. It was one of the thorny vines, which grew around his whole body and strangled him to death. Soon enough, the whole park was covered in the evil foliage, blocking off all entrances. The deadly vines even made their way through the Central Park Zoo, killing all the animals inside. Three of the cop cars reached the 72nd Street entrance to Central Park. The officers slammed on their breaks as soon as they saw the vines blocking the entrance, causing them to crash into each other. The still growing vines wrapped around one of the cars and crushed it like a tin can, killing those inside instantly. The rest of the officers got out of their cars and tried to run, but they too were grabbed by the lethal vines and killed as well.

The rookie cop, Jay Sil, was in the station bathroom when the call came through so he was late to the scene at Central Park. And he was not prepared for the sight that stood before him as he arrived. Jay ran from his car to see what had happened. His fellow officers were bloody messes, and he was soon to join them as the vines made their way closer.

Radix smiled at Nathan as he watched his victim's blood pour onto the rocky ground. Pleased, the dark man waved his arms and the vines stopped growing.

"We are now completely alone. No one can enter, and no one can leave. Watching you die will give me more pleasure than any death that I have ever delivered," Radix sadistically said, taking some of Nathan's blood on his finger and sucking it off as if he were sampling icing from a cake. "Your blood is indeed sweet.

You should feel special, lasting as long as you have. No man has ever given me such a fight."

Nathan spit in Radix's eye, his only line of defense.

"Seeing you up there brings back some fond memories," Radix continued, wiping the spit from his eye. "I was there, you know, when they hung Him from that cross. Actually, I'm proud to say that it was some of my best work. In fact, He was my first. The first time is always awkward. You don't know how to approach it, so you inch in until it feels right, then you just kind of make it up as you go along. You have to see what works and what doesn't.

"I was different then. I wasn't quite so hungry for blood. I was very timid and shy — almost nervous. Just like everyone's first time at something new. You see, I had to make sure I would succeed so I had to plan it right. What was I suppose to do? How should I kill him? I was a thinker, the son of a philosopher. The Greeks were the best at that, you know.

"I followed Him and His disciples everywhere. I studied His moves, His techniques, His way of life, and those of His followers — especially the Twelve. A pacifist, a lover of people, and the Son of God — He was indeed a curious one and hard to knock off. Many tried, but all failed. You could not just go up to this man and kill Him. He controlled demons; He resurrected people from the dead; He was no joke. But I found a way, through His own bleeding heart. Judas, the one known as Iscariot, had doubt in his soul. He feared that Christ would lead him to death and nothing more. How right he was. I played with Judas' mind, entering it as Satan had entered my own, and I took control of it. The Lamb was led to slaughter by a kiss on the cheek. That was all it took. My greatest kill, and I did not even get one drop of blood on my hands. I left Judas just after the kiss with the bag of silver coins to remind him of how cheap he had sold his soul. Shortly after, he hanged himself from a tree, sort of like how his Master was hung from a tree; but with a rope around his neck, not with nails in the hands and feet — like you. Then it is said that falling headlong, he burst open in the middle of the field that had been purchased with the blood money; and all his bowels gushed out. The strangest part, though, was that he was never found. He is still missing to this day.

"What that has to do with you, I'm not sure. But what I am sure of is that that day I began to feel pain. God cursed me for doing what I did to His Son. He made it so that whenever I am injured, hurt, or wounded I would feel the pain. The worse the injury, the worse the pain would be. I have been beheaded, turned to ash, and have had my skin ripped from my body; and trust me these are very painful things. With time, pain feels less, and now I like the pain and feed off of it. Though it does not matter how much pain I feel, I cannot die. And once again just as I did to His Son two thousand years ago, I will slay yet another savior of His," Radix walked off and grabbed his sword. "Nathaniel Salvatore, 'God grants us a gift, a Savior,' be prepared to meet your God as I pierce your side just as they pierced your Lord's."

Radix sent his sword to skewer Nathan through the side. But it was met by another sword, equal if not greater than his own — the Ravenblade.

"Radix, it seems that your game is over," Ravenblade said as Radix could do nothing but stare in shock.

Radix looked around to see Lyles, who also had a blade drawn, and Puck, who displayed his sharp teeth and claws in a threatening manner. *How could this have happened?* he wondered. How could they have gotten to this place at this time? He would get no answers from the three who stood around him. At that moment, the clock struck twelve midnight in New York and the ball had made its way to the bottom in Times Square. The painful screams that came from Nathan echoed louder than the cheers from those celebrating in the streets. The villainous Radix did his best to remain calm. But it was difficult because he could feel the cold shadow of death cast over him.

# Part II
## New Life

Far from the painful screams of her brother, Esmeralda belted out her own screams of pain. At midnight, Esmeralda gave birth to the first of her twins. It was a boy. After cutting the umbilical cord, Sister Thomastina quickly cleaned the baby and placed him in his mother's arms. All of the sisters who were present to help with the birthing watched with awe as they witnessed the miracle of life. Despite the fact that the birth was slightly premature, the boy was healthy and of normal size and weight. Intently, he studied his mother's face; and unlike most newborns, instead of crying, he just seemed to giggle. As odd as this was to all watching, including his own mother, everyone passed off this spontaneous laughter as the sign of a very happy child. Then, Esmeralda thought to herself that she had not picked a name for the boy, though, she had toyed around with a few names for both sexes, not knowing what she was going to have. At that moment, a name was whispered into her ear by an unfamiliar voice. She repeated the name, which she gave to her son.

"I will call you Gideon," Esmeralda said with a smile.

"What a strong name," Sister Thomastina complemented her, "It must have been decreed from God, Himself."

The rest of the nuns agreed with what the Sister had said. They nodded and gave praises to God for the life that He allowed Esmeralda to bring into this world. There was much rejoicing in Heaven as the angels sang, as well as in Hell as the demons bellowed. Satan smiled and held out his hand, waiting for a moment to place the child in his grasp. All yearned for an opportunity to mold this child. But Michael still stood guard with his fiery blade, ready to pierce any who tried to touch either child or mother. More was to come, for another child was still waiting to be delivered. Soon enough, the boy was taken from the mother and placed in a plastic crib on the other side of the room.

The delivery of the second child was not as smooth as the first. And contrary to what Esmeralda had thought, it was far more painful. The first problem that arose was that the child was breech. But matters grew worse when a second problem was detected. Sister Thomastina realized that the child was tangled in the umbilical cord and was possibly having its oxygen supply cut off. This meant that the baby would have to be delivered immediately. Sister Thomastina called over one of the other nuns and whispered to her. The nun walked over to a drawer and began to gather some equipment.

In a calm and reassuring tone, Sister Thomastina explained, "Now, Esmeralda dear, I am experiencing some complications with your second child and am going to have to perform a cesarean section."

Esmeralda was very concerned and a little frightened as she asked, "Is everything going to be okay with the baby?"

"Yes, everything will be fine. The sooner the child is delivered, the better the chances will be for its health."

"Then, do what you must," she said through the pain and began to pray.

The anesthesia was being prepared, while Sr. Thomastina checked to make sure she had everything she needed. But before anything could be done, Esmeralda let out a giant scream; and the baby, though breech, was sticking halfway out of its mother. With no hesitation, Sister Thomastina went to work to get the baby out safely. Once the baby was out, she quickly cut the umbilical cord and released it from the baby's neck. Esmeralda's second child was born and it was—

"—A *girl!*" Sister Thomastina joyfully exclaimed.

But the joy seemed to drop a bit as it was noticed that the child was not breathing properly. Oxygen was given to the baby girl, and she began to breathe better after a few moments. Unlike her brother, she was weak and frail. After being cleaned, she was placed on a ventilator and given some more oxygen because she was wheezing. Esmeralda had passed out from all the pain and pushing just after she heard that her child was a girl, and the new mother was unaware of the state of this child. Sister Thomastina and the other sisters thought it would be best if Esmeralda just slept now for she could use the rest. The matters of her daughter could be discussed after she was awake and had a much clearer head. As all eyes were still on the strapping baby boy, God had a special eye on the little girl. She might have seemed weak to all others who watched her struggle, but to the Almighty Father she was strong and mighty and would do some of the most wonderful things.

Time passed and with it Esmeralda slept. She dreamt of her and her children living in the peace of God's kingdom happily ever after with Nathan, her parents, and all of their family and friends. But as she slept, the story continued. The ending was not there yet, and miles away her brother was not very happy. He still hung on that cross, dying and bleeding more each moment that passed.

# Part III

## Blood and Water

"And what on God's precious green Earth did you think you were doing, Azrael?" the Archangel Michael asked as he barged into the Hall of Records.

"My job. And it's none of your concern, Michael." Azrael said.

"Everything under the heavens is my concern, especially when it's a violation of the laws," Michael responded as he slammed his fist into his palm.

"No laws were violated. I did not touch Radix or Nathan. Therefore, I crossed no boundaries. Not like you with your thrashing Radix down in Antarctica. But I'm sorry, I forgot that you can do whatever you want. Right?"

"I was obliged to protect the one wearing my medal. I did what I had to do."

"And so did I. You're just jealous because you did not think to bring them there yourself," Azrael snickered, trying to egg on the pretentious archangel.

"I just hope that they can stop that beast and make him roast for his sins."

"It burns you up that you won't be the one to finish him off."

"Stay thy tongue before it is you that tastes my wrath," the ferocious warrior angel said as he pointed his blade at Azrael.

"The Holy Father would really like that, now wouldn't He?"

The Prince of Hosts drew back his sword and gave his salutations to Azrael with a, "Good day!" and took off in a fiery frenzy.

"It is over, Radix. After all these years, you have been beaten," Ravenblade boasted.

"I still have some hours left to kill this boy. If I am lucky, he'll bleed to death before my time runs out. You see, the sun of the New Year has to rise over the land I am in before my time expires; and from the looks of it, the moon is still in the sky," Radix responded, still holding his sword.

"Then, let's fight, you maggot!" Ravenblade yelled as he made the first move.

Radix and Ravenblade were once again going toe to toe, as Nathan bled more each minute. The Spirit of the Lord was still with him, helping him to stay alive. Lyles and Puck ran over to Nathan to try to take him down from the cross. Neither of them could budge the metal posts that were in Nathan's wrists and feet for they were set deep into the thick thorny structure. Lyles couldn't even chop the cross down with his sword. The sight of his friend bleeding on the cross angered Lyles very much; and if he could not help his friend get down, then he would help his friend by fighting for him. Filled with rage, Lyles charged Radix. It was tough for Radix to parry two men with only one sword. Lyles' blind rage left him open, though, and Radix soon was able to disarm him and send him flying into Ravenblade, knocking both of them to the ground. As they struggled to get back up, Radix noticed Puck and remembered that with the Ring of Solomon he had control over Djinn. The evil man tried to get Puck to obey him, but Puck fought hard to keep control of himself. He did not want to attack his friends, and especially did not want any harm to come to his master. Regrettably, Puck had no choice. The ring had power over him — it was decreed so. As hard as the Djinni fought, he could not fight hard enough. His eyes became red with fire, and the little demon pounced on his friends tearing at them like a rabid dog. Seizing the opportunity, Radix made his way over to Nathan. It was time to finish him off.

Ravenblade kicked the crazed Puck off of him and ran for Radix, calling back to Lyles, "Keep him busy — I've got some unfinished business!"

Lyles did not know what to do. He did not want to hurt his friend. Yet he did not want to die either, and the possessed Djinni was looking to fill his belly with Lyles' flesh. Up against the cold stone wall of the castle, Lyles' sword shook, unwillingly ready to strike his comrade if need be. But in his heart, Lyles prayed that he would not have to hurt his friend and hoped that he could wake Puck up from his demented trance.

"Puck, it's me Lyles, your friend," Lyles pleaded.

"Not Puck, only Djinni. No name, no friends have Djinn. Dinner, you are. Juicy steak," Puck growled.

Meanwhile, Ravenblade stopped Radix from slaying Nathan, buying them more time as he once again waged war with the unholy beast. With skill unmatched by anyone on Earth, the courageous immortal cut through Radix's attack and sliced off the fingers of his right hand. Radix lost more than just his fingers; he lost the Ring of Solomon, and with it his control over Puck. Instantly, the hunger-stricken Djinni stopped dead in his tracks; he snapped out of his trance and fell to his knees.

"Friend, Puck sorry, very sorry. He not want to hurt friend. But ring, control it has over Djinn. Puck, nothing could he do."

"It's okay, buddy, I'm just glad you're back," Lyles said. He gave Puck a hug and patted him on the back heartily. "But this is not over. Let's go help Ravenblade stop this monster."

Now Radix was once again surrounded, but this time Lyles did not allow himself to be taken over by his rage. He patiently stood, as did his two friends. Radix was on one knee; his fingers had regenerated. The three waited for him to make a move, yet he just looked up and whispered something in Greek. Ravenblade could not hear what Radix was saying, but he could read his lips.

"He's raising the dead!" Ravenblade shouted.

At that moment as was the case in the desert, all who were dead in the park that night were raised in the form of mindless zombies; and their only desire was to feast on flesh. The three who stood against Radix could hear growling and roaring in the distance. It was the animals that at one time were attractions for people visiting the park's zoo. They were now demented vicious be? prowling through the thorny vegetation to find fresh meat. Their destination was Belvedere Castle. Being in the mindless undead state that they were in, the animals had no problem scaling over the sharp thorn-ridden vines. There was no time to waste. The ravenous creatures would soon enough arrive to devour the three heroes, who at this time decided to attack Radix while they still could. Radix rolled to dodge the onslaught of blades from Lyles and Ravenblade. With no sword to fight with, Puck fought with the only means he had. He sunk his teeth deep into Radix's side, tearing at his flesh as best he could. But the blood that Puck swallowed burned him very much, and he was forced to retreat. The battle sparked more and more. Radix was just barely standing. That was, until his cavalry came in — the gruesome, possessed pack lunged over the spiky vine walls that surrounded the castle. They stood there ready to feast; everything from polar bears, to penguins, to pythons, to monkeys, and even birds all shifted and deformed into demonic versions of what they used to be. It was quite a sight for all to behold. Even Ravenblade had never witnessed such beasts as these now were.

Over at the 72nd Street entrance of the park, Jay Sil was relieved to still be alive. Just before the vines were about to grab him, they stopped growing. But his relief would not last very long. His fellow officers who died in the grasp of these vines were now demonic zombies just like the animals from the zoo, and they were determined to make a meal of the young rookie cop. There were six of them, four men and two women, and just one of him. Jay quickly drew his gun and fired away, but the bullets just seemed to pass through them with no effect. He had no other choice but to get to the other side of the vine wall, hoping that they would not follow. So without hesitation, Jay ripped the sleeves off his shirt; and he wrapped the fabric around his hands to avoid the sharp thorns. He scaled the wall only receiving a few minor scratches, but otherwise was unscathed. His only problem when he got to the other side was that the frenzied group of zombie officers began to make their way over the vines after him. Jay shot at their hands to knock them off the vines as they reached the top.

A couple of them lost their grip and fell back to the city street. But that did not stop them. They just started climbing again. The young officer had to run and fast — so he did. He slipped under some of the jagged shrubbery and entered Strawberry Fields. The ground was still covered with snow as Jay collapsed in the center of the crossroad. His arm wiped away some of the snow on the ground, to reveal the word "Imagine." He read the word softly and then rolled onto his back to look up at the stars.

On the small stone courtyard of the castle, Lyles and Puck slashed away at the mindless beasts trying to stop them, while their friend Ravenblade continued to keep Radix occupied. Lyles struck the animals again and again but their wounds seemed to have no effect on them. It was getting difficult to survive. Demonic birds swooped down to peck at Lyles' head, while the polar bear slashed violently at his ribs. Puck aided as best he could using his razor sharp claws and teeth to counter those of the animals that he fought.

"Their heads, attack their heads!" Ravenblade shouted to his companions. "You must sever their brains! Even zombies need a brain to live!"

"You imbecile, I will kill you for that!" Radix shouted at Ravenblade for his advice.

"If you could kill me, you would have already," the immortal taunted.

Using their friend's advice Lyles and Puck began to turn the battle around. Puck jumped at the birds, biting off each of their heads. Lyles hacked off the penguins' heads that were biting his legs. As for the colossal polar bear, it wasn't so easy to take his head off. While the bear kept Lyles busy, the python snuck up behind him and wrapped itself around Lyles' body and neck, choking him. The giant paws of the growling bear came swinging at him, when Puck jumped in and took a nice big chomp on the bear's neck causing the animal to pull back. As he held on with his teeth, the Djinni stuck his claws deep into the bears brain, and then pounced onto the snake. With a swipe of his talons Puck decapitated the python freeing Lyles from its grasp. Lyles picked up his sword and slowly made his way over to the polar bear to cut off its head and ensure that it was dead. The polar bear still had some life in it and gave Lyles a crushing blow to the gut, knocking the wind out of him. Puck jumped on the beast but was thrown off. The bear lifted his paw into the air ready to slash Lyles when Radix came flying across the courtyard and slammed into the bear, knocking both of them down. Ravenblade ran over and easily chopped the head off the bear, killing it. Now all of the deranged animals had been slaughtered, and all that was left was Radix. Lyles could not get up, and Puck ran to his aid. Radix was on his feet, angrier than before, and once again drew his sword at his immortal adversary. But Ravenblade moved in fast and cut through Radix's chest with a powerful slash from his mighty sword. Many hours had passed. It was almost dawn, and Ravenblade had Radix right where he wanted him. The immortal picked up his treacherous foe and threw him up against the thick woody wall that imprisoned them. The thorns stuck through Radix's back causing him to cringe from the pain.

Radix looked at Ravenblade and started, "Do you think that you are any different from me? You and me, we are the same."

"No, we are not. I have changed," Ravenblade answered.

"Sure you have. Look at your so-called friends. They are pathetic, weak. They are nothing. We are strong; better than them, and you know it. Well, at least you used to be. You are getting soft, my friend. Look at you. You are becoming just like them. What happened to the mighty and feared Ravenblade, killer of all men, the most evil man to walk the Earth? Isn't that why you wanted to stop me, because I invaded your territory? I stole your crown!" Radix carried on. His words entered the one-time angel's brain and circled around his head, reminding him of what he had always been—

"Evil! I am Evil! And I will be the most feared man to walk the Earth!" Ravenblade shouted to the stars and took Radix's own sword from his hand and stuck it straight through the dark man's throat, deep into the thick stalk of the vine.

Radix gave a malicious grin beneath all the pain and softly said under his breath, "That is exactly what I wanted to hear," and just as he had entered the mind of Judas, Radix now entered the mind of the infamous immortal killer — Ravenblade.

Jay Sil still lay on the ground, happy to be alive, but he was in jeopardy once again. The zombiefied officers had tracked him down, and they were slowly approaching him. Jay panicked, not knowing what to do. His shots earlier had no effect on them. But then, from his vast knowledge of zombie flicks and videogames, he remembered that in order to kill the undead you must stop their brains from functioning. Being an excellent marksman, Jay Sil reloaded his gun and aimed straight between his assailants' eyes. It took a few shots, but finally all six men and women were down for the count. But the night was still not over for the young rookie.

He heard a gun go off behind him. Cautiously, he walked toward an opening in the brush and looked into the distance. It was the night watchman, another zombie, and he was packing heat. Jay stood behind the vine walls as bullets flew furiously by him. The watchman stopped firing. Figuring that the watchman had run out of bullets, Jay turned the corner to get in a few shots. To his surprise the watchman's gun was still loaded, and he connected with a shot to Jay's left shoulder. Bleeding on the ground, Jay aimed his gun as best he could and fired a few more shots at his attacker. But he missed each one. Luckily for Jay, the zombie watchman *was* out of bullets this time. Jay tried to capitalize but dropped his gun from the pain in his shoulder. The famished bloodthirsty corpse made its way over to the rookie and leaned over him. Jay, overpowered by the zombie, was pinned to the ground. It then bit him rather aggressively on the left shoulder where he had been shot. All that the officer could think of was that he would now too become a zombie, just like in the movies. That did not stop Jay from shaking the creature off of him as quickly as he could and retrieving his gun. Aiming much more precisely this time, Jay Sill hit his mark and sent the zombie watchman back to his grave.

Needing to stop his bleeding shoulder, he bandaged the wound with a piece of his pants. Once again, Jay sat on the ground and looked up; he hoped that he would not become one of the undead.

Radix — inside the body of Ravenblade — made his way toward the cross where Nathan was hanging, still alive after all this time. Lyles heard the strange talk that came from his friend's mouth when he spoke of being evil, and he knew that something was not right. Hobbling over to the immortal, Lyles grabbed him by the shoulder.

"What is going on?" he asked.

"Mind your business, kid," Ravenblade answered in a dark sinister voice and threw Lyles to the ground.

Lyles could not get up this time. He only watched in dismay. Ravenblade was now down the stairs and on the rocky platform right before the crucified Nathan. He lifted his sword into the air, which glistened from the light of the setting moon.

"No, master, no!" Puck bellowed vanishing in a flash of smokeless fire.

The Ravenblade, the sword that shared the immortal's name, was just about to stab through Nathan's flesh and kill him. That was until Puck appeared before the blade in another flash of smokeless fire and took the blow to save his master. Ravenblade looked down at the altruistic Djinni and let go of his blade. He grabbed his head and fell to the ground, realizing what he had just done. Puck could not budge the sword that was cast into his chest. Sounds of dying screams came from his lips as he departed back into the smokeless fire from which he was born.

"What have I done?" Ravenblade cried as he fought against Radix's control.

The combat that was being waged in Ravenblade's head at that moment was fiercer and more draining than any battle that he had waged by hand in his lifetime. But like all of his battles, he would not succumb; he would not let down and die. Radix's evil presence was banished from his head. Blood still gushed from Radix's throat where it was ruptured by his own blade. He opened his eyes, now back in his own body, and looked around. Ravenblade and Lyles were both on the cold, stone floor, incapacitated at the moment. The Djinni was nowhere to be found, and Nathan still hung from the cross. The sun was about to rise, and Radix could see its rays beginning to paint the horizon. This was his last chance. He pulled the sword from his throat, and tore himself from the thorns that held him up. A bloody path followed Radix, as he made his way to Nathan.

As Radix put his sword to the side of the sacrificial victim, Nathan spoke softly, "Father, forgive this man for he does not know what he does."

"I know what I do, and I love what I do. I ask for no forgiveness from your God," Radix replied arrogantly.

"Father, into your hands I commend my spirit," Nathan continued.

"No!" screamed Lyles as he stumbled down the stairs and grabbed Radix by the ankle.

"It is finished!" were Nathan's last words.

As the sun rose, Radix's blade stabbed Nathan through the side and into his heart — despite Lyles effort to stop him. Blood and water flowed from Nathan's side, and he breathed his last.

# Part IV
## The Aftermath

Radix feasted his eyes on the sun's rays, giggling like a child who had found his Christmas presents under the tree. Nathan was dead, and he had made it to the next day. He had won, once again. But then, Radix felt a sensation that he had never felt before. He felt his soul being ripped from his body. Radix had *not* succeeded. Nathan did in fact die, but it was not until the sun had already started to rise in the morning sky. God allowed Radix to see the light of day for one last time, to get a glimpse of what he would be missing where he was headed. Even more joyful than Radix had been a moment ago was Death as he collected the soul of his arch-nemesis for the past two millennia. The Root of All Evil — Radix Malorum — had returned to the dust that he came from, as did all of the things that his magic created the night before. No more would he strike fear into the hearts of men and women. Unfortunately, Nathaniel Salvatore had to play the part of the martyr. Death went to collect his soul, as well, but could not find it. This was odd. Though, it did not affect him, which made it even more odd. Death just shrugged his shoulders and left. Ravenblade and Lyles awoke to find their friend dead on the cross. They saw the pile of dust that used to be Radix and knew they had won the battle with a high price. Grieving the loss of their friend, the two men took him down from the cross, which faded away with the other remnants of that night. After they wrapped their beloved friend in Ravenblade's cloak and went to carry him off with their heads hanging low, a voice called out.

"Wait for me!" the voice cried.

It was Puck. He was still alive. The two men were happy to see their friend, but they were confused as to how this was possible. Then, Ravenblade realized that Puck was pierced in the chest. Djinn do not have hearts, and therefore cannot be killed by being stabbed through the chest. The only way to kill a Djinni was to chop off its head, which can prove to be a most difficult task as the immortal knew. Puck explained this all to Lyles since the young man was still unfamiliar with these things. The slayer turned hero, Ravenblade, gave his deepest apologies to his friends for allowing Radix to gain control of his mind and body. His lust for power cost his friend, Nathan, his life and almost cost the world a whole lot more. But they forgave him because they knew that even an immortal such as he had weaknesses such as they. Happy to see a world without Radix, the trio carried their friend off.

Jay Sil woke up. He had slept a few hours. His wound still hurt, but he was happy to not be a flesh-eating zombie. Another officer picked him up and brought him to the emergency room to have his wound treated. The police commissioner asked him to keep that night's events to himself for they seemed outrageous and unreal. Though, he knew as well as anyone that they did in fact take place. Jay Sil kept his mouth shut, but he would never forget all that he saw and was part of.

Two days had now gone by, and the rejoicing of Radix's demise was muffled by the sadness of young Nathan's death. Nathaniel Salvatore had sacrificed his own life to save that of the masses, a modern-day martyr who few would ever know about in this life. All of those who loved him dearly gathered together that day to mourn his death. The funeral was at Divine Body Church. Sister Elizabeth felt very strongly about Nathan's death. She knew of all that had transpired; she took part in the journey. Because of this, the good Sister arranged all of the funeral services herself. And with some outside help, she also made sure to have Nathan laid to rest quickly. It seemed odd to bury the body just two days from his death, but the Sister assured those involved that it was best this way. The family and friends who gathered were very sad and confused that God decided to take young Nathan when He did. No one could understand God's ways for they are above that of mortal man. There had been such sorrow and tragedy for the Salvatore family that year with the death of Maria, Giuseppe, and now Nathan. And Esmeralda could never forget the horrifying event that she had endured. That memory would be with her forever, especially now as she tightly held her newborn babies — the products of her nightmare. But these children were more than that to her; she loved them tremendously, as all mothers do, and thanked God that such joy could spring from such misery. They were the only happiness that Esmeralda had right now, as she looked over at the casket and spilled tears onto the church floor. But very few people would know the truth of all that took place during the last year. Esmeralda did not know what to tell her family about what happened, so she had to weave a tale. It involved kidnappers, and her parents and Nathan eventually getting murdered, as well as her miraculous escape while pregnant. She told them that she found a retreat house in the woods while running away from her attackers; and that she stayed there until she delivered the babies, which was somewhat true. As for questions about the father of the children, she never really answered them. She would just change the subject. But more importantly, she let everyone know how much she adored her two newborn children — Gideon and Bianca Marie. Esmeralda chose the name Bianca for the girl because of her bright white complexion, and Marie in honor of her mother Maria. From sadness came the joy of love.

Lyles had also come to grieve the loss of his good friend, Nathan, and to give Esmeralda any support that she might need. Accompanying Lyles were Kimberly, Martha, and of course the faithful and loyal Puck. The Djinni was cloaked in invisibility the whole time as not to cause any panic. The night before, Lyles had told Kimberly and Martha everything that he had experienced while he was away. He could not lie to them, especially not Kimberly; he was in love with her. As bizarre as his tale was, Kimberly and Martha believed every word of it. From their past friendship, Martha had known about Reverend Reynolds and his bout with the Devil, knowledge that Lyles was not aware of. Kimberly was also a woman of strong faith and believed very much in God and the Devil. She knew that only a monster could slaughter innocent children the way that her three little friends were killed. But both Kimberly and Martha had no way to contest Lyles story once they met Puck. They grew very fond of the Djinni, especially Martha.

The group of mourners silently cried and hung their heads low as they followed the casket's procession out of the church and into the hearse. The air was bitter and cold at the cemetery where Nathan's body was being laid to rest. His plot was next to his parents' graves, which were also quite fresh. Rose petals and tears covered the dirt that now sat upon the casket where Nathan was set to sleep eternally. The burial hit much harder than the funeral itself for it seemed more permanent, and winter's cold, dead sting only heightened the moment. Martha and Kimberly tried their best to smile as they played with the twins, while Esmeralda buried her head in Lyle's chest trying to grasp any bit of reality that she could. Lyles had been more than a friend — he was a true hero to her; and she needed his strength right now, to move on. As the frigid January wind blew the snow around the graveyard; and the cold became too unbearable, turning everyone's tears to ice; the crowd began to leave. There was to be plenty of food at one of Esmeralda's aunt's house, and all were invited. One way to fill an empty heart is to fill an empty belly, at least for the meantime. The pain would last for a while, but it would start to die down eventually. Not even pain lasts forever. Lyles told Martha and Kimberly to go back to the car with Puck, and that he would meet them there in a minute. Kimberly had borrowed her mother's car so they could drive to the funeral. Most of the people had already driven off, including Esmeralda. Lyles knelt down at Nathan's grave and said a quick prayer — asking God to take his friend's soul to a better place. Just as he spoke these short sincere words under his breath, a dark figure walked out from behind the snow-covered trees. His shadow cast over Lyles.

"Raven, you came," Lyles said both happy and sad.

"Don't be so glum. Nathan was a good man," Ravenblade said in response. "You should sing merrily of all that he did. A hero never dies, for his tales live on forever."

"It's hard to think that way when I stare at the grave of another lost friend," Lyles responded.

"After all we have fought and been through, you should know better. You should know that Nathan's soul is still alive and well, and much happier than he ever was here. I am not a man of many words, but I have a few for you. I have never had friends in my lifetime, as long as it has been. But I consider you, Nathan, and Puck among my closest family. All of you taught me how to care; and now thanks to you, I will never be the same. I can never erase the crimes that I have committed against God and humanity, nor do I look for absolution for my sins. Nathan will indeed go to Heaven, as will you — as all great heroes do. The both of you proved to be two of the greatest and most honorable warriors that I have ever known, and I have known many. But I am not too much for the heartfelt speeches, so I will go now. Please, just remember what I have said and know that your friend is not really dead. Neither he nor you will ever be. Good-bye, my friend," Ravenblade genuinely professed before he turned and drifted off, back home to the desert.

"Good-bye, friend," Lyles called back and then softly said, "You too are a great and honorable hero."

The words carried off into the frosty breeze and lifted up into the heavens. Lyles stood up, looked at Nathan's headstone, and saw something sparkling on top of it. He bent down to get a better look. It was the Ring of Solomon. Ravenblade had found it under the snow in the park and left it there for Lyles to have, for he would have more use for it than the nomadic immortal. Taking the ring Lyles placed it on his finger and walked back to the car. Soon the cemetery was empty again, except for those buried under its ground. That night, the gravediggers said that they saw angels visiting Nathan's grave. But these men were always known for telling tales after having a few too many drinks as they dug the night away. In this case they were not weaving any stories. Angels did in fact visit Nathan's grave, as did other beings — both good and evil. Late that night after all other visitors left, Death sat alone on Nathan's tombstone waiting.

# EPILOGUE
## DEATH'S PARTING SOLILOQUY

Alone I wait for the dead as I sit upon the stone of yet another fallen hero. No emotion controls my body for I have none to betray me. I have been made to see only what is black and white, though I have discovered many grays. Somewhere deep inside my empty heart, I feel for the boy who gave up everything to save his people. His sacrifice was noble, and for it he received a hero's death.

But I still sit here upon his grave, thinking of Radix and savoring the sensation of finally closing the wound that he left inside of me. But like all things that are mortal, Radix has died and gone on to his eternal resting place. His torture and torment will more than reflect the pain and suffering that he has caused all of mankind during his lifetime, but it will never undo what he has done.

Evil still lies in the hearts of men, and Radix was neither the last nor the greatest evil to plague the Earth. More will come, and more innocents will be slaughtered. I just pray, yes pray, that the mortals will one day discover their true purpose and find a way to conquer the evil for good. God had come to show them the way, but men rejected what they saw and continue to reject it every day — embracing darkness more and more. If the inhabitants of this world do not resist soon, they will fall into the darkness as other lifeforms from the distant stars already have.

But the time is almost here, and I will stay perched on this grave and wait. For I have searched and searched for this soul since he has passed; yet I have found none, nor has any pain taken over me in not finding this soul. That can only mean one thing, and I do know where this soul has gone. Even though I cannot truly feel, I am overcome by joy or the closest reproduction that I can conjure up, for this man is not dead but alive. As with all heroes, his spirit will endure forever.

# The Story Begins...

A STORY TOLD

# About the Authors

*Chris LoParco* is a writer and an artist who draws his inspiration from his love for God and his deep interest in the epic battle between Light and Darkness. He is a graduate of the School of Visual Arts, and he is an very proud husband and father.

*John Santarsiero* is a writer and a musician, who is drawn to the supernatural both in his life and in his art. He enjoys seeing the paranormal through the scientific eye, yet is very intrigued by what cannot be explained. John is also a very proud father.

*Herbert Olivera* is a writer whose influences extend from Eastern philosphies all the way to science fiction, hitting many places in between. He focuses his life around the principal idea of "goodness" and is driven by his great love for his family and friends, especially his wife and children.

Made in the USA
Lexington, KY
24 January 2012